RAINBOW'S END

Liverpool, 1904. When Ada Docherty gives birth to twins, Deirdre and Donal, in her tiny house in Evangelist Court, she has no choice but to make Ellen, her eldest daughter, bring them up, for she must work to feed seven hungry mouths. But in Dublin, Maggie McVeigh's lot is even harder, for she sleeps on straw in a tumbledown tenement. When a local woman, Mrs Nolan, needs someone to look after her sons, Maggie takes on the job and finds security and comfort—and love, too, with the eldest boy, Liam. When war is declared, life changes dramatically. Ellen, newly in love, follows her young man to France—but does he share her feelings? A tragedy sends Liam off to the trenches whilst at home wartime shortages and a constant stream of bad news affect both families. But a surprise is awaiting them . . .

RAINBOW'S END

Katie Flynn

CHIVERS PRESS
BATH

First published 1997
by
William Heinemann Ltd
This Large Print edition published by
Chivers Press
by arrangement with
Random House
1999

ISBN 0 7540 1209 3

British Library Cataloguing in Publication Data available

F

489358

Printed and bound in Great Britain by
REDWOOD BOOKS, Trowbridge, Wiltshire

For Maria Garbett,
a true friend in need, and an avid reader into the
bargain. Hope you like this one,
Marie!

ACKNOWLEDGEMENTS

My thanks to the staff of the Liverpool Libraries particularly Eileen Greenwood of Everton Library who set up meetings with Evertonians and lent me a copy of a book I badly needed. Ann Cunningham told me about her mother-in-law's girlhood, some of which I 'borrowed' for Maggie in this book. Sam Crystal's experience of the meat trade was invaluable and last but not least John Williams of the Wrexham Branch Library found the very information I needed on Armistice Day 1918.

Since I developed M.E. early in 1996 I have been afflicted by appalling memory loss, so if I've missed anyone out, I'm truly sorry.

CHAPTER ONE

January 1839

It was very cold. Snow lay thick on the flat, high terraces of the Burren which surrounded the Feeneys' small farmhouse and the pools which had formed where the nearby stream had deepened with the winter's snow had ice like lace round their edges, spreading into the centre as the cold grew more intense. Grainne Feeney, who had just checked the family's winter supply of potatoes, protected by straw and earth against snow and frost, reflected that everyone dreaded a severe winter and this looked as though it was going to be just that, since it had snowed heavily the previous evening. It was Twelfth Night, when the superstitious believe that the dead walk ... but since the sixth of January is also celebrated as 'little Christmas', all over Ireland, the children, and older people too, were looking forward to an evening spent telling tales and playing games around the fire, whilst the woman of the house prepared the finest meal she could manage, to see them through the hungry months ahead.

And hungry months they might well be, Grainne thought, going into the earth-floored farmhouse kitchen and frowning over the sacks of flour, the sides of smoked bacon and the tub of crude lard which she had stacked in the cupboard against the back door. In the roof space above her head were some precious apples carefully spaced out on a piece of board, a tub of molasses, two sacks of

1

oatmeal and a great many jars of blackberry jam, but would this be sufficient to see them through until summer came? Grainne did her best to prepare for winter, but she was never quite sure if the food would last out, and as winter advanced and the family made inroads upon her supplies, she was always apprehensive that she might be caught out. The trouble was, she was always so busy! Her father, Paddy Feeney, did his best, but he was not helped by the fact that he had lost his leg as a young man when a wound had gone bad on him. He had a wooden leg and pegged around as best he could, but even an able-bodied man with a farm such as his needed grown sons to help with the work, and Paddy's oldest son was eight. When Paddy had been young and his father and mother had had the farm, there had been plenty of hands to make light work, for Paddy was one of eight brothers. But as they grew up his brothers had decided that a hand-to-mouth existence on the farm was not for them and they had begun to emigrate, some to Dublin, others to America, the remainder to England, until only Paddy Feeney remained on the home farm set on the wild limestone uplands known as the Burren.

Paddy himself was the eldest Feeney, but the second brother sent a letter sometimes, all the way from Chicago, and the third occasionally got his wife to write from their New York home, for none of the Feeney boys could write or read. But the passing of time had loosened the strong thread which had once bound the boys and the younger brothers had long ceased to keep in touch. Paddy was fond of telling his children that they had an uncle who sold cattle food in Dublin and another who was a drover, driving cattle from all over the country to the big beast markets, besides a seaman who sailed out of Liverpool port and travelled the world, but Grainne never expected to meet these uncles of hers; they were like all the other legends of Ireland, more myth than truth. So though she read the letters with the foreign stamps on them when they arrived and carefully wrote replies, to her father's dictation, she didn't really believe in her clever uncles. They were characters from the past, no more real than Finn McCool, and had no reality for Grainne in the present.

But her mother was real to her, though she had been dead now for more than six years. She remembered her mother lifting her up when she was three or four and showing her the pictures.

Grainne adored the pictures. There were two of them, both embroidered, and the first and oldest was all done in the most beautiful, delicate coloured silks. Grainne's grandmother had made it when she had been a young girl, working for rich people with a big manor house just outside Ennis. The mistress there had been a good churchwoman who embroidered altar cloths for the church and stoles for the priest, and when she saw that Grainne's grandmother was interested, she gave her the odds and ends of silk from her work.

'Make yourself something for your dowry,' she had said, meaning an embroidered pinafore or a tablecloth no doubt. But Grainne's grandmother had made the picture, because she had been heartsick for the Burren, and she hung it on her wall in her little garret room and looked at it each day. And when William Feeney, who owned his own farm up on the Burren, had asked her to

3

marry him, she hadn't given a thought to the hardships, the child-bearing and the battle with the weather which were the lot of a farmer's wife. She had had a man from Ennis eager to marry her, a rich widower in his mid-thirties with a handsome town house and a large and flourishing seed-merchant business. But marriage to him would have rooted her firm in the town for the rest of her life, so she had had no hesitation in dismissing him. Neither did she cast a backward glance at her comfortable life with her kindly employers, nor the pleasures of living in a large, well-run household. Her mistress, who was truly fond of her, tried to dissuade her from leaving, pointing out the advantages of marrying a sober citizen with plenty of money, but Grainne's grandmother knew her own mind. She had said 'yes' to William Feeney and gone back to the Burren with a full and happy heart, and she had hung her beautiful picture on the wall of the farmhouse, to remind her of spring in winter, she told her children. And she never regretted coming home, because she loved beauty and the sea and being her own mistress, even if it was of a tiny, barren little farm and not of a handsome town house.

Then Grainne's grandmother had had her sons, and Grainne's father, Paddy, being the eldest son, had taken over the farmhouse. And when he was established and near to thirty he asked Bridget MacGuire to marry him, because he thought she was the prettiest, cleverest girl in the district. Bridget had accepted and come to live in the farmhouse up on the Burren, and she greatly admired the beautiful picture her mother-in-law had made with her silks and canvas and her clever

4

fingers, and her clear, beautiful memories of spring on the Burren.

So as she combed and carded the wool from her husband's sheep, it occurred to her that she would like to make a companion picture to the one which hung on one side of the big old fireplace. And she had dyed hanks of wool all different colours, and cut a piece of canvas to size and begun to make her own picture. For she could not have afforded silks, and anyway she wanted her picture to be hers and not just a copy of her mother-in-law's.

Her own mother's picture hung, now, on the other side of the fireplace. Grainne was never sure which she preferred—sometimes I like one best and sometimes the other, she decided now. Her grand-mother's picture showed the Burren in spring, when all the extraordinary and exotic flowers and plants, which people came from all over the country to admire, were in full bloom. She had made each little flower-face with the greatest care and attention, she had drawn the lichen with her silks, and the moss, and the whitish-grey limestone, the clumps of grass, green as spring grass must be, and even a gull's egg, mottled blue and brown, lying on that same grass.

But her mother's picture was an autumn scene and that, in its own way, was even lovelier. The sky was a pale blue, the bent silver birch gold-leafed and the flowers of the Burren the quieter shades of autumn. And Grainne loved it because the wool was their wool, from their sheep, and also because her mother had been so happy with her work, so innocently proud of what she had created.

It was a great shame, so it was, that Bridget had given Paddy five daughters before she produced

5

her first son, but Paddy had never grumbled. And when the son was finally born, what rejoicing there was! When she gave birth to a second son, the rejoicing had been even greater, but within a fortnight she had died of milk fever and the light had gone out of Paddy's eyes. He started work at sunrise and worked on until long after sunset, and apart from his two older daughters he did it all himself, for the boys were babies still and could not be expected to work with him.

Paddy often talked of his brothers, who had gone so far away, and he told the children that, had his brothers known there would be work and a place for them on the farm, they would never have left, but Grainne doubted it. Feeneys, it seemed to her, were natural wanderers; she saw it already in Sean and had little doubt that her father, too, would have left the place had he not married his Bridget young and settled down.

Farmers' children always work hard, be they boys or girls, but Grainne and Fidelma Feeney worked harder than most. Grainne had been eleven and Fidelma a year younger when their mother had died. Now they were sixteen and seventeen, old enough to be a very real help to their father, and indeed he often remarked that he could never have managed without them. There was no task they could not undertake on the farm, they sewed and cooked, kept the house decent and managed the small amount of money which came their way when Paddy drove his cattle to the November market, making it stretch to cover everything a lively young family could not do without. Indeed, since their mother's death they had done more, for they had schooled their younger brothers and sisters, teaching all of them, even Sean, who boasted that he didn't have a brain at all under his mop of curly brown hair, to add up, divide and multiply as well as to read and write a little.

Now, having satisfied herself that she had done all she could to stock up for the coming months, Grainne picked up the overflowing pig-bucket from beside the door and carried it out to the fenced-off bit of rough ground with the old stone pigsty at one end where the pigs lived with their bonaveens. They rushed towards her, snorting and grunting with pleasure as she tipped the food out on to a cleared patch of ground, and began eating at once. There was a big old sow and three youngsters snouting at the potato skins and the cabbage leaves, all looking healthy enough despite the cold. Paddy had killed the young boars in September, because he always put the sow, known to one and all as Bessy Lug, to his neighbour's boar, so the bonaveens left were all she-pigs, which would produce bonaveens of their own in time. Or if we run short of food for them we can sell them at the market, Grainne reminded herself, aware that a hard winter would stretch their supplies to the limit. There was always someone wanting a healthy young gilt in the spring to start off their own litter.

Having satisfied herself that all was well with her pigs, Grainne checked on the children, who were making a slide on the empty potato patch, shouting and yelling as they careered down it on a flattened piece of tin. It was a still, overcast day, almost uncannily still, Grainne thought. Her younger brothers and sisters were making a good deal of noise, but nevertheless she could hear the shouts of the Casey family carrying across the flat limestone

7

and the little fields which separated them from their nearest neighbours. Indeed, when Dervla came out of the cottage to call the children indoors and slipped, every imprecation reached Grainne's ears as clearly as if the older woman was no more than a couple of yards distant, instead of a couple of miles.

'Is it indoors you want me, Grainne?' Maura, who was twelve, said reluctantly when she looked up from the game and saw her sister watching. 'I'm just havin' a bit of a game wit' the others, but I'll come, if you need me.'

'No, stay out for a while,' Grainne said. She was glad to see them playing because it kept them warm, for the good God knew that their clothing was a poor protection against cold such as this. It was hard work, making clothes for six children who ranged in age from five to twelve, and often boots were a real problem, for though Paddy Feeney had his own cobbler's last and mended boots until they were more patch than anything else, new boots were more than the Feeneys could manage. But this year, with a fair price for the cattle sold for the Christmas market, a good crop of potatoes and winter cabbage and with Bessy Lug producing two large litters, everyone had pretty respectable boots. We're managin' well, so we are, Grainne told herself and turned back towards the farmhouse.

They called it a farmhouse, but Grainne reflected it was more like a cottage, with a thatched roof which was held down by ropes flung across it and anchored with great rocks from the beach so that it stayed in place even during stormy weather. The glassless windows were set a couple of feet into the thickness of the whited cob walls and there

8

were stout wooden shutters which could be closed across at night and in rough weather. It was low-built, as were all the dwellings on the Burren, and it always looked to Grainne as though it had pulled its thatch low over its eyes to save itself from the bitter winds which roared inland from the Atlantic, all but tugging the small dwellings from their moorings. For though the Feeneys farmed a dozen acres, which was quite a good-sized property for the Burren, their neighbours further inland, the McBrides, owned thirty acres and had a far larger flock of sheep than the dozen ewes and the evil-eyed ram which kept the Feeneys supplied with both wool and mutton.

There was, however, bad feeling between the Feeneys and the McBrides. Fergus McBride had an exalted idea of his own importance—did he not own his farm, and had he not married a woman who had brought a substantial dowry with her when they wed? Perhaps, but everyone knew that the McBrides' first child had not been of Edward McBride's getting, that Fergus's mother had been pregnant by another man when they married. No one thought it a matter for shame, but neither did they expect Fergus McBride to take the attitude that he was, socially, far above his neighbours.

And then there was the matter of the spring lambs. Paddy had taken his lambs into Ennis on market day and Fergus McBride was buying. He liked the look of the Feeney lambs and had been about to purchase them when someone had said they were Feeney lambs, raised on the Burren, and weren't they just grand, now? Fergus had drawn himself up to his full height, looked down his nose at his informer and had deliberately snubbed Paddy

9

before all the world by saying that he'd changed his mind; he wouldn't buy Feeney lambs because sheep reared on the poor grazing offered by the Burren had thin, rickety bones and never prospered.

Paddy, not to be outdone, had said how strange it was that McBride had been admiring the lambs for their fat sides and strong bones . . . until he had heard they came from the Burren, of course. And wasn't it stranger still that the McBride farm was right on the edge of the Burren too, which didn't say much for his own stock, did it now?

The argument had ended in a scuffle during which Paddy, very much smaller than his opponent but also square and pugnacious, had landed a good punch on his rival's high-bridged nose.

The two families had ceased to speak to each other from that day on.

With the Caseys and O'Hares, however, who were the Feeneys' neighbours in the opposite direction, a much easier relationship existed. Grainne and Sammy O'Hare had often gone egg-hunting on the cliffs, for she could climb every bit as well as he, and as she took over management of the house she and Mrs O'Hare exchanged recipes and complained when the hens weren't laying or the cow went dry.

The Casey family had sons a-plenty, unlike the Feeneys, and the oldest boys, Evlin and Durvan, were a couple of years older than Grainne and Fidelma and hung around, making sheep's eyes and trying to interest the girls in shared pursuits. But though Fidelma was friendly enough and rather liked Durvan, Grainne refused to encourage either boy. She had ideas of her own regarding marriage which certainly did not include an alliance with

10

their neighbours.

But thinking about their neighbours would not get the evening meal. Grainne put her hand on the latch to let herself into the farmhouse, then paused. Last spring, she had planted a climbing honeysuckle right by the door, and now she looked at its dry twigs and tried to imagine how it would look in summer, with the pink and gold of the flowers against the whitewashed walls and the green of its leaves making a good background colour. It's withstood the wind so far, Grainne thought hopefully; it may yet flourish. Life on the Burren was harsh, but . . . it's a grand place, so it is, Grainne thought, and I wouldn't live anywhere else but here for twenty pound. But of course she might not be able to live in this particular place for ever. Not if she married.

Grainne went into the kitchen and threw potatoes into a bowl, then poured water over them and began to scrub off the worst of the dirt. Marrying was a knotty problem, for the Feeney girls always seemed too busy with their own family to think about much else. Indeed, Grainne sometimes thought that the older they grew, the less time they had to themselves. Now that they were keeping hens, her father frowned on the collecting of seabirds' eggs, saying that it was too dangerous, that they would fall to their deaths and then where would he be? This meant that the friendly rivalry between Sammy O'Hare and herself had stopped, and though they met various young men from the area when they took the donkey down to the seashore and collected seaweed to fertilise the land, the boys were working as hard as they and could not stop their labours for long.

11

Certainly there was chat, flirting even, but Grainne, at least, did not take any of this seriously. It was not courtship; they knew each other too well, Grainne supposed.

Another reason for going down to the shore was the Feeney fishing currach. On fine summer evenings Grainne and Fidelma would set off, sometimes with some of the younger children aboard, sometimes alone, and cast out the nets, which they made on winter evenings before the fire. They followed the herring, or the mackerel, and did as well as the O'Hares or the Caseys or any of their neighbours, Indeed, the girls cut peat, swinging the big slane as expertly as many a man, piled the turves in the old tumbril and brought it down to the cabin to add to the turf pile behind their dwelling, and took no longer over it than the Casey boys. And year in, year out, they planted, tended and harvested the potato plot and grew from seed such things as cabbages, swedes and turnips to help feed the family—and all this in addition to what would have been called women's work about the farmhouse.

Despite the hard work, which started before daybreak and went on until dark and beyond, Grainne had always enjoyed her life, especially that part of it which she spent out of doors, with the wind from the sea ruffling her hair and her healthy young body rejoicing in its strength. She would have liked more freedom, but all around her people worked from dawn till dusk so why should she be any different? And then an event had occurred which was to change her life, though at first she had not recognised it as anything out of the ordinary.

It had happened last June, when Grainne had been at work hoeing the potato field. At the end of the last-but-one row she looked up and saw a young man leaning on the dry-stone wall, watching her. He was tall, with dark-auburn hair and when he grinned at her his teeth were very white and even in his brown and merry face.

'Aren't you doin' a fine job, now?' he said as she approached. 'If you've a mind to carry on workin' for a while, how about comin' over to me father's farm an' givin' us a hand wit' the hoein'?'

'I've not finished here, yet,' Grainne said. 'Seein' as how you're here, though, 'tis you ought to be helpin' me, not the other way around.'

She hadn't meant it seriously, but he had jumped over the wall, seized her hoe and worked his way along the last row, talking as he did so.

'Well then, that's easy fixed! Here I am, doin' your work for you, so mebbe you'll take a walk wit' me when this is over and done? We could go down to the shore, see if we can pick us some mussels.'

'Who are you?' Grainne had said, suddenly seized by an unpleasant suspicion. 'What's your name? What are you doin' here?'

He finished the row and bowed, flourishing the hoe at her so comically that she had to smile. 'I'm William McBride, missus. And you'll be Miss Feeney, I dare swear.'

'I'm Grainne Feeney,' Grainne had said stiffly. 'Does your dadda know you're consortin' wit' a Feeney, Mr McBride?'

'Divil a bit does he know,' came the airy response. 'And why should I care what me dadda thinks, an' me a man grown? And you, Grainne? What would your dadda say if he knew you was

13

consortin' wit' a McBride?'

'I don't know,' Grainne said slowly. 'But there's no harm in talkin', nor in walkin'. And I'm mortal fond of mussels.'

It had been the start of what rapidly became not just a friendship but a courtship too. Only it had to be kept secret, because when Grainne had sounded her father out, mentioning the McBrides, Paddy had responded with something akin to violence.

'*Them?*' he had said and spat into the fire. 'They're dort beneath me feet, so they are—dort! Don't you have nothin' to do wit' that fambly, alanna. They're all bad, all the way t'rough. Leave 'em alone, no good ever came of consortin' wit' folk like that.'

It didn't make any difference, of course, because William told her roundly that he did not intend to let two old men ruin their lives. 'You're me choice of 'em all, alanna,' he had said as they couched themselves down in the lee of a haystack and watched the sun sinking in the west in a glow of flame and gold. 'You're everyt'ing I ever wanted, an' you feel the same about me, so you do.'

'I do,' Grainne had admitted. 'But me dadda won't say we can wed, you know.'

'Then we'll wed wit'out 'em,' William said and squeezed her hard. 'I can't live wit'out you, Grainne me little beauty, nor do I want to. And don't worry, now, because we'll work it out, so we will.'

Fidelma knew about the friendship, and thought her parent was being foolish and her sister sillier for not bringing it out into the open. 'Dadda will shout and rave an' then won't he be huggin' you an' sayin' he's an ould fool an' only wants your

14

happiness,' she prophesied. 'But don't let Dadda find out for himself, alanna. Tell him straight.'

And the truth was that it was becoming more and more difficult to hide what was going on. A man in love is a generous creature and William was no exception. He was always turning up at some point in her working day, handing over small gifts with a diffidence which touched and delighted her. A box of day-old chicks, a length of ribbon, a grey kitten to live in the donkey's stable to keep the mice and rats down. Grainne loved the presents but allowed her father to think that it was Evlin Casey who was courting her.

'You're living a lie,' Fidelma warned her. 'No good will come of it; tell Dadda, alanna!'

'I will. But not yet,' Grainne said. 'We're young, still. And William's not asked me, not properly.'

And still the time went by and Grainne continued to meet William, to grow steadily more in love with him and to say nothing to her father.

Things finally came to a head just before Christmas. William had given her a present which she could not, in all conscience, hide. A gold signet ring. A token, as she knew well.

'It's the McBride ring,' William said. 'Look—see the initials—it's old and valuable. It will do until I can get to town to buy you something proper. Tell your dadda,' William said, putting the ring on her finger and kissing the side of her mouth. 'Tell him, then we can start to plan for our own lives.'

'But he can't manage wit'out me,' Grainne said sorrowfully. 'We'll be waitin' many a long year, William. You want a wife who's young, wit'out responsibility for a family of children.'

'I want a wife who's you,' William said. 'My

15

father has another son. If your father will only accept me, I'd work for him whiles we save for a wee place of our own.'

So that evening, as her father sat by the fire mending a net and she sat opposite him darning, Grainne showed him the ring and admitted that it had come from William McBride.

'But you don't know the feller,' Paddy had said, staring from her face to the ring and back to her face again. 'Oh, you could have seen him in the market, but you've not so much as exchanged a word wit' him.'

'I have. We've been meeting,' Grainne said. 'Dadda, we love each other. We—we want to marry. Oh, not yet, I know it wouldn't do, not yet. But—but some time.'

'And what'll his parents say?' Paddy asked. 'They'll never agree; they'll send the lad off wit' a flea in his ear, an' he the eldest son.'

'He doesn't care,' Grainne said. 'He loves me, Dadda, so if his father turns him out it's wit' us he'll make his home.'

'Alanna, William lives in a big farmhouse, wit' a younger brother an' sister. That's *t'ree* childer against our seven, an' the McBride childer is all grown, useful. Then they've money ... their flock of sheep is *trible* our flock ... and they've several donkeys, carts, a jaunting car ... why, they've horses, even. There, the lad will want for not'in'. Why should he t'row all that away for the daughter of a feller wit' ten acres of the Burren? I own me own land and proud of it I am, but we work hard, I sometimes t'ink, to stand still. We'll never own a proper cart, even.'

It was the first time Grainne had ever heard her

father sound wistful and it made the tears come to her eyes. She jumped to her feet and put her arms round his shoulders, giving him a hug. 'Dadda, we don't want a damned cart, nor a great flock of sheep! You're the best father a family ever had, an' so I've told William, often and often. But wit' William livin' here, helpin', don't you t'ink we'd get on better, easier?'

'He won't be used to the sort of work we do, child,' Paddy said gently. 'The McBrides have farm-workers for the mucky jobs.'

'He doesn't care,' Grainne said earnestly. 'He'll do what we do, Dadda.'

'Mebbe you're right,' Paddy said, doubt in every syllable. 'Jaysus, Mary an' Joseph, I hope to God you're right. But we'll see, alanna. When your William tells his own family, then we'll see.'

All might have been well, Grainne thought, had the two older men not met, nose to nose, a few days after she and William had broken the news to their respective families. Paddy Feeney had gone into Ballyvaghan for the wake of a local farmer and Fergus McBride was also there. Paddy assured Grainne afterwards that he had fully intended to shake McBride's hand and demand that they let bygones be bygones now that the young'uns had become rather more than friends, but he never had a chance.

McBride came straight across to him, his large face reddening, his eyes bright with spite. 'You'll be against it, as I am,' he asserted, before Paddy had so much as opened his mouth. 'My wife is distressed; I can't have her distressed. William's me eldest son, I need him as, no doubt, you need your gorl.'

'I do need me daughter,' Paddy had said. 'But they'll wait, they won't be jumpin' into marriage for a year or so.'

'A year or so! I'll not have it, d'you hear? William could marry anyone, anyone at all. You want to find a workin'-class lad ... the Casey boy would suit, I imagine ... then she'll stop dreamin' about catchin' her betters.'

'I didn't hit'm,' Paddy said defensively, when telling Grainne what had transpired. 'I just told'm neither himself nor his son was any better than the Caseys. An' I torned me back on him, so I did.'

It was only when her father began to tell her of Mr McBride's disapproval that Grainne realised what William's love had done for her. It had changed her from a shy and diffident girl into someone who was self-confident, sure of her worth. Once, she might have given in, told her father it was all right, she and William would just have to wait until Mr McBride softened towards them. Now she knew that she and William must go their own way. And if it meant William marrying her and moving into their cottage then she was willing to put up with that for a few years, rather than lose him.

But that had been before Christmas, and now it was Twelfth Night and she was looking forward to William's very first proper, official visit to her home, for he was coming for the celebrations, her very first proper guest. He had met Sean and Maura a few days ago, because they had been with Grainne and the dog Tinker, fetching in the cow and her calf, but he still hadn't met her father or the rest of the family. It will be nice for them to know each other, Grainne thought, putting the

18

potatoes into the big cauldron and pulling it over the fire. The fire heated the wall-oven beside it, and presently it would be hot enough to cook the soda bread and also the fish which she was about to prepare. Whilst she cleaned and gutted the sea bass her father had caught she went over her preparations in her head. The brack was made and ready to be cut and buttered, the poteen which her father made in his still in a small limestone cave a mile from the house was to hand, and the special cake, made with flour, eggs and dried fruit, was in the cupboard by the back door. She had brought down some apples and last time her father had gone to Ennis market he had bought chestnuts which they would roast in the embers . . . it was a real ceilidh, her very first ceilidh with a proper guest!

But before the ceilidh could start she would have to get the children and Fidelma in to help or they'd not be sitting down before midnight. She went to the door and called, her voice echoing weirdly round the snow-covered countryside, and saw Fidelma coming across the yard towards her. Fidelma smiled and waved and Grainne thought how very pretty her sister was becoming. She began to wonder whether William would notice her sister and hoped, unkindly, that he would not. Then she felt guilty for the thought and told herself that if he preferred Fidelma to herself she could scarcely blame him . . . and as Fidelma got closer she noticed how becomingly flushed she was and wondered whether it was the coming ceilidh, or whether she had met one of the Caseys, because there was no denying that that Durvan Casey was more than a little interested in the sudden blooming into womanhood of Fidelma Feeney. And then she noticed something else—that there was an odd light out there, a sort of sulphur yellow, a hell-light, which sometimes presages a storm.

Then the first child came in, red-cheeked from the cold, and Grainne set her to lay the table, and the second child was sent to fill the reed basket with turves for the fire and the third filled the water bucket, and the family swung into their evening routine as Fidelma, still prettily flushed for whatever reason, came in and said wasn't it a strange light out there, now, and had anyone brought the donkey into the byre, for sure an' the poor thing would freeze into a block of ice in the field tonight.

'I'll fetch Darky,' the eldest boy, Sean, said, carefully pouring water from the bucket into the big iron kettle. 'He'll come quiet for me.'

'I'll come wit' you,' Kieran, the youngest of the family and just six years old, said eagerly. Plainly, he wanted another chance to be out in the snow. Grainne was about to say that one was enough to fetch any donkey and wasn't Darky a dote then, who would come in for anyone, when Maura said someone should fetch down some hay from the loft and it might as well be herself, so the three of them went out into the dusk—though you could see clear as noon still because of the reflecting snow and the odd light in the sky.

Paddy came in, drooping with weariness, and was starting to ask if water had been brought in, when he was interrupted by a terrific bang which made everyone jump. One of the shutters had blown loose from the hook which held it back and was flapping freely, swinging into the room.

'The wind must have got up,' Grainne said, crossing to it. 'That's very odd, it was still as death out there five minutes ago. But we'd best close up for the night; fasten the other window, Fid.'

She leaned out to catch the erring shutter just as another gust of wind, stronger than the first, slammed it shut so she seized the second, slammed that shut too and dropped the wooden bar across the inside, which would keep them closed and barred until morning.

'What's that noise?' Fidelma said, having fixed her own shutters. 'A sort of howling ... where's Tinker?'

Tinker was a lurcher, a fine dog for the rabbits and a good friend to the Feeneys, for he lived outside most of the year and could be relied upon to bark whenever strangers were near.

'The children will have taken him to fetch Darky,' Grainne said. 'Not that they'll need him; Darky likes the byre, so he does.'

'I'll see if Tink's outside . . .' Roisin said. She was ten and sensible. She crossed the room and cautiously opened the door a crack.

Several things happened at once, then. The tallow candles, which Grainne had lit as soon as it grew dusk, went out, plunging the shuttered cottage into pitch darkness. And the door blew wide, crashing back against the wall, allowing a gale to sweep through the room, a gale so strong that it sent Grainne, who had stepped into its path, reeling into the solid wooden table and bowled the door-opener head over heels across the earth floor until she collided with her elder sister.

'Shut the door!' Paddy Feeney bellowed and sprang to obey his own command, for though

21

Grainne had heard him, she had been unable to do anything against the force of the wind which held her pinned to the table. But even as he plunged at the door the shutters blew in, and one of them sailed across the room, catching Paddy a wicked blow across the side of the head. He fell to the floor as if poleaxed and the wind rolled him across the room as though he had no more substance than a day-old chick, until he fetched up against the wall with a dull clunk.

But at least the wind's bursting of the door and shutters meant that Grainne could now see again in the faint light from the grey clouds overhead, though what she saw was daunting indeed. Fidelma was crawling towards the doorway, the younger children, no doubt terrified out of their wits, were crouching behind their father's big old rocking chair and Paddy Feeney lay still as a stone where the wind had carried him.

'Fid . . . can you close the shutters?' Grainne shouted. 'If we could close up again, mebbe we could keep the storm out.'

'They're broke,' Fidelma screamed back. 'They're in bits, so they are. Where's the boys? And Maura?'

'They'll have sheltered,' Grainne said with a confidence she was far from feeling. 'What's happenin', in the name of God?'

'It's the turblest storm ever,' Fidelma said, beginning to sob. 'I'm frightened, Gr—'

One minute they were crouching in the cottage, listening to the wrath of a storm they had not even seen approaching, the next the roof had gone. There was a bumping, screaming noise and the thatch, the ropes, the big rocks from the seashore, simply took wing and flew into the night.

And now they were at the mercy of the elements indeed! Grainne had once pushed her spade into a nest of field-mice whilst lifting potatoes and now she knew just how those terrified little mice must have felt. One moment safe and secret, secure in their neat little home, the next revealed in all their pitiful inadequacies as the spade sliced through the sod. Staring up, aghast, she could see that not only had the thatch gone but the old timber rafters were creaking and groaning . . . one was breaking loose . . .

'What's wrong wit' Daddy?' screamed Sorcha suddenly, peering out round the chair. 'Why don't he move?'

'He's stunned,' Grainne shouted, just as a beam fell from the roof, narrowly missing her head. She felt it skim her right ear and tried to scramble under the table. 'Oh, my God!'

The exclamation was torn from her; the great wind must have got into the chimney and suddenly the stove front was hurled open and long tongues of flame, scarlet, yellow, blue, were being driven across the room by the force of the gale. Orange sparks flew and before she had moved a muscle the rocking chair caught fire and a wooden bucket began to blaze. Ashes and embers took to the air, a burning grass-tuft landed in Fidelma's hair and Grainne had to crawl across to her and pluck it out before it set fire to her sister's locks.

'Out, everyone,' Grainne shrieked, trying to outdo the wind. 'Get out of here before we're kilt stone dead!'

It was no exaggeration. Two of the rag rugs were blazing and even as she tried to hurry the children out the curtains caught, the flames whooshing up them in seconds. Another beam broke loose and fell and promptly caught fire too, the flames licking eagerly along its dark, bone-dry length. The heat was enormous, and when the wind caught them, the flames and embers moved restlessly, one minute streaming in one direction, the next changing course entirely.

'Take the childer, Fid,' Grainne shouted now. 'I'll fetch Dadda out. Where's Tink?'

'He's outside somewhere,' Roisin shouted. 'I'll go after him.'

'We're all goin', but kape together,' Fidelma said. She gathered Roisin and Sorcha close to her and Maura, who was twelve, caught a fold of her skirt and, clutching each other, the four of them fought their way out into the open.

'Where'll we go, Grainne?'

'The pigsty,' Grainne screamed back. The sty was an extension of the house really, but it had no joining door for Paddy had closed it off years since. The fire would not go through a stone wall two foot thick, surely? She guessed that the roof would have gone, but the walls would stand . . . it would be a better refuge than the farmhouse with the fire raging, wouldn't it? 'Fid, if it isn't safe, make for the cavern. Go on, hurry! I'll bring Dadda.'

She crawled over to her father and caught hold of him by the shoulders. He groaned and his eyelids fluttered but he did not wake even when she tugged him slowly across the floor and out into the wild and spiteful wind. She looked around her; there was no sign of the children but when she bent to the task of moving her father once more she felt something warm nudge against her and glanced

24

round, hoping to see one of her brothers or sisters.

It wasn't a child, however, it was Tinker. He was wild-eyed, shivering, but he whined softly when Grainne said his name and as she began to pull her father across the yard—anything to get him away from the burning building—the dog followed her, limping along on three legs with the fourth held at an odd angle. I hope to God it's not broken, Grainne thought, dismayed. Tinker was invaluable to them, they relied on the dog's intelligence and obedience in many ways. He hunted for his own food, which was a saving, of course, but he also brought rabbits home when times were hard, and when the sheep wandered too far Paddy Feeney only had to tell Tinker to 'Fetch 'em out!' and off he'd go and come back with the flock, driving them proudly before him. 'He's me extry leg,' Paddy would joke. 'And me daughters is me extry arms.'

But where should she take her father and the dog? It was terrifying out here; ordinary, everyday objects became deadly missiles, picked up by the wind and hurled with all its force at anyone fool enough to be in the way. Looking around her, Grainne saw that the children were no longer in sight. She began to tow her father towards the pigsty. Then stopped. The wooden half-door had gone, completely disappeared, and most of one wall. A second glance showed her that the empty sty, for the pigs had clearly fled, was actually rocking as the wind howled around it.

Another glance around failed to find her sisters or brothers, so Grainne got her father round the waist and staggered with him across to the big old bramble patch which grew against the old stone wall which divided the yard from the trees. Inch by painful inch, doubled up against the force of the shouting wind, she half dragged, half carried him across the uneven ground. When they reached the brambles, she let go of him and she and the dog forced themselves into the hollow in the middle of the briars which Grainne had never thought to enter, though she had known of its existence since the first time she lost a broody hen within it. Having ensured that there was room for them, she crawled out again and dragged the still inanimate body of her father back into the strange shelter. She made a couple of vain attempts to bring him back to consciousness—it worried her that there was a big, dark lump on his right temple and a trickle of blood ran from it—then, feeling she had done her best for him, she told Tinker to stay with the master and set out to look for her brothers and sisters.

*   *   *

An hour later, or maybe two, she crawled back into the brambles. She had searched and called but against the terrible howling of the wind she could not have heard an answer had there been one. And she had seen nothing, save for objects bowling along the ground or hurtling through the air too fast for recognition. But she had managed to untangle from a stone wall a precious blanket, only a little burnt at one edge. This she carried back with her and when she reached her father and the dog, she put the blanket over all three of them and settled down to get what sleep she could. And so exhausted and frightened was she that she did sleep at last.

All night long the worst and most destructive storm in living memory raged. And towards dawn the inevitable happened. The sea, tossed into a frenzy of turbulence by the wind, backed up. Even as the roaring of the wind began to die down a little, the roaring of the sea took over. The stream which ran no more than a few hundred yards from the Feeneys' home came surging over its banks, the water tumultuous enough to destroy a good deal of what lay in its path.

The first Grainne knew of, it was when she was woken by Tinker whining and nuzzling against her. She sat up and felt the ground soggy beneath her fingers. Tinker whined again, then barked urgently. Blinking, Grainne forced her head and shoulders out of the briars and looked around her. In the pale grey dawn light a sea of turbulent water surrounded her, gleaming like pewter beneath the unquiet and cloudy sky. Really frightened now, Grainne wriggled back into the briar patch and once more tried to rouse her father. 'Dadda, wake up! We'll be drowned, else! Come on, Dadda, there's a flood and the wind's still howlin' . . . oh Jesus, Mary an' Joseph, let me dadda wake!'

Outside the briar patch Tinker barked again. Imperatively. Grainne wrapped her father in the now very damp blanket and, using it like a sort of sledge, towed him out of the bushes and into the open. She glanced towards the house. The water washed around it, but the fire seemed to have been extinguished—perhaps it had burned itself out? She towed her father to the ruins and stopped, aghast. The house was burnt out, empty. Any furniture which had withstood the hurricane had been swallowed up by the fire and a quick glance around her showed that the smoke-stained walls were all that remained. There were no pigs, no hens, no potato clamp, no turf pile and, worst of all, no children, no Fidelma.

*　　　*　　　*

It took Grainne the best part of an hour to settle her father in a corner of what had once been the pigsty. She roofed it with planks from the donkey's stable, which had collapsed entirely, and to keep Paddy from the encroaching water she built up a sort of platform from the loose stones which she found piled against the front of the house. From the look of them they had been blown along the plateau until the building stopped their progress, but Grainne didn't waste time wondering how they had got there, she just used them and was thankful.

At this point her father actually came round, or at least he half opened his eyes and mumbled something.

Grainne bent nearer. 'Dadda? Oh, thank God, you're alive!'

'Water,' Paddy said suddenly, the word coming out quite strongly. 'Water!'

'Indeed, there's plenty of that,' Grainne told him, and looked around her for something to carry water in, then found a battered tin scoop which had once been used to fetch flour and oatmeal out of their sacks. She went outside and got some water, then held the scoop to her father's lips.

He supped, then spat. ''Tis salt!' he said. 'Oh, 'tis

28

salt!'

'I'll get fresh,' Grainne promised, leaving the shelter once more. Tinker would have accompanied her, but she turned him back. 'No, Tink, stay wit' Dadda.'

The Feeneys had no well because the stream was near enough to use and so far as Grainne could remember there was no other source of water ... but then she remembered the little brooks which ran off the plateau in wet weather—they wouldn't be salt, surely? It was just the backing-up of the sea which had caused this.

She would have to cross the stream to get at the little brooks, though. It wasn't a deep stream, but would the flood water have made it dangerous to cross? She stood, up to her knees in water, for a moment, staring out, then took a deep breath and began to walk into the flood.

And it was all right. It reached her waist in the centre but she kept walking steadily and once free of what had been the stream bed she only had to remember what the terrain was like, with its ridges, hollows and rifts, to choose a safe route.

And the water in the tiny brooks was fresh! She filled her scoop and returned by the way she had come, though she nearly lost her precious cargo once, when her foot found an unexpected hollow.

However, she recovered without spilling more than a drop and presently was able to hold the scoop to her father's mouth and watch him eagerly empty it. 'There, Dadda,' she said as he lay back again. 'Now I'll find the rest of the childer and then we'll try to get help. I wonder how the O'Hares and the Caseys have fared?'

She wondered most of all about how the

McBrides had fared, of course, and William in particular, but did not mention it; her father had worries enough right now, she concluded, but she did wonder why William had not come to them the previous evening. She hoped desperately that the hurricane had not caught him in the open, on his way to them, but trusted to his knowledge of the countryside and his natural good sense to have saved him had that been the case. And anyway, with her brothers and sisters missing, she had work to do.

'Take care,' her father whispered as she bent to creep out of the shelter. 'Safe home, Grainne.'

The odd little phrase, which her father had used all her life to anyone undertaking any sort of journey, brought tears to Grainne's eyes. She was beginning to realise that the hurricane was not just an ordinary natural disaster, like a drought or a bad crop. It was something which would affect their lives far more deeply. But she did not intend to let her father see her tears. Time enough for grieving, now she had work to do, her brothers and sisters to find.

Once outside in the windy and rapidly brightening day, Grainne stared around her; there *must* be more than she had thought left to them, there simply must! But the harder she stared the worse their plight seemed. The stone walls of the farmhouse were there still but everything else had gone; the pigs, the front of their sty, the donkey and his leaning plank stable, the very hens and the loud-voiced cockerel had vanished as if they had never been. And the careful piling up of the dry-stone walls which separated field from field had gone too, though at least, Grainne saw thankfully, the wind had dropped stones all over the landscape which could be used to construct new walls. And though she strained her eyes not a human figure was in sight. The only bright spot, in fact, was that the flood was beginning to ebb; she could see the entire yard now, so she should be able to get over the stream easily enough.

The cavern she had advised Fidelma to run to was on the far side of the swollen stream. It was a natural limestone cave with a narrow entrance which widened out once you got inside to a large, downward-sloping cave. When you stood in the cave mouth you could hear, far below you, the swish and chuckle of an underground river making its way along through the impenetrable dark, but though she and Fidelma had often talked of exploring, they had never done so. At times of drought Paddy had threatened to go down with a bucket, but droughts in Ireland rarely last long and the rain had always come again before he had a chance to put his threat into execution.

She forded the stream, considerably heartened to feel how the tug of the water had lessened since her last foray into it, and began to climb from ledge to ledge, glancing around her as she did so. The sheep would be all right, they must be all right . . . sheep would surely have the sense to take shelter, to lie down, to resist . . .

She glanced back towards the flood and saw something bobbing along on the current. A sheep. Two, three . . . more! She had forgotten that a soaked sheep simply can't protect itself in water, it becomes waterlogged quickly and drowns.

But the cow would be all right, she was a sturdy animal . . . the calf was a heifer and worth a deal of money. Let the cow and the calf be all right, dear God, Grainne started to pray, then remembered her brothers and sisters. How could she pray for a cow and its calf when her own relatives were missing?

Grainne stumbled on towards the cave. As she got nearer and saw no one, she was suddenly filled with terror. The underground river! If the sea had backed up there, too . . . she broke into a run.

Reaching the cave mouth, she bent down and put her head and shoulders into the darkness, then went right inside because whilst she was in the entrance her body blocked most of the light so that she could see nothing. 'Fidelma!' she shouted, and heard her voice echo eerily round the rocks. 'Fidelma . . . are you there?'

No one answered. But when Grainne stopped shouting and looked carefully around her, she knew that her sisters had been here. The floor was dry and sandy, and footprints scuffed the lighter end of the cave. Grainne could even see where they had sat, had made a sort of nest for themselves.

And she could see the footprints leading into the back of the cave, where it narrowed once more into a deep, downward-sloping passage. Footprints which only went one way and did not come out again.

Grainne stood at the mouth of the passageway for some time, calling gently, but there was no response and she was too wary to try to explore further. She had no candle or means of getting a light so she could see nothing, and if the passage simply ended in a huge drop to the unseen river below then she would be mad to try. Common sense told her that she would not help the family's desperate situation by getting killed too.

Presently she left the cavern and, with a heavy heart, decided to go next to the McBrides' farm to ask for help. After all, she and William were promised to one another—he would help her even if his family would not.

So Grainne set out on the long walk. She had never seen the McBride farmhouse but knew it was not on the Burren but on the gentler land, and she assumed that because the McBrides were rich, the house would probably be undamaged, unlike the cabins inhabited by the O'Hares and Caseys, which were poor structures of sods and mud and thatched with straw, unlikely to stand against such weather. Besides, she must know what had happened to William. People of means, furthermore, were likelier to be able to assist others than peasants who would have their work cut out to help themselves.

Grainne hurried along, with the flood on her left, and saw frightening things. The bodies of hens came first, draggled and drowned, lying in pathetic little bundles on the streaming limestone slabs. Then came a cow, floating on its back and wedged against a stand of reeds, its poor legs sticking straight up into the air, its stomach bloated. Sheep, too, had been drowned or simply killed by the force of the wind, she could not tell which, but she recognised two of their own ewes and gulped back tears. It was gradually being borne in upon her that they were ruined entirely. The pigs and cattle could not have lived once the flood came, even if they had survived the hurricane. The hens had been unable to fly because their wings had been clipped so they, too, had died. The tumbril would have been carried out to sea or far inland, if it wasn't already in bits, and the stable and all its contents were gone, she had seen that as soon as she left the bramble patch earlier that morning.

But she must get help to search for the others! And unless she was in truth the only survivor, she would do so whatever the cost. If I have to go down on me bended knees, Grainne told herself grimly, I'll get the McBrides to help me search, so I will!

And presently, she had an extraordinary bit of luck. A piece of stone wall stuck out into the flood with a bent willow tree growing against it and where the two met, wedged between them, was a currach.

'Now what the divil are you doin' here?' Grainne asked it, climbing on to the wall and edging out along its length until she reached the willow. 'Dear God in heaven, 'tis our currach! How has it come here, by all that's wonderful?'

Last night, to her knowledge, it had been pulled well up on the beach below the cliff. It had been filled with rocks, because that was how they always left it, so that wind and water should not have moved it. Of course it was light, having little more weight than a large basket, but . . . could the wind have blown it up the cliff and inland?

She leaned down from the wall and caught hold of the small craft. It bobbed on the water, as though waiting patiently for her to release it from the willow's clutches. The oars were gone, but Grainne broke off a willow branch, climbed into the currach, took off her boots and pushed it out on to the flood. It would be a faster method of travel for a while, until the stream wound its way further from the McBride farm, where she would pull it well up and leave it to give her another ride going home.

But as soon as she was aboard, Grainne realised that this was not going to work. If she had been going home, the current would have aided her, but it had no intention of letting her punt herself along against the force of it. So she steered her craft near the bank, grounded it and climbed reluctantly out, boots in hand, holding the currach firmly by its bows as though it had been a recalcitrant dog, and towed it the rest of the way ashore, pulling it well up on the grass. But going home, she thought hopefully, ought to be quite possible, provided the stream remained swollen.

After that, she had to search the surroundings for big stones, for she had no intention of letting the currach float back off to sea again. Once it was well anchored she sat down, replaced her boots and set off.

There was something in the shallow water ahead of her. Something which stirred and bobbed on the current, but which was almost aground. She went towards it.

It was a child.

She knew it must be her sister, knew she was dead, but she still had to turn Sorcha's small body over and bring it ashore, lay it tenderly down on the grass so that she might try, all the while knowing it was useless, to get the water from the child's lungs, to bring life back.

She knelt on the wet grass for what seemed like hours, but was probably no more than twenty minutes, then she crossed her sister's arms across her breast and began to walk towards the McBrides' farmhouse once more. She could do

35

nothing for the child, she would deal with her later: right now she must fetch help for her father. But she wept as she walked, tears for the waste of the little life that had been Sorcha's. She had seen other little ones die, of childish ailments, from accidents, but this was different. Sorcha had been well, happy, only hours before. Now she was dead. Grainne hardly dared ask herself what had happened to Fidelma, Maura and Roisin and the boys. They had gone to bring Darky in, but the donkey was nowhere to be seen, neither alive nor dead; was it possible that they had seen the storm coming and taken shelter elsewhere?

Grainne hurried on. She told herself firmly that Fidelma was almost a grown woman and extremely sensible; she would have found shelter for herself and her little sisters. How Fidelma had come to be parted from Sorcha she dared not think and remembering that she herself had only managed to get her injured father into a brambly hollow made it clear that Fidelma might easily have lost her hold on Sorcha for long enough for the child to be quite literally blown away from her. Dear God, let the others be all right, she prayed. Let the boys have gone to a neighbour, let Fidelma, Maura and Roisin be safe! I can't bear the thought of me brothers and sisters all goin' the way of poor little Sorcha.

The sky overhead was grey still, but at least it was lighter. The wind blew a gale, though nothing like the hurricane of the previous night. Grainne was cold; her shawl had gone and she had left the blanket with her father. It would have been sensible, she told herself now, to have searched around a bit, tried to find something else to throw

36

across her shoulders, but hurrying warmed her and the thought of getting help in the search for her brothers and sisters spurred her on.

It was a good walk to the McBride place, though, and not easy going. There were trees down, hay-stacks strewn across the melting snow, dead stock everywhere. The countryside had been devastated by the hurricane and the backing up of the sea had finished off the job. As she walked, Grainne noticed dead fish on the margins of the flood-water; they had no more been able to resist the tempest than people or animals. The McBrides kept a big flock of sheep, or rather they had kept a big flock of sheep; now, large numbers of drowned sheep lay about her on the soggy land and as she walked Grainne realised that the wild creatures had suffered as badly as the domesticated. Rabbits, stoats, hedgehogs ... she saw the little bodies in amongst the fallen trees, under uprooted bushes and of course on the water, which still rolled sluggishly to her left. She had left the Burren behind her now and presently came to a wood behind which, William had told her, the McBride farmhouse was snugged down. But of that beautiful wood he spoke of there were now almost no trees left standing. And here, to her distress, the ground was littered not only with the debris from the fallen trees, but with hundreds of dead birds. Crows, blackbirds, tits, robins, sparrows lay where the wind had cast them, torn from the sky at the height of the storm, so pathetic that Grainne felt tears come to her eyes once more. Poor little birds ... poor little Sorcha, barely ten years old ... ah, dear God, what will become of me if ...

She did not finish the sentence, even in her

37

mind. To be alone was too awful to contemplate, but of course she need not contemplate it; Dadda is sickly perhaps, but he's waiting for me at home, she told herself comfortingly. He'll be well, if I can get help to repair the house so that I can nurse him properly.

So full had Grainne's mind been as she walked that she had scarcely taken notice of the changes, for this was no longer the Burren, but a gentler, milder land. There were softly sloping hills, woods, rolling meadows, cultivated fields. Though now of course the trees were almost all broken down and the fields, like their own, had mostly lost the dry-stone walls. But it's rich land, Grainne thought, marvelling at it. No wonder Dadda thought William would not want to change it for our life on the Burren.

Grainne topped a gentle rise and the house stood before her. Roofless. The thatch had been stripped, as had their own, and then the great wind had got to work on the rafters, crushing them like straws in the hand. The McBrides had a proper garden, William had told her, but where was it now? Crushed, mangled, the poplars which had fenced it to the west broken off less than a foot from the ground, the orchard of which he had spoken not only fruitless but treeless too. Not a plum, apple or pear tree was standing. And the window-glass, which she and Fidelma had envied so much when William had described his home, had been blown out, leaving the house with a blank, blind look, because the windows were larger than the Feeneys' windows.

The outhouses still stood, however, and from here she was fairly sure that fire had not devastated

38

the farmhouse. A door swung, but otherwise, if you discounted the missing thatch, it looked relatively undamaged.

Having checked as much as she could, Grainne set off down the slope of the hill. The path was so thick with fallen debris that her footsteps scrunched as she walked; a fat lot of good it was, trying to go quietly, she told herself, so you might as well put your chin in the air and stride out. They'll help, they have to! They wouldn't dare not, for surely God would punish anyone who did not help a neighbour after a disaster so all-embracing?

She reached the swinging door and banged on it. Hard, then harder. No one came. She pushed the door and called out, then walked into the room. It was empty of people, but they had not been long gone. Firelight illumined it, there were used dishes piled up by a low stone sink and someone had cast down some knitting in a chair by the fireside.

'Hallo?' Grainne called timidly. 'Is anyone to home?'

She waited. And heard faint but approaching, shuffling footsteps.

*   *   *

An hour later, Grainne reached the currach and climbed aboard. She should be back at the farmhouse, or what was left of it, in another hour, her mission at least partially accomplished. Mrs McBride had been kind enough, once she had got over the shock of learning she had a Feeney standing in her kitchen. She was older than Grainne had imagined her to be, tall and grey-haired, with a soft, foolish face and an irritating little laugh. She had a habit of blinking very rapidly when she was thinking and she was nervous, stammering as she talked, but she did not seem ill-disposed towards her visitor.

'Me son W-William's gone in to Ennis wit' his f-father,' she had said, once Grainne had introduced herself. 'Me other boy, Talbot, is out searchin' for beasts. There's none here to help wit' your s-search, Miss Feeney. Me daughter's in the dairy . . . we've found a couple of cows, she's m-milkin' 'em.'

'Why have they gone to Ennis?' Grainne had asked boldly.

'William's hurt. He went out earlier, then turned back when the hurricane c-came upon him. He reached the wood'—she sniffed and patted her eyes with a spotted handkerchief—'and a tree came crashin' down. It banged him on the side of the h-head, broke his shoulder, pinned him there on the ground for hours. We found him at first light, no breath of life, no m-movement, nothing. But his father and brother c-carried him home and he c-came round . . . he's gone to get his hurts seen to by the doctor.'

'Oh, poor William,' Grainne had said. 'I'm glad he's not too much hurt—and when they come back, may I ask you to beg William to come and visit us? The hurricane has all but destroyed us entirely.'

Mrs McBride smiled for the first time. Was it triumph? Or was she as foolish as she seemed? Grainne could not tell on such short acquaintance.

'Oh, he won't b-be able to leave his own h-home for a long while yet. He'll be busy here, findin' our beasts, makin' good the d-damage, for you aren't the o-only ones to have s-suffered. I fear W-William won't be walkin' your way for w-weeks.'

40

'Then I must find help elsewhere,' Grainne said and turned towards the door, but just as she was about to open it her hostess called her back.

'It's cold; you've not even a shawl,' she said. 'I can spare a jug of m-milk . . . a loaf . . .'

She piled food into a rush basket, but hurriedly, as though she was afraid of being caught, then flung a shawl around Grainne's shoulders. It was made of thick, soft wool and was much finer than Grainne's old one had been.

'Thank you, Mrs McBride,' Grainne said, bewildered by the older woman's behaviour. 'If William should ask, tell him we're in need, would you?'

'He's not well,' Mrs McBride said as though in answer. 'Poor William, he won't be walking your way for a while yet.'

Shrugging to herself, Grainne had set off after another word of thanks and farewell, and now the currach was homeward bound, drifting with the stream. The little craft bounced along, needing only a touch now and then with the willow-branch to guide it, and all too soon Grainne and her basket of food were back at their own farmhouse, or what was left of it.

And there she found Fidelma, with Roisin at her side, kneeling by her father and hugging him, whilst tears ran down her face.

*   *   *

'We went into the cavern,' Fidelma said when Grainne told her how she had searched for them. 'Sure an' didn't you say to do so, Grainne? But it was frightenin' outside, so it was, wit' howlings and

41

t'umps and bangs. And then Sorcha wailed so . . . she wanted to creep right to the back of the cavern, where we wouldn't be able to hear the noise so well, or feel the wetness, for we were soon soaked,' she added.

'Did she run outside?' Grainne said gently, when Fidelma stopped speaking and closed her eyes for a moment. 'I know she's dead, alanna, for I found her body not half a mile from here, in the water, floatin'.'

'Ah, sweet Jesus, I knew it!' Fidelma cried, rocking back and forth with grief, whilst Roisin wailed in unison. 'Oh, me poor darlin', me poor Sorcha!'

'Don't carry on, Fid,' Grainne said rather sharply. 'What happened, if she didn't run outside?'

'She went deeper,' Fidelma said simply. 'And she didn't come back. We had no light, it was dark as pitch in there, so after a little time, Maura went to look for her. And when they hadn't come back by first light, Roisin and I went down to the passage, callin', weepin', beggin' them to answer us.'

'How far down did you go?' Grainne asked. 'I nearly came down . . .'

'T'ank the good Lord that you didn't,' Fidelma said piously. 'For though we got t'rough the passage safe enough, it comes out near a great, rushin' underground river, like Dadda always said it did. We felt around, Roisin an' me, hopin' to catch a holt of one of the others, but there was nothin'. It's my belief that earlier, when they went down, the river was floodin', an' took them.'

'I'm sure you're right,' Grainne said. 'For that river comes up to the surface and then goes

42

underground again all across the Burren. I've heard Dadda say so many a time. Oh, Fid, thank God that you an' Roisin didn't venture too far!'

'Then . . . then you t'ink poor Maura's drowned as well?' Fidelma said, her voice a whisper. 'I hoped they'd be carried above ground an' spat on to dry land . . . oh, if only I'd kept a holt of them, Grainne! If only I'd not let go, once we were in the cavern.'

'You couldn't know what would happen,' Grainne said. 'When Dadda's stronger we'll go out and search the place. The boys haven't come back yet, I suppose?'

'Not yet,' Fidelma said. 'You've brought food though, Grainne—shall we try to light a fire and make somet'ing hot for Dadda?'

*   *   *

Before night fell, the boys came home, shamefaced, shivering. Sean had a bruise the size of a cooking apple on his brow and Kieran had a four-inch slash right across the crown of his head where a plank had fallen on him when the stable collapsed, but they were all right, they assured their sister. The two of them had been nearer the Caseys' cabin when the hurricane started, so they had sought shelter there. It had been all right at first, they had clustered round the fire with the Casey family, telling stories and joking, but then the cabin had simply fallen about their ears, which was how they had come by their wounds.

'We were a sight,' Sean said. 'Black as ink from the mud, Grainne, an' wet as mermaids. Where's Maura? She's all right, isn't she?'

43

'She hasn't come home,' Grainne said slowly. 'You didn't see . . . anything . . . as you came along?'

'Not a t'ing,' Sean said, with Kieran echoing it. 'Only dead sheep, dead rabbits, dead bords . . .'

Fidelma, listening, put her hands over her face and turned away, and Grainne hastened to comfort her. 'It's all right, Maura's a sensible girl,' she said, hugging the younger girl. 'We'll find her, I know. You see if we don't.'

But they did not.

*   *   *

It was spring in the Burren and the limestone crags were bright with spring flowers. The Feeney farmhouse, however, was still roofless. It looked untenanted and indeed it was about to become so, for the Feeneys, with their small possessions in a handcart which Paddy had knocked up with bits of plank from the stable, were leaving.

They had spent the first few days after the hurricane searching the countryside for their possessions and had found some of the things which the wind had snatched so cruelly from them on that terrible night. Their haystack had gone, whirled away to land, no doubt, on someone else's property, but they foraged further afield and found hay, gathering it up in their arms and carrying it home, to lay it in the bit of roofed shelter which they had made, for bedding, warmth . . . even to get a fire lit.

They found some pans, dented and filthy, but not past repair. And rags of clothing, some torn blankets . . . not theirs, but 'refugees' from some other domestic disaster of the hurricane. And there were dead sheep, so they would not starve, and fish, carried inshore by the wild tide and stranded on unaccustomed grass and slabs of limestone rock.

But it was not enough. Paddy did his best; he went into Ennis to try to see if someone would lend him some money so he could buy stock, a donkey, the makings of a new beginning. The trouble was that the hurricane had affected everyone. People were scratching around trying to repair their own fortunes. The Feeneys would have to manage somehow.

And then the letter arrived, with a Dublin postmark and a genial invitation to go and stay with Tomas Feeney and to find work so that they might restock the farm once more.

'It makes sense, alannas,' Paddy said pleadingly when Grainne had read him the letter. 'I know you want to stay here, but we've not even a roof over our heads, not so much as one bonaveen left to us. Tomas will see us right, don't you fret.'

The older girls had fought against it, both of them. Grainne had said that she was promised to William and intended to stay on the Burren and marry him, even if they had to live hand-to-mouth for a bit, if his parents disowned him for marrying, as they thought, beneath him. And Fidelma tightened her lips and said she'd plans of her own, so she had, and she wouldn't be goin' to old Dublin no matter what.

'Me brother Tomas says to come to Dublin,' Paddy told the Caseys and the O'Hares, who were rebuilding their cabins and doing everything in their power to keep themselves fed whilst they planted potatoes and built up some stock. 'We'll earn easier in Dublin than we can here. The girls

45

can work, I can work . . . me leg's niver stopped me workin' here, so why should it stop me there? . . . an' when we've our fortunes made, isn't it back we'll be comin', with all the speed we can muster?'

Grainne let her father make his plans because she understood that he needed to do so, perhaps he even needed to get away for a while, with two of his five daughters dead. But she told him straight that she wouldn't go with him, because she just knew that William would want to wed her as soon as his hurts healed, but then rumours began to reach her that all was not well in the McBride household. And one beautiful sunny spring day when her father's preparations for leaving were all but complete, she took her courage in both hands and walked over to the McBride farm. She knocked and Mrs McBride answered the door.

'I've come to see William—we're promised,' Grainne had said boldly. 'I must see him.'

She expected a flat refusal or an argument, but after staring at her for a moment Mrs McBride stood aside. 'He's in the front room, on the sofa,' she said. Nothing else. Neither welcome nor reproach.

A front room—how grand, Grainne thought inside her head, but she said nothing aloud, only went out of one door and through another.

And there was William. He looked just the same for a moment; dark-red hair, brown face, white teeth when he smiled. But there was something different about his smile. He looked . . . empty.

'William?' Grainne said, going near. 'William? It's me, Grainne.' Almost without thinking, her hand went to her stomach. 'William, do you remember the night we went to the barn, you and I,

46

and climbed up amongst the hay in the loft? William, I think . . . I think . . .'

Her voice died away as he stared at her, apparently unheeding. Slowly, she held out her hand and he took it in a vicelike grip. He hurt her fingers. After, there were bruises. 'Pretty,' he said. 'Pretty, pretty, pretty!'

She was frightened, then. She tried to tug her hand away and he clung, with something so pathetic in his blank face, something so akin to sadness in his eyes, that she could have wept . . . yet the emptiness was frightening, the very fact that he could look at her as he would look at a stranger so painful that she felt she could not bear it.

'Pretty, W'm . . . wanna pretty,' he kept saying over and over, and the look on his face, the sadness, the longing, became mixed with something else, a sort of brutish determination. He tugged at her hands, crushing her fingers. She cried out involuntarily with the pain. Grainne was able to tug herself free only because William saw a little beetle running across a patch of sunshine on the whitewashed wall and let go of her in order to squash it.

Grainne ran from the room. She ran from the house, but then she was ashamed, turned back and reluctantly went in through the door once more.

In the kitchen Mrs McBride was making soda bread. There was butter in a crock and milk in a bucket and the kitchen smelled warm and good. She said: 'Did he know you?' But there was no real hope in her tone, no real questioning.

'No,' Grainne said flatly. 'What's happened to him, Mrs McBride?'

'The doctors say the blow on the head addled his

47

wits,' Mrs McBride said. 'He should get stronger in himself, but he won't get his good sense back. Oh, when he heals he'll work in the fields and plough the land and shear the sheep. But he won't ever marry, or read a book, or talk sensible.'

'I'm terrible sorry,' Grainne said awkwardly. 'He—he was a lovely feller, Mrs McBride. I really did love him.'

The older woman looked across her baking at Grainne and nodded. 'I b'lieve you did,' she said. 'But it's God's will.'

'It's cruel hard on William,' Grainne said, tears trying to choke the words in her throat. 'He did love to laugh and joke, and he read any book he could lay hands on. Won't he ever read again, Mrs McBride?'

'No. Doctor says it's all gone,' Mrs McBride said. 'We've had a week or two to think about it, so I don't cry any more. He'll never leave me now, William won't. He'll stay with his mammy and daddy until we all die. He won't inherit, elder son or no, but we'll take care of him.'

That, for Grainne, had been the turning point. Now, she had no reason to stay on the Burren, none to protest that they might survive here without taking a step so dubious as making their way to Dublin city. And she found that she wanted to go now. Without realising it, she had been counting on William's help to get the farm back into shape and without that help the struggle would be so uphill that she doubted if they would ever attain a decent, normal sort of life again. They could fish, gather seaweed, trap rabbits and perhaps scrape together enough money to buy a few hens, in time another cow, perhaps. But it would be unbelievably hard—and life on the Burren was hard enough in the ordinary course of events. Once she had seen William and acknowledged that the William she loved was no longer there, she discovered what all young lovers know: that every path you have walked with your love becomes a part of the love you've shared. It was painful to her to go down to the beach for seaweed, because she had walked the length and breadth of that beach with William beside her. She no longer wished to fish from the currach, because she and William had fished together. The lanes they had wandered, the secret places they had met, were no longer beautiful, sacred, but somehow horrible, because she would never meet William there again. Or not the old William, the man she had loved. Worst of all, in a horrible sort of way, was that the *shell* of William was still here. She might meet the beautiful face and athletic body at the market, or on the winding road to Ennis. And face to face, she would see the emptiness behind his eyes, see those same eyes, which had once shone with love for her, blank, indifferent.

'I agree with Dadda,' she had said at last to Fidelma, a week or so after her visit to the McBrides. 'We should leave. There's nothing for us here.'

'I don't want to leave and I won't,' Fidelma said stubbornly. 'I want to stay near Durvan. Him and me are promised.'

'You're nothin' but a pair of children,' Grainne had said furiously. It wasn't fair! Fidelma was a child, it should be she, it should be she . . .

'You're a jealous cat!' Fidelma had shouted, face scarlet, tears starting. 'You were happy enough to

49

stay when you t'ought you were goin' to marry William. Well, I won't leave me lovely Durvan, I'll stay wit' him, his mammy likes me . . .'

'You'll come wit' us, an' give a hand,' Grainne had said coldly, implacably. 'The Caseys don't want an extry mouth to feed an' well you know it. Fid, we'll both of us have to work, so we shall, an' then, one day, we'll mebbe come home.'

Fidelma had snorted. 'Is that what you want? To work like a slave until you're an old woman and then to come home to find William even more mad than he is already? To find him drooling after you, pawing at your clothes, saying *pretty, pretty, pretty?* You want to t'ink about gettin' yourself a real man, Grainne, before you're too old to be a wife!'

'Oh, and Durvan's a *real man,* is he? Well, if he is, he ought to t'ink about gettin' himself a *real woman,* Fid, an' not a spoilt child!'

The sisters glared at each other, Grainne's fingers itching to slap her sister across her increasingly pretty, increasingly appealing little face.

'Dadda, did you hear what Grainne called me? A spoilt child, she called me, an' me only wantin' to go to me intended. She's jealous, Dadda.'

Quarrels like this sprang up all the time now, as the tension caused by their troubles stretched their nerves to snapping point.

Paddy flapped a hand at them. 'We're all goin', and we'll all come back when the time's ripe,' he declared. 'No more quarrellin' from either one of ye or I'll do something desp'rit!'

So now here they were, with their few possessions on the handcart, setting out for Dublin. Fidelma with a face like thunder, Grainne pale and sad, and the other children clinging together, clutching Tinker, sobbing quietly.

They missed their dead sisters, of course, Grainne told herself. As did she. She really did. But none of them knew pain like hers. She missed William so badly and felt such terrible sadness for him, yet still there was the longing, hot in the pit of her stomach, for their closeness, which had gone for ever.

She walked along the dusty road beside Fidelma and glanced timidly at her sister from time to time. Finally, she laid a hand on her arm. 'Fid ... I'm sorry for all the things I've said and the way I've behaved, honest to God I am. There's a reason for it, indeed there is, one day you'll understand that I can't help the way I feel. But we've got to pull together now, and I'll try me very best to be fair to you and to please you. Will you give me a kiss now, an' be friends?'

'No,' Fidelma said coldly. 'You're me enemy, Grainne Feeney. You don't want me to be happy wit' me Durvan because you can't have your loony William. Just you leave me alone an' I'll leave you alone.'

'You're a cruel bitch, Fidelma,' Grainne whispered. 'I hope to God one day you have an ache inside you that hurts you as much as it hurts me now.'

'I hope to God you go on hurting for the rest of your natural life,' Fidelma hissed, for they knew better than to quarrel aloud after their father's many threats. 'And don't think I'm goin' to live wit' you when we get to Dublin, for I am not! I'll move away from you the first chance I get—as far as possible, what's more.'

'You're not alone, Fidelma Feeney, for I don't intend to live anywhere near you whiles I've breath in me body. Right, then. It's war between us two, then?'

'War,' confirmed Fidelma between her small white teeth, which were gripping her lower lip as if they would bite it in two. 'And may you rot before I speak dacent to you again, sister.'

This time Grainne did not reply and the two of them walked on, elbows almost touching but hearts and minds a mile apart, into the soft spring dusk.

CHAPTER TWO

Liverpool, March 1904

Ellen awoke. For some time she had been dimly aware of a disturbance; faint cries, the occasional muttered curse, but she hadn't been able to wake herself up to find out what was going on. She had been late to bed, for a start, and for once the pile of blankets and old coats which covered her had felt warm and adequate, from which she deduced that the bitter cold was beginning to break at last.

Now that she was awake, however, she stirred cautiously, opening one eye and squinting towards the window. It was a paler square in the darkness to be sure, but it wasn't morning yet. Not by a long chalk. So why the fuss? The drunks had tottered home hours ago, her new stepfather was at sea, her mother . . .

Her mother! There was a baby on the way— could this noise be a sign of its imminent arrival?

Ada Docherty had said only last evening that her back ached and that the baby should not be long now. Ellen sat up, reluctantly pushing the covers back and letting her bare feet dangle inches above the floor. Because she was the only girl in the family she had a tiny box of a room to herself, whilst her brothers—Dick, Ozzie, Fred and Bertie—shared the larger room next door. It wasn't bad being the only girl in some ways—you had a bed to yourself for a start, the boys shared, four to an ancient, creaking wooden bedstead—but it did mean you were the only one who helped your mam. Boys sometimes ran messages and carried water, but for the most part it was the girl who worked around the house, even when she was only ten, as Ellen was, with brothers whose ages ranged from Dick, who was sixteen and working, to Bertie, who was eleven and therefore the nearest to Ellen in age.

There had been quiet since Ellen sat up and she was actually considering rolling back into her warm bed when she distinctly heard her mother's voice. Faintly, she was calling Ellen's name. Immediately Ellen jumped out of bed, ran across the icy-cold floorboards and out of her room. She closed the door quietly, though; she didn't want to wake the boys, who would sleep through anything when you needed them and woke at a whisper when you didn't. Boys, in Ellen's experience, had a short way with sisters who woke them from a good sleep. Not that she would hesitate to wake them if the need arose, of course. They weren't bad, her brothers, but they didn't know their own strength. A playful clout from Dick or Ozzie could really hurt, but if she cried they called her names . . . Mammy's pet, teacher's boot-licker . . . which could hurt as badly as a clip round the ear, so by and large Ellen avoided conflict or even disagreement with brothers so much bigger and stronger than she.

'Ellen, love, can you come?'

The faint voice from the direction of her mother's room had Ellen rushing across the landing at once. She shot open the door and went over to the bed. Her mother lay on it, propped up by a couple of pillows, her pretty, night-black curls draggly now, her beautiful face streaked with sweat and the colour of cheese, a sort of yellowy grey. She was endeavouring to take off a stained woollen jacket and Ellen, feeling the cold already invading her own nightgown and underclothing, remonstrated gently.

'Did you ought to tek 'em off, Mam? You'll freeze.'

On the bed, Ada Docherty smiled faintly, but continued to struggle out of the garment. 'It's awright, chuck, I'm like an oven,' she said breathlessly. 'The baby's comin', you see, Ellie, so I want me clean nightgown, the one wi' the lace collar. Can you find it up for me an' help me into it? Then you'd best gerroff and fetch Mrs Bluett. I'm a bit long in the tooth for havin' babies so your dad paid for Mrs Bluett to come for me lyin' in before his ship sailed. So we might as well . . .' Her breath was suspended for a moment and colour invaded her pale face, then faded again.

'Oh, Mam, it hurts you,' Ellen said, easing the jacket down her mother's arms. 'Babies do hurt. Me pal Shirl said her mam shrieked out ever so! Can I do somethin' to help? Shirl rubbed Mrs O'Connor's back, she told me.' She crossed the

54

room to the little wooden chest of drawers with the Sacred Heart on top of it, where she knew her mother kept her clean clothing. She found the nightgown and returned to the bed, where her mother was trying to disentangle herself from a couple of petticoats. 'Oh, Mam, Mrs Bluett won't mind you keepin' warm, don't tek 'em all off!'

'It's best,' her mother said firmly. 'Oh Gawd, here it comes again!'

As Ellen watched, the veins on her mother's forehead swelled as she fought against shouting out, and as the pain faded the two of them managed somehow to get Mrs Docherty out of the petticoats and into the nightgown, though it wouldn't go down over the swollen mound of her stomach.

'Never mind, chuck,' Ada said, pulling up the blankets. 'Now run off, there's a dear. Mrs Bluett may take some wakenin', you know.'

'I'll send Bertie,' Ellen said. It was dark outside and Mrs Bluett didn't live in the court; her house was two streets away. 'I'll just tell him, Mam.'

Her mother started to say go yourself, go at once, but Ellen was already back in the boys' room and shaking Bertie briskly by the shoulder. He was a good lad, Ellen considered, the least likely to hit out when roused, but even so, as soon as she had shaken him she moved back out of range.

'Bertie! Mam's started wi' the baby . . . go get Mrs Bluett, will you? And hurry, she needs help.'

'Go yourself,' Bertie said predictably, but he shrugged the covers down to his waist, causing Dick, who lay beside him, to moan and shuffle further down the bed. 'Why can't you go, Ellie?'

'Well, our mam needs me,' Ellen said. And then,

55

more truthfully: 'You don't know nothin' about havin' babies, Bertie, but me pal Shirl told me all about it, so I can give our mam a hand, see? Oh, go on, Bertie, you don't want to have to sit wi' our mam whiles she shouts out, do you?'

Bertie stared at her, his eyes round and black in the half-dark. 'I don't fancy seein' a baby come,' he admitted. 'I heared her cry out a couple o' times, but Mr Lawson said childbirth's for women, so I didn't do nothin'. But if you ran quick, Ellie, you could be there an' back before the cat could lick its ear.'

'Don't be daft, you know old Ma Bluett couldn't hurry to save her life,' Ellen said impatiently. Boys, she told herself, would come up with any old rubbish just so's they were the ones what stayed in bed and you were the one what went out into the cold. 'Come on, Bertie ... Mam's moanin' somethin' awful.'

'Oh ... awright,' Bertie said. 'I'm awake now, I s'pose. What'll you do whiles I'm gone?'

'Boil a kettle, get our mam a drink, fetch out the baby clo'es, rub Mam's back,' Ellen said rapidly. 'Hurry, Bertie!'

Bertie, muttering, climbed out of his nest and made for the door. He was fully clothed—the weather had been bitter for weeks—but downstairs there were boots; he would need boots at this time of night, even if they were several sizes too large, with holes at toe and heel. With three brothers older than himself Bertie was used to wearing hand-me-downs.

Ellen followed him downstairs. She didn't make the mistake of trying to wake the others. Dick, Ozzie and Fred were all right so far as it went, but she didn't think an appeal to their better natures would get her far. Family feeling came a long way behind what they would call *looking after number one,* so she would not disturb their slumber. Mind you, Ellen told herself as she came down the stairs, Dick did hand over half his wages to Mam—he was a porter at Exchange station—but the other two boys froze on to any money they earned as of right. And Dick was getting interested in girls, spending ages staring at his reflection in the bit of mirror above the sink whilst he combed his hair this way and that and squeezed the spots which had suddenly begun to appear on his chin.

'I brung you some water in,' Bertie said as she entered the kitchen. He had donned a couple of pairs of extra socks and was pulling on a pair of boots, Ellen was glad to see. Not his own—Bertie's boots were awaiting replacement, being too small and having cardboard covering the gaping holes in the soles—but Ozzie's, probably. Ozzie worked as a delivery boy after school and at weekends for a local butcher; he did all right. 'I fetched some in afore I went to bed,' Bertie continued. 'It'll do you till teatime.'

'Thanks, Bertie,' Ellen said with real gratitude. All the boys knew that she didn't much like the dark, not since she and their stepfather had been attacked coming up from the docks one night. Of course the men who attacked them hadn't been interested in a small girl, Mick had said afterwards, they had been after a seaman's pay, but the blows which had rained down upon her had hurt just as much as if they had been intended to fall where they did.

'Awright. I'll be off, then,' Bertie said now,

getting to his feet. He went to the front door and took down the ancient, much felted overcoat which hung there. 'I dare say Dick won't grudge me a loan o' this.'

Ellen, heaving the old black kettle over the fire and belabouring the embers with a poker to bring it back to life, muttered breathlessly that he probably wouldn't. The three older boys were always borrowing each other's clothes and there was invariably an outcry, but with luck Bertie would be back long before his brothers stirred.

The door creaked open and banged shut, and Ellen heard Bertie's footsteps ringing out on the icy paving slabs, then fading as he turned out of Evangelist Court on to Prince Edwin Lane. She calculated that it would take him perhaps five or six minutes to reach Mrs Bluett's house on Netherfield Road, which was next door but one to the Queen's Arms on the corner of Cornwall Street. But it would take twice as long to get back, because Mrs Bluett was a stout woman, nearer seventy than sixty, who had never been known to hurry. So Ellen would have plenty of time to take the orange box, lovingly lined with pieces of blanket, the little clothes her mother had prepared and the cup of tea she was making up to her mother's room before old Ma Bluett arrived, shouting for kettles, clean linen and a bottle of stout.

Shirl had told Ellen that Mrs Bluett expected a bottle of stout. ''Tis hard work, you know, birthin' a babby,' she had said. 'The old gal likes to wet her whistle afterwards. Me da fetched her a whole crate when she birthed me brother Willie. He were rare pleased to 'ave a boy, see?'

'But you said the midwife didn't bring the baby,'

58

Ellen had pointed out. 'I thought she did, but you said the mam has the baby under her pinafore and that was why my mam was gerrin' so fat. So if your mam brought the baby, why didn't she get the crate of stout?'

'I dunno,' Shirl had said. 'But it were me mam our da shouted at when he saw the marks on Willie's face, only Ma Bluett told 'im they'd fade, an' they did, so that were awright.'

Ellen, waiting for the kettle to boil, thought that perhaps she wouldn't be a mam when she was a grown woman after all. It sometimes seemed as if mams got all the kicks an' none of the kisses, as if they couldn't do right, in fact. On the other hand, she'd had a nip of stout from her mam's glass once and hadn't liked it above half, so perhaps she wouldn't be a midwife, either. I'll have a shop, Ellen decided, and sell puppies and kittens. That 'ud suit me right well.

A moan, gurgling up to a shriek, came echoing down the stairwell and Ellen hastily grabbed the tin in which the tea was kept—the food was all covered because of black beetles and mice—and tipped a few of the small black leaves into the mug, then added water from the now hopping kettle. Ellen loved the tea-caddy; her real father, not Mick Docherty but Tommy Rathbone, had brought it back from foreign parts. It had a picture of the old Queen on the side and it smelt deliciously of the mysterious east. Usually she bent her head over the tin as she took the top off and inhaled deeply, but now she was in a hurry. Having stirred the tea briskly until the colour deepened, she fetched a tin of condensed milk—half empty already—from the cupboard and poured a syrupy spoonful into the

59

brew. Picking up the mug with both hands, she remembered that she should really have used the teapot, but she was in a hurry, her mother needed the tea now. Of course there were tea-leaves at the bottom of the mug, but if her mother drank slowly enough she might not get a mouthful, and at least it was hot and sweet.

Ellen climbed the stairs carefully, holding the mug before her, and entered her mother's room. Ada was lying back, the frilled nightgown in place, even though the lace collar had somehow got twisted so that the bow of ribbon was under one ear. Ellen handed her the tea and straightened the bow, then stood back.

Ada smiled wearily at her daughter, held the mug to her lips and began to drink thirstily. 'Ah, that's better,' she said presently, lowering the mug. 'Puts heart into you, that does. Oh, hell an' damnation, here it comes again!'

'Let me rub your back, Mam,' Ellen said anxiously, taking the mug and standing it down on the bare floorboards. It astonished her to hear her mother swear, for Ada was fond of telling her children that bad language was never necessary. 'Shirl said it helped when a baby's a-comin' to rub your mam's back.'

'Shirl's right, queen,' Ada said as Ellen began to rub. 'Have you brought up the baby's box? And the clothes?' She sat up on one elbow and peered over the side of the bed. 'I want them clothes ready for when Mrs Bluett gets here; and the box, of course.' She stiffened, then clutched at the hard mound of her stomach. 'Ah, Christ, I'm too old, that's the trouble. I never had pain like this when I birthed the rest of you. And I had your gran standin' by, advisin' me. Oh, I do miss me mammy!'

'I 'spect you've forgot what the pain was like before, Mam,' Ellen said, going to the chest of drawers for the baby clothes. 'I'm ten; ten years is a long time. An' . . . an' you ain't the only one what misses Gran.'

Gran had lived with them until her death two years earlier, and Ellen had been very fond of the old lady with her broad Irish accent and her fund of stories and home-made remedies. She had been a good cook too—Ellen remembered the glorious wedges of potato cake, the creamy scrambled eggs on thick rounds of toast, the loaf of brack spread with butter. And she had loved animals, keeping a pig and some hens in the tiny backyard.

But since her death, things had changed. Ada had reluctantly allowed Ellen to keep a couple of hens but she'd put her foot down over a pig.

'Your gran was brought up on a farm,' she had explained. 'She understood all about animals and would have been unhappy without them, but you're a city gel, like me, you can manage very nicely on food from the corner shop.'

So now Ellen got the little baby clothes, lovingly made by her mother during the waiting period, out of the chest of drawers and laid them on the foot of the bed. 'There y'are, Mam,' she said. 'Ain't they pretty, though? Lucky baby, eh?'

'And Mick's younger'n me,' Ada mumbled after a moment and Ellen realised that her mother had not listened to a word her daughter had said but was giving voice to her own secret worries. 'He's a prince, is Mick—what did he see in me, eh? A woman nearin' forty, wi' five kids . . . I'm past me best, there's no denyin' it. S'pose he meets

61

someone younger, someone who's still got her bloom on her? Suppose he leaves us? Oh, dear God, I couldn't bear it if Mick left me all alone again! Ten years I been alone, 'cept for your gran, strugglin' to bring up me fambly right, wonderin' what I'd do wi' meself when they left home, then your gran died an' I din't know which way to turn ... and Mick came along and made me see I'm not finished yet ... I hope to God he doesn't want a baby a year, though ... I'm too old for babies, I told him just the one, then we'll have to find a way ...'

She mumbled off into silence and Ellen, who had been half listening as she moved around the room, went back to the bed and began to rub her mother's back again, making soothing noises as she did so.

'Don't you worry, Mam, you ain't too old for anything! An' we all love Mick, you couldn't have found a better feller. He won't go away, he likes us and we likes him.'

'Oh! Well, that's good,' Ada said and Ellen realised that her mother had forgotten she was there, had been unaware, in fact, that she had a listener. 'Lean out o' the window, queen, and see if there's any sign of Mrs Bluett. The pains are changin', they're gettin' mortal close.'

Ellen breathed on the frost flowers which obscured the glass and made herself a little porthole; she had no intention of opening the window as her mother had suggested and letting in that ice-cold air! 'I can't see anyone ...' she began, then stopped short as the woman on the bed gave a strangled shriek and hauled herself into a crouching position.

'Oh Gawd, it's comin', it's comin', an' there ain't a bleedin' thing I can do about it,' she moaned. 'Quick, Ellie—knot me shawl round the end of the bed an' give me the end of it.'

'Right you are, Mam,' Ellen said briskly. What a blessing it was that Shirl was the eldest of her family and had assisted at so many births; what a blessing she had insisted on telling Ellen in great detail about each one, furthermore! Mind, I didn't think it was good at the time, Ellen remembered, knotting one end of the shawl round the sturdy iron bedpost and handing the other to her mother. All that heaving and grunting and blood and stuff just sounded frightening. But now it was coming in useful; she remembered Shirl telling her how she and her mam had tugged on opposite ends of a length of rope until the baby 'popped out', as Shirl had put it.

Having done her duty with the shawl, Ellen stood back, trying to remember what she should do next. The baby would be washed in warm water so she should go down and bring a kettle up, then there was the clean sheeting which would be wrapped round the child like a shawl ... the clothing was for show until the baby was a lot bigger, her mother had told her ... and of course the stout. A bottle, not a crate, rather to her disappointment. Even if the new baby was a girl her mother had declined to provide the midwife with a crate of stout.

'Your gran brought you an' the others into the world an' she never needed no stout,' her mother had said. 'Still an' all, if that's what Mrs Bluett wants ...'

So the stout waited, downstairs because Mam

63

said she wanted Mrs Bluett stone-cold sober till afterwards.

'Aaargh!' her mother shouted suddenly, as though the noise had been wrenched from her. 'Aaaargh!' She was squatting forward, the covers had fallen back and Ellen saw that her stomach had a strange, pointed look and was as shining and slippery with sweat as her mother's face.

And what a face! Ada was a pretty woman with a bright colour and small features, but now her lips were drawn back in a grimace, her eyes were screwed tightly shut and her teeth were clamped on to her bottom lip with such force that a trickle of blood ran down her chin. She looked frightening, her daughter thought apprehensively, and even as the thought crossed her mind, Ada's face began to flush, veins stood out on her wet forehead and she began to heave on the shawl until the bedpost started to creak ominously.

'Hey, Mam, have a care,' Ellen said anxiously. 'Don't you go tryin' too hard or you'll beat Mrs Bluett to the winnin' post!'

'I know, I don't wan . . . but I can't . . . aaargh!' Ada said breathlessly. 'Go an' find Mrs Bluett, chuck . . . this ain't no place for a kid. Oh, the sweat's stingin' me eyes somethin' cruel!'

'I'm stayin'; I shan't leave you, Mam,' Ellen said stoutly. 'I'll mop the sweat.' She grabbed one of the sheeting squares which were piled up beside the bed and drew the soft material gently round her mother's scarlet face; it came away sodden. 'Shall I rub your back?'

'No, no, no,' Ada sobbed beneath her breath. 'Go 'way, go 'way . . . aaahhhh!'

'Oh, Mam, what's that?' Ellen said suddenly.

64

'Mam, you're bleedin'! There's blood on the . . . oh, oh!'

'It's the baby,' Ada said in a hoarse whisper. 'It's comin', chuck. Bring me a bit o' sheet over to wrap it in.'

Ellen rummaged through the pile and had just selected a decent-sized piece when the bedroom door creaked open. Mrs Bluett took in the situation at a glance and went towards the bed. 'Well done, Ada . . . let's be havin' you, littl'un,' she said cheerfully. 'Yes, 'ere 'e comes, pink an' beautiful!' And whilst Ellen watched, her mother gave one last, convulsive heave and the midwife leaned forward and picked the baby up, then held it by its tiny legs and gave it a brisk slap across its small pink buttocks. The baby gasped and yelled, and Mrs Bluett turned it right side up again and reached for the piece of sheet. She laid the baby on it and produced a small pair of scissors and a piece of what looked like pink string from the pocket of her thick winter coat. 'There you are, Ellen, a little brother for you,' she said, working away. She straightened and patted Ada's knee absently. 'A beautiful child, for all your fears, queen.'

Wrapping the baby firmly in the sheeting, with its arms clamped to its sides, she turned once more to her patient. 'Now we'll just fetch out the afterbirth, an' your Ellen can mek us a nice cup of tea,' she said. 'I told young Bertie to bring a kettle up . . .'

The door rattled as though Bertie had heard, but did not open. Ellen went across and opened it. Bertie stood there, eyes apprehensive, the steaming kettle in one hand, an enamel bowl in the other. 'She awright?' he said. 'Wharris it?'

'A boy,' Ellen said gloomily. 'She's awright, though she's tired. Oh, well, another girl would ha' been nice.'

She turned back to the bed, where her mother lay with the brand-new, pink-faced shrimp of a child in the crook of her arm, smiling down at it. 'Bertie brung the water, Mrs Bluett,' Ellen said timidly. 'Where d'you want it put?'

'Pour some into the bowl so's I can clean your mam up,' the midwife said. 'What'll you call this one, then?'

'Oh, I thought Donal; that was me dad's name,' Ada said. 'What d'you think, Ellie love?'

Ellen, who was sick and tired of being the only girl in a family of boys, sighed but said dutifully that Donal seemed just fine and watched as Mrs Bluett took the swaddled baby from her mother and put him into the blanket-lined cardboard box which stood by the bed. She peered inside at the pink-faced scrap, then put out a cautious finger and stroked the soft down on the baby's head. 'It's got the softest head, Mam,' she said. 'All covered in goldy-brown down.'

''E'll grow proper 'air soon enough . . .' the midwife began, but suddenly stopped speaking and stared at Ada's exposed stomach as though seeing it for the first time. Ellen, staring too, saw that her mother's stomach was moving gently, as though it had a life of its own.

''Ello,' Mrs Bluett said slowly. 'Wharrave you gorrin there?'

'What?' Ada said drowsily. Her eyelids were already half closed; she was plainly exhausted. 'It's the afterbirth, acourse.'

Mrs Bluett shook her head and then, moving

66

with amazing swiftness for one so large, she hooked both hands under Ada's armpits and heaved her back into a sitting position once more. 'I'm sorry, chuck, but there's another kid still to come,' she said positively. 'You're havin' twins.'

'Twins? I don't *believe* it,' Ada said groggily. 'I'm too old . . . it ain't right a woman of my age havin' a child at all. It can't be twins!'

But even as she said it Ellen could tell by the expression which crossed her mother's face that she knew it was true and sure enough, with remarkably little effort this time, presently another baby was being swung by its heels, smacked and wrapped.

'An' this 'un's a gal, chuck,' Mrs Bluett said triumphantly as she placed the second baby beside the first. 'Nice to 'ave a gal, eh?'

Ada glanced cursorily at the second baby, wrapped in sheeting and awaiting its turn in the enamel bowl. 'It's a judgement on me, that's wharrit is,' she moaned. 'It's God's way of punishin' me for marryin' a young feller instead of strugglin' on alone. Why, I haven't even gorra box to put this 'un in, lerralone clothes for its back. God's punishin' me, that's clear as clear.'

'Oh, Mam, it isn't a punishment, what've you ever done wrong?' Ellen said at once. 'You work hard, an' bring us all up proper. An' I've always wanted a sister.'

Ada snorted. 'Oh, chuck, at my age I thought I'd be able to tek things easier. Norra lot, I don't 'spect miracles, but a little easier,' she said bitterly. 'An' what've I got? Twice the work, twice the dirty washin', twice the food to find. Dear God, how am I goin' to manage when Mick's at sea?'

'You'll manage, queen,' Mrs Bluett said robustly,

67

pouring water into the basin for the second time in half an hour. 'You're a big, strong woman, you've a good daughter, a grand man, and sons bringin' money in. You'll manage a treat, once you get used to the idea.'

Ada sighed but said nothing more whilst Mrs Bluett was in the room. As soon as the midwife went downstairs, however, to have her bottle of stout before getting off home, she turned to Ellen. 'I can't tell Mrs Bluett, queen, but I'm goin' to tell you, so's you understand. Mick's a grand feller, but he's got parents in Ireland dependent on him. He can't let them down, see, so the money has to be split two ways. I understand, 'cos nothin' would have made me let your gran go short. But I thought, wi' Dick thinkin' about movin' out and Ozzie leavin' school come summer, that I'd be able to manage with a new baby. But two of 'em! There's no way I can take two of 'em round wi' me when I'm sellin' flowers in Clayton Square, or buyin' them from the wholesalers.'

'But I thought you wouldn't do that no more, not now you've married Mick and you've got Dick's money comin' in,' Ellen said, puzzled. 'I know that was what you said, Mam.'

'Yes, but I didn't reckon on two of 'em, nor I din't know me friend Peg were goin' to offer me her pitch,' Ada said patiently. She glanced over the side of the bed, then stiffened. 'That last 'un . . . look at that hair!'

Obediently, Ellen looked. She had seen the second baby's tight, dark curls, wet from its bath, but now that she looked closer, the hair was drying, and it was a bright, carroty red. 'Ooh, what a lovely colour,' she said. 'It's pretty, though, ain't it, Mam?

68

Wish mine were red, 'stead o' brown,' she added.

Ada, who had been lying back against her pillows, struggled upright again. 'Mick won't like it,' she said worriedly. 'I've got black hair, same's all you kids, an' Mick's fair. What'll he say? Oh Christ, what'll he *think?*'

'Why should he think anything, 'cept that it's pretty?' Ellen said. 'Men don't mind what colour hair babies have, do they?'

'No-oo, but . . .'

'Then just you stop worritin', Mam,' Ellen advised her parent. 'It ain't good for you to worry. I'm goin' to tek the babies downstairs now, so's you can get some sleep. I'll have 'em wi' me in the kitchen, whiles I see Mrs Bluett off and mek you a nice cup of tea.'

She picked up the box, which was surprisingly light, and went carefully down the stairs and into the kitchen. Mrs Bluett was sitting in front of the fire, sipping stout from a chipped teacup, and Bertie was filling the kettle again from the enamel bucket under the low stone sink. He had not gone back to bed, Ellen realised, because he would be required to escort Mrs Bluett home presently, when she announced that she wished to go. He looked up as his sister entered the room and put the box carefully down on the table. The babies lay packed close as two little sardines in a tin, fast asleep still.

'Twins, eh?' Bertie said. 'An' one of 'em's another bleedin' useless girl!'

He was grinning as he spoke but Mrs Bluett, making herself comfortable before the fire, frowned at him. 'Don't you go bein' nasty about your sister, young Bertie,' she said sharply. 'Your

69

mam could do wi' some help since she's give birth to twins, and from whar I know of lads, she'd be better off wi' a score of gals.' She turned to Ellen. 'Take your mam up a cuppa, queen,' she said. 'If she's asleep, leave her be, but I reckon she could do wi' a wet.'

Ellen made the tea, poured it out and then stood staring at the midwife and wondering how best to phrase her question. Mrs Bluett, glancing up at her, said: 'Well, queen? Spit it out—wha's on your mind?'

'It ain't me, it's me mam,' Ellen admitted. 'The last baby's got red hair. What's wrong wi' red hair, Mrs Bluett?'

'Nothin' in this world,' Mrs Bluett said comfortably. 'Why, don't your mam care for red'eads?'

'She doesn't think Mick likes 'em . . . Mick's our dad now,' Ellen said conscientiously. 'He's a nice feller, but the boys won't call him Dad, so I don't, either. He's . . . well, he's . . .'

'He's only eight years older than our Dick,' Bertie said, settling the kettle over the fire.

'Ah,' Mrs Bluett said. 'What did your mam say, chuck?'

'She said what would Mick think when he saw the baby had red hair,' Ellen said, after some thought. 'She thought he'd be cross, I could tell.'

Mrs Bluett glanced at Bertie, who stared, round-eyed, back at her, and then she laughed. 'The rest of you are dark,' she said. 'Mick's got light 'air, ain't 'e?'

'Yaller,' Bertie said succinctly. 'Like one of them day-old chicks they sell in St John's market.'

'Yes, well there you are, then,' Mrs Bluett said

70

rather obscurely. She finished her stout and climbed laboriously to her feet. She went across to the box on the table and checked that the babies still slumbered, then turned back to Ellen. 'I reckon your mam thinks Mick'll want the baby to tek after 'im, like. But you know when you mixes paint?'

'Blue an' yeller meks green,' Ellen said promptly. She loved using paints in school, though the opportunity came seldom. Her teacher believed in discipline, the three Rs, children being seen but not heard, and not much else.

'Aye, you've gorrit, chuck,' the midwife said, struggling into her heavy coat and wrapping an immense muffler round her neck. 'And with 'air, it's the same. Black—that's your mam—and yaller—that's your dad—make red, in 'air. Just tell your mam that and she'll likely stop worritin' about it.' She turned to Bertie, staring open-mouthed at her as she expounded this new idea. 'Now you're to tek me arm goin' acrost the cobbles,' she said severely. 'A woman my size could do damage if she slipped on that ice.'

'To the cobbles?' Bertie asked innocently, then dodged as Mrs Bluett aimed a swipe at him. 'Come on, then, Missus, 'cos the dark's fadin' awready.'

Mrs Bluett turned and winked at Ellen. 'Your brother don't want 'is pals to see 'im arm in arm wid an old woman,' she said. 'Go up to your mam with the tea, queen, an' then get back to bed or you'll be good for nothin' come mornin'.'

Ellen saw them across the court, then closed the door and returned to the kitchen. Once more she made tea, but before taking it upstairs she took another look at the babies, snug in their cardboard

71

box. 'Ain't you a pretty pair?' she whispered. 'Your daddy will love you both, he'll think it's pretty, like what I think. Now you stay there quiet an' presently I'll come down an' fetch you up to my room an' we'll all of us sleep till mornin'.'

She carried the mug of tea up to her mother's room, but Ada was sleeping, so Ellen put the cup carefully down on the box which served as a bedside table and tiptoed out again. Going down to the kitchen, which was still warm from the fire glowing in the range, she decided that she could do with a hot drink herself and probably, when Bertie came back, he would feel the same. Tea was expensive and not something she particularly enjoyed, so she made two mugs of hot water with a spoonful of conny onny in each and was enjoying her own drink when Bertie came quietly in through the back door.

'It's bleedin' cold out there,' he said, taking the proffered mug and wrapping his hands round it. 'And that ole woman's heavy as a cart-horse; I had to lug her all the way up to Kepler Street, what's more, acos when we got to her house there was this little kid from Kepler Street sayin' as how his mam had started wi' the baby, an' would the old gal please come. I tried to gerraway,' he added morosely, 'but she had a grip like a vice on me arm, so I din't have a lorra choice.'

'Well, never mind, an' our dad'll be pleased with you for helpin',' Ellen said craftily. Of all the boys, Bertie was the one who liked and admired Mick the most, possibly because he couldn't remember their real father, who had been swept overboard when Bertie was barely five years old. 'Want to look at the littl'uns?'

'Babies are babies, they all look alike to me,' Bertie said, but he came over to the table and peered into the cardboard box. 'Cor, where did that 'un get them curls from?'

'That's the girl; the boy is called Donal,' Ellen said importantly. 'Mam didn't name the girl, though. What should you like her to be called, Bertie?'

'Ginger,' Bertie said promptly. 'Or Fido, if you like.'

'Don't be horrible,' Ellen said. 'What really?'

But Bertie would not be swayed. 'They'll call her Ginger whatever I say,' he pointed out. 'So why not start out with it? She'll like it better'n Carrots, I dessay.'

'Anyone who calls her Ginger will have me to reckon with,' Ellen said darkly. 'Elizabeth's nice, don't you think?'

'Lizzie. Skinny Lizzie. Ginger Lizzie,' Bertie said thoughtfully. 'Yeah, Lizzie ain't too bad.'

'Oh, you!' Ellen said, giving up. She finished her drink, then went over to the box. 'Come along, twins, we're goin' off to bed,' she said. 'Night, Bertie; see you tomorrer.'

'It's tomorrer now,' Bertie pointed out. 'What'll they have for breakfast, eh? You'll be cookin' bangers an' mash for 'em, I dessay.'

'Babies have milk,' Ellen said. 'Their mams give it 'em.' She knew very well that her mother would breast-feed the twins because Shirl's mam breast-fed all the little O'Connors, but she didn't want to get involved in a technical discussion with Bertie— you never knew just what boys really knew and what they didn't, she thought confusedly. He might easily plead ignorance so he could trick her into saying something she shouldn't. And besides, she realised suddenly how very tired she was; and there was school to be faced in the morning, unless her mam would let her take a day or two off to keep an eye on the new babies.

It was a nice thought, but she really was tired out, so she picked up the babies and trailed slowly up the stairs and into her own room. There, she put the box down beside her bed and climbed between the blankets, then looked down at the two little faces below her.

They looked as alike as all babies did, but not so very alike, she decided. Donal had rather a snouty little nose and full, pouting lips, but the girl twin had a nose like putty and a little rosebud mouth. And the box, for all its blankets, didn't look all that warm. The babies were crammed close in their swaddling of sheets, but as they breathed in and out their breath showed as steam.

'You'll be warmer in here wi' me, babies,' Ellen whispered, dragging the box on to the bed and tipping the contents rather unceremoniously amongst her blankets. 'You don't want to be in that cold old box when you could be snuggled down wi' your very own big sister.'

One baby made a snorting sound, the other gave a little purr, but their eyelids remained tightly closed. I like them, Ellen decided, putting her arms round both children and cuddling them close. I like them very much. They're like beautiful dollies, except they're smooth and warm, and I can feel their little chests moving when they breathe.

She had intended to lie awake for a little, considering what names she would have given the babies had she been able to choose, but weariness

74

overcame her. Presently, all three children slept soundly in the narrow bed.

CHAPTER THREE

Dublin, March 1906

Liam Nolan came out of the front door cautiously, because it had snowed in the night and self-preservation indicated a degree of care when emerging into a white and chilly world, but even so the first snowball narrowly missed his nose and the second one splattered on his chest, damping his uniform jacket.

'Stop that!' Liam called sharply. 'I'm goin' to work, you divil's spawn, just you leave off snowballin' me this minute or I'll be whackin' your bums to a pulp, so I will!'

'But forst you've got to catch us!' a mocking voice shouted, the words echoing round the narrow, canyon-like street and bouncing off the tall tenements which housed such a multitude of children. Not that Liam had any doubts about the identity of the snowball throwers; he knew who they were all right! 'Come on, Liam, catch us if you can!'

'If I don't get to work on time you won't have no soda bread,' Liam called, sidling down the steps and on to the pavement. If he scooted for it he could be round the corner and up Thomas Street before they whopped him with another snowball. If he hadn't been going to work, of course, he'd have chased the little divils and let them have some of

75

their own medicine, but as it was, diplomacy would have to be tried because the thought of getting soaked as well as freezing wasn't one he fancied, and the Post Office inspectors didn't think much of messenger boys who wasted their time with snowballs and came in soaked into the bargain.

So Liam cleared his throat and adopted what he hoped was a friendly, reasonable tone. 'I *was* goin' to bring back somethin' nice just for the pair of ye, but if I'm late, an' soaked wit' snow . . .'

He paused. At the mere mention of something nice one of the twins' heads had appeared round the corner of the house opposite. He couldn't tell which one, because they were so alike—and didn't they make use of it, now?—but you couldn't mistake that shock of hair. They were the naughtiest children in their block . . . the naughtiest in the street. For all he knew, the naughtiest in all Dublin and wasn't it unfortunate, now, that he'd landed them for younger brothers?

'Liam . . . we didn't t'ink . . . are yez soaked, now?'

That was Seamus, always the more thoughtful of the two. Liam, who had played with the idea of dodging round the corner and then vengefully making the biggest snowball in the whole world and hurling it with all his force at his erring brothers' smouldering heads, decided not to bother. For one thing they had probably got a great pile of ammunition ready to hurl, and for another . . . well, though they were divils there was no real harm in the twins.

'No, I'm only wet on me chest,' he called back, therefore. 'I'm off now, fellers, so no more messin'. Right?'

'Not till you come home again,' a voice answered. 'Then you'd better be wearin' your posh cape or you'll get a drubbin', Liam Nolan!'

'Garvan, I know your voice,' Liam said warningly. His cape was at the GPO, waiting for him; if I'd known it was going to snow I'd have wore it home, he thought longingly, now. But failing protective clothing, he resorted once more to threats. 'You aren't the only one who can make snowballs, you . . .' He ducked as another missile came whizzing across at head height, then ran, hearing Garvan's cackle of laughter ringing out behind him.

As Liam hurried along the roadway, scuffing the snow with his regulation boots, he thought about how much he liked his job and how lucky he was. When everyone was needing work and looking for work he had heard on the grapevine that the Post Office were wanting messenger boys. There were a grosh of school-leavers just like him, many of whom had sat the examination for Post Office messenger, but of the three hundred applicants only ten had been taken on, he and his friend Paddy amongst them. He could still remember rushing home, grinning from ear to ear, and telling his mammy how they'd put him on a big old bicycle because he'd sworn to heaven that he could ride one, and watched him climbing aboard in the great, bare Post Office yard.

'Oh, be Jaysus,' his mother had said, clutching her heart. 'But you've never rid a bicycle, Liam! Did ye fall much? Are you hurt bad?'

'I hopped round the yard on me one foot, scootin' wit' the other, and then I got me leg over it and hoisted me bum into the saddle,' Liam said.

'And then I rode that bicycle round and round that big ould yard. I kept aboard it out of *terror*, Mammy, in case I should be made out a liar. And devil a bit did I fall, though me heart was hammerin' loud enough to deafen me. So the fellers that could ride the bicycle sat down to the examination, and ten of us passed and got the messenger jobs, an' me an' ould Paddy are workin' men, so we are.'

'And who knows where a job like that may lead? Who can tell how high you'll climb in a job like that?' his mammy had said dreamily, when he'd told her he would be paid half a crown a week and would get a uniform too. 'Why, you could be a postmaster, Liam me darlin'. Oh, we're goin' up in the world, so we are, wit' you a reg'lar wage earner, an' your brother out of school as often as he's in to earn us a bit from the papers, an' me wit' the dressmakin' . . . oh aye, we don't do so bad.'

'I'll be in line for postman if I don't blot me copybook, an' in a year or two the twins could be earnin' a few coppers an' all,' Liam said hopefully. The twins needed a job, in his opinion, to keep them out of mischief, or at least to concentrate their minds a bit. 'Kids start at seven or eight on the newspaper sellin', you know.'

'Not Seamus and Garvan,' his mother had said firmly, however, abruptly coming out of her dream. 'They're me babies, so they are. Let them have some childhood, Liam.'

Liam had said, uncomfortably, that he didn't mean . . . and his mammy had tousled his hair and said wasn't he as good a boy as ever walked now, without a mean bone in him? And she had reminded him that he hadn't worked on the papers himself until his twelfth birthday was passed, which was fair enough.

So now Liam hurried off to the GPO on O'Connell Street, still proud as a peacock over his job though he'd been in it a year, and decided that he would try and get a bag of fancy bread from Kennedy's on his way home from work, when they were selling off the end-of-day stuff, for weren't there bound to be telegrams to deliver in this unseasonal weather, and didn't the telegrams sometimes bring a nice little bit of a tip from the recipient to the messenger boy? And though his younger brothers might be terrible naughty, there was no real harm in 'em, and he had promised something nice if they stopped harassing him.

Presently he came down on to Merchant's Quay and fell in with Paddy, also hurrying to work. And when they arrived at the Post Office they fetched their capes, pulled on the woolly gloves their mammies had knitted for them—for gloves were no part of the uniform, unfortunately—and went into the office for the first telegrams.

*   *   *

'When I grow up, Garv, I'm goin' to be a messenger boy. How about youse?'

The twins squatted behind the half-door of the broken-down tenement on the end of their row, with the snowballs piled up behind them, waiting for their next victim. Though the most impatient of kids in the normal way, they were like cats when it came to stalking prey; they could wait patiently for hours if, at the end of the wait, they could catch a mouse. Or, in this case, fire snowballs at some

79

unsuspecting victim.

'Well, I won't be a newsboy,' Garvan said decidedly, having given the question some thought. 'The bike's nice, I'd like the bike, so I would. But I'd want to go where I wanted to go, not where I was sent.'

'Uhuh,' Seamus agreed. 'But when you're workin', Garv, you can't always choose to do what you want, you know.'

'If I can't choose I shan't work, then,' Garvan said placidly. He reached into a pocket and withdrew two small, wrinkled apples. 'Want one?'

'Where d'you get 'em? Nicked, are they?' Seamus asked, but without much hope of being answered. Garvan had difficulty with the concept of ownership and sometimes he was pursued down the street by folk who wanted to teach him the difference between 'mine' and 'yours'. Seamus considered nicking to be fair game in some circumstances and not in others, but he wasn't as strong a character as Garvan so he usually went along with what his twin wanted.

'Ould Nellie,' Garvan replied, handing over an apple. 'They rolled off her cart as she was pushin' it into her front room. I was holdin' the door for her.'

'Mebbe they were for her tea,' Seamus said sadly, regarding the apple with watering mouth. 'Mebbe I'll take it back, Garv.'

'She *give* 'em me for holdin' the door,' Garvan said patiently, through a mouthful of apple. 'I didn't have to nick 'em.'

Half the apple immediately disappeared into Seamus's mouth and for a moment the only sound was a contented crunching. Then the twins

80

exchanged glances; another crunching came to their pricked ears . . . footsteps!

With one accord both boys reached for the pile of snowballs behind them and inched forward until they could see who was approaching through the crack in the half-door as it swung on broken hinges.

'It's a girl,' Garvan whispered. 'Give it to her, Shay!'

'How big?' Seamus whispered back. 'If she's little, we'd best wait. Her mammy will kill us hard if we soak a littl'un.'

'Big enough,' Garvan hissed. 'Ready . . . steady . . . fire!'

Seamus saw the hem of a tattered skirt and skinny, pallid calves ending in skinnier, grey-blue feet. The feet were bare, so clearly it was a child and a poorly clad one at that in this bitter weather. Seamus, with a shirt, three ragged jerseys and a very worn man's overcoat, cut down more or less to fit, shivered for the child outside. Why, he and Garvan even had boots, now that there were so many earners in their family! He didn't recognise the girl's grey hem; there were so many kids in the tenements that there was small chance of recognising one from a glimpse through the crack in the door, but whoever she was she did look pathetic . . . he decided to save his snowball for bigger game.

Garvan, however, had no such scruples. Everything he did, he did with all his force and now snowball after snowball left his hand at deadly speed and smashed into its target . . . who dropped whatever it was she had been carrying and proceeded to wail and also, alas, to curse.

'Oh, oh, *oh!* Stop that, ye wicked wee buggers or

81

I'll come in there and tear the hairs from your bleedin' heads, so I will! Oh haven't ye soaked me to the skin, an' me wearin' me only dacent skirt an' it all covered wit' snow . . .'

The diatribe stopped abruptly. 'Got her full in the gob,' Garvan said gleefully. 'That'll teach her to call names!'

Seamus was starting to remonstrate when the half-door was pushed back and a virago came vengefully down upon them. She was carrying a very old string bag full of knobbly objects—they were wrapped in newspaper so he could not see what they were—and wearing a limp grey skirt and a very large, rather holey shawl, wrapped tightly round her head and shoulders, completely hiding her hair and most of her frame. But the twins were soon less interested in her appearance than her actions, for she seized them by the hair and brought their heads together with so much force that Seamus, at least, promptly saw stars.

'I *knew* it would be you, you wicked little animals, and hasn't the devil marked you for his own, so he has, which everyone in the Liberties knows? Oh, if I was your mammy I'd see to you, so I would!'

'Thank the good Lord you ain't our mammy,' Garvan growled, trying to kick out at her skinny bare legs with his large boots, only she was too agile for him and continued to whack his head against his brother's whilst nimbly keeping out of reach. 'Let go of us, you wicked bitch!'

'I shall not, for you've soaked me for sport, you little worms, wit' never a t'ought for how I was to get dry,' said the girl, if she was a girl, for her strength seemed, to the astonished Seamus, to be

82

the strength of a woman grown. She gave their heads one last, resounding bang, then pushed them disdainfully away from her so forcefully that they landed on their backs amongst their carefully manufactured ammunition. 'I hope that will teach you not to snowball ladies,' she finished, dusting her hands with the air of one who has just completed a satisfactory job.

'Ladies?' Garvan howled, untangling himself from his twin and sitting up. 'If you t'ink you're a lady you're very much mistook! You're just a kid, that's all!'

For the first time, Seamus was able to take a good look at their attacker and saw that Garvan spoke the truth; she was just a kid. She was older than they, of course, perhaps as old as ten or eleven, but very definitely still a child. In fact, she looked weak, Seamus thought wonderingly as the girl turned on her bare heel and strode towards the half-door. Who would have thought that a weak little young wan like that could pack a punch which could send stout fellers like himself and his twin reeling! But Garvan, never one to let good sense stop his mouth, was still muttering and the girl, who was half-way out of the door, turned back.

'Now, you two,' she said severely. 'I'm goin' to see your mammy presently. I'll not go snitchin' on you, but no more lyin' in wait for girls, see? Or your mammy shall have the whole story out of me, so she shall.'

'You don't know our mammy,' Garvan sneered. His hand had sneaked out and found an undamaged snowball and he was pressing it and squeezing it into a ball of ice with his hot, indignant hand. 'Our mammy's a real lady, so she is—not like

83

you!' The girl took a step towards him and Garvan stepped back, just to be on the safe side, Seamus assumed.

'I do so know your mammy, I'm on me way to visit her now, this minute,' the girl said calmly, but she did not come any nearer. Seamus was relieved; he had often noticed that no matter how good he might be, when his twin was bad any punishment was apt to be shared between them. 'Put that iceball down, Garvan Nolan, or you'll very soon find out what a good wallopin' means.'

And with that parting shot she withdrew completely and they could see her padding across the snowy cobbles and heading . . . oh *God,* Seamus thought miserably . . . heading for the tenement which housed the Nolan family.

Garvan shied his iceball through the doorway but, Seamus saw happily, it was not even vaguely aimed at the angry young girl.

'Missed!' Garvan said and looked slyly at Seamus under his white lashes. 'I say t'anks be to God, Shay, that we don't have any ould sisters in our house!'

'T'anks be to God,' Seamus echoed, making the sign of the cross. 'She's a furious young wan, eh, Garv?'

'We whopped her wit' our snowballs, that's why,' Garvan said, but he sounded worried, nevertheless. 'Why's she goin' to our house, Shay?'

'Dunno,' Seamus admitted. 'Shall us go back now, Garv, an' find out? Mammy'll tell us, when the gorl's gone.'

'Who did she put me in mind of?' Garvan said dreamily, ignoring his brother's remark as though he had not spoken. He placed his iceball carefully

84

on top of the mangled snowballs, then wandered over to peer round the half-door. 'I know! She's one of them lousy McVeigh gorls, all cropped heads an' no knickers.'

'Is she?' Seamus said doubtfully. All girls looked alike to him, particularly when they were wearing a shawl. 'There's hundreds of 'em though, Garv ... gorls, I mean ... so how d'you know which is which?'

'The McVeighs are all no better'n they should be,' Garvan said virtuously. 'They're all dirty and they breed hoppers; mammy wouldn't want us gettin' near a McVeigh, I'm tellin' ye, Shay. So she won't be goin' to our house to see our mammy, not that young wan!'

'Well, she's gone into our hallway,' Seamus felt bound to point out. 'Who'll she be visitin' then, Garv? Do the McVeighs tell lies? Gorls don't, usually.'

'How d'you know? You don't know any gorls.'

'I do! I know Peggy and Maeve.'

'They ain't gorls, they're our cousins,' Garvan said. 'Oh, come on, she won't be long, then we can go and ask our mammy what she wanted.'

'But you said she wasn't goin' to our house, you said she must be visitin' someone else in the block ...' Seamus started to say and got his ear pulled hard for his pains. He shouted and threw himself at his brother and a fight ensued which ended abruptly, as such fights always did, with Garvan saying breathlessly: 'Awright, awright, pax. Twins shouldn't fight, mammy says.'

'Awright yourself,' Seamus said. 'She still hasn't come out, Garv.'

'Aw, she must've. She'll have come out whiles we

scrapped,' Garvan said optimistically. 'Come on, let's go back up.'

Their flat was on the fourth floor, which meant a good trail up a lot of stairs. Garvan set off but Seamus lagged behind.

'Or shall us go to school? It's time we left, if we're goin'.'

'School? Us, go to school?' Garvan said scornfully. 'Wit' that wicked ould Father O'Halloran an' his ould cane, slashin' at everyone? 'Sides, it 'ud be a waste of the snow.'

'Mammy says we'll never learn nothin' if we don't go to school,' Seamus said, but he didn't say it with much enthusiasm. The teacher who was in charge of the small boys was a fat, easygoing woman called Sister Bridget, but Father O'Halloran, who taught the bigger boys, was not above meting out punishment to small boys who misbehaved or became too much for the sister to cope with. Naturally, both Seamus and Garvan knew the feel of the O'Halloran cane too well for their comfort.

'Well, if you want to go . . .' Garvan said craftily. 'We'll get our dinners from mammy and then we'll think on.'

But when they reached the landing from which their rooms led they could hear, through the door, the murmur of voices.

'It's that gal,' Garvan said crossly. 'She is talkin' to our mammy. She's a horrible young wan, I hate her. When she comes out I'm goin' to push her down the stairs an' I hope she breaks her wicked neck, so I do.'

'Oh, shut up,' Seamus said good-naturedly. 'Come on, let's go and find if anyone else is mitchin' off school today.'

'What about our dinners?' Garvan said. 'Oh, I suppose we can come back later, pretend we've been in school all mornin'. Where'll we go, Shay?'

'Dunno. Let's see who else is out.'

The two boys clattered down the stairs, the strange girl, and her visit to their mother, no longer important, soon forgotten.

*   *   *

Maggie McVeigh paused on the landing outside the Nolans' rooms and glanced down at herself. Her grey skirt was neat enough, her shawl, though holey, clean enough. Her feet were pretty dirty, but how could they be anything else? They had already this morning carried her down to Francis Street, to the dairy for milk and then to the bakery for soda bread, and washing them in the ice-cold water which was all that would be available in the McVeighs' dirty, overcrowded rooms wasn't exactly appealing in weather such as this.

But her mammy had said 'be neat, be polite, sure an' isn't this the best opportunity to better yourself that a gorl ever had?' and Maggie thought reluctantly that her mother was probably right. Because rumour had it that the Nolans were well-to-do and ate every day.

The McVeighs were poor. Mary McVeigh had once been heard to remark that she'd sooner be dead than give birth to any more children, but she went on bringing them into the world anyway. Maggie had an awful lot of brothers and even more sisters, and the youngest, Lonny, who had been in her charge until a week ago, had been a great favourite with everyone.

But Lonny had caught a fever and died just before his second birthday, and it had been only days after that dreadful event that Mrs Nolan had approached Mrs McVeigh. Mrs McVeigh had been lining up to use the mangle in the shed next door to the privy at the bottom of the yard, whilst Maggie, under a load of wet linen, had been waiting patiently for her turn and trying hard not to think about Lonny, about his sweetness, the way he clung to her, the charming pink of his cheeks when he had been well . . . and the awful brightness of his eyes and the waxen hue of him when he had been sick unto death. It was then that Mrs Nolan came into their yard, picking her way amongst the assorted livestock and various children, and began to talk in an undertone to Mrs McVeigh about her difficulties, whilst Maggie had been an apparently unnoticed eavesdropper.

'Mrs McVeigh, I've a problem and I was wonderin' if you might be able to help me out?' Mrs Nolan had started. 'I was askin' a friend whether she knew anyone who might be able to help me out around the house, like, an' she mentioned you. The t'ing is, I need a bit of a hand now, wit' another littl'un on the way, me man gone and me wit' only sons. You'll have heard me husband died a month back, so I'm workin' at the dressmaking too, as you know. But me work doesn't pay well enough so I can't afford a wage, though I promise ye that any girl who comes to me shall have her keep, the same food as we eat ourselves, and a day off now and again. I don't mind that she'll still be in school, indeed I don't, since it's before and after her lessons that she's most needed. So if you've a daughter you wouldn't miss . . .'

It wasn't an unusual suggestion. Maggie had friends who lived with cousins or aunts because their own parents simply had no room for them. But she had somehow never thought it would happen in her family, and hadn't they managed, so far? But if she expected her mammy to turn down such an offer then she was doomed to disappointment.

'You can 'ave Maggie,' Mrs McVeigh had said eagerly. Too eagerly. Poor Maggie had felt very real dismay. What had she done that her mother should cast her aside, give her to a stranger so willingly? It hadn't been her fault that Lonny had died, she'd done all she possibly could . . . she'd missed weeks of school over him, given up her chance of a good attendance medal, hung about up at the market to carry the heavy baskets home and earn a ha'penny or so. What else could she have done?

'Which one's Maggie?' Mrs Nolan had asked. 'Is she strong? Healthy? I need a strong, healthy girl, Mrs McVeigh.'

'She's me finest daughter, a good, bright girl, an' she'll be eleven come the summer,' Mrs McVeigh said at once. She didn't say *she's standin' not four feet from ye*, which she could well have done, but Maggie realised that her mother would want her to look her best for a prospective employer, and a chilled, half-naked child with cropped hair and an armful of wet sheets was not likely to make a good impression. 'She brought our Lonny up as though he were her own, but he died, God love 'im, not a week since. She'd be that glad of another littl'un . . .

89

I'll not be havin' no more, not now Mr McVeigh's been took so bad.'

'Well . . .' Mrs Nolan said undecidedly. 'Well . . . send her round, would you, Mrs McVeigh? I'll see if she'll suit.'

What about her suitin' me? Maggie had thought angrily as the two women parted. *What if I teks one look at 'er an' decide I'd be better off at 'ome?* But she knew it wouldn't make any difference. If her mammy had decided to let her go then she had little choice but to obey. Well, no choice, in fact. Their dingy rooms were overflowing with children. She and her sisters slept in a flea-ridden pile of straw in the kitchen-living-room, the boys slept on two large pallets in the only other room, sharing it with their parents. And Mr McVeigh was coughing blood; Maggie had seen it on the rags which he held to his mouth when a spasm overcame him. Once he had been a great, six-foot-tall docker, strong as an ox, fierce, intemperate. But then the illness had come upon him and now he was meek, no longer able to work, waiting. Maggie never put it into words, of course, but she knew what he was waiting for. Death. Easement from the painful, racking cough, the sickness, the hunger when there wasn't enough food to go round and he wouldn't take his share because he knew he'd bring it up later,so it would do him no good.

When they got home with the mangled wash, Maggie had asked her mother whether it might not be better to send Aileen, who was thirteen and due to start work soon anyway, or even one of the younger girls, who were not much use about the house as yet.

Mrs McVeigh, not a demonstrative woman, had

90

suddenly dumped her share of the sheets on the rickety table and put her arms round her daughter. 'Oh, alanna, I'm sorry,' she said, her voice thick with unshed tears. 'But the trut' is, I'm desperate for how to keep goin'. One less mightn't seem much, but it'll ease the burden a bit. And Aisling Nolan's a good woman. We were in school together, many long years since. She'll treat you fair. Aileen could be earnin' for us soon, so I don't want to lose her, an' the others are too young an' giddy. Look at it this way; you'll have a bed all to yourself, you'll not be asked to miss so much as a day's schoolin', an' you'll be give dacent food every day of the week, so you will.'

Put like that, it sounded heavenly to Maggie. Since her father's illness, food had often been in short supply, though her mother and the two older brothers still at home had done their best.

But ... 'So many mouths,' Declan had said, giving his mother all the money he earned as a bottle washer at the bottling plant, though Mrs McVeigh always handed him back a sixpence for his dinners. 'And Daddy needin' all sorts we can't give him.'

'All right,' Maggie had conceded at last, having thought it through. 'Mammy ... it's not 'cos Lonny died, is it? I did me best, honest to God ...'

Her mother had hugged her again and this time the tears had simply gushed from her eyes. 'Oh, God love ye, as if I'd blame me little gorl who did everyt'ing she could to save him! Alanna, if you're set against goin' ...'

So of course then Maggie had cried and assured her mammy that she was not against going, that she quite saw she would be better off and that she would come home often, whenever she could.

'Be a good gorl for Mrs Nolan, now,' her mother bade her, dabbing at her tears with the hem of her apron. 'And if they're unkind to you . . .'

So now, outside the Nolans' rooms, Maggie stiffened her back, drew herself up and knocked.

A voice from within called 'Come along in wit' ye' and the door was opened. Mrs Nolan stood framed in the doorway. She was about the same age as Maggie's mammy, Maggie knew, for they had been in school together, but she didn't look it. She looked a great deal younger, with skin like milk, smooth, pale-gold hair and a pair of large, chilly blue eyes which looked Maggie critically up and down. But she must have accepted what she saw, for she suddenly smiled faintly and gestured Maggie inside.

'You'll be Maggie McVeigh, your mammy said she'd send you. Come along in wit' you.' She led Maggie through into a living-kitchen, but how different from the McVeigh accommodation! There was a blackened range with its doors open so you could see the fire burning brightly within, a round table made of wood so highly polished that it looked like dark water, upright chairs of the same wood with seats upholstered in what seemed to be needlework, a piece of carpet on the floor, all reds and blues, wonderfully rich, and red velvet curtains at the windows. And there were pictures on every wall, paintings in gilt frames, depicting everything you could imagine or desire. A farmyard, a cottage with a thatched roof and a garden full of wonderful flowers, two children with long ringlets playing rather soulfully with a brown-and-white puppy and a great many beautiful religious pictures. Our Lord gazed down at a group of children, He fished from a corracle with the disciples around Him, He scattered the moneylenders in the temple. Looking around her, saucer-eyed, Maggie saw two comfortable armchairs with bright cushions on each, one either side of the range, little tables, each bearing a burden of prettily painted delft, an object which she guessed must be a sewing machine and . . . a piano!

'I dare say you aren't used to a room like this,' Mrs Nolan said as Maggie stared. 'Well, I'm proud of me room, so I am, and I want it kept nice. It'll be your job, Maggie, to polish the table and chairs, brush the upholstery, clean the winders, wash me delft in warm soapy water, dust me piano . . .'

'Oh, I will, Mrs Nolan,' Maggie breathed. The room was like a little palace, even the wash-stand with the jug and ewer on it and the buckets beneath were clean and shining and looked as though they were never used. 'Sure an' isn't it the loveliest room in the world, now? And is it yourself plays the piano?'

'No, I don't play, but me late husband, Cathal, used to tickle the ivories as he called it,' Mrs Nolan said proudly. It was easy to see the piano was Mrs Nolan's pride and joy—and why not, indeed, Maggie thought. She had seen pianos in the smart shop windows on O'Connell Street but never in a private home. 'Mr Nolan gave me the piano for a weddin' gift when we married, so he did,' her new employer told her. 'And even if it isn't the loveliest room in the world, it's a nice room and I'm mortal fond of it. You're not a breaker, are you, Maggie? I couldn't share me home wit' a breaker.'

'I don't think so, Mrs Nolan,' Maggie said. 'But

it's not certain I am, because in our house there's not a great deal I could break. Mammy doesn't have much delft.'

'No. Well, you like me room, so I hope you'll have respect for dacent t'ings. Best come through, see the rest.'

Maggie, tiptoeing behind the older woman, saw with awe that the Nolans had all the rooms on this particular landing. The biggest was the living-kitchen, obviously, but there were three other rooms on the same floor. Three bedrooms, and them with only the four sons and themselves to use them! The Nolan boys slept in the first, their mother in the second and the third—a tiny slip of a room which measured about six feet by four—was intended, Mrs Nolan said, for Maggie herself.

Maggie stood in the low and narrow doorway and stared. A real bed, very low, with little wheels, and a real blanket . . . and a pillow, an object which only Mr McVeigh's illness had introduced into the McVeigh household. There was even a piece of window—not a whole one because the room had been made by chopping a slice off the larger room next door—and there was a picture on the wall as well. A beautiful picture of a strange country where wonderful flowers grew, and the lichen on the flat slabs of stone and the little curled ferns which grew between them were so real that Maggie felt she should have been able to smell the fresh sweet country scent of them. She went over to the picture and looked at it closely, and saw that it hadn't been painted at all, it was even cleverer than that. It was made of threads, it was embroidered, as altar cloths were embroidered, and close up it was even more beautiful than from a distance.

'Sure an' it's a grand little room,' Maggie said, when she saw that Mrs Nolan was waiting for her to comment. 'I like the picture; where's it of?'

'That's Clare,' Mrs Nolan said. 'Me gran was from there, way back. The picture was hers, though I don't know for sure that she made it. I've a feelin' it were give to her by someone.'

'Sure an' that *is* strange, for me own Gran was from Clare, I've heered me mammy sayin' so many a time,' Maggie said. 'Well, whoever made that picture was clever. But she was sad, I'm thinkin'. For I t'ink there's somethin' sad about it, even though it's beautiful.'

Mrs Nolan looked surprised. 'Sad? Well, it's a long way from Clare to here, so the person who embroidered it might have been homesick,' she acknowledged. 'My mammy used to say it was a beautiful place, and I know she wanted to go there one day, though she never did . . . but I'm a city person, meself. I can't imagine livin' anywhere but Dublin.' She squeezed into the room and lifted up the blanket, turning it this way and that. It was rainbow-coloured, having been made of knitted squares.

'Now I do know who made this—it were me gran, she used to sit by the fire knittin' away, then she crocheted the squares together. It's been mortal cold these past few days, but I dare say you've a coat?'

She didn't say it with any real hope; it was plain she didn't expect an affirmative, and indeed, Maggie did not possess such a garment. She looked from the bed to Mrs Nolan and then back again. A coat? What had that to do with cold, or blankets for that matter?

'I spread the boys' coats on their beds in winter,' Mrs Nolan explained. 'This is a good blanket, but I wouldn't want you to be cold.'

'I won't be cold,' Maggie promised fervently. 'Sure an' I'll be warm as a bug in a rug under that lovely blanket. We don't have blankets at home, much.'

'Ye-es, but at home you've your sisters to keep you warm,' Mrs Nolan said. 'Oh well, I'll find you up something, no doubt. Now come into the kitchen; we've a deal of talking to do.'

*   *   *

Twenty minutes later, Maggie left the Nolan household. She had been told what was expected of her and was not at all worried by the amount of work, for didn't she work every bit as hard at home? No, what worried her was those twins, the good God confound them! She was to be responsible for them and that meant seeing that they attended school, that they were properly dressed and behaved themselves, and that they did not interfere with the new baby, when it came.

'For Garvan and Seamus are high-spirited boys,' Mrs Nolan said and for the first time sounded a little worried, a little less than perfectly self-confident. 'Sure and all boys are divils, but bein' twins, me little boys are a rare handful. I've only worked from home since they were born, but I'll be workin' properly again as soon as the new baby arrives. And aren't I a first-rate seamstress in me own right? But workin' from home I don't mek the money, so when me friend axed me to go into partnership in a shop . . . well, I couldn't rightly

96

refuse. Which is why I'm willin' to give you a home an' your keep, in exchange for a bit of a hand around the place.'

'I see,' Maggie said. 'What's your hours, Mrs Nolan?'

'Oh, the usual. Eight o'clock in the morning, Monday to Saturday, till seven in the evening, the same. Sunday off,' Mrs Nolan said airily. 'Whiles you're in school the boys will be in school too, except for Liam, who's workin'. And I'll take the new baby to the shop with me, because I'm in the work-room, makin' hats and alterin' dresses, so it won't annoy the customers.'

'I see,' Maggie said again. It occurred to her that she would not so much be giving 'a bit of a hand', as running the home, but that didn't worry her. When her mammy was poorly after having a baby, hadn't she and Aileen run the home between them? And the McVeighs were a large family, whereas the Nolans were a small one—she should be able to manage.

It was only her responsibility for the twins, in fact, which worried her as she made her way home to tell her mammy what had occurred and to fetch over anything she wanted to take to her new home. She hadn't liked to tell Mrs Nolan that her possessions were one tatty black skirt and a shawl even more riddled with holes than the one she wore at present. Mrs Nolan had asked if she would prefer to bring along some of her own bedding, but Maggie had just muttered that she would manage, thanks. She did not think that her new employer would think it amusing if she turned up carrying an armful of flea-ridden straw.

It wasn't far from the Nolan building to the

rundown tenement where her own family lived, but it might have been in another world. The Nolans lived just off Thomas Street, but the McVeighs were further off it still, down a noisome little dead end known as Dally Court. Because the tenements were so tall, very little daylight came into the court, so it was always dusk, even at noon, and the houses leaned perilously, as though the garrets were trying to get close enough to whisper secrets. Here there were no cheerful little huckster shops with their goods in big sacks and the shopkeeper dipping into them with a little tin shovel, because there would have been no point. No one came down Dally Court because it led nowhere and the people who did live there had so little money that they could not have bought the goods displayed. Instead, there were hens and a couple of geese scratching, and a lean, bristle-backed pig rooting. Dirty, whey-faced children clad in rags had scratched a piggy bed in the snow and now they were kicking a flattened tin from square to square, shouting to one another as they did so. 'Tip the piggy,' they shouted. 'Tip the piggy, Alis . . . ah, hasn't it touched the line now—you're out, you're out!'

One of the children spotted Maggie and came running over to clutch her hand. She was Maggie's youngest sister, Carrie. 'Maggie—where's you been? You goin' to play piggy wit' us?'

'Not today, alanna,' Maggie said gently. 'I'm goin' to work today.'

'To work? But youse in school, Maggie,' the little girl pointed out. 'You like school, you said.'

'So I do, but I'll be earnin' money . . . in a sort of way.'

'Money!' The child's small, pointed face grew

98

thoughtful. 'Wish I could earn some money, Maggie. Will you buy bread? Cakes?'

'If I can,' Maggie said steadily. 'Aileen will be workin' soon, too. She'll buy food.'

'An' won't you be in school no more?' the little girl persisted. 'When I'm big I t'ought you'd be in school wit' me.'

'So I shall,' Maggie said. 'Leave me go, Carrie, our mam wants me.'

The child stepped back obediently and before Maggie was even in the house the game had restarted, with Carrie taking her turn to tip the piggy.

I wish I really was going to earn some money, though, Maggie thought to herself. It would be wonderful to have a penny or two to spend now and then. She envied her older brothers who had left home and gone to England to earn real money and still did their best to help out at home, but she, too, was doing her best. Just by leaving home she was helping.

Maggie crossed the hallway and set off up the stairs, which weren't easy to climb because the angle at which the tenement leaned meant that the stairs had come adrift on one side and had a drunken tilt. What was more, you could look right down to the ground floor through the holes in the treads ... and right up to the roof, if you tipped your head well back, through the treads above you. Still, she thought, trudging onwards, even if she wasn't being paid at least she would be fed, which would mean she might be able to lay her hands on some spare food—or smuggle the odd slice of bread, or cake, or whatever Mrs Nolan gave her, into her clothing. Then she could bring it back for the kids.

The thought heartened her, because no matter how beautiful their home, how lavish their table, the Nolans were virtually strangers to her. The rooms in No.14 Dally Court might be crammed with people and empty of possessions, but Maggie, Aileen and their mother saw to it that the place was kept clean. Lugging all the water up three long flights of stairs was backbreaking work, but although the fleas never completely left them, and bugs appeared as soon as the winter cold eased, at least the floors, what bedding there was and all their threadbare clothing were always fiercely clean. Mounting the third flight, torn between a feeling of satisfaction that she was about to help her mother in the best way possible and an almost equally strong feeling of loss, Maggie tried to tell herself that Dally Court wasn't much of a place, that she would be much better off with the Nolans. But she could not deny that the two small rooms on the third floor had been home to her for almost eleven years and that counted for a good deal. Change is never nice, Maggie thought confusedly; but a change so . . . so total . . . well, she should not expect it to be easy.

At the third landing she stopped and waited for a moment to get her breath, then opened the door which led directly into their living-room. The kids were either at work or at school, only Biddy, who suffered from bad chests and was laid up at present with a deep and barking cough, was present, sitting with a blanket round her as close to the stove as she could get, whilst Mrs McVeigh stirred a concoction in a small pan over the stove. Mr McVeigh was asleep on the broken-down sofa, well

100

wrapped in blankets and old coats, but he still looked half frozen, his daughter saw sadly. How she wished she could bring home the butter, the fresh milk and the vegetables which the doctor said their father needed! But little hope of that as a skivvy to the Nolan family!

Maggie crossed the room and stood by the stove, watching the potion bubbling in the pan. It smelt good, peppery, clovey, with licorice predominating. 'I'm startin' tomorrer, Mammy,' Maggie said, as her mother looked up from her work. 'Mrs Nolan said it would be all right, so long as I weren't a breaker, and I don't *think* I am. She—she seems nice enough.'

'Oh, me little darlin',' Mrs McVeigh said and reached for a tin mug. She poured the bubbling liquid into it and wrapped it in a length of soft cloth. 'What will she be wantin' you to do, now?'

'She wants housework, of course, and them twins minded, as well as the new baby when it comes,' Maggie said rather gloomily. She had just remembered the snowballs. 'Them twins is *divils*, Mammy.'

Her mother laughed and handed the cloth-wrapped mug to Biddy, who wiped her nose on her blanket and took the drink, holding it between her two cold little hands.

'Don't think of 'em as twins, Mags,' Mrs McVeigh advised. 'They're no better an' no worse than any other kids, each of 'em has his good points and his bad. Just you treat 'em like two ordinary little boys and take notice of the differences between 'em, an' before you know it they'll love you like we do. Now you look froze; I'll make you a hot cup o' something.'

'I don't think they'll ever love me, Mammy,' Maggie said sadly. 'I whupped 'em for soakin' me to the skin wi' snowballs, that's the trouble. Because I wanted to look me best for Mrs Nolan, that's for why.' She saw Biddy beginning to smile and smiled too. 'I cracked them evil little heads one agin' t'other,' she admitted. 'They roared, so they did.'

'Do 'em good,' Biddy piped. 'They's bullies, they is. They pull plaits if you're a gal an' ears if you're a feller, so long as you're smaller than them.'

'Both of 'em?' Mrs McVeigh enquired. 'Is it the both of 'em what pull plaits an' ears? Or only one?'

Biddy raised the tin mug to her mouth and took a cautious sip, then lowered it again. 'Dunno,' she admitted. 'They's twins . . . us casn't tell one from t'other.'

'There you are, then,' Mrs McVeigh said triumphantly. 'Oh, Maggie'll be fine once she's sorted the boys out, indeed.'

*   *   *

'All I'm askin', Mammy, is who told you?' Garvan's voice was plaintive now, with the suspicion of a whine in it. 'Who told you Shay an' me weren't in school today? Aw, Mammy, where's the harm in mitchin' for one little day? We're there often enough, so we are . . . why can't we mitch off when the snow's down, an' there's fun to be had?'

The twins and their mother were in the living-room, Mammy getting the tea whilst the twins sat at the table, laboriously copying their letters on to two small slates. Because an unknown someone had told Mammy that they had not been in school

102

for several days—it was more like weeks—she had made them produce their slates and given them an alphabet to copy. Furthermore, she had insisted that no food would be forthcoming until they had both got all twenty-six letters off pat.

Mammy was never strict, always indulged them, so at first Garvan had pulled faces at his brother and Seamus had drawn stick-men on his slate and deliberately squeaked with his pencil in the hope that Mammy would get fed up, give them their tea and let them play, but for once it hadn't worked. Mammy had tightened her lips and, when they persisted, had actually smacked them across their heads—as if she meant it, too!

So now, Garvan had decided to find out who had snitched on them, and if it was that skinny ould gal . . . well, they'd make her sorry, see if they didn't. Of course he couldn't *say* any of that with Mammy still within smacking distance, but there are times—a good many—when twins don't need words and this was one of them. Seamus knew that Garvan was plotting revenge just from one glance at his brother's red curls.

'Mammy? Who told on us, eh? Was it a feller? Father O'Halloran, or Mr Betts from up by the school? Or was it one of the nuns? Or . . . or just some ould gal who wanted to get us in trouble?'

Their mother was cutting a loaf of bread into thin, even slices. Seamus watched whenever he paused for a moment in his copying and even more closely as his mother began to spread the beautiful golden butter with the little drops of water on it smoothly across the pitted surface of the bread. She was still cross with them; Seamus could tell by the firm way she drew the butter across the bread, as well as by her tightly closed lips and the way her eyes sparkled when she glanced across at them.

'Mammy? Who told on us?' Garvan said again, all gentle persuasion and coaxing. 'C'mon, who was it, now?'

Their mother finished buttering the last slice of bread and looked up. She flicked the top off a jar of jam without once looking at it, then dug the knife into that too, and began spreading it thinly across the buttered slices.

'What d'you mean, *some ould gal?*' she said. 'Why should *some ould gal* come to me and tell stories about my sons?'

'We saw a young wan come into the house earlier,' Seamus put in, since Garvan didn't answer immediately. 'A strange gal, Mammy.'

'Oh *did* you?' Mammy said, in a rather ominous tone. 'Well, that girl came to see me, not to tell tales on you. She's comin' to live here, that's why.'

'A strange gal, livin' here?' Garvan had exclaimed. 'Why, Mammy? We don't want a gal in our house! And *that* gal's a horror, so she is! She . . . she might smack us, you know, when you weren't around to stop her.'

'I t'ink you need someone to smack you now an' then, Garvan, since you've taken to mitchin' off school,' his mother said severely. 'I'm goin' back to work, you see, boys, which means I'll need a hand around the house, and when the new baby comes I'll need someone here when I'm out.'

'We could help,' Garvan said eagerly. 'We could, couldn't we, Shay? We'd rather, Mammy, honest to God we would.'

'Oh aye? When you've never lifted a finger in this house from the day you were born?' his mother said. She laughed. 'Sure an' you'd be as much use about the place as a one-legged parrot.'

'New baby?' Seamus said suddenly. 'What new baby, Mammy?'

His mother went on spreading jam, but even as he watched, faint colour stained her cheeks. 'Oh, had I not mentioned it? We're havin' a new baby, so we are, and babies mean work. So Maggie McVeigh is comin' to live here. No messin', no tryin' to get me to change me mind. She's comin', and that's that.'

'Maggie McVeigh? But Mammy, she'll kill us dead, so she will, the moment you're not watchin' to keep us safe,' Garvan said, honest alarm in his voice.

Seamus, remembering the way the skinny girl had seized their heads and banged them together until they saw stars, could sympathise. He added his pennorth. 'She hits hard, that Maggie McVeigh; she bowled us over like . . . like cherry wobs this mornin'.'

His mother's busy hands were stilled. She raised her head and gave them a long, cool look, her eyes resting first on one, then the other. 'This mornin'? When you were supposed to be in school, studyin' your letters? When you'd been give a ha'penny for milk to go wit' your bread an' cheese?'

Garvan gave Seamus a look which said 'You fool!' but it was too late; Seamus had given the game away and he thought it would be worth it, if they could persuade their mother that Maggie McVeigh was not fit to be given charge of two people as precious as themselves.

'Yes, Mammy, we were mitchin' this mornin', but you knowed that already,' Seamus said. 'An' that young wan roared at us an' came in where we was playin' an' grabbed us by the hair and banged our skulls together till we near on was kilt.'

'And what did you do to her?' Mammy asked.

And then, of course, Seamus remembered what had been done to Maggie McVeigh and knew they were in deep trouble. 'Nothin',' he muttered. And it was true, wasn't it? He hadn't thrown a snowball or laid a finger on that young wan, it had all been Garvan, as usual!

'Nothin'? You expect me to believe that a quiet girl like that one simply fell on you and cracked your heads together for nothin'? You must t'ink I'm as mad as bedlam.'

'I din't do nothin',' Seamus repeated . . . then dodged and threw his arms protectively round his head, for his gentle, loving mother had cast herself at him across the table which separated them and was smacking his head with every bit as much enthusiasm as Maggie had displayed earlier.

'You're a liar, Seamus Nolan, and I can't abide a liar,' she said breathlessly as she smote. 'And she never said a word, that young wan, never a word, so don't get the idea into your head that she told on you, for she did no such thing. Snowballs, was it?'

And then, to his brother's astonishment, Garvan, who believed in looking after number one, spoke up. 'Seamus din't t'row so much as one snowball,' he admitted. 'It were me, Mammy. I *pelted* her, so I did. So don't you be after hittin' poor Seamus.'

His mother stopped hitting Seamus, which was a relief, then gave Garvan a great, swingeing blow around the ear.

He swayed, then gulped back tears and picked up his slate once more. 'So that gal Maggie's

106

comin' to live here,' he said, squeakily, tracing a letter q on to his slate. 'Well, we probably won't see her often, 'cos we'll be in school.'

'You will indeed, for Maggie's first job of a morning will be to take you there and hand you over to your teacher,' his mother said, striking both boys dumb for a moment. 'And now, if you've finished copying your alphabet, I'll put the tay in the pot and as soon as Liam's foot sounds on the stair, we'll eat.'

*   *   *

Much later that evening, when they were in their bed, Garvan kicked Seamus in the back, then dived under the covers, knowing that Seamus would do likewise. In the stuffy warmth of the bed, he said: 'That Maggie gorl, Shay; she won't be livin' here long, I'm tellin' you. We'll make her miserable, so we will, an she'll up sticks an' go back to that fleapit she comes from.'

'I dunno,' Seamus mumbled. 'She's a strong gorl, Garv. Mebbe she'll make *us* miserable, if we behave bad. Perhaps, at first, we'd do better to be careful.'

Garvan snorted. 'Careful! No, that won't work. We'll put salt in her milk an' stingin' nettles in her bed an' we'll dirty the floor after she's cleaned it an' . . .'

'I'm not,' Seamus said. He suddenly felt quite sure that Maggie McVeigh was not a girl to trifle with. She might live in a slum with heaps of brothers and sisters and they might have no money and they might wear rags . . . but she could wallop!

'Please yourself,' Garvan said with fine

indifference. He was thinking, Seamus knew, that whoever did the deeds, they would both take the rap for them.

So Seamus took a deep breath and decided to scotch that one. 'I'll not be blamed, Garv, for plaguin' the girl, I tell you straight. I can't stop you doin' it, but I can tell Mammy and Liam it weren't me.'

'You wouldn't!' Garvan said. He sounded scandalised, as though not getting the belting intended for your twin was a wrong thing. 'You're me brother—you're me *twin!*'

'And you're *my* brother, and *my* twin,' Seamus countered. 'You shouldn't want to see me beat for your doin's.'

There was silence for a moment; this was clearly a novel idea to Garvan and he was spending time chewing it over. Finally, he spoke. 'Oh. Well, we'll wait a week or two if that's what you'd rather. G'night, Shay.'

'G'night, Garv,' Seamus said and they emerged simultaneously from under the blankets like two seals surfacing. 'Phew, it were hot down there.'

Garvan mumbled a reply and presently both boys slept.

*   *   *

By the time Liam and Kenny, his twelve-year-old brother, came up to bed the twins had been asleep for an hour or two. They had squiggled right across their truckle bed and were lying half out of the blankets despite the cold, so Liam covered them up, then he and Kenny shed their outer clothing and climbed into their own bed. Just before bedtime, Liam had run a message for Mammy, down to the huckster shop three doors along. They had been closed, but Mrs McAllister had opened up at his knock and sold him some milk. Mammy had decided that she should drink milk before settling for the night, because of the new baby, and because he'd run down to the shop through the snow, Liam's feet were like blocks of ice. That's why I can't sleep, Liam thought, tossing restlessly. It's not because of that girl Mammy's bringing here, it's because I've got awful cold feet.

Their mother had told them all about the girl who was coming to live with them, and Kenny, who sometimes played with a couple of Maggie's brothers, said he thought she would be all right; useful, in fact. Liam could tell that Kenny's main preoccupation was to make sure he personally wasn't saddled with housework or put in charge of the twins, particularly the last. Provided someone else did the housework and looked after the twins he had no particular objection to sharing his home.

Liam, on the other hand, was not at all keen. I've got a job so's I can give Mammy a hand wit' the others, his thoughts ran. Not so's she can bring someone else into our family! Why does she want to work, anyhow? Wasn't he the man of the house now his father was dead. She said when she married again that she wouldn't need to work, an' that pleased her, so it did. But now she says there's another baby on the way. Well, that was possible. Dear God, Liam thought, turning over restlessly and cracking his knee against Kenny's shin, suppose Mammy has twins? Hadn't she had one set, only six years ago? Suppose this baby were to be twins?

Thank God for Maggie McVeigh I'd be saying then, Liam thought sourly. Perhaps Mammy had a point; perhaps a girl would be useful, you never knew. He put his feet down the bed but that was too cold, so he drew them up again and placed them carefully against Kenny's warm ones. Kenny snorted but did not snatch his feet away and presently Liam's toes began to thaw out.

Soon, he slept.

CHAPTER FOUR

Liverpool, Summer 1909

'Dee! Deirdre Docherty, just you come here this minute or I'll tell our mam you've been a wicked gal again!'

Poor Ellen's shout went unregarded. Deirdre and Donal heard her as it happened, but they had better things to do than to go running after elder sisters! Indeed, the work—for they both thought of it as work rather than play—totally occupied their waking moments just now and had done for three whole days, a record in itself.

When Ellen's voice came to their ears the pair of them were stealing earth. They had acquired—well, stolen—a large hessian sack from the general shop on Netherfield Road owned by the Harvey family—Joe and Essie Harvey were their bosom friends—and had carried it to the triangular-shaped garden at the top of Everton Brow, where they had laboriously filled it with soil.

It had taken days to fill, even after they had

stolen—'Borrowed,' Donal insisted, but 'Stolen,' his twin said proudly—the metal scoop which Mrs Harvey used to get rice, lentils or dried fruit from the huge sacks which leaned in front of the counter into rustling blue paper bags for the customers.

The length of time was partly because Deirdre would not permit Donal to ask anyone for help. This was a secret, their own secret; if they let other people into the plot, well, it wouldn't be a secret any longer, would it? And five-year-olds, no matter how determined, cannot dig earth at any great speed when they are doing it secretly.

Fortunately, however, there were some sizeable bushes in the triangular garden. The twins crouched beneath them, often very hot, and patiently scooped earth into their sack. And quarrelled. 'Little birds in their nest should agree,' Ellen chirruped sometimes—and got baleful glares from the quarrelling ones. Their sister, who was rather nice in many ways, did not seem to realise that quarrelling was a part of life and not to be easily cast aside. Besides, if Donal hadn't rebelled now and then, Deirdre would have grown bored with always getting her own way and might have looked for another companion. And no matter how fiercely they quarrelled—sometimes the quarrel became a fight, with redheaded Deirdre pulling hanks out of dark-headed Donal's hair whilst he, not to be outdone, seized her curls and tugged till her eyes watered—they always agreed to differ in the end, because they knew full well that there was no one on earth quite as good as your own twin when it came to playing, or running messages, or getting into hot water.

So the twins had spent all their spare time, for

two whole afternoons, filling their precious sack, and by mid-afternoon that day the sack had at last been filled to capacity and the first snag had presented itself. Neither one of them, nor both combined, could move it more than an inch or two.

'It's too bleedin' heavy,' Deirdre groaned, heaving until sweat ran down the sides of her small, freckled face. 'Why didn't you tell me it 'ud be too heavy? You're a feller, you should know about heaviness.'

Donal regarded his sister open-mouthed. 'Wha-aa-at? Who was it said she'd do it alone if I weren't careful? It were know-all Dee, that's who.'

'Well, you try to lift it alone if you think you can,' Deirdre said, deliberately misunderstanding him. 'Go on, show us!'

'We can't either of us do it,' Donal said, giving the sack a contemptuous kick. 'We'll have to empty some out, it's the only thing we can do.'

He could see that Deirdre would have dearly loved to quarrel with him over this—all that hard work for nothing—but she just heaved a martyred sigh and pushed the scoop reluctantly into the sack. After removing three scoopfuls, she glared at Donal and seized one ear of the sack. 'Right. Come on, pull!'

It didn't shift an inch. Grimly, the two children fell on their knees and systematically emptied the sack until only about a third of their precious soil remained. Then, arguing horribly, coming to blows twice, they began the long and tedious job of towing it home.

So naturally, when they heard Ellen hollerin' from the corner of Prince Eddie and Netherfield Road, they took no notice. How could they? Ellen

112

would instantly have made them take the sack back to Brow Side and empty it out. She would probably have made them scatter the soft mound of earth which they had taken out of their sack and for which they intended to go back the next day. And—here Deirdre looked down at herself for the first time—Ellen would undoubtedly have had harsh words to say about the condition of them, plastered with soil as they were.

'Deirdre! D'you hear me, you bad girl? Come home at once or it'll be the worse for you both.'

Deirdre gave a tiny squeak and tugged the sack sideways so that Donal, perforce, followed. She could actually see Ellen now and if Ellen looked to her right she would see the twins! Small hope of being mistaken for anyone else with hair the colour of a hot coal, Deirdre thought bitterly. She should have rubbed soil into her head as a disguise, but unfortunately it hadn't occurred to her. Or perhaps fortunately; it might take some getting out and Ellen could be turrble cruel with a scrub-brush and a bit of soap in her hand. Nevertheless Deirdre had acted so quickly that she and Donal and the sack were diving down the entry towards the dairy before Ellen had had a chance to look in their direction.

'Phew, that were close,' Deirdre said, wiping a filthy hand across her filthy brow. 'Did you see our Ellen, Don? She were just goin' to look our way, you know—I saved us trouble then, Donny!'

'Mm,' Donal said. 'Ay up, here comes the ole feller; what'll we say?'

An elderly man was approaching them, leading a pony across the yard. It was the one which hauled the milk cart in the mornings and Deirdre, who could think on her feet faster than anyone else Donal knew, beamed confidently up at the man. ''Ello, mister,' she said. 'Gorrany hoss-muck to spare?'

She cast a glance at the sack and Donal, despite himself, was filled with admiration. It would have been natural enough for a child to collect horse-manure from the street and try to sell it up one of the better roads, where the houses had gardens and would buy manure to spread on their vegetable plots. No one could tell you off for that, apart from your mam of course, who could scalp you for any reason, specially for ruinin' your kecks an' tekin' the soles out o' your boots.

'We-ell, looks as though you've got plenty to be goin' on wit',' the man said, smiling at them. ''Ow far've you brung that little lot?'

'Oh, miles,' Deirdre said airily. 'But we're nearly home now.'

'Come back tomorrer,' the man advised them. 'I'll put some by for ye.'

Donal and Deirdre thanked their saviour profusely—for whilst they were talking to him they had both seen Ellen stalking angrily past the entry—and wearily picked up their sack, or rather got hold of it by the open end, and began to tow it back towards the roadway.

Once on the street again, Deirdre bade her twin 'Gerra move on!' and hustled him down Roden Street, along Garden Lane and into Prince Edwin Lane. 'There, you see, Donny, if you doesn't ask you doesn't get,' she said breathlessly. 'Now we've gorra get this lot over that bleedin' wall. Come *on*, Donny!'

She broke into a run and Donny, who had begun

114

to say that he was coming on as fast as he could, shut his mouth and saved his breath for panting as they tore up Prince Edwin Lane and began to scramble up the wall of Number 17a.

About three weeks ago, Donal and Deirdre had had cause to go into the backyard of 17a to recapture a ball which one of them—it was, of course, Deirdre—had shied over the crumbling and blackened brick wall. If there had been other kids of their own age around they probably wouldn't have gone, because everyone in the court knew that the old man who lived there had horns and a tail and ate kids for tea, as well as refusing completely to throw back any balls which happened to have landed in his miserable yard, but there were no small kids playing out that afternoon. It was bigger boys, and one of them, a fat youth with a squint and two front teeth missing, had said that the twins were scared to get their ball back.

'Us fellers goes over all the time,' he boasted. 'Whaddyer fink 'e'll do to ya, eh? 'E's the devil awright, but we ain't skeered o' the devil! He's skeered of us, the mis'ruble ole bugger, knows we'll purra stone through 'is bleedin' winders if we wants. So I'll go over for ya, willin'—an' I'll keep the bleedin' ball, wha's more.'

The ball had been new and an especially fine one. The twins' dad had bought it for them last time his ship came into dock for a refit. Donal and Deirdre had exchanged petrified glances and had simultaneously made up their minds. They didn't believe for one moment that the big boy had ever scaled the wall and come face to face with the devil. Some might, but not he. However, if they didn't go, they'd lose the ball for sure, and if they did, they

115

could get their ball back and win fame! So, chins up and hearts fluttering painfully, they approached the high, blackened wall behind which the devil was said to lurk.

'He can't kill us,' Deirdre whispered as she made a back for Donal to climb up first, for though normally the leader, she did not intend the fat boy to say that the Docherty twins were yellow, not either of 'em. 'Me mam would tell the scuffers if he tried to kill us an' they'd stretch his neck for him. Anyway, he's old, even if he does have horns an' a tail . . . the tail'll gerrin the way if he tries to run after us, Donny.'

It was impossible to say whether these strange remarks gave Donal courage, but as soon as he was astride the wall he leaned over to give his sister a heave up. Thus ensconced, they sat there for a moment, looking about them. The house was tall and thin and extremely filthy, the windows so cobweb-covered within and so bird-bespattered without that the twins felt considerably bolder.

'I don't see how he'll know we're in his yard, if we goes quiet,' Donal whispered. 'If we can't see in, how can he see out? Once we're on the ground . . . Holy Moses, look at all that ole rubbish!'

Deirdre looked. The yard was absolutely filled with what looked like a lifetime's hoarding. Tottering stacks of old newspapers, more tomato and orange boxes than either twin had known existed, piles of hessian sacks, old bicycle wheels, broken bricks, ancient beer bottles . . .

'He's a Jew,' Deirdre gasped. 'Or a retired pawnie. *Look* at the stuff he's got hid away here, Donny!'

The rag-and-bone men who patrolled the streets
116

might or might not have been of the Jewish faith, but they were commonly believed to be Jewish, as were the pawnbrokers, who were such good friends to the people of the back streets. But a moment's reflection told Donny that a rag-and-bone man or a pawnie wasn't likely simply to fill his backyard with such stuff. Still, he did not intend to quarrel with Deirdre; it wasn't the moment.

'Yeah, mebbe,' Donal said. The truth was he did not care if the house owner worshipped Buddha or was truly the devil, so long as the ole feller didn't catch them on his property. 'Look, there's our ball. Come on.'

He slid off the wall and Deirdre, not wanting to be left behind in case the fat boy thought her a coward, swiftly followed suit.

The ball was conveniently lodged in the highest box on one of the piles, so that they had been able to see its scarlet-sorbet beauty excellently well from their perch on the wall. The snag was that having identified it, they could not reach it. When they jiggled the boxes they swayed perilously, but could not fall over for the press of other things around them. And when Donal attempted to climb up, near-disaster threatened.

'Woah, Donny, you'll have the lot on your nut,' Deirdre warned him in a hissing whisper. 'Good thing it is that the boxes is between us an' the winders. No one can't see we're here.'

'The winders is *filthy,*' Donny hissed back. 'No one can't see out of 'em, I shouldn't think. Now you give me a back-up an' I'll reach into the box an' . . .'

Deirdre obeyed and it was at this inauspicious moment, when she was bent double and Donny was standing in the small of her back, reaching for the topmost box, that a voice said: 'What the 'ell d'you t'ink you're doin', ye rogue, ye!'

Donny jumped, but even as his bare feet scrabbled for a purchase on his sister's cotton back she jumped too and the next moment the twins were a jumble of arms and legs on the floor.

'Run, Dee—I got the ball,' Donny screamed, even as a long, skinny arm reached out and a thin but sinewy hand caught him by the ear. 'Run, run . . . tell me mam I's cotched!'

'Lerrim go!' snarled Deirdre, shaking with terror but with no intention of leaving her twin. 'Lerrim go you wicked ole devil!'

'Why should I so?' queried the voice which—presumably—belonged to the hand now gripping Donal's right ear. 'Sure an' aren't ye trespassin', the pair o' ye'? An' me an ould feller just wantin' to be mindin' his own business in the twilight of me years.'

Deirdre poked her head around the stack of boxes and there was the devil himself. Only he didn't look much like a devil to Deirdre. He had thick white hair and a white beard, his skin was tanned until it was as brown as leather and he was wearing a blue shirt and black trousers. Deirdre, scrambling to her feet, followed her instincts, as she usually did. 'How d'you do?' she said politely. 'I'm Deirdre Docherty an' me brother's Donal, an' we've come for our ball if you please.'

The old man looked down. He might have been smiling, but Deirdre wasn't too sure and it's a certain thing that he didn't let go of Donal's ear. 'Ball? Ball? I see no ball.'

'It lodged in one of your fine boxes, mister,'

118

Deirdre said. 'We was after reachin' up for it when you cotch . . . when you called out. I had to mek a back for Donal, 'cos we aren't too tall . . . oh, Donal, did you say you had it safe?'

Donal, still with his ear held captive, said nothing but opened his fingers to show the shiny red ball.

'Ah, I see it now,' the old man said. 'Why didn't you come to me front door, like Christians, an' ask if you could have it back? Sure an' when I was a kid that's what I'd ha' done.'

'But everyone knows you won't give balls back,' Deirdre pointed out. 'Everyone knows, mister.'

The old man had very bushy white eyebrows over sparking, dark-blue eyes. Now the eyebrows climbed up as though they wanted to leap into their owner's thick pelt of white hair and hide.

'I won't? How d'you know, ye spalpeen? For you've not come to me door, that I'll vow.' He chuckled. 'Yours isn't a face a feller would forget in a hurry; no indeed.'

'We've not had the ball long, mister,' Deirdre said. 'And everyone says you won't give kids their balls back . . . they say there are hundreds in your house, you must have a room full of 'em.'

'Niver a one,' the old man declared. 'I'm not sayin' there aren't balls here, in me backyard, but I've niver a one in me house. What would I want wit' a hundred rubber balls, indeed? Do I look as if I play cricket, or rounders, in me kitchen of a night?'

He sounded serious, so Deirdre and Donal gave the matter their serious consideration, too.

'No, mister,' Donal said finally, seeing that his sister wasn't about to commit herself. 'I don't 'spec' you do. But it's what they say, see?'

The old man sighed and let go of Donal's ear. 'Ah, what they say! Well, that'll larn you to judge for yourself, not from other people. Go on, get off wit' ye.'

But Deirdre was no longer so keen to leave. She prodded the nearest pile of boxes with a bare and grimy toe. 'Why d'you keep all them boxes, mister? An' the papers, an' the bottles? Are you a rag-'n'-bone?'

This time the old man did laugh, though he shook his head. 'No, I'm not a rag-an'-bone, not yet, any road. I've been a lot of t'ings in me life so I have ... farmer, cattle drover, seaman ... but never a rag-an'-bone man. And now, young leddy, young gent, I'm a searcher.'

'What's that?' Deirdre demanded. 'I ain't never heered of a searcher!'

'It's not a job, exactly,' the old man said. 'But it's what I do. I'm searchin' for someone my Daddy knew long ago.'

'Are you goin' to give them twenty pound?' Donal asked. 'Is it fambly you're after searchin' for?'

The old man shook his head. 'No, not fambly, exac'ly. Nor there isn't no twenty pound, but there's somethin' more important. When my father lay dyin' he told me of a great wrong done by his fambly to a young woman, an' he axed me to see that the wrong was put right. Only when he told me I was young, an' I had me life to lead, an' I t'ought I'd look into it tomorrer, always tomorrer. An' then one day I realised I was old, an' I'd done nothin', so I started in to search. But I don't rightly know who I'm searching for any longer, 'cos gorls

120

marry an' change their names, which meks 'em difficult to get aholt of. I've put a notice in the *Echo,* but there's been no answers. I guess time covers over all sorts, but after all I've done I'm beginnin' to believe the fambly I'm seekin' isn't in Liverpool, any more than it was in Dublin, or London, or New York.'

'And you've hunted in all them places?' Donal asked, much impressed. 'You must want to find that fambly, mister.'

'I do,' the old man said quietly. And for a moment he just stared at the tall, blackened brick wall as though he could see through it, through the mean streets beyond and out to where the Mersey joined the bounding blue ocean. Then he gave himself a little shake and addressed the children once more. 'But here I am an' here I'm stuck, till my ship comes in.'

'What ship's that?' Deirdre asked politely. 'Our Dad's a seaman, he's gorra ship, it's the *Princess Indira* at the moment. But he changes,' she added conscientiously. 'Sometimes he's aboard one, sometimes another.'

'Aye, I know. But I didn't mean that kind o' ship. I meant that I'm stuck here until me luck changes, because I'm cleaned out—penniless. I can't move on until I make some chink.'

'Sell this stuff,' Deirdre said, gesturing around her. 'You'd gerra lorra money for it, mister. We'd help you, Donal an' me,' she added. 'We like sellin' stuff, don't we, Donny?'

'We've never tried,' Donal growled. ''Sides, folk don't give kids much. You want a barrer, mister.'

'Mebbe I does and mebbe I doesn't,' the old man said. He sounded tired and sad. He turned

121

away from them, towards the house, then turned back. 'I'd like to clear this lot out, though; then I could have a bit of garden. I'm good at growin' crops, always was. And it's a big yard.'

'An' you could have lodgers, 'cos it's a big house,' Deirdre suggested brightly, looking up at the long, thin height of it. She knew it was easily the biggest house in the road, unlike their own home in the court, two up and two down. 'Our mam wanted a lodger, only our dad said no, too many kids.'

'Tell you what,' the old man said, ignoring this suggestion. 'Why don't we work together, the t'ree of us? You can give me a hand pilin' this lot on to a barrer or a handcart or some such, an' then I'll let you have a bit of me yard for to play in. An' I'll tell you what I know about the fambly I'm searchin' for, an' you can do some searchin' too.'

'Ooh,' Deirdre had said, her voice heavy with longing. 'Ooh, what we'd like best in the world, mister, would be a bit of dirt of our own. We could have a garden then . . . we live in one o' the back to backs,' she added. 'No yard, even; shared lavvy, an' all.'

'Right, then, is it a bargain?' said the old man, and when they nodded he spat on his hand and held it out. 'Shake, partners.'

After that they'd exchanged names. The old man was Bill, he told them, and the family he was searching for was—or had been—called Feeney. And Donal said he would find out about barrers, or handcarts, and they'd give Bill a hand wit' clearin' the yard.

Now all that had happened some weeks ago, but with their usual feeling that they should keep their doings to themselves, the twins had told no one about their new friendship. They had worked like a couple of slaves in Bill's yard though, helping him to clear out, and at last there was a piece of ground, six foot by eight foot, clear enough to be used.

'But the soil's sour, you'll not get anything to grow in it,' Bill said disappointedly when he brought a spade to dig it over for them. He wrinkled his nose. 'Cat's lavvy, that's what this is.'

'What should we do?' Deirdre had wailed, disappointment in every syllable. 'I wanted to grow spuds for me mam to boil for us dinners.'

'Eh, that's the Irish comin' out in ye,' Bill said, chuckling. 'Get some dacent soil from somewheres, alanna, wit' a bit of hoss-muck, an' you'll grow taters fit for a quane, so you will.'

Which was how Deirdre and Donal came to be struggling over Bill's wall that afternoon, with a sack of stolen soil from the public gardens swaying between them.

'Tomorrer we'll get that hoss-muck,' Deirdre said, as the sack plopped into Bill's yard and they followed it. 'Empty it out, Donny, then we'll tek the sack back wi' us an' hide it for tomorrer.'

'We're in a bit of a state,' Donny said later, as the two of them, having stowed the empty sack away down a jigger, strolled with what innocence they could muster along the paved middle of the dark court. 'What'll Mam say?'

'She'll be busy wi' the new baby when she gets in,' Deirdre said rather glumly. She could not understand why her mother had insisted on bringing yet another baby into the family when they had one already, and the one they had was awful fond of screamin' his head off come bedtime. Mam

123

took the newest baby to work with her, because she was still feeding him, but poor Ellen was in charge of the two-year-old. The twins called him 'screamer', or 'snotty Sam', and resented him bitterly. 'It's Ellen we'll have to watch out for.'

And she was right, for no sooner did Ellen set eyes on them than she shouted, 'Where've you been, the two of you? Oh, no . . . you're *filthy,* wait till our mam sees them kecks, Donal . . . is that *earth* caked on your skirt, Dee? Get in the yard, an' mek it quick because I've not got time to bath either one of you, so it's under the tap wi' you both.'

'We'll wash ourselves, Ellen, you watch Sam,' Deirdre said with dignity, but Ellen merely snorted.

'Sam, bless him, is sound asleep in bed. As for lettin' you wash yourselves, something tells me you wouldn't end up much cleaner than you are now,' she said, seizing each twin by the hand and dragging them across the paving to the end of the court, where the big old cold-water tap was situated just beside the double-seater lavatory. 'Come on, I'll swill you down, you can soap yourselves if you do it proper, then I'll rinse you off.'

There was a large enamel bucket standing by the tap for this specific purpose. Deirdre tried to point out that it was a chilly afternoon, that they'd done no wrong, had they, only got a bit of dirt on their . . . and the ruthless Ellen stripped her small sister's smock dress off and threw a bucket of water over her, effectively stopping her mouth. She then did the same to Donal, who gasped but heroically did not yell. Deirdre, screaming, decided she was glad she wasn't a boy. A scream warms you up, she told herself, filling her lungs for a real good 'un. A scream helps to make the cold water bearable.

'For Christ's sake stop batterin' that child,' moaned a voice from the nearest dwelling. 'Or I'll come an' batter you, so I will. I'm workin' nights at the brewery this week. Can I not have a moment's peace?'

'That's Mr Feeny,' Ellen remarked. 'He's tryin' to get some sleep before his shift starts. Will you shut up, Deirdre, or will I shut you up wi' a chunk of carbolic in the gob?'

'I hate carbolic,' Deirdre grumbled. 'Why can't we have Pears? The little girl in the advertisement likes it, I can tell.'

'She doesn't eat it,' Ellen pointed out, working up a fine lather between her two hands and slamming them, palms down, on to Deirdre's defenceless face. 'Keep your eyes shut or it'll sting, 'cos soap does, whether it's called carbolic or Pears!'

'Ellen,' Donal said as he was treated similarly. 'Ouch! Ellen, I'm tryin' to ax you . . .'

'Right. Rinsing,' Ellen said, ignoring her little brother's frantic attempts to speak with a mouthful of suds. 'Here it comes . . . close your eyes and hold your breath or it's drowned you'll be for certain sure.'

The bucket swung, the long loop of water encompassed both shivering twins, then Ellen stood it down and passed each child a small and grubby piece of towelling. 'There! Now give yourselves a good rub and tek a run round the court. Mam will be home soon, so I'll go back indoors and put the spuds on to boil. And you two can come wi' me, an' when you're dry and 'spectable, you can lay the table, butter the bread . . .

125

stuff like that.'

'All right, Ellie,' Donal said peaceably. He tucked his small hand into hers. 'You know you talked about Mr Feeny just now . . .'

'Well, I didn't talk about him, I said he was doin' nights, that was why he shouted at Dee for screamin',' Ellen said, pattering up the steps and in through the doorway. 'Why, Donal? D'you know the Feeny kids? I know there's a lot of 'em, but I've not spoke to any of 'em, only Mrs Feeny.'

'We've gorra pal, he's quite old, he's searchin' for someone called Feeney,' Donal said. His twin, wrapped in her towel, tried to kick out at him, to warn him to shut up, but Donal saw no reason why he should take any notice of Deirdre. Hadn't taking notice of her always got him into trouble, now, and didn't he share the blame with her equally, even though it was almost always she who did bad things?

'Well, it's a common enough name,' Ellen said. She pointed to the horsehair sofa. 'Sit!'

'We aren't dogs,' Deirdre grumbled, but she sat down as Ellen fussed around, getting them clean clothes and throwing their dirty things into the low stone sink in one corner. 'When's tea?'

'When it's cooked,' Ellen said. 'Now. Just what have you been up to?'

'Nothin',' Deirdre said at once. It was her firm belief that if you denied everything you might well get away with something.

'You didn't get that dirty playin' hopscotch, or cherry wobs,' Ellen said firmly. 'Oh, Deirdre, you've not been down by the floatin' road?' She pulled a clean and much darned smock down over Deirdre's head and handed her a pair of flannel

126

drawers. 'Put them on, chuck, while I get Donal sorted.'

'Where's the floatin' road?' Donal asked eagerly. A floating road sounded good sport, and it had to be a mucky place where a kid could find mud. Donal, diligently digging, had kept going because if there was a game he loved it was mud pies, and when they had found enough soil for the garden they wanted in No. 17a, he fully intended to make mud pies with any soil left over.

'Never you mind,' Ellen said, however. 'No, you wouldn't have gone down there, you've only got little legs. You know half the time I forget you're only five and not even in school yet. I wonder what poor Mam will do wi' the pair of you when I get a job?'

'She won't scrub an' slap,' Deirdre said hopefully. 'Mam loves us, don't she, Donny?'

'Yes,' Donny replied with total conviction. 'But you won't gerra job till we're in school will you, Ellie?'

'Probably not,' Ellen said. 'Probably I'll stay in the blee . . . I mean I'll stay in the house until I'm fifty, the rate I'm goin'. Mam earns more'n I can, that's the trouble, an' someone's gorra keep an eye on you kids. Now once an' for all, Donal, what were you doin' this afternoon to gerrin such a filthy state?'

'Playin',' Donny said promptly. 'Hopscotch, kickin' the can, relievio . . .'

'What, just the two of you? Oh, come on, Donal, pull the other one!'

'All right, Ellen, it was mud pies,' Deirdre said. 'We was shopkeepers, we took it in turns, an' we sold mud pies. Everyone does it.'

127

'But everyone don't gerrin that state,' Ellen told them. 'What did you do, *eat* the perishin' things? I tell you, I'll give you mud pies if you come in like that again. I'll be washin' every stitch on your backs afore I go to bed tonight, an' I've better things to do, I tell you straight.'

'Sorry, Ellen,' Deirdre said and heard Donal echo her words. 'I'll lay the table, shall I?'

'Yes, queen, if you wouldn't mind,' Ellen said, and Deirdre smiled lovingly at her elder sister and thought that Ellen was really nice most of the time and only cross occasionally. When we deserve it, Deirdre thought, and trotted over to the dresser for the cutlery, astonished at her own frankness.

*   *   *

Ellen made the twins their tea and packed them off to bed, though she was resigned to them scampering downstairs again the moment they heard their mother and the boys come in from work. But at least it meant they were ready for bed, so she could eat with Mam and the boys, then she and Mam could tell each other all about their day. Though I'm still not at all sure what them divils were up to, Ellen reminded herself. Mud pies, indeed! If it had really been mud pies, then why in the name of heaven hadn't Donal told her so first go off? No, it was worse than mud pies, though she couldn't for the life of her imagine what it could have been. It isn't as if we've gorra yard, or a piece of ground of our own at all, Ellen thought, humping the kettle over to the sink and pouring boiling water over the twins' plates and mugs. Oh, well, at least they're safe in bed now.

There was a nice piece of mutton and some vegetables stewing in a pot over the fire and her mother had made the bread last night. Ellen wasn't bad at it, but she didn't have her mother's touch, so Ada usually made the bread, then Ellen took it down to Samples and they baked it. A couple of hours later Ellen would go down with her mother's big basket and collect it, sweet-smelling and wholesome, and pay the few pence the baker charged for the service. Sometimes Ada made currant bread ... Ellen's mouth watered at the thought ... and then they feasted, because with more money coming in, food was easier to obtain and more interesting too. And the boys really enjoyed having meat once or twice a week, instead of cheap fish or blind scouse.

Ellen lifted the lid and prodded the neck end of mutton and shifted the pot sideways, so that it wasn't getting the full heat. It was done; now it could simmer until the family were ready to eat. Then she cleared away the remains of the twins' tea—bread and jam and rice pudding—and staggered over to the sink with the pan of potatoes. She drained them, then left them, still in the pan, on the draining board to finish cooking so that they would be dry and floury by the time the boys and Mam were in.

Next, Ellen went for the big pitcher of milk and poured some into the small enamel pan kept specially for the purpose. She would boil Toby's milk and stand it in a bowl of water to cool, then she would make bread and milk for Sammy and wake him up and let him sit on her lap whilst she spooned it into his eager mouth. Going up the stairs and bringing Sammy, heavy and rosy with

129

sleep, down on her hip, Ellen decided, not for the first time, that her mother, working all day with the flowers in Clayton Square or spending the early evening trudging round the theatres with a basket of fruit, was to be envied, even though she knew that Ada worked long hours and that sometimes the game wasn't worth the candle. In the hungry months of January and February, when flowers were scarce and expensive and fruit was the same, Ada sometimes came home as dusk fell with such a heavy step and such a pale face that Ellen got quite frightened, but as the evenings lengthened and flowers became more plentiful so her mother smiled once more and seemed happier.

She didn't take Toby on her evening excursions, though. She left him with Ellen and the boys ... not that the boys would have lifted a finger to help had the house been afire, Ellen thought bitterly. They had their own ploys and certainly did not intend to get lumbered with a baby brother. It was Ellen's job, they pointed out if she complained or asked for help. They did their jobs, let her do hers!

But oh, lucky Shirl, Ellen thought often. Shirl had a job! She was the eldest girl but not the only one in the family, as Ellen was (you couldn't count Deirdre, who was a holy terror rather than a girl), so when Shirl found work in Gaddishes Dairy her mother had simply deputed Lizzie, Shirl's younger sister, to 'tek on the fambly', as Shirley put it, and Liz had no choice but to obey.

So, though both Shirl and Ellen knew that working in a shop was hard, they also realised it was a lot easier and pleasanter than running a family as large as either the O'Connors or the Dochertys. It isn't as if the damned boys leave

130

home, Ellen thought bitterly now as she mashed the potatoes with milk and butter. Look at 'em! Dick was twenty-one and courting Nellie Hardy; he had a decent job now, but he seemed to have no thoughts of leaving home as yet. Ozzie worked as a porter on Lime Street Station as Dick had done, Fred was at the brewery and even Bertie, a badly paid clerk in the Royal Liver Insurance down on the Strand, took it for granted that they would live at home.

Money-wise, therefore, the Dochertys were much better off than they had been—better off than most of their neighbours. Though there had been some grumbles, lately, from the boys about the cramped little house and the shared lavatory and single cold-water tap.

'We could afford somewhere better,' Dick told his mother over a cooked tea, made by Ellen, of pigs' trotters, cabbage and potatoes mashed with butter and liberally peppered. 'Everyone in this family is earnin', apart from Ellen, the twins an' the littl'uns. Other families move house, Mam, when their circumstances change.'

'I'll think about it,' Ada had said. 'But you're right, Dickie, we are a bit cramped here. And houses are always comin' up for rent. Yes, I'll think about it.'

But so far as Ellen knew, thinking about it was all she had done. The trouble was, of course, that Mick was home so seldom and Ada liked to consult him about everything. Come to think of it, Ellen reminded herself, it's been a while since Mick came home . . . he'd not seen the new baby, Toby, since the kid was about three weeks old and Toby was five months, now. Ellen liked her stepfather, but

131

she couldn't help thinking, wistfully, that she would like him even better if he didn't give her mam any more babies. She was still a trifle vague as to what part Mick played in their arrival—he was never around by the time the babies were born—but she knew well enough that women without husbands didn't have babies and women with husbands did.

Not that I'd wish Mick a scrap of harm, she reminded God hurriedly, in case He was listenin' in, like. He's a grand feller, is Mick. Only if Mam keeps on having babies I'll never get free of the house, I'll never get a job! And when Dick and Ozzie leave home we'll be strugglin' again, if the babies keep coming and coming.

But Shirl seemed to think that babies would stop coming quite soon, of their own accord. 'Your mam's past forty,' she said. 'Women don't catch so easy once they're past forty.'

She made it sound as though having measles and having babies were more or less the same, but even so, it was hopeful.

'More, more,' Sammy said, as Ellen popped the last spoonful of bread and milk into his mouth. 'More, Eyyie, more!'

'You'll end up fat as a pig, Sammy,' Ellen said. 'I know, you can have some of the twins' rice puddin'. Here we are—ain't you a lucky feller?'

She put Sammy on the floor and went and filled his empty bowl with rice pudding. Sammy, who had never to Ellen's knowledge turned down any food, promptly devoured the rice pudding and looked round hopefully. 'More, Eyyie?' he said. 'More?'

Ellen was just about to tell him he'd had enough when the door opened and her mother came into the room. Her big basket was empty, save for a

132

couple of tired-looking bunches of Canterbury bells, and she had popped baby Toby into it. He was asleep and her mother, Ellen was glad to see, was smiling.

'Well, here we are again,' she said cheerfully. 'Done well today, I have. Wharrabout you, queen? Kids been good?'

'Sammy's all right, but the twins got filthy,' Ellen said. 'I'll just make a pot of tea, Mam.'

She put Sammy down on the ground again and he heaved himself up by the nearest chair and waddled over to his mother.

'Mammama . . .' he said adoringly, attaching himself to Ada's long black skirt like a small limpet. 'Mammamama . . .'

'Yes, you're a good little lad,' Ada said. 'See the baby, Sammy? He's a good lad too, isn't he?'

Sammy peered into the basket and made cooing noises, then grabbed a bunch of Canterbury bells and tried to ram them into his mouth.

'That 'un would eat the cat if it sat still long enough,' Ellen said. 'Can baby go straight up, Mam? I've boiled his milk an' cooled it; the bottle's standin' on the drainin' board.'

'You dish up, I'll get the pair of 'em settled,' Ada said. 'You're a good gel, Ellie. And when I come down I've got some news for you.'

Ellen watched her mother disappear up the stairs rather uneasily. What sort of news would it be? Oh, *not* another baby, she thought hopelessly. If there's another baby I'll never get free, never!

But at that point the door banged open again and the boys came in, Dick and Ozzie first, then Fred, with Bert last of all. They made the kitchen seem very small indeed, but by the time they'd

133

taken it in turns to wash at the sink (Bertie always said he shouldn't have to wash because he was an office worker, but since he managed to get himself smothered in ink that didn't seem a very good excuse to Ellen) the food was on the table and Ada was coming wearily downstairs.

'I told the twins I'd batter 'em if they come down them stairs,' she said, sinking into the creaking wooden chair at the head of the table which she always used when Mick wasn't home. 'I had a good day, but I'm wore out. I'm not doing the theaytres, not this evenin'. I reckon I deserve an early night for once.'

'Reckon you do, Mam,' Ellen said, since the boys were so busy filling their faces that they ignored the remark. 'What's your news, then?'

'Oh, that,' Ada said. She smiled at Ellen conspiratorially, as though they were both in the secret instead of only one of them. 'What d'you want most then, Ellie?'

'Want? Well, to get a job,' Ellen said eagerly. Her mother smiled at her. She knew how desperately Ellen longed to earn some money and have some independence.

'Oh, you're a one, queen. Don't you remember you were sayin' t'other day you could do wi' a bigger bedroom?'

'Mam! Oh, Mam, d'you mean . . .'

There was an immediate outcry from the boys once they realised what their mother was getting at.

'You've gorrus a new 'ouse!'

'Oh, Mam, does it 'ave a lavvy of its own?'

'Where is it? There's a real nice 'ouse on Upper Beau what the landlord's lettin'.'

'It ain't that one, this one's on Mere Lane,' their

134

mother said triumphantly. 'There's a parlour, a kitchen, three bedrooms on the first floor an' a lovely big garret, divided into two. I thought Ellen could have the big half of the garret, wi' the babies,' she added. 'Which would leave the bedrooms for the rest of us.'

'Mere Lane?' Ozzie said blankly. 'Where the'ell's that when it's at'ome?'

'Oh, Oswald, you must know Mere Lane! It's off Heyworth Street, up by the Iron church. Go on, you must know it.'

'Well, I don't,' Ellen said, terribly disappointed. People didn't move long distances, there was always a bigger house to rent in your own neighbourhood. 'Why can't we go to Upper Beau, Mam? That's nice an' near.'

'Well, for several reasons. One is 'cos the Mere Lane house is very reasonable,' Ada said, ticking off her comments on one hand with the forefinger of the other. 'And two, we'd be on a tram route, which 'ud mek life a lot easier for all of us what have to get to work. And three, we'll be near your Auntie Anne.'

Nobody groaned; nobody dared, Ellen thought. But there was a speaking silence.

'What's wrong wi' me sister Anne?' Ada asked crossly. 'Come on, Ellen, why are you lookin' like that?'

'We-ell,' Ellen said slowly, glancing hopefully at her brothers. Surely they would chip in, get her out of having to be unpopular? 'We-ell, it ain't that we don't like Auntie Anne, Mam, it's just that she . . . she doesn't have much time for us.'

Ada's elder sister had married the middle-aged owner of the tea-rooms in which she worked, and after the wedding she had thrown herself into the formidable task of proving that she was not 'just a waitress', as her husband's relatives thought. She had taken over the day-to-day running of the tea-rooms, and had not even let the births of her three children get in the way of her business, which had prospered.

Auntie Anne's elderly husband had died long before Ellen was born, and her two daughters and her son had all married and moved away. But Auntie Anne, now a rich woman with four very successful tea-rooms and a chop-house in Liverpool, never made a secret of the fact that she thought her younger sister had been improvident and foolish to marry her first husband and produce so many children, and downright stupid to marry a second time, and a seaman at that, who was seldom home, who had elderly parents to support and whose Irish brogue and sparkling blue eyes failed to charm one down-to-earth Liverpudlian at least.

'Time for you? Why should she have time for you, Ellie?' Ada leaned across the table and patted her daughter's hand. 'Only teasin' you, queen, I does know what you mean, but it's you'll benefit from Auntie Anne bein' so near us. She's offered to give an eye to the babies, so's you can work once the twins is in school.'

'Oh, Mam!' Ellen squeaked. 'Oh Mam, that's grand ... but I didn't know Auntie Anne liked kids!'

'She don't, particularly,' Ada said, looking rather self-conscious. 'But she's started up a new business venture an' she thought, if she gave an eye to the babies ...'

'What?' Ellen demanded, instantly suspicious.

136

'Oh, I knowed there were a catch!'

'Well, she thought you might like to work in her shop,' Ada said in a rush. 'She's gorran eye for a bargain, has your Auntie Anne. She's goin' to start a confectioner's shop.'

'What's that mean?' growled Dick, seeing that no one else intended to admit to ignorance by asking. 'Sweets, is it?'

'Cakes; fancy ones,' his mother said briefly. 'She's been buyin' 'em in for years for the tea-rooms, but now she's decided to mek her own. And naturally, if she's mekin' for her tea-rooms, she might as well sell straight to the public. But she says she's too old to get behind a counter at her time of life and her children are all livin' too far away to help . . . so it occurred to her that she could trust Ellie wi' the till an' that. An' I said, if she'd give an eye to the babies . . .'

'Auntie Anne's gorra house out at Seaforth though, hasn't she?' Bertie said suddenly. 'That ain't very near Mere Lane—or is it?'

'Auntie Anne's goin' to live over the new shop,' Ada said quickly. 'There's a big old house on Heyworth Street; she's usin' the front part for the confectioner's shop an' the rest for livin' quarters.'

'Then she'll be on the premises,' Ellen said in a hollow voice. 'She'll be checkin' up on me every bleedin' minute of the day . . . she'll probably mek me give an eye to the babies while she goes an' interferes in the shop.'

'She won't!' her mother said, sounding affronted. 'She's gettin' a bit long in the tooth for that sort of carry-on. No, she'll leave it to you, Ellie. An' . . . an' her manageress.'

'If she's gorra manageress, what does she want

137

wi' our Ellen?' Bertie asked, spearing a potato and carrying it carefully to his plate. 'Sounds a rum ole go to me, Mam.'

'It's . . . it's because she ain't too trustin', I think. She's always handled the money at her shops . . .'

'Oh come on, Mam, she 'ad four or five shops at one time,' Dick put in. 'She couldn't be in four or five places at once, norreven Auntie Anne!'

'Oh, all right, jump down me throat,' Ada said irritably. 'She's worked wi' folk till she knows 'em well, seemingly, then purrem in charge, like. But this time, she don't reckon she can. So . . . so she's axed me to be manageress, an' our Ellie to be on the counter. An' I shan't interfere wi' you, Ellie, you may be sure o' that.'

'Oh, Mam! It 'ud be grand to work wi' you, an' I wouldn't mind if you did interfere a bit,' Ellen said. 'Why didn't you tell us you were there too, though?'

'In case you didn't fancy the t'ought of working wi' me,' her mother said frankly. 'An' also because I'll be keepin' an eye on the bakery most o' the time, whiles you'll be sellin', so we shan't be together that much. But Anne did say as how we'd keep it in the fambly, so far as we could, an' the head baker's to be Mr Renwick, who was the cook in her very first tea-shop.'

'Gawd, 'e must be old,' Fred said. 'E'll probably drop dead afore pay-day.'

'He's not much older than your aunt,' Ada said crossly. 'He's not much above fifty-five. So we're movin' to Mere Lane; right?'

'But I don't want to leave 'ere,' Bertie said, putting into words what they were all thinking, Ellen suspected. 'All me pals are 'ere, Heyworth

138

Street's miles away, I ain't never even 'ad a friend from them parts.'

'The shops are good,' his mother said after a moment. 'And folk is folk, Bert. You'll mek pals soon enough.'

'Shops! What's wrong wi' the shops on Netherfield Road, that's wharr I say,' Fred put in.

'We're goin' to live in Mere Lane,' his mother repeated. 'It's no use carryin' on, Fred. You all wanted to move somewhere bigger. Well, now we're goin' to do just that. We'll be out of here at the weekend.'

'The weekend?' Dick's face grew cunning. 'But you've not told Mick yet, Mam! He won't like it if you up sticks wit'out tellin' him.'

Ada's face usually softened at the mention of her husband's name, but now, if anything, it hardened. 'He's got no say,' she said briefly. 'He ain't been home for months.'

'But he's at sea, Mam,' Ellen said quickly. 'He can't come home, you know he can't—you telled the twins he couldn't, I heard you.'

'Well, that's as maybe,' Ada said grimly. 'But if he ain't here, he's got no reason to object if we ups sticks. Anyway, it's settled. I've hired a couple o' handcarts, so you boys needn't mek any plans for Sat'day evening, nor yet Sunday. We'll be moving all our stuff then.'

'I wonder what the twins will say?' Ellen said to Bertie as the two of them washed up the pots. Bertie was more helpful than the older boys and gave a hand when he had nothing better to do. 'They'll be affected more than any of us, Bert. They'll be goin' to a strange school, an' all, wi' strange kids, an' leaving their pals behind. I bet they doesn't tek it lyin' down!'

*   *   *

The twins, when told that they were about to move house, were at first delighted and then furious.

Ada had chosen to tell them as they ate their tea, thinking that they would be too busy eating to worry much over the whereabouts of Mere Lane, but she had underestimated her children. Deirdre and Donal looked at one another and put down the jam sandwiches they had been devouring.

'Mere Lane? That ain't round here,' Donal said. Ellen, watching them with a good deal of sympathy, thought she saw Donal's cheeks whiten beneath the dirt. Mam's forgotten how those two get around, she thought. They know every street, every tiny terrace, every court, even, within a mile or so. But they've not gone as far afield as Heyworth Street, not yet. 'We don't wanna go far, Mam, we like it here, wi' our pals.'

'It'll be fun, movin',' Ada said brightly. 'You'll love it, Heyworth Street's ever so lively, we'll be near your Auntie Anne . . .'

'But we thought you meant round here, not movin' miles away,' Deirdre wailed. 'There's heaps o' houses round here, Mam—why, we've gorra pal, me an' Donny, what's livin' in a *huge* house . . . we could ha' moved in wi' him!'

'You'll soon settle in,' their mother assured them. 'Why, the school in Kepler Street's so close you'll be able to see the house from your classroom, very like, you'll just cross the road an' you'll be there! An' . . . an' Heyworth Street an' Mere Lane aren't miles away from here, honest.

140

When you're bigger you'll be able to walk back easily . . . or even catch a tram, 'cos trams run along Heyworth Street.'

But the twins, who were always eager for a tram ride, suddenly seemed to have lost interest in that particular mode of transport.

'We don't have enough pennies,' whined Deirdre, whilst Donal, not to be outdone, reminded his mother of the many times she had told them that the best way to grow tall was to exercise their legs.

'I can't help it,' Ada snapped. 'We're goin', an' that's all there is to it. Now gerron wi' your tea.'

'I've had enough,' Donal said sulkily. He crammed the last piece of bread into his mouth and turned to his twin, speaking thickly through it. 'Gerra move on, Dee. There's people we've got to tell.'

'Not today,' Ada said firmly. 'Today it's bed next. You can tell people tomorrer.'

The twins, grumbling, made for the stairs, but Ellen was not altogether surprised, when she went up after half an hour to see how they had settled, to find their bed empty; the small birds had flown by the usual route . . . they had waited until their mother and sister were too involved in making the evening meal to think about them and had stolen down the stairs and out of the door like a couple of shadows.

'Just wait till they come home,' Ada said grimly, when Ellen came downstairs and told her that the twins weren't in their bed. 'I'll leather the pair of 'em.'

'They're real upset, Mam. It might be best to turn a blind eye this once,' Ellen said gently. She

141

knew how the twins were feeling because she felt very odd about leaving the area herself, and for her it was an adventure, with a job at the end of it and the tantalising prospect of freedom, eventually.

'Oh well, mebbe you're right at that,' Ada said. 'But honest to God, Ellie, the way everyone's carried on you'd think we was goin' to the ends of the earth. We're still in Everton, you know.'

'I know,' Ellen said. 'We'll all settle to it, Mam, in the end. Just give us time.'

CHAPTER FIVE

Dublin, Summer 1909

Maggie was cleaning. She rather enjoyed cleaning when there was no one else in the house and she could pretend that it was her own place, and it was always best just after she'd fed Ticky his dinner, because afterwards he went down for a nap. But she was faced by a dilemma at present and whenever she was alone her thoughts reverted to it.

She was fourteen, so of course she had left school. Her mammy never said anything outright, but when Maggie went home for an hour or two, she looked wistfully at her daughter's clothes and once or twice she had remarked that now her husband was dead and there were no more babies, she had expected things to get easier, but somehow . . . with only Aileen and Cairell earning amongst the girls, and Brendan among the boys, money seemed almost as hard to come by as it ever had.

And then, looking up at the ceiling or down at

her own hands, Mrs McVeigh would say it seemed mortal hard that Mrs Nolan, who didn't have a daughter to her name, should have a willing little soul to clean and cook and make and mend, whereas she, who had a great many daughters, should have to limp along somehow, almost unaided.

Maggie knew this wasn't true, that her sisters did a great deal to help their mother, but she was also bright enough to realise that this was her cue. Her mammy thought she should offer to leave Mrs Nolan, Ticky and the twins, to say nothing of the other boys, and try to get decently paid work so that she could bring the money back for the family pot. And of course once she was living at home the housecraft which Maggie now excelled in and in which Mrs McVeigh was so sadly lacking, would be useful as well.

But the honest-to-God truth was that Maggie didn't want to go home. Not any more. Once, she would have welcomed it; she remembered too well those long nights when she had laid, snivelling, in her bed, desperate for the feel of Aileen's warm back against one side and Carrie's bony knees the other. But gradually she grew less lonely. Once Ticky was born, for instance, he shared her bed and his warm, strong little body was a great comfort to a lonely young girl who missed her sisters. He was a happy child, eager for love, and Maggie loved him dearly. And it wasn't only Ticky, either; against all her expectations, she had become extremely fond of the twins. They were naughty, she admitted that they mitched off school, told lies and were generally difficult to handle, but she very soon discovered that they could be every bit as nice as

Ticky if you were patient with them and treated them firmly but with affection.

She was pretty sure they had intended to drive her out to start with and she was never totally sure what had changed their minds. It certainly wasn't when they saw how fond she was of Ticky, for the twins didn't like babies and had no patience with small children. She thought sometimes that it was when they discovered her in John Street church spending a precious ha'penny on a candle, which she had lit for her father when he had been taken into hospital. Neither the candle nor the fervent prayers which went with it had done any good, he had died two days later, but she thought it possible that their changed attitude had dated from that time.

Or had it been the dog? The twins had come home one afternoon with a disgusting dog in tow, the most draggly, half-starved, ugly mongrel you could imagine. Garvan, who was proud of his nastiness and had been smacked and shaken by Maggie for throwing stones at cats, had plonked himself down at the kitchen table and said very loudly: 'It's *our* dog, mine an' Shay's, an' if anyone tries to hort him again we'll kill'm, so we will.' And he had burst into tears.

'Oh, Garv,' soft-hearted Maggie had cried, putting her arms round his shaking shoulders. 'Who's hurt the poor feller, then?'

Garvan, his voice shaking, told her that the dog had been thrown into the Grand Canal, alive but 'wit' his four legs tied together, an' a rope round his mouth so tight it near strangled him'. He and his brother had fished the animal out, believing it to be dead, and whilst they were deciding to have a

144

funeral and where they should bury the poor dead creature, the dog had moved, actually moved, after God knew how long in the water.

'We *hate* whoever hort him,' Garvan said at the conclusion of his story. 'And we *will* keep him, won't we, Shay?'

Seamus agreed that they wanted to keep the animal and Maggie, who knew nothing at all about dogs and was in fact rather afraid of them, stared doubtfully at it. It was leggy and loose-limbed, with a shaggy, fawn-coloured coat and a long, pointed nose. Its ears were large and lay flat until Maggie spoke to it kindly, whereupon they came erect like two small wigwams, giving the dog an even stranger appearance than before.

'Well . . .' she began, wondering how best to disillusion the twins, for taking care of the dog and feeding it and taking it for walks, if that was what you did with dogs, would undoubtedly fall largely to her, and her hands were already full, what with Ticky and the twins themselves. Then the dog had smiled at her. It really did, it smiled, showing a set of beautifully white teeth and a gently lolling pink tongue . . . and behind all the rough-looking fur, its eyes, limpid and very dark, seemed to beam with affection.

'Oh, I don't know . . . what'll your mammy say?'

'If you say you want to keep it, Mags, then Mammy won't stop you,' Seamus observed. 'She was tellin' Mrs Platt only the other day that you were a real comfort to her, so you were, goin' on about how you looked after smelly Ticky an' all.'

'Did she?' Maggie said, feeling her cheeks warm. It was nice to feel that she was appreciated, from time to time. 'Well, all I can do is ask. And you

145

mustn't call the dog "it", fellers. He deserves a nice name.'

'Yes, if we call him somethin' holy then Mammy won't turn him away,' Seamus observed. 'Shall we call him Saint Augustine?'

'That's a nice name,' Maggie said, trying to keep a straight face. 'But a bit of a mout'ful it is to be sure ... your mammy might prefer somethin' shorter.'

'We'll tell her his name's Saint Augustine, an' see what she says,' Seamus decided. 'So long as she lets us keep him ...'

There was such naked longing in his voice that Maggie was taken aback. The twins seemed to her to be much loved and rather spoilt, not the sort of children to long for a pet of their own with quite such desperation. It was only later, when she was in bed with Ticky snuggled up beside her, that she had realised something. The new baby had definitely put the twins' noses out of joint as they say. Mrs Nolan adored little Ticky, played with him, sang to him and refused to let the twins interfere with their small brother in case they inadvertently hurt him. Had this attitude made the twins doubt their place in their mother's affections?

So Maggie decided that she would try to explain to Mrs Nolan that the dog was rather important to her small sons—and indeed, by the time her mistress returned from work that night, he had the entire family on his side. Liam, coming in tired and rather cross after a long day delivering telegrams in the rain, had been charmed by the dog's smile and had taken him out and washed him under the tap so that he would make a good impression on his mother when she returned.

Kenny had liked him, too. 'We've never had a dog,' he had said. 'Sure an' lookin' after him might keep those divils out of mischief.'

He meant the twins, Maggie knew, and by the time Mrs Nolan returned she and Kenny and Liam had brushed most of the tangles out of the dog's coat and fed him on scraps which he wolfed eagerly but with a sort of natural courtesy which Maggie found touching.

'It's as if he wanted to make sure no one else had more right to the food,' she said, awed. In her admittedly small experience animals grabbed what they could and ran for it. 'Aren't you a lovely feller, then?'

The lovely feller wagged his long, draggly tail and lay down on one of the rag rugs which Mrs Nolan made as she sat before the fire on long winter evenings. And when Mrs Nolan arrived home everyone pleaded so eloquently, and she was so amused by the creature's saintly name and the way he smiled, that his inclusion in the family was more or less a foregone conclusion. They called him Gus, it being more suitable, Mrs Nolan said tactfully, than Saint Augustine, and loved him almost as much as he loved them.

But regardless of whether it was Gus or her father's death which had influenced the twins, Maggie no longer had any doubt that they regarded her with affection. They were nine years old now, and still capable of great wickedness, but they loved their family and they included Maggie as a member of the clan, whilst still acknowledging her right to spend time with the McVeighs. Maggie did not think that it ever crossed the twins' remarkably similar minds that she might one day return to

Dally Court and she herself did not feel the slightest wish, any more, to do so.

One reason was that she enjoyed life with the Nolans; but another, which she tried very hard to keep a secret, was her feeling for Liam.

After a bad start, he had taken to her, there could be no doubt of that. At first, when the twins' wickedness had caused her to shed many bitter tears, he had been brusque with her, telling her that if she couldn't win their affection then she might as well give up and go home right away. But then, as she did her best to take his advice, he had begun to give her a helping hand, at first grudgingly, then more willingly. He had warned her that Garvan, in particular, did not much care what he did or whom he hurt so long as he got his own way, yet advised her to concentrate on treating both brothers equally.

'For Seamus sees neither rhyme nor reason in anyone not loving Garvan simply because he's a holy terror,' he had explained. 'I tell meself over an' over that they'll improve wit' age, but I can walk away from 'em. You can't. Best try seein' the good in 'em—and it is there, if you search.'

Maggie had done as he advised and very soon she loved both Seamus and Garvan with an exasperated affection which was proof against most of their ordinary naughtiness. As Liam had hoped, they did improve with age. And gradually, over the three years, Liam had fallen into the habit of spending time with Maggie, until now he treated her almost as an equal, despite the fact that she was fourteen and he eighteen and therefore a man.

Maggie knew he wasn't handsome in the accepted sense, that he probably wasn't as good-

148

looking as Kenny, who had his mother's thick, creamy-fair hair and light-blue eyes. Liam was dark-haired, dark-eyed and rather serious. He had a thin face with a long chin and he suffered—as did many boys of his age—from occasional spots, but to Maggie he was everything that she most admired. He was quiet, loved reading, the countryside, tram rides, long walks, and this despite the fact that he no longer dashed about Dublin on the heavy bicycle, delivering telegrams, because he was now a postman. You might have thought that all the walking he did in his work would have put him off doing it for pleasure, but it hadn't. And besides, there was more to being a postman than delivering the mail. Liam told Maggie about sorting the letters, learning about the various postal districts and, finally, about the actual deliveries. The rich houses where huge dogs bounded out at you, barking fit to bust. The people who hadn't spoken to their neighbours for twenty years and so would not pop round with it if you delivered a letter wrongly by accident. Others who asked him in on cold days for a hot cup of tea and a cut of soda bread. Others still, usually the immensely rich, who would not dream of exchanging a word with a postman, let alone encouraging him to cross their threshhold. And when he was tipped for delivering a longed-for letter from a son or a lover he bought little treats and shared them with her.

So he likes me, Maggie concluded. I don't know if he likes me in the right sort of way, but what other way could there be? Her friend, Dympna, had a young man now and said, wisely, that not all men who liked you wanted to take it further. Still, it's nice to be liked. I value his friendship, Maggie'd

149

told herself. But if I go home, live with Mam, get a job ... will he like me then? Or will he find someone else to talk with, walk with? We'll hardly ever meet, because the sort of job I could get wouldn't mean much time to meself and Mam would expect me to help at home, like the others.

So staying with the Nolans was what she wanted to do, which made it hard that clearly duty meant she should do the opposite. Everyone knew life wasn't easy, so by rights she should be going back home to Dally Court. She could earn money, help her mother in the long struggle to bring up the remaining younger children ...

Maggie finished a vigorous scrubbing of the hall lino and turned back into the living-kitchen once more. Once there, she took a hard look at her scrub brush. It had had it. It was semi-balding and with what bristles it still possessed leaning almost flat to the wood, it had barely finished this job and would, Maggie thought, never do another. But there was money in the teapot on the mantel for just such emergencies—she would buy a new one presently when she had finished the housework. Money wasn't short in the Nolan household. Mrs Nolan was doing well, the dressmaking business in which she was a partner was thriving, and both Liam and Kenny were in work. I'm sure she could afford to pay me a bit, if I asked, Maggie said to herself. Cleaning and cooking and looking after the twins was no joke, there weren't many girls of fourteen who would be happy to do it without pay. The only snag to asking was that in three years Maggie had got to know Mrs Nolan very well indeed. She liked her all right, but had long ago realised that her employer had no idea just how

150

hard Maggie worked. If she asked for money as well as her keep there was a strong possibility that Mrs Nolan, who spent freely on her own home and family but who was quite mean in other ways, would very likely say she'd get another schoolgirl to do the job and out Maggie would have to go, back to Dally Court. And even though Mrs Nolan would speedily discover her mistake, because the job had grown with Maggie so to speak, the die would have been cast. Mrs Nolan would not acknowledge herself to be in the wrong, which would mean everyone would be unhappy. The twins, Ticky, Liam and Kenny, Mrs Nolan, Maggie . . . and the poor little schoolgirl, of course.

Maggie crossed the kitchen and picked up the linen basket. She had a line of washing out and there was a good, stiff wind, so it should be dry by now. She would fetch it in, then nip out to the nearest huckster shop and buy a new scrubbing brush—which would mean waking Ticky, but he'd been asleep quite long enough—and be home by the time the twins got in.

Maggie ran down the stairs, closely followed by Gus, who seldom left her side whilst the twins were in school, and went round to the backyard. She took the prop down and began unpegging the washing, which she piled in her basket. Before I come along, Mrs Nolan sent the washin' out to Mrs Forbes in the next block, she reminded herself. So even by doing this, I'm savin' her a bit. Oh, I wonder if I dare ask for a bob or two, as well as me keep?

She toiled up the stairs again with her basket of sweet-smelling linen and piled it on a chair; she would iron it later, shoving the flat irons into the

151

heat of the fire, testing them, being careful, as Mrs Nolan liked.

She had not turned out to be a breaker, either. The china ornaments on shelves and tables were intact, save for one or two which the twins had seen off in their youth. Ticky wasn't as boisterous as Garvan and Seamus had been, he had only recently begun to walk, so they'd managed to avoid breakages for a while now. Maggie went further along the landing to the room she and the baby shared. He was asleep, rosy-faced and snoring slightly, in the very centre of the bed, his hands curled into sleepy fists, his mouth open. But he woke, sweet-tempered and serene, when she called his name, and allowed her to get him up and dress him without a murmur of protest.

'Come on, me fine feller,' Maggie said when he was dressed in his tiny boots and a wool jacket. 'We're goin' shoppin', Ticky, Mags an' Gus here. If you're good I'll buy you some peggy's leg to chew on.'

'I be good,' Ticky said solemnly, but his eyes sparkled and his mouth curved into a cherubic smile. 'I be *bery* good.'

'That's me boy,' Maggie said, hoisting him on to her hip. She fetched her shawl and made a sort of sling of it, to take his weight a bit, then the two of them raided the teapot, selecting a sixpenny piece, and went down the stairs.

The huckster shops were all tiny, but they sold an amazingly wide variety of goods and Maggie knew she would have no difficulty in replacing her scrubbing brush. She went into Mrs Pete's, though, because Mrs Pete was crippled and needed the money. The tiny shop was dark and smelled of

152

candle-grease and potatoes, but Mrs Pete, sitting behind the counter crocheting, glanced up and smiled as Maggie, with the baby on her hip, entered. Gus, who knew the rules, sat down in the doorway and apart from peering in accusingly from time to time, as though curious to know just what she was doing on the forbidden territory, he made no attempt to move from his place.

'Faith, if it isn't little Maggie McVeigh an' the bouncin' boyo,' Mrs Pete said, leaning foward. 'Is it more soap you're after wantin'? Mrs Flynn said ye'd a fine line of washin' flutterin' in the breeze when she come by earlier.'

'No, not this time, Mrs Pete,' Maggie said politely. ''Tis a new scrubbin' brush I'm after needin', an' a sugar stick for the baby, if you please.'

'An' one for yourself, alanna?' Mrs Pete said. 'You work so hard you should be give a sugar stick now an' agin.'

'I'll take a bite of the baby's,' Maggie said diplomatically. Mrs Nolan wouldn't think much of her if she found she had been buying herself sweeties with the housekeeping money. It was different buying them for Ticky, of course, and she could have bought for the twins without risking a telling off. But not for herself.

'Please yourself,' Mrs Pete said. She fished around in the tall glass jar which stood to one side of the counter and brought out a brown sugar stick. 'There y'are, me fine feller! And a biscuit for that blessed dog 'cos 'e's never raised his leg on me doorpost. Now I'll show you me scrubbin' brushes, alanna, and you can choose.'

'I'll have that one,' Maggie decided, having subjected the three brushes on offer to a close scrutiny. 'It's no use me gettin' a real big one, not wit' the little hands I got on me. Oh, and have ye such a t'ing as a half-pound of beef drippin'? I'm after fryin' the spuds tonight, to go wit' the cold meat left over.'

Mrs Pete found a bowl of beef dripping and hacked off a chunk which she popped into a brown paper bag and handed to her customer. 'There! Best beef drippin' you'll buy this side of Anna Liffey,' she said complacently. 'Have you give your Maggie a bit o' that sugar stick yet, young feller-me-lad?'

Ticky, thus prompted, stopped gnawing his peggy's leg and shoved it inexpertly in the rough direction of Maggie's mouth. Maggie removed the sticky thing from the region of her left ear and gave Ticky a hug, then bit a piece off the end of his stick.

'Thank you, alanna,' she said. 'Thanks, Mrs Pete.'

'He's a dote, that littl'un,' Mrs Pete said. 'Not like some.'

Maggie handed Gus his biscuit, which was crunched down eagerly, and turned in the doorway to smile at the old woman. She knew that Mrs Pete had suffered more than once at the hands of the twins. 'Oh, Garvan an' Seamus aren't as bad as they were,' she said tolerantly. 'They're settlin' down as they get older, so they are.'

She left the little shop and headed for their tenement, and as she did so, felt the glow of excitement in the pit of her stomach which meant that the boys would be coming home from work quite soon. Well, Liam was the one who brought about the glow, not Kenny, if she was honest.

'Want to stay down for a bit, Ticky?' Maggie
154

asked the baby in her arms, who cooed at her and said 'Ess, ess!', not, she knew, because he particularly wanted to stay in the yard, but because he agreed with most things said to him. 'Right you are, then,' she said. 'Tell you what, Ticky, we'll take a walk, shall us? Just up the road a wee way.'

She turned into the road, hesitated a moment, then began to walk. Towards the quays, of course, with the Liffey running brown beside them. Because it was a nicer walk, that's why I've come this way, Maggie told herself; no other reason. She and Gus strolled along in the soft evening sunshine. They came to the Ha'penny Bridge, crossed it, ambled along Bachelor's Walk and turned down O'Connell Street.

It was a lovely evening and a good many of the shops were doing a brisk trade still. O'Connell Street was a rich and fashionable area, and now Maggie and Ticky watched, fascinated, as trams charged along and cabs tried to keep out of their way, pedestrians scuttled for the pavement and a boy selling the *Herald,* barefoot, hoarse from shouting, padded past them, still calling his wares.

'We'll go a bit further, Ticky,' Maggie said. She rather wished she had changed her work-dress for something a bit nicer, but although Mrs Nolan kept her decently clothed, she was not over-generous with such things. She passed on clothing of her own which was no longer good enough to wear in the shop and Maggie altered it to fit, with a good deal of help from Mrs Nolan it must be confessed. So by careful husbanding and loving washing Maggie now possessed a good skirt, blouse and wool jacket, a work-dress, several white pinafores and a gingham dress which she wore when the Nolans took her out

155

on the spree somewhere.

A huge fat woman, selling tight little posies of wild flowers from a huge basket, winked at Maggie and chucked Ticky under the chin. 'What a dote,' she said. 'Well, what does he t'ink of O'Connell Street, then? Four bunches a ha'penny!' she added, her voice suddenly swelling in volume until it drowned out the thunder of the trams and the rattle of the cabs and sounded, to Maggie's startled ears, like the last trump.

'He likes it,' Maggie said, when she realised the woman was waiting for an answer. 'He's come to meet his big brother out of work, so he has! Safe home.'

'Safe home,' the woman echoed and moved ponderously on down the street, her long, black skirt swishing up the pavement dirt as she went.

Maggie hesitated here to look at an enticing window display, but she dared not give it too much time in case Liam came past and she missed him, so she looked admiringly at the beautiful boxes of chocolates for a moment, then turned her footsteps resolutely towards Henry Street—for was not the General Post Office on the corner of Henry Street and O'Connell, and wasn't it time that Liam emerged from there?

But she did not hurry; Liam had to come this way, unless he was walking home with a friend and going by some other route, and Maggie had no intention of allowing him to know that she had come out expressly to meet him. She had an uneasy feeling that if he knew, this would not please Liam at all; quite the opposite. He would be embarrassed by such an overt show of affection. No, she must meet him by chance.

So she loitered, but nevertheless she was almost level with the GPO when she saw him coming briskly along the pavement. She pretended interest in a nearby window, and surprise, too, when Ticky suddenly shouted: 'Lee, Lee, dere's Lee, Mags!' and looked round with, she hoped, well-simulated surprise. 'Oh, Liam! Good, you can carry your great brother for a bit, give me arms a rest,' she said as soon as Liam was near. 'Did ye have a good day now? Tell me about it—we was just about to turn for home anyway, since it will soon be time to put the dinner on.'

'I've been luggin' a heavy post-bag all day, now the gorl expects me to lug a heavy lump like you, Ticky,' Liam said. 'Why can't you walk?' But he took the baby in his arms and pretended to groan under the weight, and the three of them walked on, with Gus walking so close behind Maggie that whenever she slowed her pace she felt his cold nose bump into her bare leg.

'We'd best step out,' Liam said presently. 'I'm goin' out tonight with one of the fellers. What's for dinner, anyway?'

*   *   *

Liam had seen Maggie and the baby as he came out of the side entrance of the GPO, and for a moment he had hoped he might scuttle past them, get away without being seen. But then Ticky had spotted him and he'd known the game was up. He would have to walk right down O'Connell Street, along Bachelor's Walk, across the Ha'penny Bridge and all the way home to Meath Street with a girl who wasn't his sister and who regarded him, he was

157

beginning to believe, with a very unsisterly affection.

What a complicated thing life was, Liam thought to himself, taking the baby and falling into step beside Maggie. She was a nice girl, there was no doubt about that, she worked hard for his mammy and took good care of his horrid little brothers, but ... did she have to fix her interest on meself, he groaned inwardly as they walked. Why in God's good name didn't she like Kenny, who was nearer her age than himself, or some other feller? When she had first come to live with them, what with her cropped head and her skinniness, he had felt terribly sorry for her. Resentment had been swallowed up by pity, and also by admiration for her courage for the way she fought to understand and be assimilated by them. Until, in the end, everyone discovered that they loved Maggie McVeigh like a sister and wouldn't want her to live anywhere but with them.

Like a sister, though. That was the part which he was beginning to believe that Maggie just didn't understand. He had noticed, vaguely, that she was much better-looking, with soft, fawn-coloured hair which matched her eyes and smooth, healthy skin. But despite the fact that he was on the shy side he had a sneaking fondness for bold girls, with a good line in sparkling and bright, fashionable clothes. Not that he had ever taken one out, but a feller could dream, couldn't he?

He was fond of Maggie though, thought her a brave, resourceful kid with more intelligence than most. Liam, studying for the Post Office exams, had not disdained her help both in understanding the questions and in learning by heart the answers. He

158

borrowed books from the library and passed them on to Maggie to read so that they could discuss them ... and for all she was a gorl, and a very young one at that, she took ideas aboard very readily ... sometimes Liam suspected that she did so more readily than he.

So he enjoyed her company, liked to be with her. But not walking down O'Connell Street, where any of his pals might see him with a child of fourteen and tell him he was cradle-snatching. Alone in the country, or on top of the tram, or sitting before the fire on a winter's evening, working away at a crossword puzzle or a quiz in one of the newspapers, that was grand, but he had no desire whatsoever to kiss her, hold her hand or, in fact, to have any physical contact with her whatsoever.

And he just knew that she fancied herself in love with him! She smiled at him with extra sweetness, chose the tastiest titbits for his plate at mealtimes, hung around outside his work, or anywhere else he might possibly be. She never imposed on him or butted in—if he was with a friend she faded into the background—but he was beginning to be aware that she expected something more of him. In her own way she was waiting for him to make a move— and he didn't want to! Damn it, she was his sister in all but blood, couldn't she see that? Didn't she realise?

'Tell her, you fool,' his friend Roy had said brusquely when Liam had confided in him that he rather thought Maggie had ... well, expectations. 'Tell her she's too young, that you think of her as a sister.'

Liam had tried, though not terribly hard, perhaps, because he couldn't bear to hurt her feelings. Maggie's feelings were all too regularly trampled on by other members of his family for Liam to feel comfortable about doing the same. But he had begun to realise that unless he did say something she would simply get her hopes higher and higher. And what was more, she wouldn't leave and go home to her own mammy.

In many ways, of course, Liam didn't want her to leave. But he had recently been rather appalled to realise that his mammy didn't pay Maggie anything, not even now she'd left school when, in theory at least, she was able to earn. He had tried gently remonstrating with his mother but she had simply said briskly that girls were ten a penny, that she clothed and fed Maggie and that if the girl was not happy the remedy was in her own hands.

'You mean she could leave, Mammy?' Liam had said incredulously. 'But she's used to us ... we're used to her. She suits us very well and I'm sure we suit her. Besides, the twins adore her, so they do.'

'That's why she won't leave,' his mother said simply. 'She's grown used to eating and being decently clothed. If she went home, even if she earned, her mother would keep her poorly clad and hungry.'

'Mammy!' Liam had cried, scandalised. 'You don't mean that ... Mrs McVeigh's a decent woman, you said it yourself. Surely to God she wouldn't see her own daughter go short?'

'Oh, Liam, think before you speak,' his mother had said wearily. 'The poor woman's a widow with a lot of kids. She can't afford to feed and clothe them properly, and haven't you noticed that women spend on their sons and depend on their daughters? Young Maggie's been well treated here

160

no matter what you may think. I can't see her giving it all up so she can go home and skivvy for her mother and brothers and have to do a job as well. And see almost none of any money she earned,' she added.

'No-oo, I can see that,' Liam had said. 'But aren't we takin' advantage of her, Mammy? You don't pay her a penny piece, that I do know. And she works harder than any of us.'

'I'm takin' advantage of her for her own good,' his mother said firmly. 'Anyway, she hasn't suggested a wage.'

Her tone said that if she did she'd be sorry, Liam thought, and he gave up the struggle. If he interfered he would make things worse for Maggie, he realised. So he left well alone and was as kind to Maggie as he could be.

Which had probably started the trouble, he thought ruefully now, as they crossed the bridge with its delicate, wrought-iron arches outlined against the pale evening sky. But Maggie's only a child; one of these days she'll grow up and take a real fancy to someone and know that I'm just a friend and a brother, or as good as. And until that day dawns, I shall just have to do me best to keep her at arm's length without actually saying or doing anything to hurt her feelings.

*   *   *

Maggie was the last to bed. She cleared up after their meal, tidied the kitchen, then went and sat by the fire with the others. And when they had gone to bed she damped down the fire, tidied round again and went into the kitchen to make sure everything was ready for breakfast. They usually had porridge, which meant that if the family got up at seven Maggie must be at work by six, lighting fires, pulling the porridge pot over the flame, taking the butter off the stone slab in winter so that it was possible to spread it first thing.

But it was July, and though Irish summers were by no means necessarily hot or sunny, they were usually warmer than winters. So she didn't have to start quite so early and the only fire she needed was the one they cooked on. Accordingly, Maggie set about her tasks and as she worked, she let her mind dwell pleasurably on the latter half of her day.

First, she thought about the walk with Liam. How kind he was, how good to his little brother, playing horsie all the way from the end of O'Connell Street to the yard outside their tenement! And he had talked kindly to her and, indoors, had helped her to get the supper on the table, though rather to her disappointment, as soon as they had finished eating he excused himself.

'Me an' Roy are goin' fishin',' he said grandly. 'Shan't be in till the small hours.'

With that he had disappeared, and though Maggie had hung about for as long as she could he had not come home.

Still. He had been nice, which was what mattered, Maggie thought, piling ash on top of the fire in the old black range. And when we come out of Mass on Sunday, who knows, he might take us— the littl'uns an' meself—off to the seaside again!

The trip to the seaside had taken place whilst her affection for Liam was still easy and comfortable, before he had become a sort of icon to her, and it was a treat which she often relived in

162

her mind, sometimes before falling asleep, often when she had just woken up and realised that it was not yet time to get up. But squatting on the floor brushing spilt ash from the rug was not ideal for pleasant dreaming, so Maggie finished her tasks, briskly swilled her face and hands with a small amount of water out of the enamel jug and headed for the door. Gus, who had been sprawled leggily on the rug, waiting for her, immediately got to his feet and loped in her wake—he knew that Maggie would go down to the yard before making for her bed.

Maggie and the dog tiptoed quietly down the stairs and out into the night. Above her head, Maggie saw a million stars pricking the dark blue-black of the sky and a slender white eyelash of moon. She hissed 'Go an' pee then, Gus, there's a good feller' and went around the corner. When she came back Gus, very black in the starlight, was wandering back into the yard—he had taken the opportunity of a quick sniff round the alley, Maggie guessed—so the two of them made for their beds once more, though she did glance wistfully towards the alley as she went. Liam might have been coming in—but he wasn't. Maggie and the dog padded up the stairs as quietly as they could and let themselves into the Nolan living quarters.

Gus slept in the kitchen at nights, on a pile of newspapers collected and scrumpled up by the twins and refreshed every week or so. Now, the dog climbed on to his bed, blinked at her, turned round a couple of times and settled. Sighing, Maggie checked that all was well in her little kingdom and headed for her own room. Ticky would have been asleep for hours but when she climbed in beside him he always made a delicious purring sound and snuggled up, making her feel wanted, needed.

I'd miss this lovely room if I went home, Maggie told herself, taking off her pinafore and her working dress, and hanging them on the hook which Liam had put on the back of her door. She glanced contentedly round the room. It was all so nice, so ... well, so different from Dally Court. Even with the McVeigh children growing up and no more babies coming along, even without the strain of an invalid husband, Mary McVeigh could not manage her finances. Indeed, she scarcely tried, having given up long ago.

Maggie picked up her hairbrush—an item which her mother would have raised astonished brows over—and began to brush her long, straight hair. She brushed and brushed until it had bushed out round her face, crackling with electricity like an exotic chrysanthemum halo, then braided it into one long, thick plait and knotted a piece of string round it. Just as she was about to climb into bed, she remembered her picture. Mrs Nolan had said she might have the picture for her own, when she had found Maggie crying once, and Maggie valued it more than anything else she possessed.

She went over to it. It was a picture of Clare, Mrs Nolan had said, but to Maggie it could just as well have been fairyland—or heaven, come to that. She stared at it for five or ten minutes, filled with strange longings. She had been into the country with the twins and a couple of times with Liam, but the countryside just outside Dublin simply wasn't like the place in the picture!

'It isn't painted, it's embroidered; you've never seen anythin' like it,' Maggie had assured her

164

mother. 'I love it, an' I'm *sure* it really is like that; no one could imagine anythin' in such . . . such detail. But when I'm old, married, and . . . and rich, I'm goin' to go there, see it for meself.'

'Oh, sure, an' pigs can fly,' her mother had said and laughed at her crestfallen expression. 'Never mind me, alanna. If you want it badly enough, mebbe you'll get there yet.'

Now, Maggie stroked the picture gently with her forefinger before turning away and getting into her bed.

'I wonder why she didn't go back to Clare, the granny,' she muttered to herself as Ticky rolled, purring, into her arms. 'Well I won't be put off, no I won't. I'll go back to where she made that picture, so I will, because when you want somethin' badly enough you can move mountains . . . Father O'Leary said so many a time. And . . . and mebbe, one day, I'll make a picture of me own.'

*　　　*　　　*

Next morning, when she woke, Maggie's first thoughts were of the picture. She had dreamed about it—or had she? Already the dream was fading, becoming less real. Probably I dreamed about the country because I'd been thinking about it before I went to sleep, she decided, and climbed out of bed, leaving Ticky rosily slumbering.

It didn't take her long to dress and to pad quietly through into the kitchen. She knocked as much ash as she could off the fire with the old scrub brush and blew on the embers with the bellows until the hearth—and herself—were covered in a fine film of ash and the fire was beginning to blaze up. Then

165

she mixed the oatmeal with water and pulled it over the flames.

The kettle, filled by Liam the previous evening, was already on the hob. As soon as the porridge was ready that would be put over the flame, then Maggie would begin to cut the flat round of soda bread into wedges and to butter them. Ever since money had grown easier the Nolans, and Maggie herself, had eaten butter, keeping the maggie ryan for such things as puddings.

Maggie laid the table and went back into her room for Ticky. He had woken up but, good little soul that he was, was simply squatting on the bed with his favourite toy, an extremely ugly monkey which the twins had come across in a pile of jumbled-up old clothes in the Iveagh market.

'Up you get, me lovely feller,' Maggie said. She picked up the child and dressed him, then carried him on her hip into the kitchen and set him down on the rag rug, close by Gus, who obligingly moved up, then leaned forward and gave Ticky a very wet lick. 'Now you sit there an' play wit' Gus until the porridge is cooked.'

'Ess, ess, ess,' Ticky said happily. He adored porridge, with brown sugar sprinkled over it. Gus, who was also fond of it, watched Maggie closely as the porridge began to bubble and Maggie drew it half off the heat and started to stir it. The twins always gave him their dishes to lick, and sometimes, if he was lucky, Ticky lost interest and insisted that Gus shared his food. Gus cocked his ears and stared intently at the saucepan. You never knew, accidents could happen, his expression seemed to say. For some reason best known to herself Maggie might well turn round and suggest he saved them trouble and ate the lot!

I'm not going back home to live, not if me mammy begs me ever so, Maggie decided suddenly, looking at Gus's hopeful expression, at Ticky's sweet, round, rosy face, and at the clean and pleasant kitchen. Why should I go back? Mammy was quick to put me forward to be Mrs Nolan's skivvy, but now she can see I might earn a bob or two she wants to change all that, to have me at home again. And what sort of wanting is that, when it means bringing your child down? Mrs McVeigh had plenty of children to help her and the fact that she'd done nothing to train her family in tidy ways and good management was scarcely Maggie's fault.

For Maggie realised, even if her mother did not, that she had a good deal to thank Mrs Nolan for. Mrs Nolan had taught her to wash the delft in warm, soapy water and to rub it dry with a soft cloth until it shone. She showed her how to launder clothing and bedding, how to iron it just right with the heavy flat irons heated before the fire, to fold it at once, flat and neat, and pop it into a drawer. In the beginning she had gone down on her hands and knees and instructed Maggie in the art of scrubbing a floor until it fairly squeaked with cleanliness, and how to polish linoleum with wax polish until you could see your face in it. She had stood in the kitchen by the hour together, showing Maggie how to bake bread, how to make pastry, how best to cut stew meat to make a good meal for a family. She had taken her marketing with the big basket, warning her of this trader, commending that one, but always making sure that Maggie knew how to tell good from bad, quality from quantity.

In a way, it would be disloyal to Mrs Nolan to go

creeping off home, Maggie told herself. Yet she knew in her heart that she would not be so loyal to Mrs Nolan had her life not been so pleasant with them, and ... and had Liam not existed. Only I don't see why I should leave just because me mammy hints, and can't be bothered to teach Aileen and Carrie how to do things properly, Maggie thought. I know I'm bein' selfish, but I was sent away when I didn't want to go, now I'm bein' tugged back when I'd rather stay. Oh, what'll I do?

The twins, careering into the room without their boots and with their hair in spikes all over their heads, put an end to such soul-searching, however.

'Maggie, Garv's took me boots!'

'Maggie, the boy's a liar, so he is! I've not laid a blessed hand on his bloody boots, he's lost 'em himself, now it's me he blames! Oh, give him a slap acrost the head, Mags, teach him dat liars niver prosper!'

'Garv, you *know* you've took me boots ... where've you hid 'em? Come on, give 'em back or I'll kill you dead—*and* we'll be late for school.'

'Garvan ...' Maggie started to say, only to be interrupted,

Liam came into the room and took Garvan firmly by the ear. 'Where've you put 'em?' he said. 'Come on now, a straight answer or you'll have one ear the length of a donkey's, so you will.'

Maggie waited for the shriek of protest, the innumerable stories, but instead Garvan said crossly: 'They're on the windowsill. Oh, you're a poor sport, Shay, to make such a fuss. Why didn't you search for 'em, eh?'

'Why should I?' Seamus said reasonably, heading out through the kitchen doorway again. 'I

168

knew Mags 'ud make you tell.'

'It wasn't me, though,' Maggie said. She began to spoon porridge out of the saucepan into earthenware dishes. 'Liam did it.'

'He's a bully, so he is,' Garvan said, but without rancour. 'Eh, that Seamus, he can't take a joke.'

'Well, not over boots,' Liam put in. 'Boots is serious things, Garv. And what cause did ye have to balance them on the windowsill, now? T'wouldn't do 'em much good to be knocked into the yard, would it?'

'Now that I'm in here, there's no one to knock 'em anywhere,' Garvan said truthfully. He picked up a dish of porridge and took it over to the table. 'Mammy gone yet?'

'No, not yet. Why? Do you want her to take you to school instead of me?'

Once, Maggie had accompanied the twins to school every day, but now they were much more reliable. What was more, the term was coming to an end in a couple of days and the long summer holidays stretched before them; she was pretty sure, therefore, that, accompanied or not, they would attend school until it finished and they brought home their reports.

'Don't matter,' Garvan said airily. He sat down on a wooden stool and dug a spoon into his porridge. 'Not much longer, eh, Mags? Then you'll have us home all day—we can go fishin', swimmin', explorin' . . . we might even do some 'tater pickin' I suppose.'

'Poor Maggie,' Liam said. 'Rather you than me, Mags.' He sat down on the stool beside his brother and began to eat his own porridge. 'I like the summer meself, mind. I t'ought we might go down

169

to the coast for the odd day . . . would you like that, Maggie?'

'Oh, I would,' Maggie said longingly. 'I do love the sea, Liam.'

'Uhuh, me too,' Liam said, through a mouthful of porridge. 'We might go fruit pickin' an' all, you an' me.'

Maggie gazed at him. Was this the first sign of genuine softening towards her? She was sure he liked her, but had noticed that he avoided being alone with her. Now, however, he seemed unworried by the thought of a twosome.

He smiled across the table at her, his face teasing, his eyes full of affection. 'What's up, Mags? Don't you fancy pickin' fruit? It's good fun on a hot summer's day—not so good when it's rainin', mind, an' it usually rains.'

Maggie found her voice. 'I don't t'ink rain would bother me,' she said huskily. 'I . . . I'd love to go fruit-pickin' wit' you, Liam.'

CHAPTER SIX

Liverpool, Summer 1909

Moving day was fine, which was a bonus, Ellen reflected, helping her brother Bertie to lug their belongings out of the old house. Outside, Ozzie and Fred put their backs into hefting the furniture on to the handcart, whilst Dick and his pal Martin prepared to push the first load all the way to the new house on Mere Lane.

Ada was masterminding the removal, of course,

but then she intended to get over to the new house just as quickly as she could—and she would travel a good deal quicker than the lads, who were taking it in turns to push the two well-laden handcarts—so that she could make sure the furniture went where she wanted it rather than where they found it easiest to dump.

'Check through, Ellen,' her mother called to her as the last object was loaded on to the handcart. 'Mek sure everythin's out, then give the floors a brush round. Mrs Emmett won't want to start cleanin' our muck when she comes in.'

'Awright, Mam,' Ellen called. 'I'll have to borrow a broom, though.'

'Damn!' Ada said. 'I forgot—our broom went wi' the first load. Never mind, chuck, nip over to Mrs Edwards, she'll give you a borrow of one.'

'Right,' Ellen said. Her mother had loaded Sammy and Toby into a big, broken-down perambulator with some bits and pieces which were too precious to go in the handcarts and was preparing to follow her older sons. 'Where's the twins, Mam? Did they go wi' the fellers?'

Ada looked round. 'Ain't they wi' you? Dear God, them kids! They'll be off playin' somewhere ... give 'em a yell, there's a good girl. I'm not hangin' round waitin' for them to turn up, though. If they've not caught me up by the time I reach Prince Eddie they'll have to come wi'you, queen. Oh, an' don't forget to bring me washing line!'

Because the houses in the court were back to backs, the Dochertys had a line which they looped across the court and attached to the house opposite. Mrs Edwards, who lived there, did the same, which was convenient because if the

Docherty washing was out and it started to rain it was quick enough for Mrs Edwards to take it in when she rescued her own—and vice versa, of course. But you didn't up sticks and leave a perfectly good line hanging across the court, so Ellen had been deputed to bring the line and the prop with her when she finally left the premises.

'I bet them little blighters have gone off somewhere, playin',' Ellen muttered to herself, going across to the Edwards place. She knocked briefly on the door and Mrs Edwards answered it. She was a large, weary-looking woman in a print dress, with two children clinging to her skirt, but she lent the broom willingly and followed Ellen into the court, chatting as she did so.

'Well, we shall miss you, our Ellie, that's for sure—you're a good girl; your mam's lucky to 'ave you to look after the littl'uns. Mind, they say the Emmetts are decent enough—they've been livin' in a bigger 'ouse but now the kids is grown they could do wi' less rent, so . . . where's them twins, then? I din't see 'em goin' off wi' your mam, nor wi' the lads.'

'I don't know,' Ellen said wearily. 'Mam said to shout 'em . . . I will, but you know what they're like. They'll turn up at the new house, come supper time.'

'What's it like?' Mrs Edwards asked. 'I never been up that end much. There's all I want on Netherfield Road, I always say.'

'Dunno,' Ellen admitted. 'I ain't been up there either yet. But I'm goin' as soon as I've brushed through an' taken the line down. No point hangin' about for them perishin' kids.'

'If I sees 'em, I'll tell 'em to go up to Mere

Lane,' Mrs Edwards offered. 'They know the way, acourse?'

'They'll find it,' Ellen said rather grimly. What a moment for the twins to choose to go missing, but how typical of them! 'They've tongues in their heads, as I know all too well.' She went through the open doorway into the empty house. 'Ta-ra for now, Mrs Edwards. I'll pop over before I go.'

'Aye, do. I've a little somethin' for your mam—I meant to give it 'er meself but one minute she were 'ere an' the next she were gone ... I did think as 'ow she'd pop in, say goodbye,' she finished rather aggrievedly.

'She's goin' to come back tomorrer,' Ellen said, hoping that her mother would agree to do just that. 'It's been such a rush, Mrs Edwards, but Mam wouldn't go without a word.'

'In that case, I'll 'and it over meself,' Mrs Edwards observed. 'Well, I mustn't keep you, you've work to do.'

She and her children turned and made for their own home and Ellen began to sweep. She had a shrewd suspicion that the twins had gone off to the 'friend' they had mentioned, in tones of increasing woe, over the past week, but since they had refused to tell anyone where their new friend lived she couldn't go round and demand that they come home at once.

Little blighters—and how clever they were at escaping from chores which didn't interest them! Ellen knew her mother had intended to put them in charge of Sammy and the baby once they reached the new house, and she herself had planned to get them to dust round after she'd swept—fat chance of that now. She would have to

173

wield both broom and duster herself.

Not that there was anything unusual about that. The only form of work which the twins willingly undertook was the running of messages, which they would sometimes actually volunteer to do. And Ellen knew they ran messages because it got them out of the house and enabled them to get little extras—a ha'penny between them went a long way in the sweet shop and if you were buying fruit the greengrocer might give you a fade; there was always bunce of some sort in running messages. And I was so pleased when me mam had a girl, Ellen remembered ruefully. Fat lot of good she's been so far! Still, Deirdre was young yet. Young kids in other families might pull their weight, but it was different with twins. It was hard to ask Deirdre to knuckle down when no one ever expected Donal to do his share of housework, so Deirdre might just as well have been a boy for all the use she was.

Ellen banged the broom crossly around the back kitchen and steered the resultant pile of dust and bits and pieces towards the doorway. Never mind! She was going to live in a big new house and start a job of her own very soon now. She would be earning money, getting away from the kids . . . why, she might begin to do the things other kids talked about—visit a picture house, go to a theatre, even. Visions of herself with the girls who had been at school with her, but who had left her behind in the entertainment stakes, whirled pleasurably round in her head.

It wasn't until she had finished brushing and was dusting skirting boards that it occurred to Ellen that, living right across on Mere Lane, she would be an awful long way away from her school pals.

But it won't matter, because I'll make new pals once I'm working, she told herself, going to the door to shake her duster. It's going to be a different life over on Mere Lane!

*   *   *

'But we're goin' miles away! We shan't be able to work in our bit o' garden, nor shan't we be able to see you,' Deirdre wailed. 'We're gonna run away from home, ain't we, Donny?'

The twins were sitting on wooden stools in Bill McBride's kitchen, with a buttered cob in their left hands and a tin mug of cocoa in their right. Deirdre looked at Donal and knew the misery on his face was reflected in her own. What a blow! No sooner did they have somewhere completely private to play, a special friend of their own whom no one else knew about, than their heartless, selfish family decreed a move. Not to a larger house, which would have been welcomed by them as much as any, but to a different district! People, in their experience, simply did not undertake moves such as that. It would mean a different school, different schoolmates, different shops . . . Deirdre remembered the happy times they had had with Joe and Essie, the ha'pence they had earned by carrying baskets of groceries home for elderly people, and her tears, which had dried whilst she considered how cruel her family were, broke out afresh.

'We will run away, won't we, Donny?' she reiterated urgently. She might be the one who said what they were to do mostly—well, she was—but she knew very well that she would never make a

175

move of which her twin really disapproved. So now she looked at him appealingly, trying to gauge his reaction to this suggestion.

'No point in you runnin' away, alanna,' Bill said, picking up his own cob and taking a bite out of it. 'I shan't be here for much longer, God willin'. I've got nowhere wit' me search, I'll be movin' on as soon as I'm able.'

'But you've got no money, Bill,' Donal said. 'You told us you got no money that first day when we come over your wall.'

'As soon as I'm able, I'll move on,' Bill repeated. 'It may not be for a while yet, but I'll not be here for ever. Besides, you can't run away from your mam—an' what about this Ellen that you t'ink so much of? What 'ud she say if you runned off?'

Silence greeted this remark whilst the twins thought about it. Finally Deirdre spoke. 'Well, all right then, we won't run away,' she said grudgingly. 'But we'll sag off school, so's we can come an' see you, won't we, Donny?'

''Spec' so,' her twin said, his eyes brightening. Plainly, what he thought of as a legitimate excuse to play truant was a far more attractive proposition than running away from three square meals a day and a doting Ellen. 'Oh aye, we'll come back awright when school's in. But now's the holidays. We can come back when we wants.'

'It's a long way . . .' began Deirdre, to be promptly contradicated.

'No it ain't. We's gettin' bigger all the time, Dee, we can walk it if we gets Ellen to mek us sarnies. Or we could skip a leckie.'

'That's dangerous, lad!' and 'We's too diddy yet, you know we is,' came simultaneously from Bill and

Deirdre. The practice of skipping leckies was popular amongst kids who wanted to go somewhere but had no money for a proper ride, but recently a boy hanging on to the back of a tram had suffered an appalling accident when the tramdriver had had to jam on his brakes to avoid running over a stray dog. The boy's hold was broken by the abrupt stop, he fell off and the cab following had gone straight over him.

'Oh, all right then, we'll walk,' Donal said defiantly. 'But whiles you're here, Bill, we'll come an' see you. How's the sellin' goin'?'

'Did ye not notice how clear the yard is? I'm goin' to plant tomatoes agin the back wall, so I am, for I've plenty room now. An' I did what you said: I borrowed a handcart for a few pence an' took all the jam jars an' bottles back, which brought in a bob or two, an' then I chopped all the wooden boxes into firewood an' sold that to the feller in the shop on the corner. He's got a notice on it now, "Chips, a penny for two bundles," so that's a help.'

'Wharrabout the rags?' Deirdre said eagerly. 'Did you tek 'em to the tatter wi' the barrer what stands on the corner of Great Homer? Our mam says he gives as good a price as anyone.'

'I did,' Bill acknowledged. 'Now if you're goin' to come back an' see me from time to time, why shouldn't you be as much of a help to me up there as you've been down here, indeed? You'll be in a different area, see, an' the fambly I'm seekin' might be anywhere. Any luck wit' Feeneys?'

'We went round axin',' Donal said. 'Most of 'em come from Ireland way back, but there weren't no one who knew the Burren. One feller I axed—his name was Bobby Feeney—said if you hailed from

177

Clare then you'd best try America. He said as an awful lot went to America when the famine came. Those that din't die, that was.'

'The folk I'm askin' for left before the famine,' Bill said. 'Have you ever heered o' the Big Wind?'

'No,' Deirdre said. She got off her stool and went over to Bill, who was sitting in the only armchair in the room. It was old and rather dirty, but in one short week Deirdre had discovered that it was the most comfortable chair she had ever sat in, so now she squiggled on to it beside Bill and looked hopefully up at him. 'G'wan, Bill, tell us.'

'Well . . . it's a long story, now. What time does this great move o' yours tek place?'

'Oh, they'll be gettin' stuff out and pilin' it on the cart for hours yet,' Deirdre lied cheerfully. 'Plenty o' time. So long as we're home for our tea.'

'Oh. Right,' Bill said. 'Want another bevvy, Donal?'

'No, I's all right,' Donal said. He came over and squeezed on to the chair on Bill's other side. 'Go on—we do love a tale, don't we, Dee?'

'Course we do,' Deirdre confirmed impatiently. 'G'wan, Bill!'

Thus encouraged, Bill started his tale. 'Well, a long time ago, seventy long years ago, before I were so much as a twinkle in me daddy's eye, the children in Ireland were playin' out, for snow had fallen in the night an' it were mortal cold. That evenin' were Little Christmas, when there's a big meal prepared an' families all over Ireland play games round the fire an' enjoy theirselves . . .

*   *   *

178

Deirdre drew a deep, ecstatic breath. 'What a 'citin' story! What did they do, Bill—them girls an' their sisters an' brothers what you telled us about—when they seed they had nothin' left, not so much as a hen or a lamb or a bonaveen?'

'There weren't nothin' they could do,' Bill told her. ''Cept to up an' leave, acourse.'

'Leave? But it were their home,' Deirdre breathed. 'It were beautiful, weren't it, Bill? An' that Grainne, she didn't want to go, did she?'

'No, she didn't. None of them did. But they had to, see? Because the big wind had taken everyt'ing; the animals, the feedstuffs, their home, their food . . . everything. And though he didn't say anyt'ing to his childer until long after, Paddy Feeney had gone to his neighbours, the rich ones ye understand, and asked for a loan.'

'And what did they say?' Donal asked. 'Surely they wouldn't say "no", after such a terrible thing as a hurricane?'

'But they did say no,' Bill assured them. 'The families had been bad friends and Fergus McBride wanted to get rid of all the Feeneys, d'you see? He wanted them out o' the way. He mebbe even coveted their farm, for though the Burren seems a poor sort of place, the grass which does grow there is rich an' good. Sheep thrive on it—do you remember I told you that Fergus wanted Paddy's lambs at market, until someone told him they were Feeney lambs? So if you could get the knack o' farmin' it properly, the land repaid you. But in any event, Fergus wouldn't lend Paddy a penny piece, and it's my t'ought that he stopped others lending too, for he was a powerful man in the community. So the Feeneys went away.'

179

'An' came to Liverpool,' Deirdre breathed. 'An' they're still here, only you can't find 'em! Ain't that romantic, our Donny!'

Donal grunted derisively, but Bill shook his head at her.

'No, alanna, 'tis more sad than romantic I'd say and they didn't come to Liverpool. Not then, not immediately. They went to Dublin, where one of Paddy's younger brothers lived. I don't know for sure what was in Paddy's mind, but I'm thinkin' that Dublin was just a stopgap, that he always intended moving on—immigratin', as so many Irish have done in the past. I t'ink he thought they'd stay a whiles, mek money for a passage to America or Australia or some such, an' then move on.

'But the girls, Grainne an' Fidelma, put a stop to all that. They'd quarrelled, you see, because Fidelma wanted to stay an' marry Durvan Casey, a neighbour's boy, but Grainne simply wanted to get as far away from Clare as possible. And when they reached Dublin Grainne just disappeared. The story goes that she left a note, sayin' she'd gone to seek her fortune an' that they weren't to follow her, but Roisin, the youngest girl, suspicioned that her sister might ha' been expectin' a child, an' couldn't stand the shame of bearin' it out of wedlock in a big city.'

'Why d'you say that?' Deirdre demanded. 'If the family sort of got lost track of, how would anyone know?'

Bill grinned at her. 'You're bright as a button, so you are! As it happens, the folk of the Burren knew about the Feeneys first because Roisin wrote, occasionally, to one of the Casey boys an' telled him what she knew an' suspected. But the other reason's a bit more personal. Me eldest brother

180

met Paddy, a good while after the Big Wind, when folk had almost stopped wonderin' about the Feeneys.'

'Met him? In Dublin, Bill? Or did he come back after all?'

'He came to Cork, to Cobh harbour, in fact, and me brother was after buyin' cattle in Cork an' didn't they walk slap-bang into one another in the street? Paddy told Talbot that he were off to America, himself an' the three youngest children. He said Grainne had taken herself off to Liverpool an' was married an' settled there, an' Fidelma was stayin' in Dublin, 'cos she were sweet on some young feller there. Bitter he was, for he must ha' realised that there were no point in returnin' to the Burren wit' his two eldest children gone. The others were growin', but they'd not manage to pull the farm around wit'out Grainne an' Fidelma.'

'Gosh,' Deirdre said, awed. 'So that's how you know so much, Bill! I wonder what happened to Fidelma, though? And Grainne, of course,'

Bill shrugged. 'The dear Lord knows, alanna. Perhaps Fidelma an' her young man went to some other part of Ireland ... the potato famine came along ten years later, you know, and it's entirely possible that they may have died, starved to death when the potato crop failed. As for Grainne, she wrote to her daddy when he was in Dublin, but once she was wed an' settled she'd not try to get in touch again.'

'Then ... then who told you the first part of the story, Bill?' Deirdre asked, having thought the matter over. 'You said when we first come over your wall that your daddy had done the Feeneys a great wrong, so you must be a part of the story yourself. Oh, oh ... I know! Your name's McBride,

181

an' that was William's name, wasn't it?'

'That's it. Fergus McBride was me daddy,' Bill said. 'I came along late in their lives and they called me William because the other William died before I was born. I t'ink it was always on me daddy's conscience that he'd refused Paddy Feeney a loan, knowing how it was wit' Paddy's daughter Grainne an' his eldest son. Me mammy would always have it that Grainne was carryin' William's child. An' I'm the last McBride, so I am, for neither Talbot nor me sister had children, though me sister wed young, an' died young, too. So me daddy axed me to seek 'em out, particularly Grainne Feeney, if I could find her.'

'An' what would you do if you found her?' Deirdre asked eagerly. 'Is there a pot of gold, Bill? 'Cos you said more than twenty pound.'

Bill laughed and rumpled Deirdre's bright ginger curls. 'There's a thrivin' little farm up on the Burren, acushla. Me brother Talbot has it now. When it was too late, when the Feeneys had disappeared into Dublin like a raindrop into a puddle, Fergus began to t'ink on what he'd done, an' he was ashamed. He set to an' he rebuilt the farmhouse, the pigsty, the stable, everything. An' he started in to farm up there, just puttin' a few sheep on the land at first, then cattle. He told me he pretended he'd bought the farm off Paddy for a song, but he never did; he was waitin' for Paddy or one o' the youngsters to come back so he could hand it over.

'But Paddy never did come back, an' it began to lie heavy on me daddy's conscience, because it looked more an' more as though he'd driv Paddy off by refusin' the loan, and then taken the land for himself. And I can't deny there was talk,' Bill admitted, looking hunted. 'I heered it meself, an' I t'umped a feller on the nose, so I did, who was talkin' big in the pub one night about folk who walked into farms when the famine was over an' the farmers dead an' gone. He said the McBrides were one of the many who'd profited from the miseries of their neighbours. And I were right to t'ump him, so I was,' Bill added righteously. 'For there was no t'ought in me daddy's head but to give the place back to Paddy in a dacint state, when he come home, an' to show him he was sorry for refusin' the loan.'

'An' who told you that Grainne came to Liverpool, then?' Donal asked. 'Who said Fidelma disappeared, come to that? How could you know, if you never found any of 'em, Bill?'

'Well, as I told you, Paddy could neither read nor write, but the children could, all of 'em. And the youngest girl, Roisin, never forgot the Burren or how happy she had been there as a small child. She wrote letters to the Caseys, who she remembered quite well, and of course the Caseys talked, told people that the girls had both run away and that Grainne was believed to have gone to Liverpool. I don't know precisely how Roisin knew she'd gone to Liverpool—mebbe Grainne left a note, or told someone—but know she did. Paddy planned to follow her, find her, but so far as we heard he never did. He died of a fever in 'fifty-five, during the great hunger, so there was no hope, after that, of my father being able to tell him how sorry and ashamed he was. He thought to do it through the daughters he had most wronged, or the sons, perhaps, but even the sons have disappeared. Well,

183

they probably went to America, which is the same, so far as I'm concerned.'

'But they won't have changed their names, they'll be Sean and Kieran Feeney for the rest of their lives,' Donal pointed out. 'You could find them, Bill.'

'Yes, possibly I could, though America's a mortal big country to find a couple of farmers in,' Bill said. 'But the debt my father wanted to honour was either to Paddy or to the eldest two girls. They'd made the place what it was, you see, through sheer hard work. And of course William was promised to Grainne. Fergus knew that he should have helped Grainne for his son's sake if nothing else.'

'And when you find 'em they'll have a farm of their own,' Deirdre said wistfully. 'We'd love to be farmers, wouldn't we, Donny? We'd have pigs an' cows an' that, an' we han't even gorra dog. I wish it were us, but now we know the whole story we'll try harder than ever to find 'em for you, Bill,' Deirdre finished. She sat up, then wriggled off the chair. 'Donny, we'd better go; Mam isn't goin' to be too pleased wi' us when we find this Mere Lane. And . . . Bill, we'll be back. We promise, don't we, Donny?'

'We promise,' Donal said fervently. 'In a day or two, Bill. When we've got ourselves settled in.'

CHAPTER SEVEN

Ellen finished her house-clean and went round to Mrs Edwards to give back the broom and to unhook the clothes-line and roll it up. She was much hampered by the prop, but it was a good one and her mother would not be best pleased if she left it behind. Those wretched twins, she thought wrathfully, as she juggled with prop, clothes-line and a bag of pegs which she had found sitting behind the door as she went to swing it closed. I'll tell'em what I think of 'em, the wicked little layabouts!

Mrs Edwards took back the broom, sniffed dolefully and asked her whether the twins had turned up yet.

'Not yet. I'll give a holler presently an' see if they come runnin',' Ellen said. 'Oh thanks, Mrs Edwards, that is kind!'

Mrs Edwards had given her a rustling brown paper bag containing a number of raisin buns, and a hug and a kiss as well. 'We'll miss yez,' she said, her grey eyes filling with easy tears. 'Eh, you brung up them kids without no 'elp from anyone, jest about. An' when our Jimmy and our Kath were with you I always knew they was all right. Well now, come back an' see us sometimes, queen.'

'I will,' promised Ellen, quite overcome by so much emotion. ''Bye for now, Mrs Edwards.'

She shouted for the twins a couple of times without very much hope, then set off on a tour of the neighbourhood, asking whether anyone had seen her brother and sister.

'Not today, chuck. An' you can't miss that red 'ead,' the man in the corner shop said, weighing sultanas into small blue bags. He raised his voice so that his customers could hear. 'Anyone seen them Docherty twins?'

But no one had, so Ellen set off on her journey to the new house with her mother's directions ringing in her ears.

'Along the lane to Netherfield Road, turn left. Keep goin' right to the top of St George's Hill, turn right down Priory Road and at the end of it, you're on Heyworth Street. Turn left along Heyworth Street and go along it a goodish way until you see the Heyworth Street school. Opposite it, so that's a right turn, is Mere Lane. See? Easy!'

It was one hell of a trudge though, Ellen thought, trudging. But once she got on to Heyworth Street it was so interesting that she forgot her aching arms and legs. Nice shops, she thought approvingly ... and then came to her aunt's cake shop. It wasn't open yet, wouldn't be open until the following week, but Ellen lingered outside it, peeping through the glass. Someone had painted swirls of whitewash on the inside to try to stop folk peeping, but with a bit of jiggling around she could just about make it out. A long counter, a smart piece of linoleum on the floor, shelves behind the counter ... and stands in the window for the cakes to be displayed on.

And I'm goin' to work there, Ellen reminded herself, feeling a warm glow of satisfaction steal over her. Working at last—and in a shop as smart as the one she was standing outside! Not a bad beginning, she told herself approvingly as she moved reluctantly on at last. The customers at such a smart shop would no doubt be smart as well, and Mam had said they would sell only the best and most expensive cakes and pastries.

Still, standing around wouldn't do anyone any good and the prop, as well as getting heavier and heavier the further she walked, was also a menace to other pavement users. Ellen had already caused cries of dismay when she'd spotted a pet shop with a window full of rabbits and pigeons and had swung thoughtlessly round, her prop sweeping two ladies' hats off their heads at the height of its parabola and striking a man so hard amidships on its downward path that he had goggled at her, his breath whumped out of him as the prop took its malicious revenge on everyone within reach.

'Jeez, I'm awful sorry,' Ellen had cried, conscience-stricken. 'It were the rabbits, see . . . are you much hurt, mister? Look, have one of me raisin buns, that'll bring the colour back to your cheeks.'

The man had muttered something about her carelessness, but he had taken one of the proffered buns, eaten it in two bites and smiled at her in quite a forgiving sort of way. 'It were the shock,' he said, adjusting his cap on his head and preparing to set off along the pavement once more. 'It ain't often as I'm swep' off me feet by a young person like yourself!'

The ladies had been rather more indignant and had refused her offer of a bun with more haste than good manners, Ellen thought. They felt they had been made to look foolish, she realised, fussing around them, fetching back the hats and dusting them off with the peg bag before watching them placing them tenderly on their smooth heads. And no one likes looking foolish. She had stood the prop down during this operation and had had to grab it hastily back, since she had leaned it against the wall alongside a hardware store and a customer, who had been examining the galvanised buckets and watering cans, had wandered over to it, a hand stretched out, no doubt about to take it inside and ask the price.

187

'Sorry . . . the prop's mine, I just stood it down for a second,' Ellen gabbled, snatching her property and holding it defensively to her bosom. 'It were the rabbits in the winder . . . they took me eye, an' me prop got out o' hand . . .'

The customer said it were the best prop he'd seen for a day or three and went inside the shop and Ellen looked round for her victims, but the ladies had taken the opportunity whilst she was otherwise engaged and had hurried off, no doubt clutching their hats. Since there was nothing more she could do Ellen continued breathlessly on her way, thinking that the journey had certainly not been a dull one. She was sorry the ladies had not accepted the bun of apology, but there you were; they looked like the sort of people who thought it not at all the thing to eat in the street, and the man had proved to be both understanding and, in the end, forgiving. I'll have to be content with that, Ellen thought, being careful now and trailing the prop behind her as her footsteps got slower and slower. Oh, shan't I be glad to see this Mere Lane Mam talked about!

And just as she was beginning to wonder whether her mother had missed out some essential part of her instructions she saw a building which looked exactly like a school and right opposite it . . .

'Mere Lane!' Ellen said joyfully, stopping dead in her tracks. 'Thank Gawd for that . . . Mere Lane at last, and Mam were right, it's nigh on opposite the school.'

As she crossed the busy road, Ellen reflected that it really would be a blessing to be so near the school. At the moment, Sammy and the baby were too small for such things, but later it would only be

188

a few yards' walk for them. And the twins would not have to be accompanied, even for the first day or so. They could scarcely miss a school so conveniently near.

'Now let me see, how far down was Auntie Anne's shop?' Ellen asked herself next, starting to walk down Mere Lane. She could see that the houses were a good deal bigger than those in the court ... but before she had had time to wonder which house was theirs a voice hailed her.

'Ellie, you've tek your time, haven't you? Where's Dee and Donny? Come on, Mam's now puttin' the kettle on.'

It was Bertie, who had been about to enter the house, she imagined, when he had seen her coming slowly up the road.

'Oh, Bertie, I haven't seen hide nor hair o' the twins,' Ellen said worriedly. She, the prop and the peg basket sidled in through the doorway, and in a quick glance round Ellen saw that they now possessed a front parlour as well as the back kitchen, the door of which was thrown open to reveal a very much nicer room than the one they had lived in in Prince Edwin Lane. 'But they know the way, don't they? Only it's even longer than I thought.'

'Yes, it's a tidy walk,' Bertie admitted. 'Pushin' that handcart was no joke, I'm tellin' ye. Look, you come in an' have a cuppa, an' if the twins aren't back by teatime I'll go an' roust 'em out. They're probably playin' with the Harvey kids, knowin' them.'

'No, I don't think so. I asked around,' Ellen said. She walked into the back kitchen and dumped the peg bag and the clothes-line on the kitchen table, which looked quite lost and lonely in its new, larger home. 'Mam, Mrs Edwards gave me some raisin buns an' she said she'd gorra little somethin' for you, only you hadn't gone in to say goodbye. So I said you'd go back in the next couple o' days, say cheerio to her then.'

'Yes, I mean to do so,' Ada said, picking the heavy kettle off the hob and pouring water into the old brown teapot. 'Cut the loaf, Ellen, we'll have a jam butty to keep us goin' till supper time.'

'You've done wonders, Mam,' Ellen said presently, sitting at the kitchen table with a cup of tea before her and carving chunks off the loaf. 'Eh, in't it big, though? An' a parlour—we *are* goin' up in the world!'

'I'm goin' to furnish that parlour real nice,' Ada said, half closing her eyes and putting both hands round the cup of tea, though it was a warm day. 'We're a way from Paddy's market here, more's the pity, but we can still lug things back on a handcart. I'm goin' to have decent chairs, a sofa, all sorts in that room.'

'How'll we afford it?' Ellen said. 'I don't suppose Auntie Anne'll pay us much, d'you?'

'Well, not at first,' Ada admitted. 'But we've got the boys' money comin' in, queen, an' we've plenty of space. I thought we might have a lodger in a few weeks, when we've settled.'

'Oh Mam, norra lodger,' Ozzie exclaimed, much dismayed. He had just entered the kitchen through the back door, which was a novelty in itself to someone who had lived all his life in a back to back, Ellen thought, carrying what looked like a sack of coal in his arms. 'There's only three bedrooms an' the garret, we don't want no one else

190

livin' here.'

'Well, we'll see,' Ada said diplomatically. 'But three rooms an' a garret means we do have a room we could let. There's you big fellers up in the garret, me an' Mick in the back room, an' Ellen an' the littl'uns in the tiny room. That leaves the dacent front one empty.'

'Wharrabout the twins?' Fred asked. 'You can't count them in wi' us, Mam. Oughtn't they to have a room?'

'Deirdre will share wi' Ellen, it's only Donal in wi' you,' Ada pointed out. 'But don't worry too much about it. We may not need a lodger after all.'

Ozzie muttered something. Ada leaned across the table and clipped his ear, then said: 'I didn't hear that, Oswald. An' just remember, I don't want to hear it, neither.'

Ellen, who really had not heard what Oswald said, opened her mouth to ask him to repeat the remark, but decided against it. Her mother's smack had reddened Ozzie's ear and the side of his face quite remarkably and Ellen did not wish to be the recipient of another such slap. But when her mother sent her up to look at the bedrooms, and Ozzie slouched up with her, she had her opportunity. 'What did you say just then, Oz? What made our mam clip your lug, I mean?'

'I said as Mick was all the lodger we needed,' Ozzie admitted. 'He's never here, Ellie! Why, apart from givin' our mam four kids, what does he do for us? We don't even get his allotment and I'm norrat all sure I believe in them old parents of his. He's just tekin' advantage of our mam.'

'He meks her happy, Oz,' Ellen said after a pause for thought. 'She's all lit up when he's home, as if she was a young gel again.'

'Oh aye. But you notice she din't say she couldn't mek a move wi'out askin' him this time,' Oswald said. 'If you ask me, our mam's gettin' fed up wi' havin' a feller she hardly sees. He came back when Tobe was a couple o' weeks old, an' we've not seen him since. Mam's done this move all by herself as far as she could . . . we helped, acourse, but it ain't the same. Mam needs her husband now an' then.'

'Oh well, he's a seaman,' Ellen pointed out. 'They're hardly ever home from what I've heard. Which is my room?'

'That 'un,' Oswald told her. 'We're up that ladder . . . it'll be grand, bein' up there, just us fellers.'

'And Donal,' Ellen reminded him, peering into her tiny room. 'Oh, Oz, ain't it grand? Just me an' Dee in here.'

'An' Sammy. An' Tobe when he's big enough to leave Mam,' Oswald reminded her. 'Mek the most of your room, Ellie, 'cos it won't be yours alone for very long!'

*   *   *

'I never knew we had so much stuff, Mam,' Ellen said wearily that evening, as she began to unload another orange box crammed with bits and pieces. 'Aren't you glad we've gorra bigger house, eh?'

'I am, but I'm deathly tired,' her mother said, collapsing on to a chair. 'Oh, I just hope Bertie lays a good one on those twins when he finds 'em. How could they stay out so late an' worry us so?'

'You know the twins. They won't have spared a thought for us till supper time,' Ellen told her

192

mother. 'Oh! What's this?'

She held the small object up. It was wrapped in newspaper and tied with pink string and it was about twelve inches long by nine inches deep. 'Is it a book?'

Her mother glanced at the parcel, laughed and shook her head. 'No, it's norra book, queen. Unwrap it. If you like it you might as well have it on your bedroom wall. It was me mam's, and her mam's before her, I believe.'

Ellen was just beginning to untie the pink string when the back door burst open. Bertie entered the room, dragging a twin by either hand.

'They were dawdlin' along Heyworth Street eatin' oranges as though they had all the time in the world, Mam,' he said indulgently. 'I wouldn't waste me breath worryin' about kids like these, I never knewed 'em to get lost yet!'

'We *were* lost,' Deirdre said indignantly. 'As lost as anything, weren't we, Donal? Mam said Heyworth Street but we couldn't 'member nothing else, so we axed people where was the Dochertys' new house an' they didn't know an' when I cried ever such a nice lady bought us a wet nellie each an' the man in the shop said we could have a norange, too. You have to *eat* oranges, you know,' she added, staring haughtily at Bertie. 'Even when you're lost an' frighted, you have to eat an orange or it goes bad on ye.'

'You're really very . . .' began Ada, to be interrupted by a squeak of excitement from Ellen.

'Mam! Oh, Mam, it's the prettiest thing I ever did see! Can I really have it to hang on me bedroom wall? Where's it of?'

Ada was opening her mouth to reply when

193

Deirdre, who had gone over to see what Ellen was exclaiming over, spoke. 'That's the Burren,' she said matter-of-factly. 'I wonder who drew it? I wish I could have it, Mam.'

There was a moment of complete, total silence, when Ellen felt she could hear the new house holding its breath. Then she said slowly, 'The Burren, Dee? Where's that when it's at home?'

'It's Ireland; in Clare,' Deirdre said. 'We've gorra pal who told us about it.' She turned to Ada. 'What's for supper, Mam? That ole orange din't fill us up proper, did it, Donny? We's starvin', so we are.'

'Mam?' Ellen said, bemused by all this. 'Mam? Is it what she said? Is it Clare?'

'That's right, it's the Burren,' Ada said, frowning. 'But how on earth did Dee know that? Or . . . have you seen another picture of it, queen?'

Deirdre shook her head. There was an orange line round her mouth, Ellen saw, and her face was grimy with the day's doings, but she wasn't messing about, she was quite serious. She had never seen another picture like this one, she just . . . just knew.

'But it isn't drawed, nor yet painted,' Ellen said, after looking carefully at the picture again. She would not have been surprised had she seen, printed in a corner somewhere, the words *The Burren,* which would account for Deirdre's unusual knowledge, but a closer study had proved the picture to be untitled. And what was more, it was, as she had just said, neither drawn nor painted. It was embroidered with what looked like very fine, soft wools, in the most glorious autumn colours. It glowed . . . that was the best way to describe it.

'Nor it is, it's wool,' Deirdre said after another

194

glance at the picture. 'Mam, what *is* for supper? I s'pose you've had yours,' she added in an injured tone. 'I s'pose you couldn't wait for Donny an' me.'

'I've a good mind to send you to bed without another bite,' Ada said, remembering her grievance. 'But you can have the same as us—jam butties, a cut of cake and some cold apple pie. I've not had time to cook since unlike some, I've been busy moving us in all day.'

Donal sat himself down at the table and reached for the jam butties, but Deirdre lingered a moment to look around the kitchen. 'It's big,' she said, sitting down on her stool and helping herself to a buttie. 'Bigger'n the other house. You'll have to get a bigger table, Mam. An' more proper chairs, 'stead o' these stools.'

'When you've eaten, you can go straight up to bed,' Ada said, refusing to be drawn into light conversation. 'And tomorrer the two of you are bleedin' well goin' to help for once in your lives.'

'And you aren't goin' to bed until you've had a good wash in nice cold water,' Ellen said cruelly. 'You're sharin' my room, Deirdre Docherty, so you'll be clean if nothin' else.'

She was still very curious as to how Deirdre had recognised the picture so unerringly, but she was also cross. Trust the twins to come in late and take everyone's mind off their lateness and naughtiness by doing something as strange as recognise a picture of a place they had never so much as set eyes on before. Trust them to wriggle out of so much as laying a table or washing up a cup or a plate!

But later, when she was getting the twins to bed, she gave voice to her curiosity. 'Dee,' she said,

195

whilst scrubbing her small sister's filthy face and hair with red carbolic soap and a good deal of cold water. 'How come you knew that place, the Burren? I mean what did your pal say about it so's you knew it at once like that?'

'Dunno. He said slabs of limestone . . . *ouch*, that was me eye, Ellie . . . an' lots of rocks . . . Ellie, if you put soap in me bleedin' mouth how'm I s'posed to answer you? . . . an' heaps an' heaps o' wild flowers,' Deirdre said. 'Aaaargh, you're takin' the skin off me nose . . .'

'Oh, is it skin? I thought it was more filth,' Ellen said cheerfully and rinsed her little sister so thoroughly that Deirdre was wetted all over. 'You are a funny kid, Dee. Now get into bed and go to sleep; the rest of us have had a very tiring day.'

'So've I,' Deirdre said, jumping into bed in her white cotton shift. 'Bein' lost is awful tirin', Ellie. Where's the picture goin' to go?'

'Over me bed, when I can get Dick or Fred or Ozzie to hammer a nail into the wall for me,' Ellen said. But actually she hammered the nail in herself, with the heel of her boot, as soon as she had seen Donal into bed in his shared garret. He was inclined to be tearful at being parted from his sister until Bertie told him it was a sign that they were both growing up, then he climbed into bed and pulled the blankets up round his chin quite happily, though he warned Bertie, in all seriousness, that he kicked and sometimes bit in his sleep, as well as shouting out and occasionally punching anything near him.

Bertie, who was no fool, said amiably that he was the same himself, which caused Donal to look a trifle alarmed, but by the time Ellen left him he

196

had apparently realised that Bertie had been calling his bluff and settled down to sleep.

In the tiny room, with Sammy in his orange-box cot already fast asleep, Deirdre lay on her back in their bed watching her sister hanging the picture and telling her whenever it hung crooked, and just as Ellen was seriously considering losing her temper and shouting at the younger girl Deirdre suddenly fell asleep and rolled on to her side, snoring slightly.

'Well, thank God for that,' Ellen muttered and stood back to admire her handiwork. The picture looked really good against the whitewashed wall; you would never have known that it had been wrapped in newspaper and shut away in an old box for years and years.

Later, downstairs in the back kitchen once more, Ellen got out her work and sat down opposite her mother. The lads were all out, so it was peaceful, with just the two of them working away in the fading light. Presently, Ellen got up and lit the lamp, then she asked her mother why she had never brought the picture out and hung it before. 'It seems such a waste, because it's so pretty,' she said. 'I know you said our old house was small, but there were plenty of bare walls that it would have looked nice on, Mam.'

'Yes, to be sure it would, if I hadn't forgot all about it,' her mother agreed. 'I brought it wi' me when I first got married because me mam said I could, but your da couldn't abide it. Said it depressed him. An' I was keen to do what your da wanted, so I put it away, thinkin' I'd bring it out again when I had kids of me own an' one of them could have it. Only somehow, I never did,' she

197

ended.

'Wasn't it strange, Dee recognising it?' Ellen said, picking up her knitting. She was making a wool blanket out of knitted squares and whenever she had a few pence, which wasn't often, she would buy old woollen garments at one of the markets and unravel them, then wash and stretch the wool and knit it up once more.

'Yes, it were odd,' her mother agreed. She was darning her stockings, a task with seemed never-ending to Ellen. Sometimes her mother's stockings were more darn than anything else, but new ones were a price, so she darned on. 'Odder, when you think that I wouldn't have known the Burren from what my mam told me. Which wasn't much. I wonder who this pal is they talk about?'

'Well, it's a big secret now, but they'll get tired of it one day and it will probably all come out,' Ellen said. 'He'll be Irish, of course. Have you noticed, when she's been with that particular pal, Dee comes out with little Irishy bits? This evening she said "We're starvin', so we are".'

'All the kids do it,' Ada said. 'You know somethin', Ellie? Whenever I see you workin' on that blanket you remind me of me gran. She were always makin' somethin' wi' wools or bits o' material. She wanted to mek her own picture, like the one you've hung on your wall, but I don't think she ever completed it. When she died one of your aunts took it, otherwise I'd suggest that you finished it. You like fiddly, pernickety sort of work, don't you?'

'Yes, some,' Ellen agreed rather cautiously. Dochertys learn not to agree to liking any work if they can help it, she thought. 'Do you like 'broidery

198

an' such, Mam?'

'Never had the time,' her mother said. 'Have you been out to the yard yet? A lavvy of our own, queen, an' quite a decent plot o' ground! There's a jigger round the back an' all, we've gorra little gate set into the back wall so's we can go in an' out that way. It's awright, ain't it?'

'It's lovely, Mam,' Ellen said sincerely. 'We're goin' to find this house suits us much better than the last. An' I'm sure when Mick comes home he'll love it too.'

She was watching Ada's face as she said it, and to her surprise her mother's expression grew melancholy at her words. 'Yes. If he comes home,' she said. 'It's been a long while, Ellie. An' he's not written.'

'But he hates writing,' Ellen said quickly. 'You know he does, he's always said so.'

'Aye. But he's never been away for quite so long before. An' I'm not gerrin' any younger, the kids tire me out more . . .'

'Oh, Mam, you're worryin' over nothin', 'Ellen assured her. 'Mick'll be back . . . come to that, when did you last write to him?'

'How can I write? I dunno where he is,' Ada admitted. 'Or d'you mean to address the letter to the old folk? Because all I know is they live somewhere in Ireland . . . it's not much help, that.'

'But Mam, you must have *some* idea,' Ellen said, scandalised. 'You know the name of his ship, where it sailed to this time! You could . . . you could get in touch with the shipping line, find out where the ship is now.'

'Yes, of course. Yes, I'll do that,' Ada said, looking more cheerful. 'But . . . near on five months, Ellie! It's a fair old length of time for a husband an' wife to be apart.'

Ellen agreed that it was indeed and continued to knit, but presently she looked up. 'Mam . . . Mick's real fond of the twins, wouldn't you say?'

'Aye, he is,' Ada agreed. 'He loves kids, does Mick.'

'Yes, he does. He's ever so proud of Sammy as well, wouldn't you say?'

'I would,' Ada said. 'What're you gettin' at, queen?'

'Well, he loves you ever so much, I can tell that even if you can't. But . . . you can't think he'd leave the littl'uns, can you?'

After a moment a big smile broke over Ada's face, completely transforming it. 'Eh, Ellen, you're right,' she breathed. 'I'll go down to the shippin' office first thing Monday mornin'.'

*   *   *

Next day, the twins were given no chance to escape but were put to work at once, much to their annoyance.

'You'll clean the cabbage for dinner, you'll help Ellen wi' mekin' beds an' tidyin' rooms, then you can start in to tidy up the yard,' Ada told them. 'I'm not havin' the pair of you slidin' off here whenever you've gorra mind, like you did in the court. The cabbages are in a basket out the back; git movin'.'

'We don't wanna,' the twins whined with one voice. 'It's Sunday, we wanna play out.'

'Do as you are told,' Ada said, enunciating every syllable with great clarity. 'Bertie, get me some coal in. It's in the shed.'

200

'A shed?' Deirdre's eyes brightened. A shed had definite possibilities, particularly if they could somehow be given the chance to tidy it, or even to take a look at it. 'I didn't know we had a shed, Mam! Can we help Bertie? Coal's that heavy . . .'

'DO AS YOU ARE TOLD,' Ada said again, this time in capitals. 'Fetch the cabbages an' don't let me see you sneakin' off or it'll be bed all day an' no dinner. Go on, off wi' you.'

The twins trailed sulkily out and came in again, lugging the basket with various vegetables in it. They selected the cabbages, laid them on the kitchen table and returned the basket to the yard.

'Good. Ellen, you finished them spuds yet? Right, move over then, so's the twins can clean the cabbage. An' I'm warnin' the pair of ye,' she added ominously, 'that if I find a caterpillar still in it when you've done . . .'

'Or half a caterpillar,' Bertie suggested, coming in with the hod full of coal.

'Yes, or half a caterpillar,' Ada agreed, 'then you'll be in real trouble.'

Deirdre, despite herself, giggled. And as she and Donal separated the cabbages into single leaves and extracted some interesting insect life, she whispered to her twin that even cleanin' cabbages couldn't tek all day and they'd be free some time.

'And it's not as bad as it would have been in the court,' Donal reminded his sister philosophically. 'We've an indoor tap here . . . no sharin', either. It's awright, ain't it, Dee?'

'Not bad,' Deirdre agreed. She had found a fine caterpillar which was exactly the same green colour as the inner leaves and was wondering whether she could ensure that it got cooked and also reached her mother's plate and not someone else's. Mam, she decided, would almost certainly shout and yell, but it would serve her right for keeping them in, and imagine if she ate it! What smirks she and Donal would exchange, how they would laugh!

But of course there were too many risks and anyway, when she picked it up the caterpillar turned round and looked at her with its big, bulbous eyes and Deirdre knew she could never consign it to death by boiling water. No, she would take it somewhere nice and release it, to live out its life until it died of old age. She slid it into the little pocket on her pinafore and patted it kindly. Stay there, caterpillar, and Deirdre will see you right, she told it silently.

'Deirdre, what are you doing? I said clean the cabbage, not moon over it.'

'I am cleanin' it, Mam,' Deirdre protested. 'No one can't moon over a bleedin' cabbage! Anyway, I've finished my share now, the rest's Donal's.'

'You will clean that cabbage until it's *all* clean, not just half,' her mother said sharply. 'Never did I know a more difficult kid! And then git up them stairs, your sister's waitin'!'

*   *   *

It had been a rotten morning, Deirdre thought as the family sat down to dinner. She and her twin had seldom worked so hard, but the cabbage looked nice, the 'taters were big and floury and the best end of neck had been cooked until it fell off the little bones and was far easier to eat. Deirdre saw, vaguely, that it wasn't such a bad thing to help in the making of a good dinner. But despite the fact

202

that everyone was feeding their faces and no doubt enjoying the food, no one had commented on the lovely clean cabbage. She sighed, knowing herself unappreciated, but rammed a piece of potato into her mouth just as a tiny movement on her blue-and-white gingham lap attracted her attention.

It was the caterpillar! Perky, inquisitive, it had climbed out of its nice safe pocket refuge and was steadily marching up her stomach.

Deirdre looked round. No one else had noticed; they were all too busy eating. Her hand stole down and gently encompassed the caterpillar. She leaned forward and speared another piece of spud. Then spoke in a carefully surprised tone. 'Oh, look, Mam, what just crawled off of your plate!'

The caterpillar was humping quickly across the table. Ada gave a squeak and shot her chair back. Dick and Ozzie laughed. Ellen began to poke worriedly at her own helping of cabbage. And Fred reached across the table . . .

'Don't!' Deirdre shrieked. 'Don't, Fred, it's a *joke,* honest! It's me lickle pet caterpillar, don't you go hurtin' him! I only put him there to tease our mam!'

She and Donal dived simultaneously, Donal reaching the caterpillar seconds before Fred's thumb descended. Deirdre grabbed Fred's hand and bit it, Donal scooped the caterpillar up and ran for the back door, and Dick reached out a long arm and grabbed Donal by the collar.

'Bring it back—I'll teach the pair of ye to go bringin' livestock to the table,' he shouted. 'Mam wants it dead, don't you, Mam?'

'Just take it away,' Ada implored. She did not like creepy-crawlies. 'Take it away at once, d'you hear me?'

'Kill it,' roared Fred. 'The little bugger bit me thumb near to the bone!'

Deirdre shrieked again: her best shriek, the one like a steam train going into a tunnel. Ellen ran for the back door and opened it and Donal, still held captive, threw the caterpillar as far as he could. The last Deirdre saw of her friend was its tiny shape soaring up against the blue sky ... then down, into the weeds which flourished at the bottom of the yard.

'The *caterpillar* bit you, Fred?' Ellen was asking in a worried voice. 'Are you awright, la'? Not feelin' the heat? 'Cos somethin' tells me caterpillars aren't very well off for teeth. Now if you'd said it *gummed* you ...'

'You know what I meant,' Fred growled, but he was laughing, Deirdre could tell. 'Deirdre's got teeth—I'd like to ram 'em down her throat right now, mind.'

'You've thrown away me little pal,' Deirdre wailed, making the most of the opportunity. 'Now we'll have to spend hours searchin' for it, Donny an' me.'

'You're not bringin' bleedin' livestock to this table ...'

'You're more trouble than you're worth, the pair of ye!'

'To the bone, Mam—look, them's her teeth marks!'

The infuriated chorus of her elders made Deirdre blink. She had planned on disruption, but not on such a scale. I don't know me own cleverness, she thought, awed. Why, I reckon I could start a bleedin' *war* if I had a mind!

'All right, all right, you've all had your say, now let's gerron with dinner,' Ada said at last, when the noise had died down. 'There's a spotted dick wi' custard for them as are still hungry.'

Everyone was and to the twins' great relief everyone, including them, was served, though as she put the dishes in front of them their mother gave them a penetrating look. 'Now eat that up and then try and find somethin' quiet to do this afternoon,' she said. 'Because it's Sunday, so I'm goin' to have a nap. Ellen, take the littl'uns for a walk, would you?'

'Oh, Mam,' the hapless Ellen said. 'Must I?'

'It's all right, Ellen, we'll go an' play out, we'll be back in time for supper,' Deirdre said eagerly, but at this their mother, beginning to eat her own pudding, shook an admonitory finger at them.

'No you don't! You had me worried out of me life yesterday, gettin' lost an' all, so today you'll be wi' your big sister. And behave—understand me? If you want any supper at all, that is.'

Deirdre knew the die was cast. She heaved an enormous sigh, then gave in. 'Awright, Mam, we'll go wi' Ellen an' the babies. Is there a park somewhere round here? Can we go there, Ellie? Can we, can we?'

'If I can find one,' the kind-hearted Ellen assured them. 'But first you're goin' to help wi' the washin' up.'

*   *   *

As soon as the meal was cleared away and washed up Ellen put the babies into the big old perambulator, bade the twins hold on to the handle, one to a side, and started off. It was a fine afternoon and although she hadn't planned to spend it babyminding, it didn't really matter all that much. It wasn't as if she had any pals of her own to go around with—yet. That would come later. For now the twins were usually good company when they were doing something they liked and she had promised them a park, if there was one in the vicinity, so a park would have to be discovered.

She pushed the perambulator along Mere Lane and, at the end, hesitated. She could go left, up Heyworth Street, but she had gone that way the previous day and could not recall passing a park. Perhaps it would be best to turn right, then, and go up St Domingo Road?

After a moment's hesitation she turned right and was glad she had done so when she passed the Free Library. Unlimited books, and so close, she thought, hugging herself. She had missed books terribly since she left school; this would make up for the lack.

Presently they passed a very large building surrounded by trees and grass. 'St Edward's College', it said on a board. A little further and there was a church, then another building with a great deal of ground around it. But no park, not yet.

'Never mind,' Ellen said, when the twins whined a bit. 'We're bound to come across a park soon.'

And then, as they were crossing Penrose Street, they heard the music.

It was loud and catchy, and it seemed to be coming from in front of them and sure enough, when they hurried, they saw ahead of them the black-and-red uniforms and the marvellously trumpeting trumpets of a Salvation Army band.

'Catch 'em up, catch 'em up,' Deirdre screamed, breaking into a trot but not letting go of the perambulator handle. 'Ooh, they's better than a park!'

'They're probably going to a park,' Ellen supplied, hurrying as hard as she could. 'We'll foller 'em, that way we might kill two birds wi' one stone.'

And follow them they did, until they were so close that they were in danger of driving the perambulator into the legs of the last players in the procession.

Ellen was right. When the band came level with Devonshire Place they swerved smartly to the left . . . and there was the park! Green grass, a few bushes . . . space to knock a ball about, or run, or play relievio . . . or just space to listen to a band.

The band were clearly expected for a small crowd had gathered, a good many of them children. The musicians formed a half-circle and started to play, and Ellen and her motley crew found a patch of untenanted grass, sat down on it and stared.

In the perambulator, Sammy craned his head to see, but Toby was not pleased that the gentle rocking of a perambulator in motion had suddenly ceased. As the trumpets began to play a joyful hymn Toby added his own voice to the music.

He simply bellowed, Ellen thought, terribly confused, as people around her advised her to 'Shush!' She plucked Toby out of the perambulator and put him over her shoulder, where he bawled louder than ever . . . and Sammy, suddenly bereft of his companion, started too.

'Pick Sammy up, Dee,' Ellen hissed.

'What?' Deirdre said absently. She was beating time to the music with a piece of twig, pretending she was the conductor.

'Pick Sammy up,' Ellen said loudly.

'Do *what?*' Deirdre repeated.

Ellen, sure that her small sister had heard every word, took a deep breath and shouted. 'PICK . . . SAMMY, UP!'

Her voice drowned out the band, which chose that moment to sink to a dramatic, but soft, note. Ellen felt her face grow hot and acting quickly, before she forgot herself in front of everyone and clipped Deirdre across the ear, she dumped Toby back in the perambulator and plucked Sammy out of it.

'Put me *down,* Ellie,' Sammy shouted, tears running down his hot, red face. 'I wanna *walk.*'

Toby was screaming again, so it seemed easiest and best to stand Sammy down, hissing at him to sit quiet now and watch the lovely fellers play, and to seize Toby out of the perambulator once more. What relief! Toby stopped screaming as though she had turned off a tap and Sammy stopped too. And set off, on fat little legs, across the grass towards the band. He held his hands out and beamed . . . but 'Grab him, Dee!' poor Ellen shouted, if you can shout in a whisper. 'Don't let him . . .'

Deirdre came out of her conducting trance and dropped her twig, then began to chase Sammy, but too late.

Sammy attached himself to the nearest object, which happened to be a black-clad leg, and beamed up at the owner far above him. 'Sammy wan' up,' he said with disastrous clarity. 'Sammy wan' up *now!*' And he proceeded to scramble up the black-

208

clad leg.

To do him credit, the young man only stopped playing for a moment whilst he bent down—a perilous undertaking—and plucked Sammy up into his arms. And Sammy sat there, enthroned, and peered at the young man's face with great interest, now and then patting the distended cheek so near his own.

Poor Ellen! Deirdre was too small to be of much help here, so she had to come forward and take the erring Sammy off the trumpet player herself. Or rather try to, for in the event Sammy refused to come. Limpet-like, he clung, resisting all Ellen's gentle attempts to wrest him from his refuge.

Ellen stepped back, knowing her cheeks were now scarlet, feeling the perspiration beginning to trickle down the sides of her face. Just at that moment she would have loved to give her little brother a good, hard wallop—how could he behave so badly? But help was at hand. The hymn ended and one of the musicians detached himself from the rest and began to take a tin round the audience, many of whom promptly melted away or discovered urgent business elsewhere.

The trumpet player put down his instrument and smiled at Ellen. 'Phew! He's a handful, this little feller! Well, Sammy? D'you want to play me trumpet, is that why you come over an' climbed me as if I was a perishin' tree? Come on then, gi's a blow.'

'I'm so sorry,' Ellen said, even more confused now that she saw the young man was extremely handsome, with golden-brown curly hair and twinkling hazel eyes. 'They was asleep, you see, an' when they woke they wanted to get out o' the pram, an' then Sammy . . . well, I never knowed him be so naughty.'

'Oh, he ain't naughty, he's just bein' himself,' the young man said easily. 'Just let him have a go wi' me trumpet, then he'll very likely want to play on the grass.'

He held the trumpet to Sammy's lips and Sammy took it in his mouth and dribbled and chewed and finally blew, then sat back and beamed all round.

'Well, you are a clever feller,' the trumpeter said. 'Goin' down now, are you? Your sister wants to play "ring a roses" wi' you, young feller-me-lad. Ah, what's that I hear?'

It was the bell of an ice-cream cart trundling around looking for business. The twins and Sammy turned eagerly towards the sound of the bell but Ellen clapped her hands to her hot cheek. 'Oh blimey, I ain't gorra penny piece,' she groaned. 'I'll gerrem out o' here afore you start to play agin, 'cos when they know they can't have ices there's bound to be ructions.'

'Oh, I'll mug 'em for an ice each,' the young man said easily. 'An' you an' all, Miss . . . what's your name?'

'I'm Ellen Docherty,' Ellen said shyly. 'An' them's the twins, Deirdre an' Donal. The baby's Toby an' t'other . . . well you know Sammy already!'

'True. And to keep the record straight I'm Alfred Tolliver, but me pals call me Tolly. Come on, then, Ellen, here's some cash, you go an' buy the ices.'

'Thanks, Mr Tolliver,' Ellen said shyly. 'I'll pay you back next time I see you—I start a job, Monday.'

'No need; and I'm Tolly, remember? Callin' me "mister" like that. How old d'you think I am then, eh?'

'Oh, eighteen?' hazarded Ellen. 'Nineteen?'

Tolly laughed. 'That's 'cos I'm tall. I'm norra lot older than you, I dessay. You'll be fourteen? Fifteen?'

'Fourteen,' admitted Ellen. 'How old are you then, mist . . . I mean Tolly?'

'I'm fifteen,' the lad admitted, for Ellen now realised that he was only a lad; it was the uniform and his height which had made him seem older. 'Where's you workin' then, come Monday mornin'?'

'At a brand-new confectionery shop on Heyworth Street,' Ellen said proudly. 'Where does you work, Tolly?'

'I'm at Flett's the jam factory on Black Bull Lane; I'm a clerk there,' Tolly said. 'I'll come wi' you to get them ices or I'll be back playin' again afore I've handed me money over. Come on, kids, see who can git there first!'

They ran, Tolly pushing the perambulator, then they all sat on the grass and ate the ices, and Tolly accepted a mouthful from Sammy, who seemed to have taken a real liking to him, though he had to be careful, he said, because he was in uniform.

They had by no means finished their treat, however, before the band started to form up again. Tolly got to his feet, brushed himself down and grinned at Ellen. 'Got to go,' he said. 'See you around, I 'spec'.'

'Where's you goin'?' shouted Donal. The twins also liked Tolly, Ellen realised, as she herself did. 'Can we foller on behind? Will you play agin?'

211

Tolly turned back for a moment. 'We'll be goin'
back to the Citadel, now,' he said. 'That ain't on
your road, Donal. Be good now, an' do what your
sister tells you.'

'Awright,' Donal called back. ''Bye, Tolly! See
you around.'

*   *   *

Well, Ellen, that's give you somethin' to think
about, Ellen told herself as she climbed into her
bed that night. All the twins had talked about when
they got home had been Tolly, who had bought
them ices.

Ada had looked at her daughter, startled, and
she had smiled. 'Well I never,' she murmured.
'D'you know, Ellie, I hadn't noticed before?'

'Noticed what?' asked the unsuspecting Ellen.
'Do I have a smut on me nose?'

'No, nothing like that. I'd not noticed how grown
up you're getting, nor how pretty you've become.'

'Pretty? Me?' Ellen said, thoroughly startled. No
one with four elder brothers and three younger
ones can have any illusions about their looks. 'Oh
g'wan, Mam, I'm not pretty.'

'You are,' Ada insisted. 'You've got lovely brown
curls, beautiful blue eyes and a neat little figure.
Yes, you're pretty.'

The only boy present, Bertie, had made a few
rude remarks at that, but under his breath; he
didn't fancy a thump round the lug from Ada, or
from herself, Ellen supposed. And after that Ellen
had been too busy to dwell on either her mother's
remarks or on her new-found friend. But later, as
she got into bed . . .

Am I really pretty? she thought. I liked Tolly ever so, but did he like me? Why should he? Although he's only fifteen he looks much older, and he plays the trumpet beautiful and wears a lovely uniform . . . what am I to him?

A pretty girl, said a little voice inside her head, but Ellen refused to listen to it. No point in even thinking it, she told herself severely, But on Monday I'll be a working girl, norra kid at all. I'll have a good job in me aunt's cake shop and, even if I'm bored serving customers and helping in the bakery, I'll have a bit of money to spend. Surely then fellers will take me seriously?

And presently she went to sleep and dreamed of a tall bandsman with dancing dark eyes and a beautiful deep voice . . . even though, in her dream, he took no notice of a small, brown-haired girl whose only claim to fame was that she had the naughtiest brothers in the whole world!

*   *   *

About a month later, Ellen knew that working in the cake shop had been a bad mistake, but with work so difficult to find—and even more difficult to keep—she had very little choice but to grit her teeth, square her shoulders and continue to serve the customers, and trek between the bakehouse and the shop with huge baskets of her aunt's wares.

The money was not brilliant, but it was not bad, either. Many of Ellen's schoolmates were paid far less for far harder jobs. The trouble was that the other girls in the shop and bakery kept aloof from Ellen, whispering in corners and never including her in their jokes or conversation.

'They think I'll tell tales of 'em to me aunt,' she said furiously to Tolly one evening when the two of them were strolling home after a band concert in the park. 'As if I would, Tolly! Why, I work twice as hard as the rest of 'em to prove I've not got the job just 'cos the boss is me aunt, an' they snigger behind their hands an' pile even more work on me. I near broke me back wi' the weight of bread in me delivery basket yesterday, an' Aunt never gi' me a word o' thanks. I tell you, Tolly, I'm off out o' it as soon as somethin' else turns up.'

'Clerkin' in a jam factory ain't a lot o' fun, either,' Tolly said mildly. 'I'd like to do somethin' more worthwhile meself. Tell you what, Ellie, we'll keep our eyes open, you an' me, an' if either of us sees a job that 'ud fit the other, we'll tell. Two heads is better'n one, I'll be bound.'

'Oh, *yes,*' Ellen breathed happily. 'Why, we might even gerra job in the same shop, or factory or whatever, Tolly! You've made me feel much more cheerful.'

'Good; same here,' Tolly assured her. 'Dead-end jobs make borin' workers; we won't be borin' much longer, Ellie!'

CHAPTER EIGHT

Dublin, December 1912

Maggie came carefully down the stairs in Dally Court, trying not to make them wobble too much and stepping gingerly over the gaps, and on the bottom step her sister Biddy was sitting, with a basket of shopping beside her. Maggie slowed.

'Sure an' what are you doin' there, Biddy me darlin'?' she asked. 'I thought Mammy said you'd gone round to see Albert, didn't she? I've just come from there, an' she said somet'ing about Albert an' yourself, so she did.'

Biddy, who had once been so sickly, had grown into a beauty. At just sixteen, she had all the boys after her, particularly Albert McCann, whose father owned a chemist's shop on Thomas Street and was thought to be a great catch. But now, hearing her sister's voice, she turned and smiled up at her with a good deal of mischief in her glance. 'Oh, you know our mammy,' she said tolerantly. 'If she's so fond of Albert, why doesn't she marry him herself? Faith, who does she t'ink I am? I'm not throwin' meself away on a feller wit' his nose always stuck in a book.'

'We-ell, he's got a grosh o' money, I'm told,' Maggie said thoughtfully. 'An' he's handsome enough, if you don't mind the specs.'

'Well I do mind 'em, so I do,' Biddy said pettishly. ''Tis Patsy Craven I like, Mags me darlin', but whether or not he likes me is another matter. Anyway, I'm goin' to the pictures wit' him tonight, whether Mammy likes it or not.'

'Oh dear,' Maggie said apprehensively. Her mother had grown bitter and difficult over the past few years and spent a good deal of time grumbling that her daughters neither understood nor appreciated her. It's all right for me, Maggie told herself now, because I can walk away from it, so I can, but the others . . . oh, dear.

'You may well say, *Oh, dear*,' Bridget said ruefully. 'You're away from it, Mags. And now you're workin' . . .'

Maggie had begun to work for a wage, as against simply working for her keep, when little Ticky had started school. It wasn't much of a job—she sold fruit three days a week for an elderly woman dealer on Thomas Street who wanted to retire but still needed some money coming in—but at least she earned some money and it got her out of the house.

In fact, Mrs Nolan had also started to pay her a small wage when she had her fifteenth birthday. She could still remember the day and her own surprise.

'Fifteen, eh, Maggie?' Mrs Nolan had said, smiling at her. 'Well, well, I never thought you'd still be wit' us when you hit fifteen!'

'Nor me, Mrs Nolan,' Maggie had replied, returning the older woman's smile. 'But we're used to each other, wouldn't you say? Oh, I know if I went you could replace me easy, now the twins is older an' Ticky's near on school age, but . . .'

Mrs Nolan looked thoughtful. 'Could I, though?' she said. 'I'm t'inkin' you wouldn't be so easy to replace, Maggie McVeigh. You fit our ways awful well, so you do.' And she had produced a small envelope from her pocket and handed it to Maggie across the kitchen table, for Maggie was baking and Mrs Nolan had just finished washing up the breakfast dishes.

Maggie took the envelope. It'll be a birthday card; the first she's ever give me, she thought to herself as she opened it. Still, better late than never, I suppose.

Except that it wasn't a birthday card. It was a shiny florin. A birthday present! Maggie thought as she stammered out her thanks, but this, too, proved premature.

'No, Maggie, it ain't a birthday present 'cos I'd clean forgot it were your birthday,' Mrs Nolan said truthfully. She was often truthful to the point of bluntness, as Maggie well knew. 'It's a weekly wage. You'll be gettin' two bob a week from now on. You earn it.'

Maggie had been grateful, but when the chance came she told Mrs Nolan that she would be working a couple of days a week for old Mrs Collins. 'She's too old to do it all herself, now,' she had said. 'I'm to help her set up the stall an' tek it down, an' two or three days a week I'm to help sell. But she knows I must be home when Ticky an' the twins get in for their tea, and I'll keep an eye on them when the school holidays come around. Only . . . I can't give me mammy much out of two bob, grateful though I am to have it.'

'All right, alanna,' Mrs Nolan had said. 'In summer the childer play out . . . and someone will always keep an eye on 'em for an hour or two, come the winter. Indeed, the twins can look after Ticky; they're old enough.'

They were. Younger children than they looked after whole families, but Seamus and Garvan were still very much a law unto themselves. You never knew what they would do next, save that it would be naughty.

So Maggie had gone round to Dally Court and told her mother that she would be giving her two shillings a week in future, and for the first time for ages Mrs McVeigh had smiled and looked a little animated. 'Two shillin'! Well, it won't go far, but it'll buy a loaf or two,' she said grudgingly at last. 'You're not a bad lass, Maggie, but if only you'd come home . . .'

'Oh, go on, Mammy, you're really pleased,' Maggie had said, laughing. 'You'd rather have me money than me company any time—admit it!'

But this Mrs McVeigh refused to do. 'All right, now Mrs Nolan pays you I dare say you're better off stayin' put,' she had said. 'But you could come home more often, alanna, have a jangle wit' me an' your sisters now an' then.'

Maggie had vowed that she would try to go home whenever she had a few hours free, but somehow she didn't. She had grown away from Aileen, Carrie and the others, and even Bridget seemed remote from her. As for the boys . . . well, she hardly ever saw them and they showed no more interest in her and her doings than they did in the carryings-on of any other stranger.

So now she advised Bridget to keep her feelings about the chemist's son to herself unless she wanted to be nagged morning, noon and night, and went on down the street, around the corner and headed for home, because she hadn't considered Dally Court her home for several years.

Back in the Nolans' rooms, she prepared the evening meal and wondered how late Liam would be getting home tonight. It was December, which meant he would be busier than usual, but she needed to talk to him.

She and Liam were still good friends. Perhaps, she thought wistfully, they were even a little more than good friends. The slight awkwardness which he had so obviously felt when she was younger seemed to have dissipated and now he often took her around, once dancing, twice to the picture show, countless times out to Phoenix Park or into the country or to the seaside. But she rather suspected that Liam treated her only as he would have treated a sister and she knew she could not blame him. She had been brought up with him from the age of eleven—she was his sister in all but blood.

When the meal was ready and only needed dishing up Maggie got her coat and went down the stairs and out into the yard.

Ticky was playing with half a dozen other kids, but he came running over to her as soon as she appeared, his face breaking into a big smile. 'Eh, Mags!' he said. 'Oh, I'm starved, so I am—any soda bread to spare? If I go up now can I have a cut wit' some butter on?'

'When the twins come home tell them . . .' Maggie began, then saw the twins hurtling past the house with Gus in hot pursuit. She sighed. 'Oh, sweet Jaysus, I'd better go an' call them. Shan't be long, Ticky.'

She hurried after them and caught them up as they were about to go into a tenement block just down the street. They both looked guilty when she called their names but came over to her anyway.

'Boys, go home an' get yourselves an' Ticky a cut of soda bread an' butter it,' she said briskly. 'I'm goin' to meet Liam, we've t'ings to discuss.'

'Right, Mags,' Garvan said. 'Any cake? We're starvin', so we are.'

'No . . . well, perhaps a tiny piece,' Maggie said, relenting. 'I can't bear the thought of me laddos goin' hungry. An' keep an eye on Ticky till I'm back.'

The boys agreed to do so and Maggie hurried off. Liam was a postman now, doing an out-of-town round, so he had a bicycle with a lamp which he lit as soon as it began to get dark. But he should be just about ready to leave now and he wouldn't bring the bicycle home. If he left it downstairs it was too tempting for the kids and they'd ride it and buckle the wheel or slip the chain or do some other damage. And carting it up three steep and narrow flights of stairs and finding somewhere to put it was no joke, either. So Liam always walked to and from work.

Maggie reached the Post Office and waited, standing discreetly in the shadows. She didn't think Liam would be shamed by her presence any more—she was seventeen, after all, and not bad looking—but she didn't want anyone thinking she was hanging around on O'Connell Street. Bad girls did that, she understood, though she had never knowingly seen one. All the girls walking up and down the pavements looked very like herself— innocently enjoying the displays in the brightly lit windows, staring at the fashionable men and women, the bustle of traffic in the wide roadway.

Liam emerged from the Post Office presently, looking tired, but his face lit up when he saw her. He came over to her, grinning. 'Mags! Just the person I wanted to see—shall we buy a paper of chips to walk home wit'? It's cold enough to need 'em to warm our hands as well as our stomachs.'

'Yes, lovely,' Maggie said. 'But Liam, I want to ask you something. I didn't come all this way just for the pleasure of your company, indeed I didn't!'

'Oh, thank you,' Liam said, pretending to bow. 'Useful for my wide knowledge of human nature, but not much good to share a bag of chips wit', is that it?'

'True,' Maggie said, shaking her head. She loved the way his eyes slitted when he laughed, and a line appeared beside his mouth! But it was no use wishing—at least they were firm friends. 'Liam, it's almost December.'

'I know that,' Liam said. 'What you might call me heaviest month.'

Maggie knew what he meant, because postmen did not only deliver letters and parcels, they collected them, too. When Liam went out to a farm with the letters he would be given parcels of eggs, fowls still in their feathers and fish, wrapped in rushes, to deliver in Dublin itself.

'Yes, yes, poor old Liam,' she said, patting his arm. 'But you know old Mrs Collins?'

'No. Who?'

'Oh, Liam, you know perfectly well, so you do! She's the old shawlie I've been helpin' out wit' the sellin' a couple o' days a week. You know, I put her stall up, an' bring it down o' nights, an' sell sometimes so she can have a rest.'

'Oh, yes. What about her?'

'She wants me to stay on her pitch overnight for to get her Christmas licence. I said I would—why not, it'll be good—but I've not told your mammy yet. She can be—funny—about t'ings like that.'

'Do those women really sit out all night?' Liam asked incredulously. 'Whatever for? Why not go along early in the mornin', like they usually do?'

'Because Christmas is the best month of all,' Maggie said patiently. 'You know that, Liam, in your job! And it's not just the women, men have to wait out too. If they waited till the mornin' they'd not get a pitch at all at all, but waitin' overnight and payin' first thing, the pitch is yours for the whole

221

month.'

'I see. Well, Mammy won't mind, I don't suppose. Why should she?'

'Because I've never spent a night away from your house since I first come there, all them years ago,' Maggie admitted. 'My mammy moans on about how I never go home for a day or two, but . . . well, I've never asked, you see. And your mammy pays me now . . . she may think I ought not to stay out at night.'

'But you work,' Liam pointed out. 'Two or three days a week, you work, don't you?'

'Yes. But only when it suits Mrs Nolan,' Maggie admitted. 'Oh, that's all right, Mrs Collins understands, but I—well, I wondered if you could tell your mammy for me.'

'Me? Oh Jeez, Maggie, I can't do that. Mammy will think it's interferin' I am and I don't want to set her against the idea.'

'No-oo, I do see that,' Maggie acknowledged. 'Then will you be there, an' come in on my side if there's a fuss?'

This Liam agreed to do and the two of them continued to walk down the street, admiring the marvellous window displays as they went.

They reached home at last and Liam was as good as his word. Maggie explained that Mrs Collins, who was getting too old and stiff to spend the night on a cold pavement, wanted her to stay on the pavement in Henry Street overnight to apply for her trading licence first thing in the morning, and with no more than a token query as to how she would manage to get back in time to get Ticky ready for school Mrs Nolan agreed that she might go.

'There you are, alanna,' Liam said that night as the two of them walked Gus around the streets so he wouldn't disgrace himself in the kitchen. 'You didn't need me to put in a good word for you—it wasn't so bad, was it?'

'No, it was all right, really,' Maggie admitted. 'I'm really lookin' forward to it now your mammy's said I may go.'

*   *   *

It was an icy cold night, but the wind which had made Maggie's eyes water earlier had dropped by midnight, when all the traders settled down with their blankets to laugh and crack the night away. Maggie had soon begun to enjoy herself. Everyone was so happy and jolly, full of jokes and laughter, though they all thanked the good Lord that it wasn't raining or blowing a gale. It wasn't snowing, either, but it was cold enough, Maggie thought, looking up at the stars twinkling in the black night sky. But it wouldn't snow, because there were no clouds . . . there would be a sharp frost, though.

Strong tea and hot chips had been eaten two or three times during the evening and Maggie speedily became friendly with a lad of about her own age who was sitting for his uncle, who sold what he described as 'fine timepieces, as fine as any on sale in O'Connell Street'. His name was Connor, Conn for short, and Maggie suspected him of being an Irish tinker for his skin was dark and his eyes black as pits, and his accent was so broad that she had difficulty in understanding him at first. But whatever his background he made her laugh, bought her tea and suggested that they share

223

blankets, to everyone's amusement, for Maggie was still at an age when her blushes all but burned her up.

So the night passed, and Conn told Maggie that she was the prettiest girl in Dublin, so she was, and had she ever wondered what it was like to take a turn around the houses wit' a fine feller like him? And Maggie laughed and said no, she'd not, and thanks all the same but she'd stick by her pitch, and the other traders told Conn he'd got a long way to go before he could fool a McVeigh.

But the best of times must end and dawn broke at last, a faint grey streak in the east, and gradually the light grew stronger and stronger and someone went for more tea and came back and announced that the feller from the council was on his way and they'd better have their money ready.

Maggie felt for the five shillings in her pocket— it was a great deal of money for a licence, but it lasted all month, so it did—and handed it over in return for the piece of paper and the metal token. Further down the road she could hear the first newsboys starting to shout . . . something about a disaster, of course . . . and a cock crowed, then another and another.

Then she put up Mrs Collins's board and set up her stall and waited until the old woman, well-wrapped against the cold, came trundling round the corner. 'You've got me pitch—you're a good girl, so you are,' she said happily. 'Off you go now an' get the littl'uns ready for school. See you tomorrer.'

As Maggie walked homewards, rather wearily, for she had had an exciting night, there was a patter of footsteps behind her and Conn came hurrying up. He took her arm. 'I'll walk ye home, acushla,' he said breathlessly. 'Did ye hear what they were sayin' back there?'

'No, what?' Maggie said with only a little curiosity. She was beginning to feel tired and to want her breakfast.

'Why, a tenement's falled down, so it has . . . there's a grosh of people been killed. Have you ever heard of such a thing? A house fallin' down?'

'No, I never did. Are you sure you got it right?' Maggie said, slowing her pace for a moment. 'Which street was it?' She tried to remember whether there had ever been any creaks and groans in the house in Claymore Alley, but it was hard even to imagine such a thing. She looked interrogatively at her companion.

'Well, now, it had a funny sort o' name, so it did,' Conn said thoughtfully. 'Someone said 'twas between Francis Street and the Coombe, but that was just rumour. Where do you live, Maggie?'

'Claymore Alley,' Maggie said. 'Just off Thomas Street. It . . . it wasn't Claymore Alley, was it, Conn?'

'No, indeed,' Conn said at once. 'Now I've got it! It was somewhere called Dally Court, wherever that may be. Why, what's the matter, gorl? You've gone quite pale.'

'I . . . I've family livin' in Dally Court,' Maggie stammered. He must have got it wrong, he must! But she could not help remembering those stairs, how they swayed no matter how gently you walked up them, and the great cracks in the outer walls. 'I'd better go round there at once, Conn . . . no need to come, I . . . I'll manage fine wit'out you.'

'No indeed, I'll come wit' you,' Conn insisted.

He took her arm. 'Shall we run, alanna? I can see you're worried to death.'

*   *   *

They arrived, panting, in Dally Court to find complete bedlam. The tenement in which she had been born and raised was a great, still smoking pile of bricks. Neighbours were digging around, moving bricks, calling . . . and bodies were laid out in a neat row over by the next block.

Maggie stood very still, clutching her throat, then recognised one of the searchers. 'Patsy!' she called. 'Patsy, it's me, Maggie McVeigh. What's happened? Where's . . . where's me family?'

Patsy Craven came over to her. His face was black, save for two white trails which ran from either eye. He was crying.

'Maggie? Sure an' 'tis yourself,' he said brokenly. 'They're dead, all of 'em. Not one saved so far . . . Biddy's gone, Carrie, your mam . . .'

Maggie said, panting, 'I don't believe you! You're coddin' me!' and broke free from Conn's restraining arm. She ran across to where the bodies had been laid and fell to her knees, gabbling a prayer as she did so. And saw for herself.

Biddy, her face smooth and calm but her body hideously broken. Carrie, the same. Clodagh, the same. Her mother, the same.

Maggie gave a terrible scream and began to say it was all her fault, that if only she'd agreed to live at home . . .

A voice, gentle, persuasive, was in her ear, an arm was around her waist. 'Come along now, there's no good in talkin' like that. Come on, I'm

226

goin' to tek you home, you can't do no good here. Dear God, your hands is like ice . . . here, put this on.'

Something warm was thrown round her shoulders and the arm around her waist steadied her, then began to lead her away. She made no effort to break free, she just kept crying and saying over and over: 'If only I'd come home! If only I'd been with them I could have warned them . . . Oh, if only I'd been livin' at home!'

*   *   *

Liam had to pass Henry Street on his way to work, so he popped in to see whether Maggie was still there, but she wasn't. Old Mrs Collins cooeed to him, however, 'Well, if it isn't young Liam Nolan, lookin' fine as fivepence in 'is uniform. Huntin' for Maggie, are you, me laddo? Well, she's gone off to get them brothers of yours off to school, so you've missed her.'

'Never mind; how did she get on last night?' Liam enquired, more out of politeness than anything, because he guessed by the fact that Mrs Collins's stall was up and doing that Maggie had stayed the course. Not that he had any idea that she might not have done so; not Maggie. She wasn't a girl to give up easy and she was looking forward to her night on the pavement, he knew it. To stay out all night was an adventure for a girl, he supposed tolerantly.

'She got on very well, very well indeed,' Mrs Collins said and gave a sudden sharp cackle. 'Found 'erself a feller, so she did.'

'What, here?' Liam said, gesturing around him.

Most of the stall-holders were elderly.

'Aye, here,' Mrs Collins said, ruffling up. 'We ain't all in our dotage, ye cheeky varmint! Other people beside meself got a helper in . . . they went off together, did Maggie an' Conn.'

'Who's Conn?' Liam asked. Despite himself his voice was redolent of suspicion, with just a touch of outrage. He might not want Maggie himself, but it now occurred to him that he didn't want anyone else to have her either. Not that she would have shown an interest in another feller, now he came to think of it. She never had, so why should she do so now?

The old man who sold watches had been setting his wares out enticingly on a piece of worn black velvet, but hearing Liam's question he stopped what he was doing and pushed his old cap to the back of his head. 'Conn's me nephew from Connemara, come into town to visit for a while,' he explained. Then he leered at Liam. 'They spent the night together, did Conn an' Maggie McVeigh. They went off together when it got light, an' all.'

'She'll have took him back to Claymore Alley, no doubt, for a mouthful o' breakfast,' Liam said. He meant to sound sarcastic but merely succeeded in sounding spiteful. 'Well, I must be on me way.'

He was half-way down the street before it occurred to him that he'd not asked one rather important question. He turned back. 'This Conn,' he said loudly. 'How old would he be? Thirteen? Fourteen?'

'Twenty, an' he's a handsome lad, so he is,' the old watch-seller said. 'Black hair, eyes like coal . . . oh aye, the maids all try to catch our Conn's eye, but your Maggie did it wit'out even tryin'.'

228

Liam nodded casually and retraced his steps, telling himself that it didn't matter if Conn was as handsome as a film star, Maggie wouldn't go throwin' herself at the feller's head. And if she did, wouldn't it be a blessin' in disguise now, for it would nail, once an' for all, her ideas about bein' in love wit' himself, so it would.

The trouble was, it preyed on his mind. All through the long, cold day, as he cycled out into the countryside, delivering letters, accepting parcels, until he finally rode in again in the dark with his lamp almost obscured by the bobbing forms of geese and ducks tied to his handlebars and eclipsing his big bicycle basket, Liam thought about Maggie. In fact, by the time he turned his steps for home he was getting in quite a state. How dared she! It was all very well to fall in love wit' a feller an' make his life a misery, but then to turn round an' go off wit' someone else, someone she'd not set eyes on until a few hours ago ... well, that was enough, Liam told himself crossly, to annoy a saint.

As he passed Henry Street the traders were packing up their stalls. Mrs Collins had gone, though her board still lay on the pavement, advertising the price of cabbage and how many oranges you might have for tuppence. Liam didn't want to appear too interested in the traders, so having checked that Maggie was not amongst them he went past with his head averted. She would be at home then, getting the evening meal; he'd find out all about this feller Conn quite soon, then.

As Liam began to cross the Ha'penny Bridge a newsboy came towards him with a pile of *Dublin Heralds*. He was shouting something in the usual garbled fashion of such boys about a great disaster,

229

but Liam was not tempted to buy a paper. There was always a great disaster somewhere and his own small disaster was occupying all his attention right now. Maggie's defection. And this Conn feller whom she apparently found so attractive that she'd gone off with him when Mrs Collins had arrived to take care of the stall.

Along the quays, into Church Street and along Thomas Street Liam trudged. His arms ached from wrestling with the weight of his overladen bicycle, his legs from the effort of pedalling it along. And his heart ached ... not, he reminded himself, because it was in any way involved with Maggie or whom she liked or disliked, but because he was disappointed in her, so he was. Fickleness was a feminine attribute, everyone knew that, but he'd not suspected that Maggie could be fickle.

Reaching Claymore Alley, he slowed; doubtless the twins would be around somewhere, playing with their pals. He would ask them, casual-like, whether they'd met Maggie's new friend, what he was like and so on. The twins would tell him.

The only snag to this plan was that the twins were not in evidence outside the tenement building, nor was Ticky. Liam looked, but he couldn't see them anywhere. Other kids were playing; there was a football game in progress between the buildings and despite the fact that it was dark a group of girls were playing pen the pig under the gas light, but there was no sign of members of his own family.

Sighing, Liam made for the stairs. He did not suppose that Maggie would see him and immediately begin to tell him about this feller, this nephew of a common watch-seller, but no doubt

230

she would get round to it if he asked about her night out, made a joke of it.

He opened the door which led into the kitchen. His mother was there, hanging over the stove. She was flushed from the fire, but she looked . . . odd. As though . . . as though she had been crying.

Liam went into the room. 'Mammy? Where's Maggie?'

His mother looked up. Her mouth trembled and she put a hand to her throat.

'Mammy? What's happened? Where's Maggie?' Liam said, thoroughly alarmed. His mother was not a woman to weep unless she had cause. And she was definitely crying—now that he was near enough he could see the tears trickling down her cheeks.

'Oh, Liam,' she quavered. 'Have ye not heard? Have ye not seen the fly-sheets? That bleedin' buildin' in Dally Court—bad cess to the landlord, I say—it's fell down. There's thirty people dead.'

Liam felt an icy coldness creep all over his body. 'Maggie?' he croaked. 'Is Maggie . . .'

'Oh, God be thanked, not Maggie, she was keepin' Mrs Collins's place all night in Henry Street, don't you remember? But her mammy, her sisters . . . the buildin' fell down durin' the night, they was all killed.'

'Oh, Jaysus!' Liam ejaculated. 'Oh, the poor kid—where is she now, Mammy?'

'She's seein' to t'ings. I ought to give a hand, but there's none but meself, now, to make a meal, an' Kenny's gone after her, to see if there's anything he can do. Liam, you've always been a good friend to the gorl—you go round there! She's at Dally Court, they're still movin' the rubble, tryin' . . . oh, all

231

those poor people!'

Liam was still wearing his thick uniform coat. He turned in the doorway and was half-way down the stairs before his mother's voice came floating after him: 'Liam, bring her home! Tell her we love her, tell her that this has always been her home and always will be. Bring the poor darlin' home!'

*   *   *

He found her easily enough. There were a team of them, friends, neighbours, relatives, all digging in the wreckage, moving the towering piles of brick rubble with the tenants' small possessions scattered or crushed to matchwood amongst them. Maggie was working away with the best, her hair tied back with a length of string, her sleeves rolled up. She was dirty as a coalman but she smiled palely at him and Liam realised that the work was stopping her from brooding.

Kenny, working away beside her, called to him, 'Hey, Liam . . . have you come to give a hand?'

'Aye. And to tell the pair of ye to get off home while I take over,' Liam said bluntly. 'Maggie, me darlin', you've been here all day Mammy says. It's time you took a break, so it is.'

'Can't,' Maggie said briefly. 'There was a sound just now from under here . . . we have to clear it all, every brick.' She turned back to her work, saying over her shoulder, 'We've had thirty-one of out here now. Fourteen injured, the rest . . .' She didn't have to complete the sentence.

'Any . . . any McVeighs saved?' Liam said after a pause. The question had to be asked and perhaps bluntly was best.

'No,' she said simply. 'But Aileen left home a while back, she's workin' in Dun Laoghaire. I've sent a telegram, so she knows. But the others . . . they were all in bed. They may not even have known what was happening, . . . and Conn reckoned it would . . . would have been quick.'

It was not the moment to ask about Conn and Liam, to do him credit, was not tempted to do so. Instead, he glanced across at Maggie as she bent to her task once more. She was pale, dirty and weary, but he could see the grim determination shining through. Liam waited until his brother straightened for a moment, then looked interrogatively at him and gestured towards Maggie. Kenny nodded and said in an undertone, 'Let her work; it's best.'

With a sigh, Liam took off his warm coat, rolled up his sleeves and began to move the rubble. 'Right; it's all hands to the pump, then,' he said cheerfully. 'Where's the twins?'

Maggie straightened for a moment, a hand to the small of her back. 'They've gone for chips, an' cups of tea,' she said briefly. 'They've worked as hard as grown men, Liam, honest to God they have, but you move the rubble faster if you've a hot cup of somethin' inside you. I don't suppose you've had your meal yet?'

'No,' Liam said briefly. 'But I'll live.'

She nodded. Together, the three of them attacked the next mound of broken bricks.

*   *   *

It was a big wake and the landlord paid for everything, though they said he left the money with a friend; he certainly did not come near Dally

233

Court whilst the clearing of the rubble continued, nor did he send messengers to find out how the clearers were getting on. He had been constantly warned about the state of the building and had done nothing, and now there were sixteen people dead.

Other landlords in the Liberties must have been scared for their lives, for a group of relatives, strong, angry dockers and brewery workers amongst them, went round to the Dally Court landlord's house the night of the tragedy. They would have killed him if they had caught him, but he had gone. His smart house and his neat garden were empty, and the maid who answered the door to the group said that he'd taken his wife and family away and no one knew when he would return.

'He's a murderer!' someone called out and the girl—for she was no more than sixteen—gasped, whitened and slammed the door shut.

Someone went to the authorities though, and perhaps it was they who arranged the wake and not the landlord at all. But it was given out that it was the landlord, and he was roundly cursed even as they drank his ale and ate his potted-meat sandwiches and great chunks of his gur cake.

'Miserable old skinflint, he wouldn't spend a ha'penny to save the dyin',' was the general opinion.

The landlord of the houses in Claymore Alley came round, very polite, rubbing his hands, and asked if everything was satisfactory and whether anyone needed repairs doing. Liam, who answered the door that evening, promptly said that they wanted new windows, for the old ones let in every

234

breath of wind, and much to their astonishment a workman came round a few days later and put brand-new windows in.

'He'll put up the rent now,' Mrs Nolan said, but he didn't. He dared not, the boys told her. He'd heard about the lynch mob which had gone calling on that other landlord and was still shouting for his blood.

Maggie attended the wake and told Mrs Nolan that night that she felt better for it. 'Cryin' makes your eyes red, but it eases the pain,' she said. 'And there weren't no moochers—did you notice? Everyone there was a friend, a neighbour, a workmate.'

It was the custom in Dublin for moochers to gatecrash on wakes, regardless of the age or sex of the departed, but on an occasion like this one even the greediest moocher had stayed away to let the mourners say their last goodbyes in peace.

And people were so kind, Maggie thought that night as she lay in bed with her arms around Ticky's comforting little shape. A great many people had brought flowers, though December is an expensive time of year for them, and holly wreaths had abounded. People who had known her since she was small had assured her that there had been nothing she could have done, had reminded her, but kindly, that her mammy had sent her away years ago and must now, in her heavenly kingdom, be praising God that she'd done such a thing.

'Out of all her fambly, only youse and Aileen saved,' one elderly woman said piously. 'Eh, your mammy must be proud she sent you to the Nolans—they're good to you, I dare say?'

'Very good,' Maggie had replied. Because Mrs

235

Nolan had been wonderful, she had treated Maggie like her own and the boys couldn't have been kinder. She marvelled at how fortunate she was, for even Conn, a feller she scarcely knew when all was said and done, had come calling, bringing her little presents—a rosary, money for candles, a mourning ring which he'd bought off the stalls in Henry Street.

'When you've had time to grow accustomed, we'll talk,' he had said tactfully, sitting on the sofa in the Nolan kitchen looking very large and rather uneasy in such elevated surroundings, for he had told Maggie during their night on the pavement that he had come from a turf-cutter's hut in Connemara and had mostly lived either in the hut or on the road. 'You know I'm takin' over me uncle's stall? Well, we miss you, so we do—I'd like nothin' better than to have a crack wit' you, when you're in the mood.' He had hesitated, looking shyly at her from under his thick brows. 'Will you come back, some time?' he ended.

Maggie had assured him that she would, though when she was not so sure. 'Mrs Nolan needs me wit' Christmas coming up,' she said. 'Oh, I'd rather be on Henry Street if I'm honest, but she's been so good, Conn! Do you know, a while ago when I was makin' the beds she came in an' axed me if I were still mortal fond of the picture that's hung on me bedroom wall ever since I come here to live. An' I said I was, an' she said it was mine, to do as I liked with, an' if ever I married an' moved away it could go wit' me,' she ended.

'That was nice, indeed,' Conn said. But he said it doubtfully. He could not be expected to realise, as Mrs Nolan had, how important the picture had

236

become to her, Maggie saw. Besides, he could not possibly know how . . . well, how mingy Mrs Nolan could be towards Maggie. Because she was now paid a small sum each week for her services, Maggie could not help noticing how Mrs Nolan always made sure she got her money's worth. Mrs Nolan wiped a finger along the mantelpiece to check for dust, asked what had happened to the last of the maggie ryan and soda bread, suggested that windows needed cleaning, stairs scrubbing, when Maggie knew quite well that they had been cleaned and scrubbed recently. Food was still given her, of course, but now when they had something nice for supper Mrs Nolan saw to it that Maggie had the smallest helping.

Not that Maggie cared, not really. Though she did miss the fact that before she started paying her Mrs Nolan had always provided her clothing, admittedly in hand-me-downs and new dresses made from old, but she had still clothed her. Now she was a paid employee Maggie was expected to clothe herself. Which she managed to do, at a pinch, by going to the Iveagh or the Daisy markets and buying from the dealers there. The second-hand clothes smelt of disinfectant, for it was the law that when a tugger, one of the women who went from house to house swapping delft for unwanted garments, brought clothing in it must be disinfected before it was allowed in the market, but the material was usually quite good and with a fair amount of careful stitching it was possible to turn out a decent coat or skirt.

Sometimes Maggie thought wistfully of the nice things which Mrs Nolan had made for her, but then she told herself that she was more independent now and could at least choose colours and materials, and once or twice, when she found a real bargain and brought it triumphantly home, Mrs Nolan had helped her to alter it to fit and she'd been really pleased with the garment.

However, she could scarcely explain all that to Conn, so she just told him once more that Mrs Nolan was very good to her and agreed that one day soon they must meet up again. 'But I'll tell Mrs Nolan that Mrs Collins needs me and I'll be back in Henry Street before you know it,' she assured him. 'We'll have a bit of a jangle then, shall us?'

Conn left, reminding her that the Henry Street stall awaited her, and Maggie went back into the kitchen and began peeling potatoes. Mrs Nolan preferred them peeled, though the McVeighs always ate their spuds . . .

Maggie sniffed as a tear ran down the side of her nose but she peeled determinedly on. Aileen had come to the wake and they had wept together, but Aileen had to go back to her mistress, for she was a kitchen maid in a big house by the sea, and sometimes Maggie felt like the only McVeigh left in the world. But there was no point in crying every time she thought about her mother and their sordid rooms in Dally Court. Better to imagine her in heaven, with a gold harp, on a cloud . . . only here Maggie's imagination always let her down, because she knew very well, really, that her mother wouldn't be thankin' anyone for a harp or a cloud. Her mother would want warmth, something nice to eat, her kids around her and no worry over where the next penny was coming from.

And she'll have it now, Maggie told herself, patiently peeling. The father said that heaven was what you made it, and that's what he meant, I know he did. No point in wishing; just get on with your life, Maggie McVeigh, she told herself. And right now, that means peel the spuds and put the pig's trotters into the pot or they won't be ready when Liam gets back.

*   *   *

A week after the wake Liam came in, popped his head round the kitchen door to check that his mother wasn't yet home and went to his room to get out of his uniform. He had decided to take Maggie to the Tivoli, in Francis Street, because they were showing a film with Francis Bushman and Beverly Bayne, a couple greatly admired by the young of Dublin, but he hadn't yet broken the good news to Maggie. She had gone back to the Henry Street market the previous day and he felt, he told himself, that if she could work again then she could have a bit of fun again too. He had bought some Liquorice Allsorts, because he knew she loved them, and two large oranges, and he meant to treat her to chips after the show.

He had met Conn at last. A big feller, but probably stupid, because most bog-trotters were, Liam told himself disdainfully, hanging up his uniform on the back of his bedroom door and going over to the piece of mirror on the wash-stand to comb his hair tidy after its sojourn under his peaked uniform cap. I wonder why Maggie admires those dark, oily good looks, his thoughts continued. You'd think, having been brought up with us Nolans, she'd go for a feller with lighter hair . . . someone slimmer, too. Why, that Conn looks like a

239

tinker—he probably is a tinker. Now what on earth would a girl like Maggie see in a bog-trottin' tinker?

Still, he would take her to the cinema and give her a good time and cheer her up and then, surely, she'd stop wasting her time on a ... a tinker? And once Conn is out of the picture, Liam found himself thinking, I can go back to ...

Go back to what? To treatin' the girl like a sister? he asked himself, rather shocked. Liam Nolan, what is it that you want? Is it a dog in the manger you are, not wantin' Maggie yourself but not wantin' anyone else to have her either? Now look, Liam, is she a pretty girl or is she not?

The question startled him because he realised, now, that he'd never really thought about Maggie's looks. She was just ... well, just his Maggie. Someone to lark about with, laugh with, walk and talk with. But thinking it over, he decided he liked her face. It was small, pale, heart-shaped and framed with soft, dusky curls. Her eyes were nice too. Large, grey-blue, wide-open, with lashes which were dark as her hair and curled upwards so that she often looked surprised.

A rattle on the door heralded the twins, who burst into the room and came one to either side of Liam as he stood before the piece of looking glass.

'What're you doin' here, prettyin' yourself?' Garvan said scornfully, seeing the hairbrush in his brother's hand. 'Liam Nolan's a girlie, Liam Nolan's a girlie!'

'Shut your gob, you,' Liam said. 'Or s'welp me, I'll bleedin' shut it for ye.'

'He swore!' Seamus said, trying to sound shocked. 'He swore at his little brothers—did ye

240

ever hear anyt'ing like it?'

'I know, Shay, he did indeed,' Garvan agreed. 'Oh, I s'pose he's goin' out wit' that red-haired crittur from down the road, the one Mammy says is no better than she should be.'

Liam had taken out red-haired Sally O'Sullivan for almost a year, but Sally had speedily decided that Liam wasn't good enough for her purpose. She was keen to get married, and though she liked Liam's steady job and good prospects, she didn't like what she called his 'addiction to his family', or his lack of interest in getting wed, so their affair, if you could call it that, hadn't lasted.

'No he ain't, she threw him over weeks ago,' Seamus said scornfully. 'Don't you know *nothin'*, Garv?'

'I know that if the red-haired crittur won't have him then no one will,' Garvan said. 'Poor ole Liam, you're a has-been, you're on the bleedin' shelf, an' I thought that was gorls, not fellers.'

'Get out o' here, the pair of yiz,' Liam shouted, feeling the rich beetroot shade of true wrath burning up his neck and into his face. 'I'm goin' to the Tiv an' I want to look dacint, so you can git your ugly faces out of here before I t'umps ye!'

'All right, all right, we're goin',' Garvan said, grinning. 'Wonder if you'll see Maggie there?'

There was a moment's pregnant silence before Liam said, carefully casual, 'Well, I might see her, if she's goin' to the Tiv. Why? Is she off out as well?'

'Come on, Garv,' Seamus said impatiently. 'He told us to get out, so let's get. I want me tea, even if you doesn't.'

They left, slamming the door so hard that Liam's highly prized lavender hair oil jumped on the shelf, then they clattered along the hallway, their boots loud enough to wake an army.

'Little buggers,' Liam muttered. He felt so disappointed that he could have cried. Had they meant it? Was Maggie really off to the Tiv without him? Who was she going with? Was it the abominable Conn, the Connemara tinker?

Straightening his tie, Liam gave it such a savage tug that he nearly throttled himself and hastily had to loosen it off a bit. What does it matter to me, anyway, what Maggie does, or who she does it with? he asked himself bitterly. I don't give a tinker's cuss, it's her business. But suddenly it did matter. She was *his* Maggie, so she was, and had no business taking up with Connemara tinkers, no matter how silver-tongued. He slammed his hairbrush back on the wash-stand and went over to the door, letting himself out into the hallway. He hastened towards the kitchen, still with his tie under one ear, he suddenly realised, and without a drop of his beautiful hair oil to subdue his mop of dark hair into sweet-smelling obedience. But he had no time to go back and remedy the defects; he grabbed the tie in a concealing hand, passed the palm of the other quickly across his head a couple of times and opened the kitchen door.

Maggie was standing in the middle of the room, reading the newspaper. When he opened the door she jumped guiltily and turned at once to the fire, then realised it was he and smiled. 'Phew, what a relief, Liam—I thought it was Mrs Nolan, come to cotch me not workin', and the supper scarce started! But she'll not be home for another forty minutes an' by then I can have t'ings cookin'.'

'Why?' Liam said baldly.

242

Maggie blinked. 'Why what, Liam?' she asked.

'Oh! Ummm . . . why . . . why is the meal not on?' Liam stammered, uneasily aware that this was not the answer Maggie expected. 'Why . . . why do you want to get supper started early? Is it goin' out you are?'

'I don't want to get supper early,' Maggie said. A frown wrinkled her white brow. 'Why on earth d'you say that, Liam?'

'Are you goin' out somewhere?' Liam said again, deciding that tact was not for him; a straight question and a straight answer, he told himself. That's the best way, so it is.

'Me? Goin' out? Why? Do you want me to go a message for you? Only I'd best get the food started on to cook first.'

'What on earth are you sayin', woman?' Liam asked severely. He was finding this whole conversation extremely confusing. 'Who wants a message? I asked you if you was goin' out.'

'Oh. No,' Maggie said simply. 'Are you goin' out, Liam? Is it an early supper you're wantin'?'

Liam heaved an exasperated sigh. If he wasn't careful they'd spend the whole evenin' talkin' at cross purposes, so they would. 'Yes, Maggie, I am goin' out,' he said slowly. 'I'm goin' to the Tiv, to see a fillum starrin' that feller you like . . . Francis Bushman.'

'Oh, Liam! An' Beverly Bayne?'

'That's her,' Liam admitted. 'An' Maggie, what I want to know is . . .'

'Are you takin' that Sally?' Maggie demanded. 'You've not been seein' much of her lately, I've noticed. Or are you goin' wit' Roy?'

'I'm going . . .'

'Because if you're goin' wit' Roy I wonder if there's any chance . . .'

'Will you sh . . . I mean hush a moment, woman, an' let me get a word in edgewise?' Liam said crossly. 'Will you come wit' me, Maggie? To see the fillum at the Tiv?'

Maggie stared at him with her mouth a little open and her eyes gradually widening until they looked like saucers. 'Me?' she whispered. 'But you never take me to the picture house, Liam, you know you don't. When we go out we go walkin', or into the country on a bus.'

'Yes, but this . . . this is different,' Liam said desperately. 'This time I'm askin' you to come out wit' me, Maggie. And I've bought you sweets,' he added hopelessly. He was making a mess of this, how on earth had they come to be talking at such cross purposes?

'Me? You've bought me sweeties?'

'Yes,' Liam said, far too loudly. 'An' I'm goin' to hold your hand when we're in the picture house,' he continued at full volume. 'An' very likely I may kiss you!'

He stopped, abashed. He had no idea why he had said that, particularly as the thought of kissing Maggie had never entered his mind until he had looked at her just now and seen her eyes like saucers and her mouth, dropped a little open, looking so sweet and tempting that kissing it seemed the only, the obvious, thing to do.

'Oh, Liam,' Maggie murmured. She looked down, then up at him through the thick veil of her lashes. It was a very seductive look, though it was delivered with total innocence, Liam knew that. 'Oh . . . I would like to go to see the fillum with you

244

. . . whatever you do when we get there!'

'Right. But I don't want them twins makin' a meal of it, so not a word, right?'

'Oh, yes, right,' Maggie said at once. 'I'll pretend I'm goin' out wit' Annie from next door, then if I happen to mention the fillum to the twins they'll t'ink I went wit' her.'

'Good idea. That reminds me,' Liam said, walking over to the fire and peering at the pan which Maggie was struggling to haul over the heat. 'The twins said somethin' about you goin' out tonight. Well, I t'ink that's what they said, you know what they are, though.'

'Divils,' Maggie said. 'You can't believe a word they say.'

Immensely relieved, Liam nodded a wise head. 'Not a word,' he said solemnly. 'We'll meet on the corner of Francis Street, then. I'll go out first an' you follow.'

*   *   *

Maggie was so excited that she could scarcely eat a mouthful at supper, though she put up a good showing. Then she washed up and cleared away, put Ticky to bed—the twins saw themselves off to bed now—told Mrs Nolan that she was just popping out with Annie for an hour or so, and finally went into her room and began to get ready.

It was strange, getting ready to go to a picture house with Liam, who knew her so well, knew the extent of her wardrobe as well as she and who had always made it plain—painfully plain—that he thought of her as a sister. I wonder what changed his mind, Maggie thought, as she put on a crisp

245

white blouse with a frill down the front and a tightly waisted ankle-length skirt. Rather reluctantly, she added her heavy black cloth coat and her blue wool scarf, because there was no sense in freezin' to death, not even to impress Liam. But whatever it was that had changed Liam's mind, made him decide that she was not, after all, his sister, this was her chance to make him see her as a person, a real girl, someone who was worth taking out. And if her best clothes helped to make her seem less approachable, more ... more *mysterious*, then that was all to the good, for Maggie was sure that a degree of feminine mystery was needed in her pursuit of Liam.

Not that I pursued him tonight, she reminded herself as she stole quietly down the stairs. I had no thought of going to the cinema with him ... what a piece of luck that I didn't do the wrong thing and put him off, somehow. Oh, dear God, let us have a lovely evenin', so that he wants to take me out again!

She reached the corner and stood waiting. She imagined that he would be some time, but in fact he was only seconds behind her.

He came up to her, smiled down at her and took her hand, giving it a gentle squeeze. 'Oh, Maggie,' he said. 'We're goin' to have a good time, so we are! We'll have chips after ... I do like chips when I've been to a really good fillum!'

*   *   *

It was a good film, Maggie decided ecstatically as they walked slowly home, arms round each other's waists, in the faint, sparkling starlight. And Liam had not only held her hand, he had put his arm round her and tucked a proprietorial thumb into her waistband, which seemed a very intimate act to Maggie. But she liked it; she liked it very much.

They had sat in the cinema in the interval eating Liquorice Allsorts and chattering about the film, and Liam had bought them an ice-cream each ... naturally, one behaved very correctly in the interval, because it would have been a dreadful thing, so it would, to hold hands then. But afterwards, when the picture house was dark again, when the figures on the screen were mouthing with increasing urgency at each other and the pianist's fingers were whizzing over the keys like greyhounds round a track ... then that was the time for Liam's arm to slide round her again and for Maggie to lean against him and—very daring—to rub her cheek against his shoulder.

So now they strolled and talked softly, until they reached their tall tenement, and then Liam pulled her gently into the shadow round the side of the house and put his arms round her. And Maggie, who had never been out with a feller before and was deathly afraid of doing the wrong thing, stood there like a clothes pole, waiting.

Liam knew what to do, fortunately. It's that redheaded Sally, Maggie thought sadly, she's taught him all these t'ings. Because he put his arms round her and smoothed his hand across her back and shoulders, just gently stroking round and round until she was in an ecstasy of gentle pleasure. I know why cats love bein' stroked, so I do, Maggie told herself, and purred, pressed closer to Liam and lifted her face the better to enjoy what he was doing.

247

And was kissed.

It was strange, she mused afterwards, how her body knew what to do even though her mind kept professing its ignorance. Her body curved in a very supple, naughty sort of way against Liam's, and when his mouth descended on hers her lips softened and she gave a little fluttering purr again, which for some reason made him do a number of other strange things, all of which excited her, whilst at the same time a miserable, naggy little voice inside her head said warningly, 'Careful, Maggie; you don't want to go gettin' into trouble now, do you?'

Maggie's ideas of trouble were hazy, but she did believe that in order to have a baby one had to remove one's coat and this Liam had not asked her to do. However, presently Maggie decided that she was being a little too easy; Liam's hand had slipped under her coat and though it was only caressing her neck, Maggie felt a halt had better be called whilst she was still capable of staying 'Stop!' So she gently pulled herself out of his arms and reached up and smoothed her palm down his cheek. 'Oh, Liam . . . that was a lovely evening, so it was,' she declared. 'Who'll go up first? Because it wouldn't do if we went up together; they'd never stop coddin' us.'

Liam looked down at her. In the moonlight his face was very black and white, the expression difficult to read. 'Oh . . . Maggie, Maggie, Maggie,' he murmured. 'Sure an' why didn't I realise before what a pretty t'ing you are?'

'I don't know,' Maggie said truthfully. 'I'll go up first then, Liam.'

And she turned quickly away from him, because it was the last thing she wanted to do, she could have stayed down here in his arms all night, and went into the building, across the entrance lobby and up the stairs.

Mrs Nolan was in the kitchen, making herself cocoa and a bite to eat before bed. She looked up as Maggie entered the room. 'Oh, you're back,' she said. 'Did you enjoy your evening?'

She did not sound as though she cared very much, but Maggie had had such a splendid time that she felt she could afford to be magnanimous. 'Yes, I had a lovely time,' she said demurely. 'Oh, I'd love a cup o' cocoa, Mrs Nolan, if there's enough hot water in the kettle.'

'There's plenty,' Mrs Nolan said. 'How's Annie?'

'How ... oh, she's fine, just fine,' stammered Maggie. 'Yes, she's fit an' well again is Annie. It were just a chill, nothin' more.'

'Good,' Mrs Nolan said. 'Well, I'm off to bed. Damp the fire down before you go off, there's a good girl.'

'Right, right,' Maggie said. She took off her coat and hung it over the back of a chair. Her clothes were all kept in her room but she would not go along there with the coat yet, in case she woke Ticky. And anyway, if she lingered here, laying the breakfast table, getting out the porridge oats, checking on the milk, then she might still be here when Liam came in.

But although she waited for quite twenty minutes, he did not come into the kitchen and suddenly she realised that he would have heard herself and his mother talking and would have gone straight to his room.

Feeling a little foolish, but still warmly glowing from her wonderful evening, Maggie finished all her tasks, picked up her coat and went along to her room. In their bed, Ticky was sprawled on his back, snoring. He had a head-cold, so his face was gummy and his nose had run all over it. Maggie, who loved him, got her flannel and gently wiped it clean, more or less, then turned him on to his side. He grunted but stopped snoring and Maggie stripped off her lovely blouse and best skirt and sat down on the bed in her petticoat and shift so that she could slide off her garters and roll down and remove her smart red stockings. Then she brushed out her hair, braided it and finally got into bed.

Ticky mumbled and rolled on to his back again. Immediately he began to snore. I hope to God the missus doesn't expect me to sleep wit' Ticky when he's a man grown, Maggie thought apprehensively as she tried to turn the child again and he lashed out, kicking her so hard on the kneecap that she had to bite back a cry. He's too big to share wit' me now, really, but the boys' room isn't that big. Ticky kicked out again and Maggie patiently turned him away from her, put her arms round him and hugged him into submission and soon Ticky was snoring gently once more.

There were no curtains in Maggie's little room so the starlight, and the faint moonshine, flooded in now, lighting up the picture on the wall, although it was all black and white, without a speck of the beautiful colours which Maggie loved. That picture is the only thing Mrs Nolan's ever give me, Maggie thought. I wonder how she'll feel if Liam an' me . . . when Liam an' me . . . no, if . . .

Her last thought, as she drifted off to sleep, was that if she and Liam did decide to get married Mrs Nolan would stop paying her immediately. A
250

daughter-in-law would be a nice free skivvy all over again, she pondered as she tipped into slumber.

CHAPTER NINE

Liverpool, Summer 1914

It was a beautiful summer day and Donal and Deirdre were sauntering along Heyworth Street, considering what they should do, since they were both, for once, at a loose end. Donal had suggested going swimming, but as the baths had sessions for boys and girls on separate days, that would have meant swimming in the canal, which Deirdre felt, as a working girl, she was a bit old for.

Donal could have pointed out that, at ten, she was scarcely a woman grown, but he did not.

'Little kids go there . . . or fellers,' she pointed out as they sauntered along. 'You don't see big gals like me down the scaldy.'

Donal gave a snort, but a quiet one, and Deirdre didn't challenge him. She knew that she wasn't particularly big and that ten years old was scarcely grown up, but she did have a holiday job, even though it was with Auntie Anne and not with a regular employer. And it was true that girls of Deirdre's age didn't usually swim with the fellers in the scaldy, so she wasn't surprised when Donal sighed but said nothing more. They would have loved to go down to New Brighton or somewhere else by the sea, but they had, as usual, no money. But it was so scorching . . . Deirdre longed for the feel of cool water on her hot skin and knew her twin felt the same . . .

So they had discussed various ploys but were still undecided. Donal was in favour of skipping a leckie and just going wherever it took them, but Deirdre was in a peaceful, pensive sort of mood and preferred to walk. And anyway, as she pointed out, they would probably hang on only for a couple of stops before they were spotted and pushed off, which wouldn't get them very far.

'Why don't we walk up to Stanley Park an' throw stones at the ducks?' Deirdre suggested. 'Not to hurt 'em, just to see 'em flap an' squawk.'

Donal gave her a cold glance. 'Because it's a waste of a fine day and because tomorrer you'll be workin', an' I'll be by myself again,' he said, suddenly gloomy. 'I'm not sayin' I like school all that much—when we leave I shan't shed no tears—but I does like the holidays, when I can be wi' me pals, like.'

'When we're a bit older and earnin' more from our holiday jobs we'll be able to do all sorts,' Deirdre reminded him. 'We'll go to New Brighton every weekend in summer, an' camp on Morton Shore, an' go to the cinema every night . . .'

'Mam won't let us. She'll take our money off us,' Donal said. Despite the sunshine, Donal was cross, Dee thought—and she knew why. Because she was working in her aunt's shop she did have some money, even though it wasn't very much. Donal, on the other hand, hadn't managed to get a holiday job. In fact, his discontent had started when he had applied for a job delivering laundry around the city and had been turned down on account of his size.

'Too small,' the man interviewing for the job had said briefly. 'The bike's heavy. Next!'

252

And to make matters worse, Donal's pal Rupert had got the job. Admittedly, Rupert was at least a foot taller than Donal, but when they fought—which they did often—Donal always won which meant, of course, that he was the strongest. Yet he hadn't got the job, which paid five bob a week, and Rupe had.

And it simply crowned his unhappiness when Deirdre had been taken on in the blooming cake shop, so there was Donal left alone for a good part of the summer holidays. And consequently sulking.

'Donny, you'll get summat, acourse you will, an' besides, I'm only workin' for Auntie Anne when she needs me, which may not be all that often, and anyway, we'll share the spondulicks,' Deirdre had offered when she had first started work as a counter hand. 'And Freddy ain't workin' yet. You can play wi' Freddy when me an' Rupe's at work.'

'Oh, Freddy!' Donal had said bitterly. 'Freddy's da says he can work in the shop now Billy's gorra proper job, so's he'll get used to it. In another year he'll be there full time, 'cos he's older than us.'

'Oh,' Deirdre had said, rather dismayed by this unwelcome news. Freddy's mam kept their corner shop, a positive cornucopia of good things, and when it was raining or freezing cold outside she let them—the twins and Freddy—play in the storeroom. It was better than the Harveys' store-room in which they had played as kids, with twice the goods stacked up around the walls. But if Freddy was considered old enough to help in the shop he would doubtless believe himself to be too old to play on the sacks of sugar, haricot beans and rice upon which he had bounded in his youth.

'Yes, *Oh*!' mimicked Donal. 'It's awright for you,

253

Dee, but what'll I do, by meself all day? And wi' no money comin' in,' he added gloomily.

'You'll find work, Donny, someone'll want you,' Deirdre had said bracingly. 'Look, I'm smaller than you . . .'

It was all Donal needed. He exploded. 'Yes, you're *much* smaller than me; you're a bleedin' *dwarf*, but you've gorra job, haven't you?' he had demanded. 'Gals can be dwarfs, but fellers has got to be *giants* if they want work. Oh, it ain't fair!'

Deirdre was starting to agree with him when she realised that it would do no good. Donal must be taken out of himself. So she squared up to him pugnaciously, eyes flashing. 'A dwarf? Did you call me a dwarf, Donal Docherty?'

The ensuing fight had raged all round the house and had brought Ellen down on them, but it had been worth it. Donal, nursing a bloody nose, had ended up laughing, saying she was right, he'd find something else in due course, and they had gone off to their separate bedrooms, sent by Ellen and definitely in disgrace, in perfect amity with each other. But that had been a week or so ago. And still Donal hadn't got a job. Deirdre would have liked to give hers up so they could have their last long summer holiday together, but unfortunately Mam refused even to consider it.

'I had to work on your aunt for a solid fortnight before she saw the sense of employin' another member of the family rather than a stranger,' Mam had said crossly, when Deirdre suggested Auntie Anne might find someone else. 'She's never forgive our Ellen for leavin', though I told her over an' over that Ellen was a born nurse an' wouldn't be happy to spend the rest of her workin' days in

254

anyone's cake shop.'

But in fact it had been a big surprise to all the family when Ellen had calmly announced one day that she was going to start her nursing training and might be living away from home for quite long periods when she was doing night duty or difficult shifts. The boys had been annoyed because they thought their comfort would be affected, which it was, because Deirdre had made up her mind from the start that she wasn't going to take Ellen's place in the home, not she! Of course there were some jobs she couldn't skip out on, but Deirdre made sure she did as little as possible—and as badly as possible, too.

Dusting, cleaning, washing and ironing were skipped and scamped until Ada was forced to redo them herself, and when Ellen came home after a long day on the wards she frequently found herself with a mound of tasks to undertake. 'It ain't fair, Dee,' she would say, looking white with exhaustion. 'I did it when I were your age, you should be doin' it now—an' doin' it properly, what's more.'

Sometimes Deirdre was sorry she'd been bad, but mostly she just shrugged. If they'd made Donal wash up, or iron shirts, she might have knuckled under, but they said it was women's work ... yet they also said that Deirdre was just a child. Please yourselves, Deirdre was apt to remark to herself as she left the iron too long on Ada's best petticoat or rubbed Ellen's stocking until a hole came, you're all bigger'n me so you can make me do it, but you can't make me do it proper, that's for sure.

And though Mam told them that Ellen's work was terribly hard and they should be sorry for her and do all they could to help her, Deirdre knew

255

that this was just an invention. Ellen had gone into nursing because she wanted to, so it couldn't be that bad, and besides, it was the only way she could be sure of spending a good deal of her working life near Tolly.

Ellen liked Tolly, as they all did. And when he'd given up his job in the jam factory and become an orderly at the City Hospital on Netherfield Road North, they should have realised that Ellen would follow him. After all, she had joined the Salvation Army quite soon after getting friendly with Tolly, so becoming a nurse in the same hospital that Tolly worked in seemed like a sensible move.

And Ellen looks real nice in the uniform, Deirdre thought to herself now, as the two of them sauntered along the pavement. Well, she looks nice in both uniforms. The nurses had dear little caps and starched white collars and cuffs, and there were the lovely, swirling cloak and the wonderfully white pinafores ... but she liked the Salvation Army uniform best, particularly the bonnet.

Even given the nice uniforms, however, Deirdre had not the slightest intention of following her sister's example. She had accompanied Ellen to the Citadel a couple of times, and had enjoyed the singing and the friendliness, but it wasn't for her. Ellen had always been the good one. She seemed to like taking care of people, she enjoyed washing filthy kids and removing dressings which had got stuck on and had to be eased off with great tenderness. I'd just rip 'em off, Deirdre thought cheerfully. Best way, in the end. As for slum kids, wi' dads what beat 'em up an' mams what half starve 'em, let 'em wash themselves, I say.

'She'll learn,' Mam said quietly sometimes to
256

Ellen, when Deirdre had been airing her opinions in a particularly forthright manner. 'Kids is all the same; they learn, queen. Until you've seen poverty an' need for yourself you can't understand, I dare say. We don't have much, but we're a good deal luckier than most; none of my kids have ever known what it was to go to bed hungry. Why, until you started nursing you didn't know what some of them kids has to suffer any more than Deirdre does.'

Deirdre, listening, piped up with her opinion. 'The Sally Army telled her a lot an' all, din't it, Ellie? But I don't want to go nursin', or helpin' people. I want to have some fun.'

No one ever said that Ellen had gone in for nursing to be near Tolly, though everyone thought it. Even Deirdre was mum on that score, because it was a delicate subject, like Donal's height. Ellen had known Tolly four years, she'd been a nurse for three of them and he hadn't yet asked her to go steady.

'He's got more sense,' Donal said when Deirdre had pointed out this curious omission to her twin. 'Bloomin' gals . . . what does he want wi' a gal when he's got his trumpet, a job, money . . . gals is just a nuisance.'

'But what about marryin'?' Deirdre had demanded. 'Everyone wants to marry, don't they, Donny?'

'Nah!' Donal said with great disdain. 'Bill never married, did he?'

'Not as we know,' Deirdre admitted cautiously. Bill had been gone more than three years now, and she and Donal missed him sorely. He had left shortly after their move to Mere Lane and had

257

never visited them there, and one day when the twins had gone round to see him all they found was a note pinned to the door addressed to Deirdre and Donal. It seemed his brother who had been managing the family farm in Clare had died suddenly and Bill had been called back to take over. He had been the best of friends and had appreciated their help in his search, though they hadn't managed to turn up any likely Feeneys any more than Bill himself had.

Deirdre had told Ellen all about Bill, in the end, because of the picture. When she had started work at the hospital there were some weeks when she had to live in and she had taken the picture with her. 'To remind me of home,' she had said.

Deirdre had been surprised at her own feeling of loss when she had looked up at the wall and seen the gap where the picture had hung. And that had prompted her, one night about a year ago when Ellen had been home, to tell her the story which Bill had told them.

Ellen had been intrigued, had wanted to meet Bill, so Deirdre had had to tell her that Bill had gone back to Ireland, to Clare, having given up his search for a while at least. 'He's a sailor, not a farmer though, Ellie,' she had said tearfully. 'He won't be happy rearin' sheep an' cuttin' turf, will he?'

'Perhaps he will, Dee,' Ellen said gently. 'Perhaps sailors, when they're old, long to work on the land. I've heard it said that it's so. Will he write to you, do you think?'

But he hadn't. And since they had no address for him, Deirdre and Donal had not written either. But they thought of him often and missed him too.

'Did you ever tell him about the picture, Dee?' Ellen asked her shortly after Deirdre had told her sister about Bill. 'Because it might mean something . . . I don't know, but Mam's gran might have been a neighbour. Is the Burren very large?'

Deirdre didn't know, but she had to confess that so far as she could remember she hadn't mentioned the picture of the Burren to Bill. 'I think I must have forgot,' she said, desperately racking her brain. 'I never thought . . . did our great-gran come from the Burren then, Ellie?'

But Ellen didn't know and Mam was not much help. 'She certainly thought it was a grand place, beautiful an' that,' she said cautiously. 'But whether she lived there herself, or just made the picture because it was beautiful I couldn't really say for certain. Why d'you want to know, queen?'

'Oh, I just wondered,' Ellen said vaguely. 'Dee was asking me.'

'That's right,' Deirdre corroborated eagerly. ''Member Bill, Mam?'

'I don't recall as I ever met him,' Ada said absently. She was making bread, pummelling it vigorously, and presently she would give the round loaves to one of the children who would take them down to the bakery for cooking. 'But I heard about him, 'cos you had to ask whenever he wanted to take you out.'

'We misses Bill,' Deirdre said forlornly. 'He were nice, were Bill.'

'Yes. Well, as I was saying, Mam,' Ellen interrupted. 'He's gone back to Ireland, probably to the Burren. And we were wonderin', Dee an' me, whether he might have known someone from our family, way back.'

'Your great-gran would have known,' Ada said. She picked up a handful of dough and shaped it, then popped it on to the baking tray. 'These will be ready for takin' down to Samples in half an hour, so could you give Sammy a shout, chuck?'

Sammy was an obliging child, always ready to go a message, unlike the twins.

'Oh Mam, we'll take it, Donny an' me,' Deirdre said, shamed into the offer, because Sammy was only a kid. 'D'you suppose a letter with "The Burren" on it would find Bill there?'

'Oh, I doubt it,' Ada said. 'Ireland's a big country an' the Burren's only a part of it. But you could try, I suppose.'

Deirdre had meant to write a letter, she really had, but somehow the weeks had turned into months and the months into years, and she had never got round to it. And now here she was, ten years old, with a job in her aunt's cake shop for the holidays and her twin miserable because he would be alone for most of the sunny summer days.

Deirdre stopped walking and turned to face her twin. 'Donny, stop feelin' sorry for yourself! It ain't a lorra fun in the cake shop if you want the truth, with our mam poppin' in every two minutes to mek sure I'm not doing anythin' wrong, an' Miss Jenkins screechin' if I so much as look at a cake, an' the customers so picky an' choosy. If I could choose, I'd much rather be moochin' around the streets wi' you, I tell you straight.'

'Yes, but . . .' Donal began, but was ruthlessly interrupted.

'I know what you're goin' to say, you're goin' to say I wouldn't want to be moochin' the streets alone. Well, I would, if it were that or bein' shut up in that ole cake shop all day. So there! *Now* will you mek up your mind where you want to go today?'

Donal looked at her, then down at his bare feet, shuffling along in the dust. He grinned. 'Sorry, I never thought of it like that. Right, it's your day off, so you choose.'

'How much money have we got?' Deirdre demanded.

'Dunno . . . I've got tuppence. What've you got?'

'The same. But I don't see why we shouldn't borrow some, out of our mam's teapot. I'm bleedin' workin', after all, so I can pay her back. What d'you think?'

'It depends what we's goin' to do wi' the money,' Donal said cautiously. 'What d'you wanna do?'

'Catch the over'ead rail to Seaforth Sands,' Deirdre said triumphantly. 'It's a grand day an' we don't have to be back till dark. We can fish, mek a fire, swim . . .'

'Oh, Dee,' Donal breathed in rapt admiration. 'You are a one for thinkin' things out! What about takin' the tent then, eh?'

The tent had been made out of a couple of stout sheets, a broken prop and some washing line, and the twins adored it.

Donal's grin, which had been broad enough before, practically bisected his face. 'Dee! We'll sleep on the beach—we'll leave our mam a note—an' have our brekfusses there . . . we'll live there—we could, you know.'

It wasn't the moment to remind Donal that she was supposed to start work at eight next morning. Besides, Deirdre thought hopefully, if she wasn't at work perhaps Auntie Anne would give her the push and then she and Donal would be together once

261

again. 'Right. Home now, then, an' fetch us some money,' she declared. 'An' some grub an' all. There's bound to be bread an' cheese . . .'

'We might get some fades from the vegetable market on our way past,' Donal said eagerly, ignoring the fact that they would not normally pass the market on their way to the pier head. 'It ain't stealin', Dee, 'cos we're just takin' our rightful grub what we'd ha' et at tea tonight if we'd been home.'

'That's it,' Deirdre agreed. How simple life was once you took it out, looked it in the eye and shook it into shape! Of course, money made the world go round, she'd heard people saying that, but even money wasn't unobtainable if you used a bit of intelligence. 'Come on, then, Donny, gerra move on! We don't want to lose any more time, thinkin' 'stead o' doin'!'

*   *   *

'Nurse, the third bed along . . . the top sheet isn't absolutely straight and it could be tucked in a lot tighter! Do it at once, please.'

Sister was a big, commanding woman with a big, commanding voice. Ellen flew to obey and when the patient said in a small voice, 'Not *too* tight, nurse, or 'tis worse'n a strait-jacket!' she said quietly, 'Just for five minutes, Mrs Williams, then I'll come and ease it off again. But you know what Sister's like.'

'Aye, like a bleedin' sergeant-major,' Mrs Williams said. 'Worse. Still, she ain't on the ward for long, I'll say that for 'er. Prefers to sit in 'er office, a-writin' reports.'

'Well, someone's got to do it,' Ellen said, tucking

262

in the erring sheet. 'There, it's just like a geometry lesson now, that'll please her.'

Sister boomed, 'That's *so* much better, nurse. Now come up here and take Mrs er-er's bedpan away if she's finished with it.'

'Yes, Sister,' Ellen said, scurrying. She took the bedpan, swished the curtains back around the patient's bed and walked swiftly back up the ward towards the sluice. If I ever get to be a Sister, she told herself, at least I shall learn the patients' names—it's so rude to call everyone *Mrs er-er*.

By the time she returned to the ward Sister had taken herself off once again. A twice-daily visit seemed to be her idea of how to run a ward—fortunately, the patients and nursing staff thought. As soon as Ellen was sure that Sister wouldn't pop back with another command she went round loosening sheets, passing patients their knitting or magazines and pouring glasses of water. Another of Sister's foibles was that she didn't like to see beds or lockers untidy, and since untidiness included any sign of human occupation it was a frequent joke amongst the staff that if Sister had her way the patients would all be turned out of the ward to spend the day as best they might in the corridors or waiting-rooms, so that the beds could be made up entirely flat, the locker-tops could be totally empty and there would be nothing for her nurses to do except to tidy and polish all day.

'Nurse, I'm awful sorry but could I 'ave that bedpan back? Only I din't like to say . . . not in front of Sister . . . I'd not finished me sittin'.'

'Right, Mrs Allyson. I'll bring it in to you on my way out because I should have finished half an hour ago and I really do want to get home before midnight! I'll just check that Nurse Watkin's on the premises.'

'Oh, I'm sorry, nurse,' poor Mrs Allyson said. 'I should've thought . . . but you know how it is . . .'

'I certainly do,' Ellen said fervently. If Sister still frightened her, how much worse it must be for these poor patients, who were bed-bound and unable to help themselves, and who lived in awe of most of the ordinary nurses and auxiliaries, let alone the more senior ranks. 'It isn't your fault; Sister shouldn't try to hurry you.'

She went back to the sluice and brought a clean bedpan, swished the curtains closed this time and made determinedly for the end of the ward. Nurse Brown had gone on time, sliding out quietly just before Sister's inspection was due to start, but no doubt Edna Watkin was on the premises, probably changing. It would not do to leave the ward without cover, but it really was time she was leaving. She had promised Tolly she would walk home with him, though a nursing orderly had about as much chance of getting away on time as a nurse did.

She must not run on hospital premises of course, except in a dire emergency, but most nurses had perfected a style of walking which was just under a run and which covered the ground almost as swiftly. Ellen employed this gait as soon as she had checked that Nurse Watkin was ready to take over and had explained how each patient was.

'Mrs Allyson's got a bedpan. Sister whipped her off it too soon,' she ended. 'Give her another ten minutes, then see if she still needs it, would you? Oh, and Mrs Williams's leg was oozing at two o'clock, when I checked her dressing. Better keep an eye.'

'Right,' Nurse Watkin said. She was taking notes on one of her stiff white cuffs, a practice much frowned upon by senior staff. 'Anything else, Docherty? No one been down to theatre?'

'No, though Mrs Potter will be going down tomorrow, all being well, so try to see she gets a good night's sleep. She may need some help ... she's very nervous, I know.'

'I'll do my best,' Nurse Watkin said. 'Thanks, Docherty. You're off now for a couple of days, aren't you? Get some rest. Anyone nursing under Sister Crawford needs it.'

'Thanks,' Ellen said. 'See you later in the week, then.'

She took her cloak off the peg on which it had hung and arranged it round her shoulders, but didn't fasten it. It was a lovely sunny evening, she had noticed that much every time she passed an open window, so she wouldn't need the cloak for warmth, but she knew that to go out without it would be frowned on, no matter how pleasant the weather. And anyway, it was neat and professional looking, and although she would shed her stained apron, her cuffs and stiff collar, and her little cap, she would have to retain her dress, which usually managed to get marked during the course of the day.

Outside the ward Ellen took a deep breath. She enjoyed nursing, but there were enormous disadvantages. Some Sisters were truly the angels the patients thought them, but others were really dreadful, spending as much time devising ways of humiliating their nurses as they did taking care of their patients. And doctors could be difficult too, critical, rude, overbearing. And of course occasionally there were difficult patients as well. Women who bullied you, lied, cheated, tried to get you into trouble for the sheer pleasure of being 'one up' as they put it. But they were few and far between; it was mainly the senior staff who made the lives of those working under them so hard.

I came into nursing to make people well again and that's what I am doing, Ellen reminded herself as she went sedately down the stairs, whilst all the time she was longing to break into a run or worse, to leap aboard the banister and go from top to bottom in one glorious, rapid swoop. She was late—would Tolly wait? But sometimes, her thoughts continued, reverting to their previous topic, it did seem as though Sister Crawford didn't care about the patients at all. She would willingly sacrifice their comfort, perhaps even their lives, for the sake of a neat and tidy ward and nurses who jumped to obey her slightest command.

Ellen came to the bottom of the stairs and walked across the wide foyer where patients wandered, looking up at the printed notices, and emerged through a side door into brilliant sunshine. She smiled, because it was such a lovely evening and because she had the next two days off, and saw Tolly. He had waited! He was leaning against the wall, gazing ahead of him with a dreamy look on his face and even as she watched, his fingers played an imaginary scale on his trumpet and he smiled into the distance.

'Tolly . . . I'm out!'

It sounded pretty silly put like that, but Tolly turned at once and smiled at her. He had the happy knack, Ellen thought, of looking at everyone as though they were very important to him. Once, she had read a good deal into that look of his, but not any more. Tolly was the nicest feller she knew, but she was beginning to realise that he was also a deeply contented person. He enjoyed his work, which was just as hard as hers and just, she thought rather bitterly, as unrewarding at times. He loved the Army and was willing to work for it in any way he could, and he loved his music. In fact, if Tolly had to choose it would be his music first, the Army next and his work last, Ellen decided as she walked across the tarmac which separated them. She herself would come a long way behind—not even fourth in the queue, she suspected, but tenth or twelfth.

But there; I joined the Army for Tolly's sake and ended up loving it for its own sake, Ellen reminded herself. And I became a nurse for Tolly's sake and now, if I leave, it will be because I'm not always allowed to be a good nurse, so there seems little point in it after all. There are other careers which are as useful—perhaps more useful. I must ask Tolly . . .

Her thoughts broke down in confusion; it had been so natural, so easy, to turn to Tolly with her problems, when really she should not do so. He likes you, but no better than he likes a dozen others, she reminded herself crossly. Stop being dependent on him, start depending upon yourself for a change! If you need advice about changing your job ask your mam, or another nurse . . . not Tolly, on no account Tolly.

'Ah, here you are at last! My goodness, they work you girls like navvies. I don't know how a slender thing like you stands the strain, indeed I do not. Now shall we go straight home or shall we have a bit of a walk down by the Mersey? It's such a glorious evening and I'm off for the next two days, as you are, so I thought we might walk in the fresh air for a while, buy some fish and chips, find a glass of lemonade or a cup of tea . . .'

He was smiling at her, taking her arm . . . how can I not love him? Ellen cried silently to herself. How can he not see that I love him? But if he saw, he never commented or allowed it to spoil their friendship—she should be grateful for that, at least.

'Well, Ellie? Home or the waterfront?'

She looked up at him. His curly nut-brown hair, brushed smooth when he left the hospital, was already beginning to curl again, and his hazel eyes smiled gently into hers. He was looking down at her, his eyebrows rising, his face enquiring. She could tell he was hoping she would go walking with him, would enter into his pleasure in the sunny evening. But why should she? She was tired, jaded, depressed . . . and in love. To be with him was heaven in some ways, hell in others. And she knew him so well! He would take her out, be kind and loving to her, talk to her, tease her . . . and it would mean precisely nothing.

'Oh, Tolly, I don't know! I'm awfully tired . . .'

'Right, home then,' he said. He spoke with unimpaired cheerfulness and Ellen promptly felt a mean beast. Did he want her to feel like that? She doubted it. Tolly was truly thoughtful for others, it was a way of life with him.

'No, it's all right. If we can have a sit-down when we reach the waterfront then I'll recover . . . I'll enjoy meself. In fact, why don't we catch a tram instead of walking? We'd be there in half the time . . . and I could sit down.'

The longing in her voice made him laugh but he put a hand beneath her elbow and steered her out of the hospital grounds and over to the nearest tram stop. 'You're sure? You wouldn't rather go home? Only I don't mind, honest, if you're worn out . . .'

'I'm not. Oh wonderful, here comes a tram . . . shall we go on top?'

On top was cheaper, but they enjoyed it better anyway. They climbed the curly stair and collapsed into a seat. A man and woman, already seated, smiled at them. They think we're a pair of young lovers out on the spree, Ellen thought sadly. If only they knew!

'Well, Ellie, tell me what kept you. I suppose it was that Ward Sister of yours—dreadful woman. Now I was late too, because . . .'

He went on talking and Ellen, looking sideways at him and laughing at the right moments, stopped listening and began to think about the young man next to her. He was fond of an outing after work, particularly in the summer. And in the winter he would go to the cinema or to a stage show, to a concert, to a band practice. At one time she had invited him home often, but she did not do so much any more.

Tolly had been orphaned when he was four or five and had been brought up in the Ragged Boys Home where he had been, he assured her, very happy. The boys were adequately fed, well clothed, looked after. The superintendent was a harassed but kindly man who took the boys in his charge on outings six times a year and camping in the Lake District for three weeks every summer. He was a music lover and had encouraged Tolly to play an

269

instrument. First a flute, then a bugle and finally a trumpet.

Tolly hadn't been a Salvationist as a boy either. In fact, music had brought him to the Army. He had watched and listened to the band as a lad, had followed them around the streets and finally, when he was playing the bugle well enough, he had approached them. He wanted to join them, he said, more for the music than anything.

The band leader had no sons of his own, only daughters who, though they were good Salvationists, had no interest in music. He invited Tolly along to the Citadel to a service and before long Tolly was attending every Sunday of his own accord.

And soon he was playing with the band, though only as a favour, when they were doing a band practice. His command of the bugle, they said, was excellent; he would be a first-rate musician one day.

And it went on from there, Tolly had told Ellen, when they had begun to talk about themselves. He had got a job, saved up to buy a uniform, borrowed a trumpet from one of the bandsmen and had practised, practised, practised, putting his heart and soul into his music.

But once he was fifteen he had to leave the Ragged Boys Home, because there were other motherless boys who needed a roof over their heads. So one of the bandsmen offered him a room. Tolly lived with Mr and Mrs Flaxman for three very happy years, but then they moved away from Everton to live with their married daughter and Tolly took a room in an ordinary lodging house. He was there still, not because he was

270

particularly happy, but because it was cheap, reasonably clean and because he spent very little time there. All his energies, which were considerable, were given to his music and to helping youngsters, who had no one but themselves to rely on, to come to terms with their lives.

'Here we are,' Tolly said, as the tram drew to a stop by the pier head. 'Are you rested? Shall we have that cuppa now, or later?'

'Now,' Ellen said firmly. 'I'm sorry, but if I don't sit down for a bit I'll just keel over, go straight off to sleep. Where's a tea-shop?'

'Tell you what,' Tolly said suddenly. 'Why don't we go out to Seaforth on the Overhead Railway? That way you'll be sittin' down for a while. We can find a tea-shop when we get there. And walkin' on the sands is better than walkin' here, wouldn't you say?'

Ellen couldn't help smiling. The sands! And fresh air, real fresh air, instead of air that was full of city and ferry smells. 'Oh, yes please, Tolly,' she said fervently. 'Let's go!'

They walked along to the south end of Pier Head station and Tolly bought two oranges at the Cabin, and two bars of Fry's chocolate.

'That'll keep the wolf from the door until we reach the sands at Seaforth,' he said. 'The chocolate will make us thirsty an' the oranges will quench our thirst. Neat, eh?'

'Wonderful,' Ellen said dreamily. She was in a mood to find everything Tolly said wonderful. He might never love her as she loved him, she had just concluded, but there was nothing to say she couldn't pretend and for today she intended to pretend like mad. People looked at them strolling

271

along arm in arm and they thought them young lovers—well, they would be so to Ellen as well, just for this evening.

The train rolled in and they found an empty carriage, because the main going-home rush was over. As it started off Ellen lowered the window the better to see out. Below them, in St George's Dock Gates, a policeman was arguing with a driver whose carthorse seemed to have designs on the policeman's summer helmet. The horse reached curiously towards the straw hat and the policeman, quite unconscious of the interest he was arousing, began to gesture towards the pier head.

Ellen, giggling, pointed. 'Look, Tolly, the scuffer's wearin' his summer helmet and the horse wants a closer look; wonder if it's got designs on it?'

Tolly laughed too. 'It ain't called a donkey's breakfast for nothin',' he observed as the horse craned its long neck. 'Oh, he's given the feller directions, now he's walkin' off.'

'Poor horse,' Ellen said as the horse watched the policeman going stolidly on his way. 'No straw supper today, feller.'

'That's it; poor horse,' Tolly agreed, but absently, as though his mind was really elsewhere. 'Want a peppermint? We won't start the chocolate until we reach Seaforth; that awright wi' you?'

Ellen accepted the proffered sweet, a stripy Everton mint, and began to suck, and as the train progressed she and Tolly got considerable pleasure from looking down on the docks and guessing at the names and destinations of the many ships therein.

'I'm goin' on a ship one o' these days,' Tolly said

dreamily. 'The big liners have musicians, you know, so I could go on one of them. Or I could sign on as cabin staff, steward or something. Nursing orderlies do from time to time. An . . . an' it's about time I saw the world.'

'Oh,' Ellen said rather doubtfully. At his words her heart, which had been high with the mere pleasure of his company, dropped into her boots. 'I never thought of you as . . . as the rovin' kind, Tolly.'

'No. People don't,' Tolly admitted. 'That's one of the reasons why I think . . . but we'll talk about it when we reach the sea, shall we? Here, have another mint.'

For the rest of the journey they restricted their conversation to what they could see from the window, but Ellen knew that for her the trip was spoilt. Tolly to go to sea? She could imagine nothing less likely, yet he said that was why he wanted to go, because folk saw him as a stay-at-home. And if he did go to sea, what of her? She would leave the hospital, she already knew that. Her high hopes of becoming a useful and valued member of a nursing team had foundered on the rocks of Sister Crawford's indifference and, to be honest, on the general attitude amongst a good few senior staff, that nurses were useless, inefficient and unintelligent. As a humble probationer she had accepted this attitude, but after more than three years of rigorous training she could see all too clearly that many of the people who criticised the nursing staff most relentlessly were in no way qualified to do so. They were the ones who were inefficient, absorbed in attention to tiny details whilst ignoring the larger issues and so hidebound that they could not see what was under their noses. And it was annoying in the extreme to be told to perform some fiddling and unimportant task whilst a patient, who needed your help, suffered without it for the sake of a bed with tightly tucked sheets or a floor so highly polished that it was a danger to the very people you were supposed to be helping.

So if Tolly leaves, so do I, Ellen concluded. But I can't go to sea. What will I do instead? She was about to turn to Tolly and ask his opinion when she realised two things. One was that she could not possibly let him know that she had joined the nursing profession chiefly to be near him and the other that he must never know she would leave after he did either. It would embarrass him and put their friendship on a distinctly different, and difficult, footing.

Another hospital, perhaps? Would that be the answer? But she did not think so. She had toyed with the idea of going in for private nursing, or for trying for a job with the Salvation Army—they employed ex-nurses for their children's and old people's homes—but she hadn't really given it much thought because she hadn't realised that Tolly was considering leaving.

'Ellen? Come on, queen, we get off here!'

The train had stopped at Seaforth Sands station whilst she thought. Hastily, Ellen followed Tolly off the train and down on to street level once more. There, he tucked her hand into his arm and set off in a purposeful manner for the beach.

'Come on, we'll walk first, and talk, then we'll get ourselves a cuppa and have a sit-down before going back to the city.'

'Right,' Ellen agreed. All of a sudden she could

feel energy flooding through her. The challenge of walking after a long day's work seemed worthwhile, especially if it meant that she and Tolly could talk—really talk, with no holds barred.

They walked down Crosby Road South and turned left into Shore Road. The sand stretched before them, smooth as brown sugar, and the sea was blue, the breakers foaming white.

Ellen gave a deep sigh of contentment as Tolly broke the first chocolate bar in half and handed her a piece. 'Here we go, then,' she said. 'You'd better start at the beginning and tell me just what you're going to do, Tolly.'

'I will,' Tolly said. He ate a piece of chocolate, then started to speak.

'About a year ago, Ellen, I began to feel . . . oh, I don't know . . . I suppose I began to feel that life, real life, was passing me by. We work hard on the wards, but what actual good was I doing, I asked meself. And then there was me music. I was good at what I was doing, I knew *that;* the Army teaches well and I was keen to learn. But could I make my living as a trumpet player? I doubted it, somehow. And although I went to the Citadel and joined in the services, it wasn't everything to me. I'm a Salvationist, don't get me wrong, but it wasn't the be-all and end-all of me life. And looking round at other fellers I could see that I wasn't the same as them. Not quite. Not completely. They had homes, you see, families . . . lady-friends, even. They enjoyed their work, but they saw a future for themselves which included a home of their own, a wife, a family. Which, I think you'll agree, is right and proper.'

Ellen felt her heart began to beat a little faster.

275

Tolly was getting to the point at last! 'Yes, I know what you mean,' she said sedately, however. 'Most fellers of your age are savin' up to get married, or they're already married and savin' up to have a family ... they've got plans which include a ... well, a domestic life, I suppose you could say. Whereas you ...'

'Whereas I just play me music, an' do me work,' Tolly concluded for her. 'Yes, and that's me point. You see I were only three when I were put into the home for orphan boys, an' only five when me dad died and I stopped thinkin'—which I did at first— that I'd be took out one day, to live wi' an ordinary family again.

'Well, for several years it were more or less a matter of survivin'. They fed us an' clothed us, but I always felt ... in a kind o' limbo. Neither fish, fowl nor good red herrin', in fact. Most of the fellers in the orphan home had relatives of some sort, but no one ever come forward to gi' me a day out or tek me home for the weekend. In fact, I could have been a foundling for all the relatives I had. Course, when I got bigger an' moved around a bit more, I realised that me dad's family hadn't approved of him marryin' me mam, so they'd cut him off. I don't know whether they disinherited him, I doubt there was much to inherit, tell the truth, but they certainly made it clear they wanted nothin' to do with either him or me mam. An' her family were from away ... over the water ... so they weren't much good.

'So there I was, a kid o' ten or eleven, wi' no one of me own. And then I found the Army, or they found me, an' I thought that if only I could play a bugle they'd let me join 'em an' I'd be all right.'

'And you were,' Ellen said encouragingly, as the silence stretched. 'You're all right, Tolly.'

Tolly shook his head. 'No, I'm not all right, Ellen,' he said heavily. 'Because one of the things we never were taught in the orphan boys' home was how to carry on in a family. How could they tell us? They was too busy seein' we was fed and clothed. I ain't never seen an ordinary family, let alone been a part of one.'

'But lots of people haven't, Tolly,' Ellen said eagerly. 'You saw quite a bit of *my* family at one time, though, so you've seen us at work. And what about those people you stayed with at first? The elderly couple?'

'They were kind, but they were an old couple,' Tolly said. 'It ain't the same, Ellen! And your family . . . I weren't inside it, see? An . . . an' I don't think I ever saw your dad, though you talk about him of course.'

'Well, we hardly ever see our dad,' Ellen admitted. 'My dad died way back, Mick's only me stepfather. But I don't see . . .'

'D'you know, you're the only person in the world, just about, that I could say this to?' Tolly said. 'But I . . . I don't know how to . . . to hug. Or any of that. When I try it seems as though I'm playin' at it, not meanin' it at all. Once, there was a girl I was keen on—that's when we was in the Songsters together, a while back.'

Ellen's unreliable heart did another nosedive. A girl? He wasn't going to ask her advice on how to get alongside another girl, was he?

But Tolly was still talking. 'I knew she wanted me to give her a kiss an' a hug, like,' he was saying earnestly. 'But I found I didn't want to; I were embarrassed by the whole idea. So then I thought perhaps I ain't normal, Ellen. Because it ain't normal to like a girl but not to want to kiss her. Is it?'

'I don't know,' Ellen said honestly. 'Perhaps it's something boys all say they want to do, but some of them are just like you, Tolly. Look, did you . . . did you try to give that girl a kiss or a hug?'

'No. I didn't know how to set about it, really,' Tolly admitted. 'So that's why I thought I'd go to sea. I'd get experience, like.'

'There aren't many women aboard ship,' Ellen said. 'If you're thinkin' of foreign ports, I don't know as that's a very good idea either. Why should you want to hug a Chinese girl, say, if you don't want to hug an English one?'

'No, it ain't that so much as bein' wi' fellers what know a thing or two,' Tolly said. His face, Ellen saw, was pink. 'I mix wi' other nursing orderlies in the hospital, an' with the players in the band. They don't say much, they sort o' take it for granted that a feller wants a gal an' will know what to do . . .'

'Why not talk to my brothers?' Ellen said quickly. 'Dick's been married a few years now. Or you could ask Ozzie—he's gorra lady-friend and they're marryin' pretty soon. An' the others are always on about gals. They'd be able to tell you, I reckon.'

Tolly shook his head. 'It wouldn't work, I don't think,' he said. 'It's something that will either come to me or it won't. An' if there's somethin' wrong wi' me, somethin' missin', then I'd rather find out amongst strangers, if it's all the same to you.'

'Yes, I can understand that,' Ellen said slowly. 'Tolly . . . hang on a minute.' She caught hold of his

278

arm and pulled him to a halt. Then she put her arms round him and pulled him as close as he would allow, which wasn't very close since the moment her arms went round him he began to pull away. 'Kiss me . . . go on, have a go,' she said in a kindly, sensible sort of voice. 'Just see whether you can . . . I mean whether you want to, with me, what you know so well.'

'I feel a fool,' Tolly said, scarlet now and not just pink. 'I can't . . . it wouldn't be natural.'

'Rubbish,' Ellen said firmly. She stood on tiptoe and turned her face up to his. 'Go on, try,' she said.

Tolly heaved a huge sigh and very slowly he lowered his head. He put his cold lips against her warm cheek and made a sort of squeaky noise, then pulled back, rather as though he thought she might suddenly bite a lump out of him, Ellen thought resentfully.

'How was that?' Tolly asked breathlessly. 'Was it all right?'

'No. Try again,' Ellen said. 'Kissing's warmer than that, I think. Try to do it on me lips.'

'On your *lips?*' Tolly said, sounding scandalised. 'Oh, I don't think . . .'

Ellen, hot all over with the forwardness of what she was doing, reached up and took Tolly's face between her hands, then guided him into the right position and placed her mouth against his. Guiltily, she was aware of the feel, the smell, even the taste of him, though their lips were only together for perhaps a tenth of a second, and knew a tremendous happiness and a surge of desire. Oh Tolly, Tolly, if only this meant as much to you as it does to me!

'Was that it?' Tolly asked. 'It . . . it's too close,

Ellen, I couldn't do that every day with someone. Think of the germs!'

'Didn't it do anything to you, Tolly?' Ellen asked shyly, staring up at him. 'Didn't your heart beat a bit faster? Didn't your stomach do a sort of lurch, like when you're in one of them flying boats on the fair an' it goes up too fast? Wasn't it . . . sort o' nice?'

'I dunno,' Tolly said honestly. 'Me stomach lurches when I see a bad wound, or when there's shepherd's pie for dinner an' the spud's all grey an' slimy. D'you mean like that?'

'No, I don't,' Ellen said crossly. She pulled away from him. 'Oh, go to sea, Tolly; you're probably right, that's the best way.'

'Now you're cross,' Tolly said. 'It were your idea to try it out, Ellen, not mine. I *told* you I thought there might be somethin' wrong wi' me.'

'So you did,' Ellen said. She broke away from him and began to run as fast as she could along the damp sand. Further up the beach some kids had set up a tent and were cooking something over a small fire; she just hoped they hadn't seen the exhibition she had just made of herself, that was all! I'd die if I thought anyone knew I'd made Tolly kiss me and then got cross because he didn't seem to care for it much, she thought, feeling the heat surge into her cheeks. Well, let that teach you a lesson, Ellen Docherty, she told herself, pounding along the beach. Girls who chase fellers never get anywhere . . . not when the fellers are having doubts about themselves, anyway.

Far behind her on the beach she heard Tolly shout, but she took no notice. How shall I face him, sit beside him on the train going home? she

280

thought miserably. We're supposed to be going for a cup of tea ... what'll we talk about when we're sitting in the tea-rooms? We'll just look at each other and Tolly will think how disgusting I am and I'll think ... well, I'll think that I must be repugnant to him. I'm not going back! I'll catch a bus, or walk ... but I can't go back with Tolly!

*   *   *

The twins had had a marvellous day—were still having it, in fact. They had taken half a crown—all Deirdre's next week's wages—out of the teapot on the mantel and used it, Deirdre told herself, wisely. They had bought bottles of lemonade, because everyone knows if you drink seawater you go mad, and a large bag of bruised apples and some bananas. From their mother's cupboard they had removed a large, rather misshapen loaf of bread, a medium-sized piece of cheese and a bottle of pickled onions. Then, of course, they had had to borrow the old perambulator to push their loot down to the docker's umbrella, because there was no way they could have managed it between them, not with the tent and all.

The pickled onions had turned out to be a mistake, but other than that they couldn't have done better if they'd been practising for years, Deirdre thought complacently. She was sitting on the soft sand and watching their driftwood fire burning briskly, whilst Donal poked cautiously at some mussels they had bought, cooking in an old Glaxo tin. Yes, apart from the pickled onions this was definitely the life! And she didn't see why they shouldn't stay here so long as the weather lasted.

281

She said as much to Donal. 'Ain't this jest what the doctor ordered, Donny? Them mussels smell good!'

They didn't, but it sounded . . . right, somehow, Deirdre decided.

Donal, however, was more practical. 'I don't see how you can smell anythin' bar pickled onions,' he said unkindly, for the onions had been Deirdre's idea, and it had been she who had knocked them over too, 'Every time I bleedin' *move* the pong near on knocks me out.'

'Oh, it ain't bad out here,' Deirdre protested. 'It's only inside the tent it's a bit strong, like. An' it'll go soon enough. Smells wear off, you know.'

'Not that smell,' Donal said. 'That smell's here to stay. I'm goin' to sleep outside, on t'other side o' the fire.'

'That's daft,' Deirdre said, rather alarmed. 'Whar-rif it rains? Besides, we brung the tent to sleep in, not to . . . to look at.'

'You like pickled onions,' Donal pointed out. 'I hates 'em.'

'Ye-es, but just because you hate a smell that doesn't mean . . .'

'Dee, for once in your life, don't *argufy*,' Donal said with spirit. 'I'm sleepin' on the sand, so there. Until the stink goes, tharris.'

'Oh. Right. Tell you what, Donny, what say I gerra lemonade bottle full o' sea, and chuck it at the tent? D'you reckon . . .'

'No, I *don't*,' Donal howled. 'Shurrup about smells, our Dee, an' tell me if them mussels is cooked.'

Deirdre approached the mussels with all the caution of one who has never willingly cooked so

282

much as a boiled egg in her life and stuck a piece of driftwood into the nearest shell. It was, of course, hard, but then she hadn't really expected it to soften. Well, she supposed it might have done . . . but Donal was looking at her with respect; he was sure that, being a woman, she would know everything about cooking. So Deirdre hooked a mussel out of the pan and looked in through the gap in the two shells at the little blob of rubber within. 'Just about perfect,' she pronounced, wondering whether that was really all a mussel ought to contain. 'Come on, gi's a cut o' bread an' we'll start eatin'.'

'How do we eat 'em, though?' Donal asked presently, when Deirdre had clattered the shells, and their contents, on to the perambulator cover. 'They's hot!'

'We leave 'em to cool for a bit, then we hooks 'em out o' the shells an' puts 'em on the bread, an' has a feast,' Deirdre said, crossing her fingers behind her back. This would be her first taste of mussels, though she often had crab when one of the boys brought one home. 'You'll love 'em, our Donny!'

*   *   *

In the event, neither she nor Donal was particularly keen on the mussels, but Deirdre dared not say so. She ate manfully, squashing the rubbery creatures between two thick slices of bread, and it was whilst they were washing down their 'feast' with lemonade and munching the softening apples that Deirdre spotted they were no longer alone.

When they'd first reached the sands they had

283

been not exactly crowded, but certainly well-peopled, but as the day dwindled so the beach seemed to lose its attraction and by the time the mussels were plopped into the Glaxo tin Deirdre and Donal were alone, save for the odd person walking a dog, or elderly people strolling along admiring the sunset.

But as the sun sank and the pale blue of the sky became streaked with crimson and gold, a young couple came down on to the sands. They strolled for a bit, presumably talking, and the twins took no notice of them at all due to the fact that they were further along the shore and Donal and Deirdre had pitched their tent at the very top of the beach. But then something happened which caught their attention. The couple got closer and closer . . .

'They're kissin'!' Donal exclaimed, much disgusted. 'In the open, wi' us havin' to see 'em at it! I call that disgustin'.'

'Ay up,' Deirdre said, having a long look. 'The feller's Tolly!'

'Can't be,' Donal said, shading his eyes against the brilliance of the sunset sky. 'Tolly wouldn't act so daft.'

'It is, I tell you. Well, stone the bleedin' crows!'

'An' the gal's our Ellen,' Donal said after a moment. 'Ooh, if our mam knew our Ellen was canoodlin' in public wi' Tolly, she'd be that cross!'

'It's only kissin',' Deirdre said. She stared some more. 'Oh Jeez . . . *now* what's happenin'?'

For Ellen had broken away from Tolly and was running along the beach as fast as she could go.

'Oh Gawd, has she seen us?' Donal said, but it was soon clear that she had not. She was belting along the beach, clearly trying to put as much distance between herself and her kisser as possible.

'No, it ain't us, she's fell out wi' Tolly,' Deirdre said at length. 'Our Ellen can't half run though, Donny, I hope she remembers there's quicksands out there! Wonder what he did?'

'Kissed her,' Donny said. 'Don't you have no eyes in your head, gal?'

'Ellen wouldn't mind no kissin',' Deirdre said wisely. 'Tolly's that nice ... I wouldn't mind it meself, wi' Tolly.'

Donal made a rude noise and suggested that Ellen was running because they were about to play relievio.

'Nowhere to hide,' Deirdre said, glancing around. 'Besides, they're too old for games. No, Tolly must of said somethin' what our Ellen din't like.'

'Tolly's runnin' too, now,' Donal said presently. 'Cor, watch him go! He's catchin' her up, he's catchin' her up ... she's stopped! Wonder if they'll have a set-to now, or whether they'll start all that sloppy business again?'

But they did neither. They stood there on the beach for a moment, Tolly with his hand on Ellen's arm, Ellen staring up at him, then they fell into step with one another and continued their walk along the beach.

'Funny,' Deirdre said, when Ellen and Tolly were out of sight. 'Now! Shall us have a walk up the beach afore we settle down for the night?'

'No, it's gettin' dark,' Donal said. 'I wonder if there's wolves around Seaforth?'

'Wolves?' Deirdre said derisively. 'Huh! You'll be askin' about sharks, next.'

'You don't have sharks in cold waters, I know
285

that,' Donal said. 'I know there aren't no wolves, really. But you might get big dogs. Or big foxes, I suppose.'

'You're right there,' Deirdre said, smitten by a brilliant idea. 'I wouldn't sleep out on the sand if you paid me, norrif I might find meself bein' snuffled at by a big dog. Or a fox. No, I'd sooner be in the tent.'

There was a thoughtful silence. Then Donal said: 'But that smell, our Dee! It turns me up. No, I reckon I'll kip down on the sand.'

Deirdre, damping down the fire and putting their food and other belongings away in the tent, just shrugged. There was a time for words and a time to let ideas simmer, she decided. She wished they'd brought a lamp, but they did have a candle, so she lit it from the fire's glowing embers and crawled into the tent. She dug the candle down in the sand and pulled the perambulator across the entrance. It was snug in the tent with the candlelight flickering on the white walls and the blanket they had brought spread out over the cold sand. As she settled down for the night Deirdre decided smugly that she was a good deal better off than Donal, who would have the moonlight and the black shadows, the chilly night breeze and his own wild imaginings for company, instead of the candle's friendly flicker and the warmth of their blanket. 'It's ever so nice in here, Donny,' she called enticingly, presently. 'Warm, too. Norra ghost in sight . . . is the moon up yet?'

There was no answer for a moment, then the perambulator was pushed roughly aside and Donny catapulted into the tent. His eyes were round and black with fear and his normally ruddy face was very pale. 'I were gettin' chilly,' he announced, heaving the perambulator back across the doorway. 'The wind's gettin' up pretty strong now. Come on, shove over, lemme have some blanket.'

Deirdre toyed with the idea of saying *told you so*, but dismissed it. She merely rolled over so that Donal could have half the blanket and said in a small voice: 'Tell me when to blow out the candle.'

Donal grunted, 'Don't know as you need; it'll last the night out.'

'Right, we'll leave it then,' Deirdre said. Outside, she knew, the beach would be huge and cold and empty, with the moon shining down on it and God knew what coming up out of the water to stare at their little tent. She could hear the wind—she was sure it was only the wind—beginning to whine and gust, but so long as the denizens of the deep only stared at the little tent and didn't try to get inside . . .

'Wonder whether Ellen's home yet,' she said a little later. 'An' Tolly, of course.'

'Dunno,' Donal droned, his voice heavy with sleep. 'Goo'night, Dee.'

'Goo'night, Donny.'

Peace reigned in the makeshift tent.

*   *   *

It hadn't been as bad as Ellen had feared, for when Tolly did catch her up he was truly sorry that he had sent her off, even if he didn't quite understand her flight.

'Ellen, I reckon I behaved real bad, an' when you run off I were that afraid you'd run into the quicksands,' he said, panting and breathless, but clinging to her arm and refusing to let her break free. 'I never should have told you what I did, and it were nice kissin' you, course it was, it's just that . . . oh, I believe I'm scared of the whole business . . . fallin' in love, marryin', havin' kids. And I did want you to understand why I was goin' to join a ship. You're me best pal, the only person I could tell about . . . about how I am. An' . . . an' when I get meself sorted you'll be the first to know, I promise.'

'It was my fault,' Ellen said, falling into step beside him. Tolly might never be more than her good friend but she preferred that to losing him altogether. 'I only meant to help . . . but I should have known better'n to encourage you to . . . Oh, let's forget it, shall we? I could do wi' that cuppa, I'm tellin' you, after all that runnin' along the beach.'

'Right; an' I'll mug you to a cake an' all,' Tolly said remorsefully. 'Oh Ellen, will you forgive me? Wharra way to behave!'

'Course I will. An' I'll write to you, too, when you're at sea,' Ellen said. 'Tell you what's goin' on at home, like. Keep you up to date wi' things.'

'You'll not stay in the hospital though, I guess,' Tolly said. Ellen tried not to show her surprise at this shrewd remark. 'I been thinkin' for a while now that you'd not stick it for much longer. It's that Crawford; you can't do your job proper wi' Sisters like her on the wards. Most of us have felt that way.'

'But what the dickens can I do to get away from her?' Ellen said. 'I'm stuck wi' the woman, from wharr I can see.'

'No you ain't. You could ask for a transfer; go to Matron an' explain that you've been on female medical for six months an' would like wider

288

experience,' Tolly said at once. 'They like a nurse to want wider experience, I'm tellin' you, it works nine times out o' ten.'

'An' I'm tellin' you that if it don't work I'm out,' Ellen said. 'Oh, Tolly, you may not believe me, but I'm downright glad we've had this talk. I feel a lot better about it now—about work, about you, about almost everything.'

'Me, too,' Tolly said. 'I handed in me notice this evenin', and at the end o' the week I'm goin' to put me name down as cabin staff aboard one o' the big liners.' He gave her arm an affectionate squeeze. 'But I couldn't go until I'd explained to you what I was goin' to do an' why,' he finished.

'I'm sure you're doin' the right thing, but you'll miss your music, an' the Army,' Ellen said rather helplessly. Having listened to what Tolly had been saying she realised that this was a problem which only he could solve, but she knew how desperately she would miss him.

'Yes, course I will. But I reckon I'll miss you worst,' Tolly told her. 'And I'll make new friends. Salvationists are everywhere, they say. An' . . . an' mebbe I'll sort meself out, Ellen, once I'm away from the Pool.'

'I'm sure you will,' Ellen said insincerely. She still didn't really understand just what Tolly thought was the matter, but she had sufficient sensitivity to realise that her friend was doing his best to be fair to everyone, herself included. 'You'll be fine, Tolly, just you see.'

Having got back more or less on their old footing, the two of them walked along the beach, then went inland to the tea-room they had already selected. They had an enjoyable meal and in telling

289

her all about how he meant to see the world, Tolly dispelled any last lingering traces of embarrassment between them and soon they were laughing and teasing each other as though the episode on the beach had never happened.

Though not quite as though it had never happened, Ellen thought ruefully as they climbed back aboard the train. They had kissed and she had a shrewd feeling that such a kiss should have changed their relationship in some way, made them more . . . well, perhaps more *aware* was the closest she could get. And it hadn't. She was still fonder of Tolly than anyone else she knew, but she understood, at last, that she must wait and let him find out just what it was he wanted. If it was her . . . oh, how marvellous that would be! But if it wasn't she would have to learn to live with it.

They reached the pier head when the street lamps were all being lit and went back to Heyworth Street on the first tram to come along. Then Tolly saw her to her door, saying a very sweet good-night to her on the pavement, and when, at the last minute, he caught her shoulders and kissed her brow, she smiled up at him and tried to pretend that the chaste salute was all she had ever expected from him.

'Thanks for a lovely evening, Tolly,' she said as she let herself into the house. 'See you tomorrer.'

It was quite late so she went very quietly into the kitchen . . . to find herself abruptly in the midst of a drama.

Ada was sitting at the table, whilst a policeman, with his helmet on his knee, sat opposite her, writing in his notebook. Ozzie was leaning against the mantelpiece with his hands dug into his trouser pockets, Fred was making a pot of tea and Bertie was toasting bread at the stove. Everyone looked round as she entered the room.

'Mam? What's up?'

'Oh, Ellen . . . the twins . . . they've run away!'

'They haven't run away, our mam, don't say such things, they've just gone off on the spree, little divils, I'll corpse 'em when I see 'em.' That was Ozzie, scowling and furious.

'No use carryin' on, ma'am. Kids is kids, they'll turn up like bad pennies when they're hungry,' the policeman said. 'Give us that there note, I'll read it to the young leddy, see if she can help at all.'

Ada handed over a scrumpled bit of paper and the policeman read it aloud. *'Dear Mam, Took me next Week's Wages from the Pot so we can go to the Seaside. See you when our Grub runs out, Love Ds.'*

'Oh, Mam, the little blighters, worryin' you so,' Ellen said wrathfully. 'But they'll be all right—you know the twins, they always fall on their feet.'

'Or someone else's,' Bert said. 'They took all the grub they could lay their filthy little paws on, an' all. I had to go out for fish an' chips afore I could have me tea.'

'What we're wantin' to know is which seaside they mean?' the policeman said. 'Any idea, miss?'

Ellen shook her head. 'No, sergeant . . . sorry. It could be anywhere. If they'd the money I reckon it 'ud be New Brighton . . . how much did they take, Mam?'

'A half crown,' Ada said. 'Oh, I'm that worried, Ellie! They're nothin' but a couple of babes in some ways . . . suppose . . . suppose . . .'

'They'll march in here in another hour or so, demandin' their supper an' sayin' they'd not

291

realised how late it had got,' Ozzie said. 'They won't stay out all night, our mam, they ain't that daft.'

'They took the tent,' Ada wailed. 'An' the old pram. An' the woollen blanket off Deirdre's bed, an' food, an' . . .'

'The tent?' Ellen said slowly. 'That old tent we made for 'em, wi' sheets an' the clothes prop an' that?'

Ada nodded, tears running from her red-rimmed eyes and dappling the table top before her. 'That's right, the old tent. Oh, Ellie, they could be strangled in their beds, drownded, ate by wild animals . . .'

'Mam, pull yourself together!' Bertie said sharply. 'Who's goin' to strangle the pair of 'em, eh? Not that I'd mind doin' it meself,' he added. 'But a stranger . . . well, they'd marmelise anyone tryin', wouldn't you say?'

Ada, sniffing, agreed that she had forgotten that the twins had a sharp way with outsiders, but even so, they were only little children . . .

'Little children?' Fred said. 'Little hell-raisers, more like. Anythin' what eats them two's got a digestion like an ostrich. Now come on, Mam, gi's a smile an' dry your eyes. Cryin' won't help.'

'No, and I don't think it's necessary . . .' Ellen began, to be interrupted immediately.

'Not necessary, when me kids are missin'? Oh, Ellen, you can be so hard!'

'Mam, I think I know where they are,' Ellen said. Light had dawned as soon as her mother had mentioned the tent. 'I think they're down on Seaforth Sands. Tolly an' me went down there for a . . . a walk, an' I sort of half noticed a white, home-

292

made tent right up at the top of the beach. I saw two kids . . . only I were too far away to see their faces . . . they were roastin' somethin' over a little fire . . . Mam, I'm *sure* it was Deirdre and Donal. We'll fetch 'em in no time, now we know where they are.'

The policeman closed his notebook and got to his feet. 'Well, there we are,' he said genially. 'Mystery solved, Mrs Docherty. In a white tent on the foreshore, you say? I'll get the Seaforth fellows on the telephone at once and they'll turn out and fetch your youngsters home wi' a flea in their ears. Don't you worry, you'll be puttin' them to bed in a couple of hours—and tellin' them not to do it again, I trust an' hope.'

'Oh I will, sergeant,' Ada said fervently. 'I really, really will!'

*   *   *

Deirdre woke. She couldn't remember where she was, but she was cold and there was a funny sort of noise. She sighed and opened her eyes. It was dark, but she could see something white which billowed and moved towards her . . .

Her shriek brought Donal sitting bolt upright beside her, wide-eyed. 'Wharris it?' he squeaked. 'Whassamarrer? Where is we?'

'Oh, Jeez, it's the bleedin' tent, we're on the sands in the tent,' Deirdre said, trying to calm her wildly thumping heart. 'I forgot where we was an' all, Donny, an' then the side o' the tent blowed towards me an' I thought it were a ghost . . .'

'The candle . . . who put the candle out?' Donal hissed. 'Ah, what's *that?*'

There was a faint light within the tent; moonlight shining down on them, Deirdre supposed, and now that her eyes had grown accustomed to it she could make out details. The perambulator across the entrance, the pile of their belongings . . .

'Aaaeeeaah!' Deirdre shrieked. Movement, slow, creeping movement, something coming towards her . . . 'Aaaeeeaah!'

She tried to scramble out of her blanket, sinking both hands in the sand as she did so . . . and saw that the creeping movement was water. Only water. A shining flood of it, moving across the sand, slowly engulfing everything. The candle was actually bobbing on the ripples she had caused by her movement and the blanket was wet round the edges. The only safe place was in the perambulator or up on the slight rise where she had spread their bed.

Donal had followed her lead and now they stood, side by side, grimly contemplating their surroundings.

'We'll have to up sticks,' Donal said at last, bending to pick up the now soggy blanket. 'Shove all the dry stuff in the pram, Dee, an' we'll just have to cart the rest. Come on, we'll have the tent down in a jiffy if we gerra move on.'

Deirdre picked up a pile of stuff and staggered with it over to the perambulator, shoved it on top of the apron and bent and looked outside. Then, wide-eyed, she turned to her brother. 'Oh, Donny, there's water all round us,' she quavered. 'Waves, an' all. They're almost as far as the prom . . . what'll we do?'

Donal joined her and peered out. Then he said: 'Right, we'll have to leave the tent, but we'll try to get the pram ashore. Come on!'

Deirdre followed him, gripping the perambulator firmly. She could swim, but nowhere near as strongly as her brother, and she had never swum at night, nor in the sort of sea which was sending waves at them in such profusion. And not all from one direction, either. They seemed actually to be coming in from the shore, though that was surely impossible?

She mentioned it to Donal, who said that it wasn't impossible at all, unfortunately. 'It's a very high tide,' he said. 'The waves are agin' the wall up there, before they's spent their strength, so they're bein' pushed out to sea agin to break. Look, Dee, there's gonna be a sort o' undertow, a current like. It'll pull you about a bit once we start into the water, so be prepared, an' hang on tight to the bleedin' pram. An' don't *worry*, 'cos I'll tek care of you. Right?'

'Right,' Deirdre said resolutely. She was too young to die, she reminded herself firmly and anyway, God wouldn't let a bit of fun end in tragedy—would He? No, course He wouldn't, everyone knew that He loved little children. And Deirdre, who, an hour earlier, would have denied indignantly being a little child, found that she was a very little child indeed when it came to facing the waves and the possibility—oh Gawd, oh Gawd—of death by drowning.

'Right. Off we go, then,' Donal said, unaware of Deirdre's silent soliloquy. 'An' don't forget—hang on to the bleedin' pram unless I tells you to leggo!'

Together, pushing the pram, they stepped off the soggy strip of raised sand ... and both gave a muffled scream. There was no question of hanging

295

on to the pram for either of them since as they plunged into the water a wave seized it and tore it from their grasp, at the same time taking Deirdre's legs from under her.

'Back ... get back ...' she heard Donal say frantically and scrabbled desperately to obey him. But it was too late. She was in the water, pushed around at the waves' whim, choking, gasping, forgetting everything she had learned, desperate only to find solid ground beneath her feet. She heard Donal's voice behind her, counselling, advising, then the black water closed over her head, filled her ears, tried to force its way into her mouth and nose. She fought desperately as the undertow tore at her, and for a blissful second her head emerged from the water and she gasped a mixed lungful of air and spray, then she was down again, down, down, down ... and something heavy hit her, tangled with her legs ... and she realised that she had no idea, any longer, which was up, or where the surface was. She continued to struggle, feebly, till consciousness left her.

*   *   *

One minute Donal had been hanging on to the perambulator, the next it had gone and so had Deirdre. He screamed at her to come back, then to swim ... then he plunged in after her.

He had never experienced anything like that undertow, however, and it took him all his time just to keep his head above the increasingly turbulent waves. He turned wistfully towards higher ground where he could still see the tent, just about standing, then to face the breakers once more. He couldn't go without Deirdre! He thought he saw her head break the surface to seaward, so he began slogging grimly in that direction, but in his heart he thought it was too late. We're goners, he thought, and was surprised at his own acceptance that this time they had overstepped the mark between adventure and total danger. Poor Mam, when the scuffers come round tomorrer and tell her her kids is drowned-dead, she'll be that upset.

But you shouldn't ever say die, Donal reminded himself, and kept on swimming.

*   *   *

'There's the tent . . . I hope to God they're still in it, though it must be a foot under water . . . what in heaven's name is that little black thing? Did you see it, then, in the trough of that wave?'

The first policeman, the man who had spoken, didn't wait for anyone to answer his question but began to heave off his heavy boots and to unbutton his cape.

'It's a little boat . . . no, it's a perishin' perambulator,' the second policeman said. He, too, began to take off his outer clothing. 'Bert, go and get the lifeboat out. I'll just check that pram. Give us the line.'

With no more ado he seized a length of line which another policeman was busy securing to a bollard and jumped into the water. The second policeman followed, then the third. The first policeman reached the pram and grabbed it, then they both turned for the shore once more.

*   *   *

'I reckon you're the two luckiest kids in the whole world,' the policeman told Donal and Deirdre, still very subdued after their ordeal, as they drove home in a cab. The policemen had stripped off their soaking clothes, rubbed them briskly dry, given them a hot drink from a flask, wrapped them in blankets and despatched them back home, with a sergeant to help with the explanations. 'If we hadn't happened along you'd ha' been dead meat, you know that, I suppose?'

'If Donny hadn't grabbed me be the scruff of me neck and made me hang on to the pram I'd ha' been a goner,' Deirdre said, through chattering teeth. 'I'd gone down an' down . . .' She broke off with a strong shudder.

Donal, sitting next to her in the cab, grinned palely at her and unwound his blanket to give her a consoling punch on the shoulder. 'Nah, you'd ha' struggled on somehow,' he said cheerfully. 'You're too bad to die young, Dee! 'Sides, the last time you come up you was right under the pram; you'd ha' caught aholt of it wharrever I did, I reckon.'

'I was too cold an' scared,' Deirdre said honestly. 'I don't swim too good either. Well, not in waves an' in the dark,' she added, not wishing Donal to remember the remark the next time he was off to the scaldy with his pals. 'Oh, Gawd, the pram!'

'What about it?' the policeman said.

'It's what our mam an' our Ellen takes the littl'uns out in,' Deirdre said in an anguished tone. 'Sammy's seven, he can walk, but Toby's only five an' he needs a lift now an' then. An' it's real useful for messages,' she added wistfully. 'Easier to push a sack of coal or a big bag o' spuds than to carry 'em,

I'm tellin' you.'

'Well, it may not be up to much be now,' the policeman admitted. 'But I saw one of me pals towin' it in towards the beach after we'd got the pair of you on dry land. Mebbe it'll still be usable.'

'But if it's on the beach, someone'll bleedin' steal it,' Deirdre wailed, sitting forward as though she was contemplating leaping from the cab and running back to Seaforth Sands. 'Oh, me lovely pram . . . me mam'll slaughter us for losin' it!'

'Your mam will be so glad to get you back she'll not trouble about the pram,' the policeman said. 'I just hope you'll t'ink twice before runnin' away again.'

'Runnin' away? We wasn't runnin' away,' Donal said, rather perplexed. 'We leaved a note tellin' 'em we'd gone to the seaside; we said we'd go home again when the grub ran out. That's not runnin' away, that's just havin' a bit o' fun.'

'You din't say which seaside, for a start. And if you go off, a couple of bits of kids like you, wi' just a home-made tent an' a perambulator, what's folk expected to think? No, you're runaways to the police, I'm tellin' you. You could be in big trouble for wastin' police time, I dare say.'

'We din't ask you to come chasin' after us,' Deirdre said, ruffling up. And then, deflating, she added: 'But we're glad you did, though. Ain't we, Donny?'

'Yeah, course we are,' Donal said. 'But I don't mind tellin' you, I'm not lookin' forward to facin' Mam, an' the fellers, an' Ellen.'

CHAPTER TEN

If it hadn't been for the war, Maggie thought the day after it had been declared, nothing would have changed. She would have gone on living happily with the Nolans, Liam would have stayed with the Post Office and eventually the two of them would have married, hopefully in peace and harmony.

But the war changed all that, though not in the way one might have thought. Maggie's life changed because the headlines had caught her and Liam off guard.

The two of them had been going out for the best part of six months, but they had never allowed any member of the Nolan family to know how things stood. Maggie felt it would be unwise, though she was not sure precisely why, and Liam went along with it, though occasionally he did point out that there was no real need for such secrecy.

'If Mammy knew we were plannin' marriage, she might pay you a bit more, so our savin's would grow quicker,' he said. 'Or if she didn't like that idea, you could get a proper job. I know she'll say we're too young to be thinkin' of marriage, but I'm earnin' a good wage now, so I am, an' if we save like fun we could name the day in . . . what, three years?'

Maggie thought three years was an awful long time to wait, but she knew better than to say so. It was supposed to be the fellers who found it hard to wait, not girls, but in her heart she knew—or thought she knew—that her feelings for Liam were stronger than his feelings for her. He had only asked her out the first time, she suspected, because he didn't want her going with other fellers. So she said that three years would soon pass and she would save, too, and there was the money she earned from helping Mrs Collins . . . and life jogged along very comfortably. Until the fourth of August, that was.

On Bank Holiday Monday the Nolans usually had a day out. This year, Liam fancied a day out without the kids around him. As was their habit, they had left the house after the evening service on Sunday and headed for Phoenix Park. They would walk there until it was dark and then they would go quietly back to the Liberties and find somewhere secluded for a cuddle.

So it was sitting on a bench which backed on to a holly hedge that Liam made his suggestion. 'A whole day to ourselves, from early mornin' until late evenin', alanna,' he coaxed. 'Just you an' me . . . we'll find out where Mammy an' the kids is goin' and we'll go somewhere different. Aw, c'mon, just the two of us!'

'They're goin' to Howth, on the train,' Maggie said at once, having been told by the twins a thousand times what their plans were. 'But your mammy needs me . . . and I do enjoy a family outing, so I do. Your mammy won't tek kindly to me backin' out of such a day.'

'Oh, I'll fix Mammy. We'll tell her you're goin' to visit Aileen and her feller, and that I'm off on a fishin' trip wit' me pal Olly Moss, but really we'll go to Booterstown. Tell Mammy that as Aileen's elder sister you feel bound to see the feller she's goin' to marry in his own surroundings,' Liam said, inspired. 'Mammy's a great one for a good match,
301

she'll understand you don't want your sister mixin' up wit' someone unsuitable.'

Aileen had a feller, someone who worked in the house with her. She had fetched him into Dublin one afternoon and Mrs Nolan told Maggie that she might entertain the young couple to tea and scones if she did the necessary, so Maggie had cooked and cleaned and told the twins to keep out of the way and let Ticky play with the Farrell kids, first giving Kate Farrell a bag of buns to keep them all out of mischief. And then her entertainment had started.

Aileen's Pat was the garden boy. He was large and lumpish and given to giggling, but he seemed good-natured and he certainly adored Aileen. He watched her as she moved about the room, never taking his eyes off her, and he agreed with every word she said—it was downright boring, Maggie thought, though Aileen clearly loved it. And after meeting Pat, though Maggie had fully intended to tell her sister about Liam, she found that she no longer wanted to do so. Liam's thin, intelligent face and quick movements would have made poor Pat look even slower and more lumpish, and Aileen seemed perfectly happy with Pat's affection, and to have no regrets over her suitor's lowly position in life or his obvious lack of mental agility. Though she had said something which rather puzzled her sister when Pat had taken himself off to the backyard for the usual purpose and the girls were left together for a moment.

'Course, he ain't like the Master,' Aileen had murmured, giving Maggie a sly glance from under her lashes. 'But he's a capable gardener, so Master's goin' to give us twenty guineas when we

302

wed . . . an' more, he says, when the babies come.'

'Oh? Are you going to keep on working, then?' Maggie asked, thinking that this was a very strange arrangement indeed. 'I didn't know the quality employed married maids.'

'They will for a bit,' Aileen assured her. 'Until the babies come. The double wages will be a help, and . . .' another of those sly, through-the-lashes looks . . . 'it'll be easier for the Master, like.'

But just then Pat came back and the kettle boiled and in the excitement of making tea and talking, Maggie forgot about Aileen's mysterious master. In fact, she hadn't given the matter another thought until that Sunday evening when it had occurred to her to repeat the conversation and to ask Liam, who was so much wiser and more worldly than she, what it was all about.

When she had finished her recital Liam had put his arm round her waist and given her a squeeze. 'Sure an' aren't you a simpleton?' he had said lazily. 'Your sister's havin' a gay old time wit' her master, an' if anythin' happens, there's slow ole Pat to pick up the pieces. In a manner of speakin', like.'

'Oh, Liam, what on earth do you mean? Pick up what pieces?' Maggie had asked crossly. Sometimes her ignorance weighed her down, so it did. 'And Aileen's a maid, she can't have a gay old time wit' anyone, can she?'

Liam sighed and looked around him; there was no one in sight so he bent over her and kissed her mouth. It was lovely, Maggie adored being kissed, but she knew better than to let it go on too long. That way lay trouble of a sort which, no matter how ignorant she might be, Maggie was eager to avoid. Disgrace, she thought vaguely. Pointing fingers.

303

And pushed Liam reluctantly back from her.

'There! Now whenever I start to have a gay ole time wit' you, you shove me away,' Liam said. ''Cos if you was to get into trouble there wouldn't be any dull ole Pat to pick up the pieces. See?'

'Ooh! Do you mean to tell me . . . are you tryin' to say . . .' stammered Maggie. 'Ooh, Liam, d'you mean Aileen an' the master . . . but he's an old feller . . . that can't be what she meant . . . can it?'

'It's what she meant, sure as eggs is eggs,' Liam said. 'An' if she trusts any ole feller wit' her honour like that, she's not as clever as she looks. Fellers like that, they turn round afterwards an' swear it weren't them an' not a penny piece will they part wit'. I'm tellin' you, Maggie, she's playin' a dangerous game.'

'If you're right, she is,' Maggie said slowly. 'Only that Pat—he worships the ground she walks on, so he does. I'm tellin' you, he'd marry her whatever she might have done. So she'll be all right, won't she, Liam?'

Her tone was worried and Liam hastened to reassure her. 'Indeed she will,' he said. 'And so would you be, for wouldn't I marry you like a shot if there was a baby on the way, me darlin' girl?'

'Ye-es, but it's not a good idea to have babies holdin' you back from the start,' Maggie pointed out. 'You said yourself . . .'

'I know I did,' Liam groaned. 'But don't I wish we could tell Mammy about us, acushla. Then we wouldn't have to wait so long to wed, because you could earn a dacint little sum at a proper job and 'tis time Mammy was realisin' it, so it is.'

'But suppose she thought I should live somewhere else?' Maggie said uncertainly.

304

'Suppose she says me board an' lodgin' is paid for by me workin' for her? Because it's true, I suppose, Liam me love.'

'After your mammy died she said your home would always be wit' us,' Liam had reminded her. 'Sides, you won't stop workin' for her just because you've got another job—you work now, on the market stalls.'

'Yes, but only when they're mortal busy, an' I can spare the time from the house an' the kids . . . but I suppose you're right,' Maggie said, having thought it over. 'I could earn eight bob a week in the lemonade factory, so they say.'

'Or more in one of the posh stores on O'Connell Street,' Liam supplied, grinning. He knew how Maggie loved those stores. 'We'll tell Mammy before Christmas, shall we? That we're savin' up to get wed, I mean. Why, she'll be really pleased, I'm sure, especially if you're workin' in a store by then and bringin' in good money. She's always on at me to start lookin' for a girl.'

'Well, right, we'll tell her at Christmas,' Maggie had said, getting to her feet. 'And if you really t'ink it'll be all right, I'll tell her I'm goin' to see Aileen and you say you're off fishin' wit' Olly. After all, she can only say "no", and she does know that Aileen's the only sister I've got now.'

But Liam certainly understood some things about his mother, for she had not hesitated when Maggie, without a blush, had said she wanted to go and see Aileen and Pat at their place of work.

'You go off, it's your duty,' she said approvingly. 'Tis time the older lads looked after the younger ones for a change, and it'll give you a real break, so it will. What time will you be home, Maggie? Our train gets in sixish; it would be nice if tea was ready for say, half-past the hour.'

Oh, well, Maggie told herself, when she heard Mrs Nolan telling Liam to enjoy his fishing, it wasn't the end of the world. It would mean leaving the seaside before the warm dusk had made much cuddling possible—Maggie belonged to the school of thought which considered kissing by daylight to be beyond the pale—but they would have had the best of the day.

Liam, when she told him, said robustly that he didn't care what his mammy said, she would be home by ten and that was an end to it. 'You can say you missed the train, or that you had to stay on longer to have a word wit' Aileen's mistress,' he said. 'Old skinflint—home in time to get the tea for half-past six, indeed!'

*   *   *

The twins had had an enjoyable day at the seaside, for though they missed Maggie and Liam, their two elders would undoubtedly have kept very much better order than Mammy and Kenny managed. In fact, Seamus and Garvan had managed to squeeze the maximum enjoyment out of their day, which meant that they had early abandoned their mother and Ticky and gone off along the beach by themselves, indulging in a number of pranks which Liam and Maggie would have instantly put a stop to had they been around. They flattened a number of castles, causing the builders thereof—small, dirty-faced brats with pudding-basin haircuts and runny noses—to scream with rage and disappointment, whilst indignant parents—in one case a hefty docker, which wasn't so funny—scrambled in pursuit of them, shouting threats and curses into the warm afternoon air.

Then they had gone nicking. First, it was a couple of real good spades to dig with. Fellers of fourteen had better things to do than dig sandcastles, of course, but they liked cockles, and they liked damming streams and making a canal which stretched half-way across the beach.

'I wouldn't mind bein' a navvy, Shay,' Garvan said at one point, as the water came rushing creamily along their canal. 'Machinery's good, too. I wouldn't mind doin' somethin' wit' machinery.'

'Well, we're supposed to be lookin' for jobs, Garv,' Seamus pointed out. 'But there isn't much navvyin' around Dublin right now. Nor many machinery makers.'

'You have to go to England to navvy, or to America,' Garvan said. 'What about the Navy, like our daddy?'

'Dunno. Shall us get somethin' to eat now?'

There were picnic parties all over the sands. It wasn't difficult to help themselves from an open basket or a child's hand as they passed, and then to speed on their way, cramming their gobs with stolen sandwich or cake, laughing like maniacs, spraying crumbs.

'Half the fellers on this beach is after our blood,' Seamus remarked after they had slaked their thirst with ginger-beer bought with the coins which had scattered from a fat man's pocket. They had scattered because the fat man had jumped to his feet to prevent them from snatching his small daughter's slice of porter cake. 'We'd best walk back along the prom.'

307

'We'll comb our hair first,' Garvan said. 'Comb it straight back, like this . . . wet it wit' seawater . . . then do up your shirt buttons . . . Now we'll pass muster.'

And oddly enough, they did. They didn't need to go back along the prom but walked at the very edge of the little waves and even stopped and spoke— kindly—to one of the children they had robbed. Unrecognised with shirts on and with tidy hair, they listened—sympathetically—to the story of the bad boys who had robbed the child of her new red spade.

When they got back to their own particular part of the beach, Mammy fed them on the lovely sandwiches and cake and lemonade which Maggie had so carefully packed up for them. The twins ate, because they were always hungry, and lolled on the sand and wondered aloud how Maggie was getting on.

'She's seein' her sister Aileen,' Mrs Nolan reminded them. 'That girl, that Aileen, she's no better than she should be, I wouldn't wonder. She's marryin' a feller who works at the house, though. Maggie's a good sister, she's checkin' that all's well there.'

Garvan and Seamus did not even exchange glances; they did not need to. They knew that Maggie and Liam were courting and very little they thought of it, but they would never have told their mammy. The twins were not often good, but at keeping secrets they were excellent. And besides, they were terrible fond of Maggie, so they were, and they liked Liam pretty well too, considering. They saw no reason why their mother should not approve, yet they both realised that she would not.

The twins recognised that their mammy considered Maggie to be several rungs further down the ladder than the Nolans, which meant she would not wish Maggie and Liam to court one another. So they just nodded when Mammy talked of Maggie visiting her sister and wondered silently, between themselves, where she and Liam would have gone today.

At going home time, however, they had by no means exhausted the pleasures of the seaside.

'Mrs O'Farrell is further up the beach, wit' Biddy an' Eileen,' Garvan said, panting, as he and his brother arrived back from yet another expedition along the shore. 'Mrs O'Farrell says we can go home wit' them, later on. They'll give us tea, she says.'

This blatant lie was easily swallowed by their mammy, who regarded the O'Farrells with awe and envy. Mr O'Farrell was a headmaster, no less, and Mrs O'Farrell, who had once been ordinary little Rosie Allen and had lived in a tenement not ten minutes from where the twins' mammy had been brought up, now had a maidservant and held 'At homes', which were the envy of her peers. Biddy and Eileen O'Farrell were thirteen and fifteen and plain as pikestaffs, with knobbly knees, large feet and stringy hair, but they were considered by the entire neighbourhood as 'little ladies' and Mrs Nolan was keen to be on good terms with the family.

'The O'Farrells?' Mrs Nolan said therefore, craning her neck and peering back along the beach. 'Where? Ah, I see them. Yes, of course you may stay with them, if you're sure they don't mind. You've got your return tickets?'

They had. They assured their parent that Mrs O'Farrell had been very keen for them to join the party.

'Hmm. I wonder if it might be better if I went along and spoke to them myself,' Mrs Nolan mused, giving Seamus a nasty moment, though Garvan's expression did not alter. 'After all, we *were* friends at school, Rosie an' meself.'

'Well, you could,' Garvan said judiciously at once. 'But they're a good way off, Mammy, right round the point there. And didn't you say you wanted to catch the six-ten train? You've only got ten minutes, you know . . . I spotted a clock as we came back along the shore.'

Kenny, who had been snoozing, woke up, sneezed and said that in that case they had all better get a move on and began to gather their things together.

Seamus was really impressed with his twin's coolheadedness. He watched his mother drying Ticky's little wet feet and cramming them into his hand-me-down boots, and scrabbling round to repack the remnants of food, the teapot, the cups, and trying to hurry all the while, with the thought of walking up the beach to see the O'Farrells gone as completely from her head as frost in June sunshine.

And when, presently, he and Garvan walked up the beach with them and waved them off, he saw a clock himself and turned to his twin. 'It's six o'clock now; the clock you saw earlier must have been fast,' he said. 'Good job!'

Garvan gave him a chilly look. 'Clock? What clock? I saw no clock,' he said. 'But I didn't want Mammy chasin' up the O'Farrells; did you?'

310

'No,' Seamus said. 'You'll not be a navvy nor a machinery feller, Garv. You'll be right up there at the top of the heap, so you will!'

Garvan gave his thin, unamused smile. 'Mebbe,' he said. 'We'll do it together, whatever, Shay.'

* * *

And so they had their glorious day together, though they caught an earlier train than Liam liked.

'I won't put your mammy's back up and make her cross when it's not askin' too much of us to get back a bit early,' Maggie insisted steadfastly as they walked down towards the beckoning blue sea. 'If I'm back and wit' the tea made she'll be pleased wit' me an' life will be a lot easier, so it will.'

So they made their way homeward with a feeling of quiet contentment, at least on Maggie's part, because they had had such a glorious day. It had been as though they were both children again, but with that special glow that being in love brings. Together, they had explored the shore, walking, paddling, collecting shells. They had dug a huge sandcastle and filled its moat with seawater, found flat pebbles to skim over the calm ocean, laughed at each other's efforts. Because the day was so warm and sunny Maggie soon dispensed with her jacket and sandals and strolled beside Liam, in his open-necked shirt and flannels, quite comfortable in her thin cotton dress, and found herself absurdly pleased when they were snapped by a beach photographer.

'It'll be a reminder of the wonderful day we've had together, only we mustn't let your Mammy see it,' Maggie said.

'No indeed,' Liam replied. 'She thinks we're up to quite different games today. It'd right put the cat in among the pigeons, so it would.'

When hunger had driven them from the beach they had licked ices, drunk ginger-beer and eaten a variety of seaside goodies—winkles, hooked from their shells with a pin, fat pink shrimps, cockles, bursting with flavour. The hot August sun had shone on them and they had both begun to glow from its warmth. 'Especially on me nose an' me forehead,' Maggie said ruefully, as they climbed aboard the train which would take them back to Dublin. 'Oh, but it's been the most wonderful day of me entire life, Liam! I'm so glad we did it!'

The carriages were full of other home-going people, many with small children. Liam squeezed Maggie's hand discreetly as they stood in the corridor, swaying to the rhythm of the train, happy to stand because you could get closer that way. Then, in the crush, he put both arms round her and drew her to him, so that had one fallen the other would have been dragged down as well. But they didn't fall, they simply clung, smiling blissfully, and enjoyed the journey.

They got off the train still dizzy with happiness, and headed for home, just two tiny cogs in the milling crowds, but two very happy little cogs, Maggie thought, clutching Liam's arm so that they didn't get separated. 'What a day it's been,' she breathed. 'Oh Liam . . .'

'We'll not need to split up today and go home separate, since it's not even six o'clock yet and Mammy said they'd not be back until half-past the hour,' Liam said, cuddling her hand against his side. 'If you'd not been so stubborn, Maggie McVeigh, we could still be on the beach! Still, perhaps it's better . . .'

He stopped short, tugging Maggie to a stop too, and stood on tiptoe. 'Well, would you believe it! Can ye see the fly-sheets, Mags? It looks like . . . it looks like . . .' He began to move again, tugging her along with him. 'We'll get a bit closer before I go jumpin' to conclusions.'

They reached a newspaper vendor, who was selling papers as though they were hot cakes. To Maggie's astonishment Liam handed over his coppers and held the front page of the paper in front of her eyes. Wordlessly, he pointed.

'War!' Maggie gasped. 'Well, I never did! Is it true, d'you suppose, Liam? Are we really at war wit' Germany?'

'We are. And they'll want every fit man to fight, so they will,' Liam said. 'Will I be called upon, I wonder?'

'No! Liam, you can't go, your mammy needs you, and the others too. And meself, of course. The good Lord alone knows where it will end.'

Liam folded the paper and put an arm round Maggie's waist. 'Come on, let's hurry. I'll give you a hand wit' the tea, then I'll mek meself scarce, come in later.'

'Oh Liam, you are good,' Maggie said breathlessly as they crossed the tenement hallway and began to climb the stairs. 'But you're not to think of goin' off to fight for the English—you've said enough t'ings about them these past twelve months, so why do it if you don't have to?'

'Oh, the English! Sure and it's not the English that I'm thinkin' of, but the Irish,' Liam assured

313

her. 'If I fight it'll be for the Irish—and for the King, of course. The King's a feller after me own heart—he's for Home Rule . . . everyone knows it.'

'Well, you're not likely to be meetin' the King if you go off to the war, only a lot of murderin' Germans,' Maggie said. 'Liam, promise me you won't do nothin' rash!'

They had reached the Nolan landing. Liam pulled her to a halt and glanced around him but the quiet was absolute, the sense of an empty house awaiting occupation complete. Slowly, luxuriously, he took her in his arms and began to kiss her, then to hug her so tightly that Maggie could scarcely breathe. 'I won't do anything you don't want me to,' he muttered against her ear. 'Let's go inside, pretend it's our own house and we're married folk. Look, Maggie, I might have to go for a soldier, so I might, just you remember that next time you push me away! I love you, alanna, and now we've got a moment alone, we could . . .'

'We mustn't. They might come home at any minute,' Maggie breathed as Liam pushed open the boys' bedroom door, but she did not break free of his hold and went meekly with him into the room. Her heart was thumping raggedly and her skin burned from the sun and salt wind, but she told herself that she would do nothing foolish, nothing wrong. Only it would be so nice to lie on the bed with Liam's arms around her and . . . and pretend a little.

They sat down on the bed and Liam, after some very mild caresses, began to push her gently backwards. Maggie, who had told herself that a cuddle lying down was surely no worse than a cuddle standing up, discovered that it was. It was

314

dangerous, she decided, tugging herself out of Liam's embrace. The thought of Liam going away, joining the army, made her want to . . . to give, but even lying on the outside of the bed, on the checkered counterpane, made her feel wanton and wicked, made her want something more. It was *not* the sort of thing that a sensible girl such as herself should do, she decided, struggling into a sitting position.

'Aw, c'mon, Maggie, just a few kisses,' wheedled Liam. 'Sure an' would I hurt a hair of your head now? Just relax a bit and . . .'

The bedroom door shot open. Kenny, red-faced, round-eyed, with his hair all on end, stared in at them. And before Liam had even got to his feet, Kenny had glanced over his shoulder and bawled at someone behind him, 'It's all right, Mammy, Maggie is home. She's in here, wit' Liam.'

*   *   *

It was one of the worst moments of Maggie's life, apart from when she'd learned about the tragedy in Dally Court. She sat there, with her hair half down and her face bright scarlet from embarrassment, shame and the sun, as helpless as a bird before a snake, whilst Mrs Nolan stared at her as though she could not believe her eyes.

Liam was the first to move. He got to his feet, smoothed down his clothing self-consciously and began to try to explain. 'It's war, Mammy, war's been declared! I . . . I met Maggie and we walked home together, we were talkin' . . .'

'Liam, what were you t'inkin' of? To behave so wit' a girl who's more like a sister to you than . . .'

315

'No, Mammy,' Liam said sharply. 'No! It wasn't what you t'ink. The truth is, me an' Maggie's been promised this twelve-month, only she's very young yet, an' not earnin' a proper wage here, so we thought we'd not say . . . there seemed no point in tellin' you until . . .'

'*What* did you say?' Mrs Nolan said in a dazed voice. 'I can't believe me own ears! Why Liam, an' I thought you were a young feller wit' a head on his shoulders.' She crossed the room and caught hold of Liam's hands, holding them in both hers, shaking her head and beginning to cry as she did so. 'Oh, what'll I do, wit' me children actin' like mad t'ings?' she said in a despairing voice. She turned away from Liam and seemed to notice Maggie for the first time. 'Out of here, madam, an' get Ticky cleaned up an' ready for his bed, then you can start on the tea,' she said, her voice very cold. 'I'm wantin' a private talk wit' me son.'

Maggie got to her feet and stumbled from the room, casting a last despairing glance at Liam as she closed the door behind her. She had known it would be bad, but had not dreamed Mrs Nolan would react so strongly. She wished she could have stayed, but Liam always said he could handle his mother. Now is his chance, Maggie thought. Oh, poor Liam!

*   *   *

Inside the boys' room, Mrs Nolan sat down on the bed and patted the place beside her. 'Sit down, Liam,' she said heavily. 'Now let me get this right. You're t'inkin' of marryin' Maggie McVeigh. My dear boy, my very dear son, Maggie McVeigh

316

comes from a poor slum family who've never had nothin'. If you'd a fancy for her ... well, I'd not approve, though I'd not forbid ye, either. Young men ... hot blood ... But marriage! Liam, I've fought an' worked an' scrimped to keep me kids fed an' clothed, to give you an education, a chance in life. What's more, I've been real good to Maggie, you can't deny that, but she's still just the little skivvy what takes care of ...'

'Skivvy? Mammy, Maggie's been more'n that to all of us. She brung the twins up, just about, an' she's been like a mammy to Ticky! And you can't call names on Mrs McVeigh now the poor woman's dead. She was poor, I grant you, because she had a *grosh* of kids; that's enough to hold anyone back, so it is.'

'Mrs McVeigh didn't have no self-control, that was her trouble,' Mrs Nolan said coldly. 'D'you think it was magic that kept me family small? Well, it weren't. It were because I was after havin' self-control an' common sense. And that's two things, Liam, which seem to have passed you by—control and common sense.'

'Oh, Mammy,' Liam said, outraged at such self-deception. 'It were bein' widowed young, that's what kept your family small. Self-control indeed!'

'How *dare* you speak like that to your mammy?' Mrs Nolan shouted. Twin flags of scarlet flew in her cheeks and her eyes seemed to burn through Liam with the strength of her scornful feelings. 'You, who've no doubt lain wit' a skivvy for your body's pleasure, havin' the cheek to come to me wit' talk of love, an' marryin' ... how dare you?'

'If you mean what I think you mean you're bloody well wrong!' Liam yelled, jumping to his feet. His own face was hot with rage now and his eyes reflected the scorn he had seen in his mother's glance. 'Maggie's a good girl, she's not in the fambly way, we're in love an' we're goin' to get married. That's what I said an' that's what I meant, no more, no less.'

'Over my dead body,' Mrs Nolan shrieked, jumping up as well. 'You'll not marry a pauper whiles I'm alive to prevent it.'

'And just how d'you intend to prevent it?' Liam roared. 'I'm a man, Mammy, not a lad to be persuaded or pushed about by you! I'm marryin' Maggie just as soon as we've enough saved.'

Mrs Nolan gave her son one last, furious glare, then walked swiftly towards the bedroom door. 'Then she's out of me house from this moment,' she said. 'What a serpent I've nurtured in me bosom ... but not a moment longer shall she spread her poison amongst me fine sons, not a moment! I don't care if she walks the streets or sleeps in a doorway, she'll not stay under this roof.'

'Mammy! Think what you're doin' before it's too late,' Liam shouted, amazed yet unbelieving. Surely his mother could not turn Maggie out, after all the girl had done for them? And what reason would she give neighbours, friends, when they asked? But his mother was clearly past reasoning with. She flew across the landing and pushed hard against the door of the small room which Maggie and Ticky still shared.

The door banged open and Maggie looked round, startled. Ticky, sitting on the bed whilst she washed his feet, did too. But his mother, Liam realised, was possessed by a fury so great that she could think of nothing else.

318

'Out!' she shrieked, pointing at Maggie. 'Get out of my house, you little whore!'

'Mammy, don't you dare use language like that about Maggie,' Liam shouted, scandalised. 'She's the best, most dacint . . . an' we've done nothin' like you t'ink, indeed we've not. Besides, what'll the neighbours think to hear you talk so?'

'Bugger the neighbours,' his mother said tersely. 'Did ye hear me, girl? Out of this house I say, this minute!'

'What . . . d'you mean, Mrs Nolan?' poor Maggie said, trying to pretend she had no idea what Liam's mother was talking about. 'I don't understand.'

'You! Schemin', connivin' behind me back . . . makin' up to me fine son . . .'

'Oh!' Maggie said. 'Oh, I *see*.' She stood up and looked steadily at Mrs Nolan across the space which separated them. 'Liam's told you we truly want to marry. Oh dear, oh dear, I told him you'd not like it, so I did.'

'Not *like* it? The boy's a fool,' Mrs Nolan said. 'To marry *you*, a nobody, a pauper, when he's a fine job an' everythin' goin' for him! I won't allow it, you shan't ruin his life.'

'Of course I shan't,' Maggie said soothingly. 'Besides, it'll be years before we can marry, Mrs Nolan. Shall you go an' sit down now an' I'll put the kettle on, make you a nice cup of tea?'

'You—will—get—out—of—this—house,' Mrs Nolan said, separating her words and saying each one with great distinctness. 'Out, out, OUT!'

'You've no right . . .' began Liam.

But his mother turned round so abruptly that she nearly knocked him over. 'Mind your business, Liam,' she said into his face. 'This is between me an' the girl here. You go an' put the kettle on, like Maggie said.'

'I'm not leavin' here until you apologise to Maggie an' say she may stay,' Liam said, though he could see the futility of it even as the words passed his lips. 'How can you behave so, Mammy, to someone who's worked so hard for our family all these years? Now tell Maggie you didn't mean a word of it and we can leave it a while and then have a quiet talk later.'

Maggie stood up, for she had been crouched down by Ticky's feet all the while the argument raged. Liam saw that she was pale beneath the sun-glow, but he could also see that she was angry now, and in control, no longer either shocked or surprised. 'Liam, take your Mammy into the kitchen . . . and Ticky, too, if you please. If I'm to leave I shall be busy for the next ten, fifteen minutes.' She lifted Ticky off the bed and stood him down on the landing, where he clutched Liam's leg, lips quivering, his gaze going from one face to the other.

'Don't you go packin' anythin' which don't belong to you,' Mrs Nolan said spitefully. 'God knows you've little enough, it shouldn't take you more than five minutes at most.'

'If I've little, it's because you've made sure I was so ill paid that I could never afford much,' Maggie said steadily. 'I'll take me clothing, me blanket, me picture and me books.'

'Your blanket? *Your* blanket? As I recall . . .'

'I'm taking the blanket to wrap the rest of me stuff in,' Maggie said. 'I'll bring it back if you like, but since I've slept wrapped up in it these past years, you'll not fancy it, I'm sure. A lady such as

320

yourself wouldn't want to use a blanket which has been wrapped around a skivvy like me. I'll give a knock on the kitchen door when I'm through.' Maggie didn't want to find herself accused of any theft other than that of stealing Liam's affections, and that seemed hard enough, so it did. But she knew she would have to have the coat for when winter came, and her thick shoes too. Pride was all very well, but she had bought that coat and those shoes with her own money and she would need them later on.

'I didn't say . . .' Mrs Nolan began aggressively— to find she was speaking to a closed door. 'Why, the little . . . how dare she shut the door in me face in me own house! I'll show her who's mistress here, she'll rue the day . . .'

But Liam had had enough. He caught his mother by the arm and literally dragged her, still mouthing off at the closed door, over to the kitchen. He shoved her into the room, then pushed Ticky in too and went and pulled the kettle over the fire. 'Well, I hope you're satisfied, for you wouldn't get Maggie to stay now if you prayed on bended knee,' he informed his still smouldering parent.

'Liam, me dearest son,' Mrs Nolan said. ''Tis for your sake I done it, surely you realise that? I can't—won't—have you goin' chasin' after the skivvy who scrubs me floors when you could have your pick o' women. Eh, I should have sent her packin' years ago, years ago.'

'Well, you've sent her packin' now,' Liam pointed out. 'An' I can't stand here argufyin' because I've a deal to do. I shan't be able to clear me room completely now, because I've a great many t'ings to pack, unlike Maggie, but if I start at once at least she an' me can leave together.'

'You? Leave? Don't be mad, boy, your life's here . . . you can't go chasin' after that little slut . . .'

Liam left the kitchen, shutting the door hard behind him. He was still shocked and sickened by what had happened. How could his mother have behaved the way she had? And now, to expect him to remain in the house after Maggie had been driven forth! What did his mammy really think Maggie could do, friendless as she was? All her family dead or far away, denied a decent schooling because she had to look after the Nolan kids, with only her part-time work on the market stalls to stand her in good stead. If the tragedy of Dally Court had never happened then at least the girl would have had a roof to go to, a family to help her, but as it was, she had nothing. Nobody.

Except for me, Liam reminded himself. He had taken a leaf out of Maggie's book and had spread his blanket out on the bed, and was filling it with clothing, shoes, books and other small possessions. The bigger things he would have to return for in a day or so . . . and now where would he go? No, he reminded himself, where shall *we* go? At least there would be two of them—and he had a steady job with a decent wage at the end of each week. They wouldn't be able to afford much, but they should survive, just about. Liam tied his blanket corners with some difficulty and realised his bundle was so heavy that he would not be able to carry it far without the blanket simply tearing in two. Sighing, he untied everything, then remembered to go and open his bedroom door so he could see when Maggie emerged.

Presently, his mother came out of the kitchen and glanced across at him. When she saw she had his attention she went and knocked on Maggie's door. 'Maggie! I lost me temper,' she called. 'We'll talk it over . . . come to some arrangement. I were wrong to try to send you off right now, wit'out givin' you a chance to find somewhere else to lay your head.'

After a moment, the door opened. Maggie stood framed in the doorway, the blanket neatly knotted into a bundle which hung from one hand. She moved past Mrs Nolan. 'It's all right, I'm going,' she said, as though she had not listened to a word the older woman said. 'And I've taken nothing that wasn't mine to take. Explain to the twins that I wouldn't leave 'em in the lurch for all the money in the world; tell 'em I was packed off, please.'

'Maggie, I'm tellin' you you needn't go,' Mrs Nolan said urgently. 'Put your bundle down, there's a good girl, and let's talk it over. I can't countenance your marryin' me son, but I were upset, an' that made me act hasty . . .'

But Maggie simply walked past her and set off down the stairs. Liam grabbed his own ill-packed bundle and followed her whilst, behind them, Mrs Nolan started to have very convincing hysterics, as little Ticky screamed in sympathy and the neighbours stood at their doorways, mouths agape.

'Maggie, I'm wit' you,' Liam said as they reached the lower hallway. 'But are you sure you wouldn't rather turn back, talk it out?'

Maggie looked up at him. Her eyes were wet but he could see she had made up her mind. 'No more talkin',' she said. 'Your mammy called me wicked t'ings, Liam. I'm not a bad girl as you well know an'

323

I won't be treated like one, so I won't. But you go back; she's no real quarrel with yourself.'

'Well, I've a quarrel wit' her,' Liam said, falling into step beside her as they crossed the yard and turned into Thomas Street. 'But I don't have much money right now, alanna—none, in fact. So what'll we do? Where'll we go?'

Before Maggie could answer, a figure darted across the street and accosted them. It was Kenny. 'Oh Liam, it's sorry I am I got you into trouble,' he said. 'I just didn't t'ink. When Mammy said she'd told Maggie to be home by half-past the hour . . . I'm sorry, old feller, I never dreamed . . .'

'It's all right, Kenny. But you're the feller in charge at home now,' Liam said. 'I won't be goin' back, not after what Mammy said to us. Take care of 'em.'

'And tell the twins I had no choice but to go,' Maggie put in, her voice thick with tears. 'And don't worry, Kenny. It would have happened sooner or later, when Mrs Nolan found out we were promised.'

'Right,' Kenny said. 'But you'll come back; we can't manage without you an' that's the truth.' He grinned at them both and disappeared into the courtyard.

Maggie took a deep breath and smiled up at Liam. 'I'm goin' along to Henry Street, to ask Mrs Collins if she knows of a cheap room where they'd let me stay a day or so free, until I've got a job,' she said. 'She's been good to me, has Mrs Collins. What you do, Liam, is up to you. I'll not have your mammy sayin' I've stole you away from her and corrupted you, for that is what she'll say, you know.'

'You, corrupt me? I'm a man, alanna, you're just a little girl,' Liam said. 'Well, you said she wouldn't be pleased.'

This remark brought Maggie to a dead halt. She turned to him and this time her eyes were brimming with laughter. 'Oh, Liam, if that isn't the biggest understatement I ever did hear! Come on now, best foot forward if we're to get a roof over our heads this night!'

*　　　*　　　*

The best of times come to an end, and Seamus and Garvan joined the rush to catch the last train home, getting a seat by the simple expedient of wriggling through the crowds to the front, then elbowing, kicking and scuffing their way aboard. Squeezed together, they sat with their eyes half shut, occasionally exchanging remarks in such low tones that no one else could possibly have overheard above the rattle and roar of the train, to say nothing of the conversation of fellow passengers. Indeed, Seamus thought, he wasn't sure that he always heard Garvan with his ears; it was subtler than that, a message passed on in a tiny, low whisper which still carried, crystal clear, to a receptive mind.

'That girl wit' the red hair—have you ever seen a face so full of freckles?'

'Are they freckles? There's spots on her chin. Look at her mammy, then, if you want to see freckles!'

'Be Jaysus, you're right! Horrible, isn't it now? They've blended together, and there's lumps, an' her nose is *black* wit' freckles. I don't t'ink I'll marry when I'm a man grown.'

And then, later, more serious topics.

'What'll we tell Mammy when we get in?'

'Oh, that we had a good time, that's all she'll want to hear.'

'Nothin' about the O'Farrells, then?'

'Oh, we'll say it was a good tea, if she asks.'

Satisfied that they had their backs covered, the twins proceeded to doze in their seats until they heard a porter shouting 'Tara station!' whereupon they scrambled from the train, still half asleep, and set off for home.

It was late, but newsboys still stood about outside the station, which was unusual, Seamus thought. He tugged his twin's arm. 'What's the headlines, Garv? Why are the fellers still sellin' papers?'

''Cos it's Bank Holiday and there's folk still about, you...' Garvan began, then stopped abruptly. 'War! We're at war, Shay! That's what the fly-sheets are sayin'.'

'War,' Seamus said wonderingly. 'Let's get home; someone will have bought a paper.'

Sleepiness forgotten, they hurried.

*   *   *

They couldn't believe it. They got indoors, shouting about the war, and found Mammy sitting by herself in front of the fire.

She looked up as they came in and not a word of reproach did she utter about their late return, not a question as to the O'Farrells. 'Oh ... you'll be wantin' a bite or a sup, I dare say,' she said heavily. 'There's bread an' cheese set out on the table.'

326

'War, Mammy! We're at war wit' Germany,' Seamus said importantly. It must be such a recent thing that no other member of the family knew, he thought. 'We seed the fly-sheets when we got off the train—we didn't buy a paper 'cos we thought certain sure either you or Liam would have got one . . . should we go back?'

His mother shook her head. 'No, there's a paper here somewhere,' she said, gesturing vaguely around the very untidy room. 'Seamus, Garvan, I've somethin' to tell the pair of you. Liam's gone.'

'Gone? To the war?' Garvan said eagerly. 'But that's very soon, Mammy.'

Their mother gave an irritated shake of the head, drawing her dark brows together in a scowl. 'No, no—can you t'ink of nothin' but war, the pair of you? Me boy's left home.'

'Liam? Good old Liam?' Garvan said slowly. 'And where's Maggie?'

Their mother's eyes widened. 'Why where should she be?' she said sharply. Seamus's heart missed a beat. Garvan had done it this time! But he had underestimated his twin.

'She can't be here, or the room wouldn't be in this state,' Garvan said simply. 'Unless she's ill, Mammy?'

'Oh,' Mrs Nolan said, clearly taken aback. 'Well, I've not had time to get round to . . . not that I could t'ink of cleanin' up or clearin' away wit' me lovely boy gone . . . and swearin' never to return,' she added pitifully. 'I'm lost wit'out Liam, boys. Lost.'

'Oh, Liam's a feller, he'll be back, but where is our Maggie, Mammy?' Garvan said. His voice was inexorable, his expression difficult even for Seamus to interpret. 'Where's she gone? You've telled us about Liam, now tell us about Maggie.'

Their mother sniffed, shrugged her shoulders up to her ears and heaved a deep sigh. 'Gone,' she said briefly. 'After all I've done for her, the little slut walks out of me house, takin' a good blanket . . .'

Garvan and Seamus cut straight across their mother's querulous voice without compunction. 'Gone? Where? Why?'

'She's gone because . . . you're too young to understand, mind . . . but she's gone because she'd set out her lures for Liam and . . .'

'Lures? Maggie?' That was Seamus, stung into anger. 'Maggie never lured anyone, Mammy, she was too busy and too tired most of the time. Come on now, what happened?'

Their mother moaned, then said pettishly, 'Make me a cup of tay then, Shay, for I'm dry as a bone, so I am. I've cried a river . . . but does anyone worry about me? Oh no, Ticky won't go to bed and when I make him, he won't go to sleep. Howlin' an' screamin' for Maggie until I could have slapped him. And then Kenny goes off to see if he can find Liam, an' when he gets back he's short wit' me an' goes straight off to bed wit'out tellin' me where me darlin' boy is stayin' . . .'

'Mammy,' Garvan said ominously. 'Are you goin' to tell or am I goin' to wake Kenny an' get the truth from him?'

'It's all right, Garv,' Seamus said hurriedly. 'The kettle's on now, Mammy's tay won't be a minute, then she'll have the strength to tell us what's been happenin', won't you, Mammy? Now start at the beginnin', Mammy. You got back from the seaside . . .'

'Oh, well . . . we got back, and Maggie wasn't home, or she wasn't makin' our supper, at any rate. So I started in to say she was late, an' whatever was I to do . . .'

'Get supper yourself,' Garvan said grimly, but so low that only Seamus heard. 'Why shouldn't the girl have a proper day out once in a while?'

'And then Kenny shouted,' their mother continued, oblivious. 'He said . . . the words are burnt into me mind so they are . . . he said: *It's all right, Mammy, Maggie is home. She's in here, wit' Liam.* And he was standin' in the doorway of the boys' bedroom.'

'So?' Garvan said after a moment. 'What's wrong wit' that, Mammy?'

There was a short silence; you could almost see Mammy thinking that one out, Seamus thought, amused. Because didn't Maggie make all the beds and tidy the rooms and dust and scrub? So if Liam was in the room and Maggie too, that didn't mean . . .

'They were sittin' on the bed,' Mrs Nolan said at last. 'And don't start on me, tellin' me there's no harm in that, because don't I know it, indeed? But the harm is that they're promised! Yes, promised to wed, for Liam told me wit' his own mouth so he did. Liam, me eldest son, the one wit' the best job, the one who's got a future . . . throwin' himself away on a little skivvy from the slums!'

'But Maggie lives wit' us, so if she's from the slums . . .' Garvan began in a deceptively reasonable tone, only to be immediately interrupted.

'You're not lettin' me get a word out, wit'out argufyin',' their mother said pettishly. 'Do you want to hear the story or don't you?'

Seamus poured the tea into a cup and carried it over to his mother. 'Here you are, a nice cup of tay,' he said soothingly. 'It's sorry we are to interrupt, Mammy. You go on, tell us what happened, we'll stay quiet now.'

'You're a good boy, Shay,' his mother said gratefully. She glared at Garvan, then sipped her tea. 'Well, when I heard they planned to marry, I was . . . I was shocked. Yes, an' disappointed, too. Liam could marry anyone, Shay, anyone at all! He's got a good job, the sort that simply gets better and better, he's a handsome lad . . . and to throw himself away on a . . . on a—'

'On an ordinary girl like our Maggie,' Seamus said quickly. If his mammy said one more word against her he could not guarantee to keep his brother in check. 'But Maggie's a pearl, Mammy! She runs this house like clockwork, she can cook like a dream, she can . . . but there. So what happened to make her go?'

'I told her to leave . . . but later, I begged her to stay, only she wouldn't,' Mrs Nolan said. 'Oh, I'm not denyin' I don't intend to let her marry Liam . . .'

'Liam's a man. He'll marry whoever he wants,' Garvan cut in coldly. 'You can't stop either him or Maggie, Mammy. Not if they're set on it.'

'Well, I don't have to approve,' their mother said sulkily. 'I don't have to have a scheming little vixen under my roof . . .'

'Where's she gone?' Seamus said without ceremony. 'We'll bring her home, Garv an' me.'

'Home! Sure and since when is this the home of Maggie McVeigh, whose mother had to sell her away to feed her?' Mrs Nolan said hotly. 'I paid for Maggie as someone to work here, not . . . not—'

'You promised her a home here after Dally Court fell down,' Seamus reminded her. 'Didn't you guess Liam liked her?'

'No! If I'd guessed . . . but it's too late now, me boy's gone and I don't know how I'm to get him back, not wit'out takin' that McVeigh girl an' all, an' that I will not do,' Mrs Nolan said viciously. 'Oh, go to bed the pair of ye!

'Where's our Maggie?' Garvan said quietly, but there was a chilly ominousness in his voice which made his mother blink nervously across at him. 'C'mon, Mammy, where is she?'

'I don't know,' their mother wailed. 'I do *not* know! And don't you go bringin' her back here when you find her, for she'll not be welcome under my roof! If she'd agreed to stay . . . but she went, an' took me eldest boy, so she comes back here at her peril, I'm tellin' you. Now I'm goin' to me bed. We'll talk again in the mornin'.'

*   *   *

Mrs Collins heard the whole story, tutting now and then, but she was only able to help Maggie. 'You can sleep wit' me niece, Kathleen,' she said. 'You must speak to the priest about marryin' as soon as can be, but until then you can sleep wit' Kathleen. As for you, young feller . . . there's doss houses down by the waterfront. You'll get a bed somewhere, so you will.'

'Don't worry about me, Mrs Collins, I'll be fixed up in no time,' Liam said gently when Maggie turned a stricken face towards him. 'I've a friend or two in the Post Office who won't see me on the streets, Olly Moss for one. His mammy's a nice

331

woman so she is, she'll give me a bit of blanket an' some floor space. Now, Maggie, we'll meet tomorrow, after work. All right?'

'Yes, sure. And . . . and Liam, I am so sorry. I knew your mammy wouldn't be pleased, but I didn't t'ink for one moment that she'd be as angry as she was.'

Liam squeezed her hand, then leaned over and kissed her lightly on the forehead. 'Tomorrow, at seven; outside the Post Office on O'Connell Street,' he said. 'You've no need to apologise for anything at all, alanna, for you've done nothin' wrong from start to finish. Take care of yourself, and don't *worry*. It'll all come out all right, you'll see.'

They were in Mrs Collins's tiny, cramped front room, with a pot boiling over the fire from which came a pleasant, savoury smell. The windows were steamed over, but outside, Maggie knew, the sun still shone and children played and shouted. Whilst she had lost, all in a moment, her home, her family and her reputation.

When Liam felt she was settled he said his goodbyes, thanking Mrs Collins profusely, and Maggie went with him as far as the corner, to see him off. For a moment they clung in the blue, star-spangled dusk, but then Liam gave her a kiss and told her she would be fine, so she would, and reminded her again that they would meet next day.

'But right now I've nowhere to lay me head, so I'll have to get that sorted,' he told her. 'Smile for me, Maggie!'

'Don't tek on so,' Mrs Collins said when Maggie went back into the little house, unable to hide her tears. 'Storm in a taycup, alanna. Tomorrer Mrs

Nolan will see the error of her ways, so she will . . . all them kids to see to an' her workin' in the shop all day. Oh aye, she'll come runnin', just you see.'

*   *   *

Next day, when Mrs Nolan woke, things seemed brighter. It was another sunny day and she went into the kitchen, tried to tell herself it didn't bother her that Ticky would have to be supervised as he washed and dressed, and started to cook the porridge. When it was simmering she went through to the little room where Maggie and Ticky had slept and fished Ticky out of bed. 'No, she's not come back,' she said grimly, for the first words out of his mouth were: 'Is Maggie home?' 'But we've our life to lead, Ticky me boy. Up you get now, an' come through for a wash. Then get yourself dressed. You'll go out to play this mornin' . . . I'll get one o' the bigger kids to keep an eye on you.'

'What about me dinner?' Ticky said sulkily. 'Maggie was goin' to make boxty today. Me pal Ernie was comin' in for it.'

'Well, I'll give you a cut of soda bread an' some cheese; that'll do you until supper,' Mrs Nolan said. 'I'll arrange something later, Ticky. Now be a good boy . . . I know, the twins can keep an eye on you for me.'

But Ticky was outraged by this suggestion and said he'd rather go without dinner altogether than be landed with the twins. 'They'll run off,' he said tearfully. 'They're mean to kids, Mammy.'

Then Kenny came into the room. 'Mornin',' he said affably. 'Where's Garv an' Shay?'

'In bed still, I suppose,' their mother said. 'They

333

were late in, an' argumentative. Those two would argue the hind leg off a donkey, so they would.'

'They aren't in bed; they haven't been to bed, by the looks of it,' Kenny said. He helped himself to a piece of soda bread and spread it thickly with butter. 'I reckon they're searchin' for Maggie an' Liam,' he said through a full mouth. 'If they'd woke me I could have telled 'em . . . but that's the twins all over. Never ask anyone anythin' if they can help it.'

'They asked me plenty,' his mother said bitterly, cutting another piece of soda bread. 'Nagged and nagged at me to tell 'em where Maggie was, only I couldn't, so they went off to bed . . . or I thought they did . . .'

'They'll be back for breakfast,' Kenny said comfortably. 'Don't worry, Mammy.'

But they weren't back by the time Mrs Nolan left for work and when she got home that evening, having abandoned her partner an hour earlier than usual, explaining that she had to make other arrangements for the children since her maid had left, neither Garvan nor Seamus had been seen.

'I can't understand where they can be,' Mrs Nolan moaned. 'I'm after findin' Liam . . . did they go to him?'

'They're not wit' Liam,' Kenny assured her when he got home. 'Nor wit' Maggie, or I doubt it, anyway. They've gone off on some mischief or other, but they can't get far, because they had no money, did they? Should we tell the polis, Mammy?'

'Oh my Gawd . . . the taypot,' Mrs Nolan said, and she and Kenny rushed to the pot on the mantel, in which she put aside money for rent,

334

messages and such. It was, almost predictably she now felt, empty.

'Rotten little thieves,' Kenny said, not mincing words. 'Well, they won't be back until the money runs out, Mammy, so just you stop worryin' about them this minute, d'you hear me? They're a bad lot . . . stealin' from their own mammy! Should we tell the polis, now, get them to find the lads?'

His mother was trying to decide whether to do this or not when there was a tap at the door. She fairly tore across the room and wrenched it open, hoping against hope that her erring children would be on the landing, but instead a small and incredibly filthy boy stood outside, holding a small and incredibly filthy piece of paper.

'You Miz Nolan?' he asked, scowling suspiciously. 'If y'are, dem boys said you'd gi' me tuppence for dis bit o' paper.'

He gave a rich snort and wiped his running nose on his raggedy jacket sleeve.

Knowing the twins, Mrs Nolan immediately produced the tuppence, handed it over, and snatched the piece of paper. She unfolded it, read . . . then fell back a couple of steps, uttering a keening wail. 'Oh, me sons, me sons! What'll I do, what'll I do? They've gone . . . They've left us! Oh Kenny, Kenny, fetch Liam home . . . the twins have gone for to be soldiers!'

*   *   *

Maggie and Liam had never had a quarrel, yet within a week of leaving the household they had their very first row. It was Liam's mother who caused it, of course, although in this particular

335

instance not knowingly. Maggie had asked him to go back home, she had assured him that the quarrel was hers and not his, and she thought herself to be disappointed when he did not do as she suggested, but of course inwardly she was delighted. Liam was on her side and that was the way she wanted it to be. Maggie's nerves were racked, naturally enough, because she was not living in her own home, or the place she had grown to believe to be her own home, but with Mrs Collins and furthermore she was sleeping with Kathleen and Kathleen was a kicker—not only a kicker, but a spreader-out. Maggie was used to sharing a small space with a number of people but not a very small space with a slut, and that was what Kathleen was. And the job hadn't materialised. Mrs Collins kept saying, 'You'll get somethin', my dear, don't you worry,' but so far Maggie hadn't managed to get anything except jobs on the market stall with Mrs Collins and her friends. Naturally, she was grateful for such work, but it didn't bring in the sort of money which would have enabled her to feel herself independent and Liam, far from pressing the matter of marriage, seemed suddenly to have drawn back from it. Property was so expensive in Dublin, even the tiniest room would have cost more than they could possibly afford and although a postman's wage was a good one, until Maggie herself started earning decent money there was little they could do apart from wait. So perhaps the row wasn't entirely Mrs Nolan's fault, perhaps it was also due to the stresses and strains of the way Maggie was living. Certainly at one time she would never have snapped out at Liam the way she had.

Liam had suggested, quite quietly and kindly really, that he and Maggie should go back to the Nolan house and at least talk to Mrs Nolan. 'I've seen me Mammy,' he said half defensively. 'I've spoken to her, Maggie. She's willing, if you are, at least to talk things over.'

But Maggie didn't want to talk things over. She did not want to see Mrs Nolan again—she just wanted a job and Liam and the security which at the moment was so painfully lacking. 'If you're so keen, Liam, go back yourself,' she had said, almost shouted. 'Leave me here, I've other things to do.'

And after all, when he thought about it, all he had done was obey her. He'd gone back, he'd talked to his mother and a couple of days later he had come round to the market stall in what can only be described as a state of considerable perturbation. 'You'll not believe it, Maggie,' he said, 'but Mammy says the boys have gone.'

'The twins? Where have they gone?'

There was a long pause, before Liam answered. 'They've left home,' he said gloomily. 'Me Mammy's in a terrible state, our Maggie. She doesn't know which way to turn. She wants me to look for 'em.'

'Look for 'em, Liam. Where, for God's sake? Why can't she look herself? Has she told the polis?'

'No. They left a note. They've gone.'

'Liam. Will you be sittin' yourself down now and tell me for what it is you're talking about,' Maggie said impatiently. To her it sounded remarkably like a story made up by Mrs Nolan in order to get Liam's attention. 'The twins wouldn't go—they're only kids.'

'Well, they have—they're gone. Mammy reckons

337

they've gone . . .' He swallowed. 'They've gone to the war.'

For a moment Maggie could only stare at him. 'The war! But . . . Liam, they're only fourteen! They're not even big or grown-up lookin' for their age. Nobody would take them for more than . . . well, not more than fourteen or fifteen, I suppose.'

Liam had come to her on the market stall. Maggie, looking round, was certain that everyone within a radius of fifteen feet was listening intently to what they were saying. 'Look, keep your voice down, Liam,' she said, 'or come back this evenin' when it's quiet.'

'No. I've got to tell you now. They've gone for soldiers, Maggie. They've gone to Liverpool.'

'I don't believe it.' Maggie said—but she did— she knew the twins of old. If there was one thing they could do it was make trouble and this was trouble-making on a super scale.

'Well, Mammy believed it and she's awful unhappy,' Liam said defensively. 'I've got to help her, Mags, I can't . . . I can't just do nothin'. I'm goin' over to Liverpool—I'm goin' to find them. I'm goin' to tell the authorities they're only fourteen.'

Maggie stared at him. 'Goin' to Liverpool—but, Liam, what about your job?'

'There are some things more important than jobs,' Liam said sulkily. 'I've got to go—you know I have—if it was your brother . . .'

'They nearly are my brothers,' Maggie said grimly, 'and I know what little buggers they are. Sure an' I'll be bound they just said that out of divilment. They just said that to annoy your mammy.'

'They ran away because of you,' Liam said, 'It said in the note—she'd kicked Maggie out and so they were goin' as well.'

It gave Maggie pause, but not for long. 'Liam,' she said, 'I don't want you to go off to Liverpool. I want you to wait. When did the boys go? Two days ago? Well then, wait a week.' She looked up at Liam and saw with dismay his soft brown eyes had hardened,

'Me mam is goin' . . . me mammy is goin' frantic, Maggie. Don't you understand? She . . . she asked if you'd go home.'

Maggie felt fury well up inside her. Not only did Mrs Nolan want to take Liam from her but she wanted her to retract, to go back, to behave like a skivvy, to live like a skivvy! 'No Liam, you can't ask it of me.'

'Just for a few days,' Liam pleaded. 'Just while I'm away, acushla.'

'Your Mam will spend all the time naggin' me,' Maggie said crossly. 'I can't do it, Liam, it's too much to ask.' But in the back of her mind the thought of being away from Kathleen's kicks and filth for a few days was tempting—but it would mean giving way. She knew if she went back that Mrs Nolan would keep telling her that she wanted her son back and blaming her for his loss; reminding Maggie what a good job Liam had got and generally undermining the younger girl's defences.

'Maggie, Mam is after havin' to give up her job,' Liam said in a mutter. 'You don't want that to happen—the family is fallin' apart. Sure an' 'tis a small enough t'ing to ask—just to go back for a few days while I'm in Liverpool.'

'It's a big thing,' Maggie said. 'A very big thing. I can't do it. And, Liam, I'm not askin' you—I'm tellin' you—don't go off to Liverpool. If you go off to Liverpool, then when you come back I shan't be here. It's a trick—your mammy is playin' off her tricks on us. You've got to listen to me.'

Liam tightened his lips and turned away from her. 'You're selfish, Maggie,' he said coldly. 'You're not thinkin' of anyone but yourself. I promised me mammy and I'm goin'.'

Before Maggie could say another word Liam had turned and vanished into the crowd.

Mrs Collins had turned to her kindly. 'Don't you worry, love. He'll be back. He'll be back. You might just go and have a word with the woman now.'

But Maggie couldn't see it like that. She felt it would be letting herself down. Instead she began ostentatiously piling potatoes into a pyramid on the stall with the big ones in the front—not even bothering to answer Mrs Collins, though that didn't mean to say it didn't worry her. Over the course of the next couple of days she was torn two ways— half of her truly wanted to go back to the Nolans, to tell Mrs Nolan that she was prepared to stay with her whilst Liam was away, but another part of her was firm. She would not go back to the place where she had been treated so badly, knowing the chances of being treated badly again, and that if she did so Mrs Nolan would think she had Maggie on the run.

Liam had gone. He hadn't taken any notice of her attempts to persuade him to change his mind. He'd gone. He'd been given leave from the Post Office, though they hadn't been pleased. They told him if he wasn't back promptly his job might be

340

forfeit.

'There's plenty after jobs like mine,' he said. 'Ah come on, Maggie, come on, come back to the building.'

'I'll think about it,' Maggie said heavily. So there she was now, working on the stall, sleeping with Kathleen, waiting anxiously for Liam to come home, seeing a week go by, ten days, a fortnight, knowing that she couldn't go round to Mrs Nolan to find out what had happened to Liam, whether he was back or whether he had stayed, hating the thought of giving in.

'You want to go round, alanna,' Mrs Collins had said. 'Give the woman a chance. You needn't go back there to live. Just go round and see what's happening.' But Maggie was very reluctant to do so. She could not forget the language, the words that Mrs Nolan had used, and in a way she didn't want to see what she was missing. She hadn't settled in well to the Collins house because it wasn't the sort of place she was used to.

Naturally, she couldn't explain this to Mrs Collins but Connor, working on a stall further up the pavement, had gone with her one morning for a cup of tea at a nearby tea-stall and she had confided in him. 'I'm thinkin' it's a mistake I've made all round,' she said rather wildly. 'Oh, I don't know, Conn, I don't know what I ought to do for the best.'

'Leave it 'til she's missin' you real bad,' Conn said, 'and then go back and offer to stay again but for a wage, this time. Tell her if she treats you like a skivvy then you ought to be paid a dacint wage.'

Maggie looked at him with considerable respect. 'I might just do that,' she said. 'I might.'

341

'Hey, you're lonely.' Connor laughed. 'It's not your type of place. Mrs Collins is a lovely woman but sure an' it's a tiny, filthy little house she's got there. Now come on, think sensible. Besides, Liam is going to need all the help he can get if he's lost that nice job of his.'

'Yes, I know,' Maggie said. 'I still can't think what made him do it. I'm sure the whole thing is moonshine. If you knew Seamus and Garvan like I do . . .' She didn't finish the sentence—no one knew Seamus and Garvan as well as she.

Would they really make trouble of this nature? Maggie was sure in her heart that they would. But time and unhappiness wore her down. Now two whole weeks had passed and she still didn't know what had happened to Liam. For all she knew he might have come back. He might have been working in the Post Office quite happily and was just punishing her for the way she had behaved. She ought to go back to Mrs Nolan and find out what was happening.

So that evening she went back along the familiar roads and into the familar courtyard. In fact she didn't have to go up to the flat because Ticky was playing with one of his friends outside. The little boy gave a shriek of joy when he saw her and rushed towards her. 'Oh Maggie, Maggie, we missed you, we missed you,' he gabbled. 'Where's ya bin, what's ya done? Have you seen our Liam?'

'Oh God, is he still away, love? Hasn't he come back from England?'

'No, no, and me mammy's worried sick, so she is. She says she's afraid he might have to go for a soldier for to find the twins.'

Maggie's heart missed a beat. 'Go for a soldier?

Why would he do that?'

'Well, when they get to Liverpool, it says in the letter, they scatter around a bit, so they do, and if the twins haven't give their own names, sure they could be anywhere.'

'I wouldn't be surprised if the twins were still in Dublin,' Maggie said sourly. 'Does your mammy have an address for Liam?'

'No, I don't think so. She's not in—she's gone out—that's why I'm playin' out here.'

'Oh, right. Well, I'll . . . I'll call on her tomorrow, perhaps. Tell you what Ticky—tell Mammy I came round to see her and I'll come round again in the next couple of days,' Maggie said. She wondered, though, how anyone could assume the twins would be big enough to join the army, though she supposed they might have just got ordinary jobs in Liverpool.

Back in Mrs Collins's little house she told her and Kathleen that she was going back next day to see Mrs Nolan. 'Liam's not come home yet,' she explained. 'It's worried I am, Mrs Collins. He never meant to stay away for more than a week. I do hope his job isn't forfeit.'

'You go an' see Mrs Nolan, alanna,' Mrs Collins said comfortably. 'Even if it's only for a few words. Everyone was too hasty, eh?'

Now, with the prospect of going back to see Mrs Nolan in the back of her mind, Maggie was working on the stall, piling potatoes and weighing them out into brown paper bags. It was a busy Saturday and the street was crowded. She had just called out to Connor that she wouldn't mind a drink, when she happened to glance up. Across the heads of the people around the stall on the opposite side of the

343

road she saw Garvan—or was it Seamus?—mooching along with his hands in his pockets looking as normal and ordinary as anyone she'd ever imagined. Maggie dropped the potatoes she was holding. 'Garvan,' she shouted. 'Mrs Collins, look—there's Garvan—or is it Seamus?'

Mrs Collins screwed up her eyes and peered but she didn't really know either of the twins well enough to identify them and she couldn't see at which boy Maggie was pointing.

'Hang on,' Maggie shouted at her customer. 'Hang on. I shan't be a moment.' And she plunged into the busy road.

*   *   *

Seamus strolled along the pavement in the soft sunshine keeping an eye on Garvan who was striding ahead, but not attempting to catch up with him. The twins rarely quarrelled but they had quarrelled over their return to Dublin that very morning.

After leaving the note for their mother they had lit out—though not for Liverpool or the British army. They had intended to stay away from home for a few days in order to blackmail their mother into having Maggie back. Life without Maggie, they had quickly realised, would not be the sort of life they enjoyed.

'Mammy will make us look after the kids, so she will,' Garvan had said indignantly. 'We've got to put a stop to this, Shay, before we get into real trouble.'

'Oh, Maggie will be back,' Seamus had said easily. 'You know Mammy.'

344

But Garvan had not agreed. 'She'll get some other girl,' he said. 'And Maggie knows us, she understands our ways. We've got to get her to get Maggie back.'

So they had written the note and off they'd gone into the countryside no more than ten miles from Dublin, and they lived very well there, what was more. It was summery weather, the orchards were full of fruit and the fields full of potatoes. They stole eggs from the hens, dug up spuds by night and roasted them over a fire, and generally had a grand old time of it. It might have gone on for ever if it had not been for the tinkers and the weather.

For the first few days the weather had been lovely and Seamus and Garvan had found themselves a spot in an ancient barn full of old hay where they were perfectly happy to snuggle down at night and from where they raided the surrounding farmlands. There was a decent little stream near enough for them to have water and by boxing the fox in one of the nearby orchards they were able to gather enough fruit to sell, so that they always had the odd penny in their pockets.

'Won't last,' Seamus told his twin but Garvan couldn't have cared less. He was enjoying himself and that was what mainly mattered.

The tinkers hadn't seemed a threat at first. The kids had played with Garvan and Seamus and the older people had welcomed them to muck around by the river and sit by their fire, but that was when they thought the twins had a home of their own. The very night that they met the tinkers the rain started. Fine, soft Irish rain—the sort that can go on for hours and hours—in fact Seamus thought that it had rained for twelve hours. It hadn't

345

mattered to Garvan and Seamus, snuggling down in the dry hay, but the following day they found that their rights to the barn were going to be disputed. A large gang of tinkers moved in during the day and by evening, when Garvan and Seamus, thoroughly fed-up, sought shelter, stones were thrown by the gypsies now firmly ensconced in the barn.

'We'll kip down under a hedge,' Garvan said crossly. 'We'll be all right there—'twill be fine again in the mornin'.'

But it was not and by the time evening fell Seamus had managed to persuade his twin that they had been away long enough and the correct thing for them to do—indeed, the only thing if they weren't to die of pneumonia—was to go back to Dublin and tackle Mammy.

And then, of course, on the very morning when they had intended to set out for Dublin again, the sun came out. Garvan wanted to change his mind and stay, but Seamus for once was firm. 'No, Garv,' he said, 'we agreed to go home, so we did, and so home we're goin'. If we stay away much longer there'll be no persuadin' Mammy—she'll have got someone else to replace Maggie, so she will. Don't you understand? What's more, if Mammy goes to the authorities we're goin' to be in real trouble. They'll search the Army for us. Heaven knows what could happen.'

So Garvan had agreed to go back and now they were in Dublin, walking along the busy street. But at least we're doing the right thing now, Seamus thought contentedly, following along behind. Very soon now they'd be back home and able to speak to Mammy and persuade her to do what they wanted.

346

Seamus was just considering catching Garvan up for a bit of a crack when they plunged into the market. Fascinated as he always was by the stalls, Seamus slowed a little more, peering at the various goods on display. Glancing up presently, he saw Garvan plodding along ahead as determinedly as ever so he began to hurry, his eyes fixed on his twin. He heard a shout, although he didn't hear what was said above the hubbub of the market, but he saw his twin turn his head and heard the squeal of brakes and a terrible crash. He glanced into the roadway. A horse and cart were pulled to one side and an ancient motor bus had also stopped, the driver jumping down and gesticulating wildly. Seamus saw Garvan dive into the road and followed him.

Garvan turned and looked at him, white-faced. 'Sure an' someone's been killed,' he said. 'Went under the wheels of the bus. Did ye see that?'

'Ah, God,' Seamus said, for he could see that whoever it was under the bus was dead—that was for sure. 'What happened then, Garvan?'

'Don't know—a girl—she shouted somethin'—I thought—Oh my God . . .' He stared at the still figure. 'Shay, it's . . . it's our Maggie.'

*   *   *

Liam stood on the deck of the ferry which plied between Liverpool and Dublin and watched the green land getting closer and felt the tears come to his eyes. All around him other Irish people with tear-filled eyes were straining towards land, as he was. Gripping the rail he felt quite ashamed of his own emotion, for wouldn't anyone have thought he had been away fourteen years instead of fourteen days, but he reminded himself that it was the first time he had ever been away from home, let alone across the water.

And Liverpool had been so different! In his own mind he had imagined it as being just like Dublin, though he had supposed that it must be slightly smaller, for wasn't Dublin a capital city? But when the ferry had drawn up alongside the landing stage, with the Liver Birds high in the sky above, he had been amazed and astonished by the whole place—the size of the buildings and particularly the height of them. They towered to the skies, so they did, and the docks were thronged with people, horses, carts and vehicles of every description.

Later, of course, he realised that the war was partly responsible for the crowds, for most of the people who filled the quayside were soldiers, coming and going about their business. And since he had come here to find soldiers he supposed, ruefully, that he had obviously come to the right place. But first things first. He walked up from the Pier Head, crossed the road and turned to the left, finding himself in Great Howard Street. He paid for a bed in a doss house, then went straight to the recruiting offices and talked to the friendly sergeant there, explaining that the twins were under age but had come to Liverpool hoping to join the Army. The sergeant had done his best, but he had been unable to bring the twins to mind. Boys by the dozen had been in and out of the recruiting office, for if they joined up at least they were sure of three square meals a day, and many of them were, of course, under age, though if they looked seventeen or so and sturdy the sergeant signed them on. Liam hastily explained that the
348

twins did not look sixteen—probably did not look fifteen—but even so the sergeant said it was often difficult for him and his staff to judge. However, although he was sure he had not signed up Seamus and Garvan, he promised to ask around amongst his colleagues, for it wasn't every day that identical twins walked into an army recruiting office.

Unable to do anything else for the time being Liam had gone back to the doss house, which he had chosen because it was cheap and conveniently close to the docks. Afterwards he realised that if he had searched for a year he probably couldn't have found a worse place to stay. His fellow lodgers were the scum of the seven seas, so far as he could make out. They swore, they drank and several times fights broke out. Liam decided that he would have to find somewhere a little more suitable if he were forced to stay here long.

The next day he went back to the recruiting office and much to his joy the sergeant told him that twins, and fairly young ones too, had been recruited by one of the other sergeants. The boys had joined either as drummers or buglers, he wasn't sure which, and had been sent off for training to a camp on the South Downs. He did not think, on reflection, that such boys would be sent to France but whether or not they went abroad, Mammy wanted them home, so home they must come. Liam went to the station, bought a ticket and began the day-long journey to get to the camp.

It took him a further two days to discover that the young lads, although definitely twins, were not Seamus and Garvan, and by then he was beginning to run a little short of money. What was more, he was also starting to realise that everyone at the

349

training camp was expecting him to join up—and he wished he could do so. The fellers were having a terrific time, so they were. Spirits were high, the war would soon be over and because of his wretched brothers he had had a taste of what he was missing. Companionship, adventure and a glamorous uniform, as well as the admiration which surrounded the military. Still, Maggie was waiting, as was his good job with the Post Office, so the Army would have to manage without him.

Since his journey had been unsuccessful, Liam hitch-hiked back to Liverpool—which took him another three days—and set about his search once more, though with less enthusiasm. He was now sure that Maggie had been right; she knew the twins better than anyone and she had said they wouldn't cross the water and join the Army. He had been a fool to come and was a worse fool to stay, because he suspected in his heart that the twins were still in Ireland. So he used the remainder of his money to have a decent night's sleep in the Old Fort Hotel on Bath Street and the next evening caught the ferry home. Pointless to brood on his failure, he told himself as it slid into the brown waters of the Liffey and headed for the quays. Maggie had been right, bless her, and now here he was, about to step ashore once more on his native soil.

It was bliss going down the gangway on to the quays, even though there was a faint drizzle falling. He'd rather have Dublin in the worst rainstorm in living memory, he told himself, than Liverpool in bright sunshine. Being a soldier wasn't everything after all. With a high heart he walked along the quays, crossed Grattan Bridge and made for Parliament Street. When the Castle was in front of

350

him he turned and made his way through the back ways into Francis Street and thus home to the buildings. And like a good omen, when he arrived there the rain stopped and a watery sun came out. Two scruffy kids, playing in the courtyard, eyed him curiously as he passed and, on impulse, he stopped and called out to them, 'Are me brothers back, lads—Seamus and Garvan, I mean?'

'Aye, I saw dem an hour or two since, so I did,' one of the kids told him.

Liam, shaking his head sadly at his own folly, waved an acknowledgement and made his way up to the flat. He tried the door—it was locked. Strange. He banged on it, but then of course he remembered that if Mammy was working and the kids all at school . . .

Down the stairs Liam clattered, across the courtyard and back into the road. He'd go to the market, after all it was Maggie he wanted to see most, he might as well go and find her, apologise, give her a hug.

He knew that he had parted from her on very bad terms and he remembered how hurt and angry he had felt that she hadn't gone home to his mammy when he had explained so clearly how sorry Mammy was and how badly she needed Maggie's companionship. But now that he was home and willing to admit Maggie had been right, surely they would sort things out. They would make up—he smiled blissfully to himself at the thought of making up—and then they would both go home to the buildings together. They would stop this ridiculous business—he would make his mammy see reason. Rapidly now, in the watery sunshine, Liam made his way through the crowded streets

351

until he reached the market. Most of the stall-holders were known to him, but as he walked along the pavement edge he realised that the stall he wanted—Mrs Collins's stall—was still packed up, as if for the night. There was a great canvas spread over it and neither Mrs Collins nor Maggie was in sight.

Liam looked consideringly at the stalls around. How odd, there was scarcely anyone that he knew, but a fat and cheerful young boy of about seventeen working on the next stall turned to him and raised his eyebrows. 'Can I help yiz?' he said. 'Were you wantin' some taters?'

'Where's Mrs Collins?' Liam asked. 'She's always here on her stall. Where's the others?'

The boy stared at him. 'Have yiz been away?' he said.

'Yes,' said Liam casually. 'I've been to England, so I have—only just got home. Where's Mrs Collins then, or Connor?'

'Why they're all out at Glasnevin,' the boy said. 'Everybody is.'

Liam stared. 'Glasnevin?'

'That's right,' the youth said, 'the burial ground.'

Liam's heart sank—what had happened whilst he'd been away? Someone must have died—thank God he'd asked about the twins!

'Has there been an accident?' Liam asked, his heart beating faster. He liked Mrs Collins. 'What's happened? Mrs Collins? Connor . . . ?'

'No, no,' the boy said soothingly. 'Are yiz a relative of hers?'

'No, just a friend,' Liam said hastily. 'I went to England 'cos me twin brothers was missin'. So I don't know what's bin happenin', you see. Can you
352

tell me?'

'Well, you might not be after knowing her,' the boy said doubtfully. ''Tis the young woman, you know, the gorl, the one that helps Mrs Collins with the stall. Young Maggie.'

Liam's heart stood still. 'Maggie McVeigh?' he faltered.

'That's right, Maggie McVeigh,' the boy said. 'Killed, she was, run over by a bus. They're buryin' her today. Nice gorl. Sad, real sad. And only young, so she was.'

Liam stared. He could feel cold shock creeping over him. 'A-and you're tellin' me Maggie's *dead*?'

The boy nodded uneasily, avoiding Liam's shocked gaze. 'She was run over, so she was,' he repeated. 'By a bus. I'm sorry, man. Is there anything . . . ?'

But Liam had turned away. Sick at heart, he stumbled back the way he had come. He told himself, as he went, that it was all nonsense, Maggie could not possibly be dead. He would find someone else, someone older, more sensible. He would soon discover how this horrible rumour had come about.

Yet even as he went the coldness in him grew, and the pain in his heart.

CHAPTER ELEVEN

June onwards 1916

'Donny! Hey, Donny, over here!'

Deirdre had given a really good shout, but even

so it took a moment or two for her twin to spot her. And no wonder, Deirdre thought, with the size of the queue and all.

Queuing had really got its grip on the nation now, largely because of the food shortages. And the prices! Mam had always been a canny cook, but now she had to be a canny shopper as well. Only since she was working full time in the bakery shop it was the younger members of the family who had become expert at queuing.

There were times when Deirdre didn't mind queuing, to be honest. If you were stuck in a queue, no one could expect you to do anything else. You could be sent on a message nowadays, Deirdre had reflected smugly yesterday, and if you said 'There was a queue' when your mam asked why you were so perishin' late, no more questions would be asked. Fair was fair—being in two places at once was impossible! Of course, you didn't have to spend the whole day in the line, it was quite possible to be trotting homeward with your messages intact after an hour . . . but if you didn't trot home . . .

So queues were a blessing in some ways. But not on a sunny September Saturday when your twin had got up early and gone off, and was now demanding your presence at the top of a fine pair of lungs. Deirdre thought—fleeting—about letting the queue go hang and joining Donal at whatever ploy he was up to, but she was fond of a nice stew and her mam had said if she would queue for some meat—any meat—a nice stew would be the result.

And anyway, Donal had seen her. He came bustling over, grinning. 'Hey up, Dee,' he greeted her. 'How long's you goin' to be?'

Deirdre looked ahead of her. The shop door had been getting nearer and nearer; now she reckoned another fifteen minutes would see her inside and, with luck, another five after that she would reach the counter.

'About twenty minutes to out,' she said, having done her sums. 'Why, Donny? What's up?'

Donal grinned and opened his hand. On the palm nestled a shiny silver coin.

'That's a bob!' Deirdre said. 'Where d'you gerrit?'

'Someone give it me. Guess who?'

Deirdre stared hard at her twin. He had very bright blue eyes—as did she—and at present they were guilelessly blank, but that didn't stop her from reading them. She gave a squeak. 'Our dad's come home!' she said.

Donal nodded energetically. 'That's it, our Dee. So when you've done your messages you'll gerra bob too. And Mam says we can go to the flicks, or fishin' off the Pier Head, or anything we like, so long as we don't go hangin' about at home all afternoon. She said to be back for supper at six, though.'

'Cor!' Deirdre said reverently. 'Oh, but I want to see our dad ever so!'

'Well, acourse. You'll be tekin' your messages home, an' you'll see him then,' Donal said reasonably. 'What'll it be, Dee? Flicks?'

'Nah, norron a day like today,' Dee said, shuffling forward with the queue. 'We could catch the ferry, have a day out.'

'Yeah, only it's gettin' on for noon already—I looked at the clock when I come out. An' Dad'll tek us out tomorrer, you bet your life he will.'

'Besides, Mam don't like us goin' off to the seaside, not since Seaforth,' Deirdre remembered regretfully. 'Crossin' the water means seaside so far as Mam's concerned, even if we're really only goin' to the woods.'

'Well, where, then?' Donal said urgently. 'Swimmin' baths? The scaldy?'

'No point, the scaldy's free,' Deirdre reminded her twin. 'We'll think of somethin', Donny.' The queue shuffled forward again and Deirdre shuffled with it. 'Oh, I wonder if I oughter gerra bit more stew-meat if I can, seein' as Dad's home?'

'They won't give you more,' Donal pointed out. 'You know wharrit's like. If you ask, Mr Austen'll just say *Don't you know there's a war on*? an' you'll wish you hadn't asked.'

'It's worth an *ask*, though, Donny,' Deirdre said reasonably. She was at the doorway now, her next shuffle would bring her on to the wooden floor of the butcher's shop with its thick layer of sawdust and its smell of blood. 'Oh . . . I got onions an' carrots but I didn't get no cornflour. Could you do that?'

Donny groaned but he saw the sense of it. 'Sure. How much?' he asked. 'I'll use me bob; Mam can pay me back when we get home.'

'How much? Oh, go to the Co-op on the corner of Dido Street. They'll tell you how much to get,' Deirdre decided. 'See you, Donny.'

'Shan't be long,' Donal said, scooting purposefully off up the road. Deirdre squeezed into the shop and counted the customers before her. Only five . . . she really shouldn't be long now.

'Did that twin o' yourn say your pa was 'ome, chuck?' Mrs Roberts, fat and wheezy and good-

356

natured, nudged Deirdre in the back with a cushiony hand. 'Well, well, well, we've not seen Mick Docherty for a while!'

'Well, he's dodgin' subs now, as well as bein' bombed at an' shot at, Mrs Roberts,' Deirdre explained. 'But this time, mebbe he'll have some leave. It 'ud be prime if he did.'

The line shuffled forward again whilst Mrs Roberts extolled the Navy, whether Royal or Merchant: she had sons in both. And as Deirdre came level with the counter Mrs Roberts dug her in the back again. 'Tell old Austen your da's 'ome,' she hissed. 'Mick's doin' a good job—they all are— so why shouldn't 'e get anythin' extry what's goin'?'

Deirdre, who had every intention of milking her father's return for every bit of extra meat it would bring forth, nodded. 'Right, Mrs Roberts, I'll do that. Thanks.'

And presently her virtuosity was given full rein, for she reached the head of the queue.

'Mornin', Deirdre. There ain't a lot left . . . Alf of scrag do you?'

'Oh, Mr Austen . . .' Deirdre began, then giggled as she realised she was quoting Marie Lloyd. The butcher leaned confidentially across the counter as she went on, unable to stop herself: 'What shall I do? I want to go to Birmingham, but they carried me on to Crewe . . .'

'That's enough of that, young 'oman,' Mr Austen said, but he didn't sound annoyed, she was glad to hear. 'Else you'll not get even that ' 'alf of scrag and then what'll your mam say, eh?'

'Sorry, Mr Austen,' Deirdre said contritely. 'The fact is, me dad's come into port an' I'm that happy . . . any chance of a bit of liver, perhaps? Course the scrag'll come in right handy for some stew, but liver, or kidneys . . .'

'Well, I dunno,' Mr Austen said doubtfully. ''Ow long is it since 'e were last 'ome, chuck?'

'More'n a year,' Deirdre said pathetically. 'We doesn't see much of our da, now the war's on. Oh aye, he were torpedoed, y'know, six months past, spent four days afloat in the Atlantic without no grub an' with only seawater to drink.'

Mr Austen tutted sympathetically and began to add meat to the meagre half-pound already on the big scale pan. 'Torpedoed, eh? The poor bugger— an' you don't oughter drink seawater, it sends you mad, they say.'

Deirdre considered going into a description of the maniacal behaviour exhibited by her father, but changed her mind. With my luck, she thought, me dad'll walk in here tomorrer an' have a crack wi' Mr Austen an' he'll think I'm a liar. Well, he'll know I am. Better not overdo it. 'They caught the rain in their sailor hats, I think,' she said. 'An' . . . an' they ate fish; fish is awright. Raw, acourse,' she added.

Mr Austen continued to pile meat on to the scale pan, though it had hit rock bottom some time ago, Deirdre saw with glee. Then he shot the contents of the pan into a couple of sheets of newspaper and gave her a wink. 'Aye, I've 'eard tell as shipwrecked mariners can get fresh water outer raw fish. Ah, well, nice to know 'e's 'ome, anyroad. Tell you what, you've gorra dog, haven't you? I'll put in a nice marrer bone, you can mek soup with it first, then give it to your dog. Shan't be a jiffy, chuck.'

Deirdre, who had never owned a dog, smiled

358

and nodded. You didn't contradict a butcher, particularly one bent on being generous. She watched Mr Austen go into the back of the shop and when he came out again the newspaper parcel was appreciably bigger.

'There y'are, Deirdre, and tell your da I'm glad 'e's come safe to port. Me son Geoff's at sea, in a destroyer, you know. That'll be four bob. Gorrenough gelt?'

'I got three and nine; can I owe the other thruppence?' Deirdre asked hopefully. 'Oh, you are so good, Mr Austen! Tell you what, I'll run home an' come back wi' the rest o' the money.'

'No need for that; we'll call it three and nine,' Mr Austen said, beaming. He was clearly quite carried away by his own generosity, Deirdre thought. She made a mental note to torpedo her father's ship more often. 'Tell you what, me ole lady could do wid one of them onions, if you could spare it.'

Deirdre handed over an onion willingly and after only the slightest hesitation added a carrot too, then turned and humped her now heavy basket towards the door.

'See?' Mrs Roberts said as she passed. 'Never no 'arm in axin'.'

'Thanks, Mrs Roberts,' Deirdre panted. What on earth was in the package, besides the scrag? She began to wonder whether the butcher had really only added a large marrow bone, though it seemed likelier that he'd popped in a lump of lead as well, by the weight of it. She had hoped for some kidneys or liver, which her father loved, but she was pretty sure they weighed quite light. I suppose it would serve me right for lyin' like a flat-fish if it were just a marrer bone, she thought dolefully, heaving the basket along the pavement. But there you are, all's fair in love and war and, as every adult in the world was anxious to remind her, there *was* a war on.

She reached the corner of Mere Lane just as a voice haled her. 'Dee! Are you deaf, girl? I been hollerin' an' hollerin' an' you never so much as looked round!' It was Donal, panting, red-faced, with a bag of what she presumed was cornflour in one hand.

'Oh, Donny, gi's an 'and wi' this basket,' Deirdre gasped. 'What wi' spuds an' carrots an' onions an' now a huge parcel o' meat, me arm's longer than a bleedin' chimpanzee's.'

'That ain't the only resemblance,' Donal remarked kindly, taking the basket from her. 'Still, we've done the messages, now all we've gorra do is clear off for the rest o' the day. C'mon, you said you wanted to see Da; let's gerra hustle on.'

The two of them hustled, therefore, and in no time, it seemed, were darting up the back jigger, throwing open the gate and charging across the yard and into the kitchen.

'Oh Mam, I telled Mr Austen our da was home an' he give me . . .' Deirdre began breathlessly, then stopped short. Her mother sat on one side of the table, with Mick standing behind her, a hand on her shoulder, and opposite her sat Ellen. Ellen was facing the back door and it didn't take more than the most cursory of glances to see that she had been crying. Donal thumped the basket down on the table and Deirdre said: 'Ellie? Whass up?'

'Oh, Dee, it's Tolly,' Ellen said, gulping. 'He's leavin' for France in two days' time. He'll be killed, I know he will!'

'Don't be so daft, our Ellie,' Deirdre said bracingly. ''Sides, no one don't know what's goin' to happen. Unless you know the Kaiser's gorra special sorta down on Tolly, that is, he's got the same chance as everyone else. Remember, queen, loads of fellers go to France and they ain't all killed.'

'I *know* he'll be killed,' Ellen sobbed. 'I've been havin' this dream, Dee, an' it always ends the same. It's so *real*, there's the trenches, an' the mud ... and then there's this great big enormous explosion an' ... an' somethin' comes rollin' across the ground towards the trench an' the men shout: "It's gas ... dive for cover, fellers!" an' I can't help, there's nothin' I can do ... an' I see Tolly fall ... Oh, if Tolly dies I want to die too ... I can't bear for him to be dead an' for me to go on livin'.'

'I've said it before an' I'll say it again. You've been overworkin' to the point where you're just wore out all through,' Ada Docherty said. 'As for dreams, well they may be one thing, but that there dream's a nightmare, Ellie, an' everyone knows nightmares don't mean nothin', they just come to cause us pain when we're down. Now dry your face an' give poor Mick a smile—he'll think he's walked into a wake!'

'You shouldn't ha' stuck at the hospital, queen,' Mick said gently, leaning across the table and taking Ellen's small pale hands in his large brown ones. 'I know you wanted to do your bit for the soldiers, but they take advantage. A young girl like you, workin' all hours, stayin' late, doin' double shifts ...'

'I'm puttin' down for France, that's what I'm doin',' Ellen said in a small, gruff voice which sounded totally unlike herself. 'If Tolly goes then

361

I'll go. He . . . he needs someone, honest he does, Mam. Otherwise . . . oh, why did he have to say he'd go?'

'I didn't think the Sally Army went in for fightin',' Mick said, handing Ellen a clean handkerchief. 'I t'ought they were pacifists.'

'Oh, he isn't going into one of the regiments,' Ellen explained. She dried her face and blew her nose fiercely. 'He's going to be a stretcher bearer . . . they have to go right up to the trenches—beyond them, sometimes—to fetch back the wounded. They're in deadly danger all the while they're on duty.'

'I hope Tolly didn't tell you that,' Ada said, her voice heavy. 'If so, queen, I'd like to have a word with him.'

'No, course he didn't. It were Teddy Brewer, the feller I were tellin' you about who's lost both his arms,' Ellen said faintly. 'He was saying he owed his life to the stretcher bearers who fished him out of no man's land after he'd got his . . . he didn't know Tolly had volunteered.' She blew her nose again, a fierce blast, then heaved a great sigh. 'Oh well, I feel better now I've had a good old howl,' she said. 'But I'm going to France I tell you, whether they like it or not.'

She got to her feet and kissed her mother, then gave Mick a hug. 'Sorry to spoil your first day,' she said humbly. 'It . . . it was the shock. I'm goin' up to me room now, to write out me letter of resignation and to put in for a job in France.'

There was silence in the kitchen until the door had shut behind her, then Mick walked slowly round the table and sat down in the chair his stepdaughter had just vacated. 'Poor wee lass,' he

362

said heavily. 'She's not realised she might be sent miles from Tolly, once she gets to France. Ada, she's exchanging one slavery for another, and for a worse one, what's more. Can't you forbid her? She's not strong ... tell me, are she and Tolly promised since I was last home?'

Ada shook her head. 'No, I'm sure they aren't. They're very fond of one another—whilst he was on board the *Duchess of Verona* they wrote often, and when war broke out and he came back into the hospital they were together most o' the time when they weren't workin'. I've often wondered, to tell you the truth, how things would pan out between 'em. I mean I knew they were very fond of one another, but there were never ... never a whisper of romance, nothin' like that.'

'Oh, lor'. And our Ellen's in love wi' the feller,' Mick said. 'Oh, dear.'

Deirdre looked from one face to the other. Why *Oh, dear*? There was nothing wrong with being in love, was there?

'An' there's our Ellen, nursing all sorts, officers, sergeants, sailors,' Ada said sadly. 'An' never more'n friendliness from her to them ... many a feller's fallen for her, wanted to meet when they left the ward, to take her out, to stay friends. But she wouldn't, wasn't interested. An' we're that fond o' Tolly ...'

'Aye. But if he ...' Mick paused and glanced from Deirdre to Donal, then back again. He cleared his throat. 'If he ain't the marryin' kind ...'

'Yes, well, there you are,' Ada said. She said it hurriedly. 'Now where's me shoppin', Dee?'

'There,' Deirdre said bluntly, pointing to the basket. 'Undo the newspaper, Mam. I tole Mr

363

Austen me da was home an' he put a bit extry on.'

'Extry?' Ada leaned across and unwrapped the newspaper, then sat back in her chair, eyes sparkling. 'Well, look at that, will ye, Mick!'

'Wharris it?' Deirdre said. It was all meat to her, but this particular piece looked bony and fatty and not particularly appealing.

'It's a leg o' mutton, a prime piece,' Ada said in a dazed voice. 'An' some scrag end for stew! What did you 'ave to give Mr Austen for that?' she added suspiciously. 'You din't go partin' wi' your dacent boots, did you?'

'I give him a carrot an' an onion an' three and nine,' Deirdre said. 'What 'ud ole Austen want wi' me boots, Mam? They'd be too small for him.'

'Three shillin' an' ninepence? You got that lot for three shillin' an' ninepence?' Ada said unbelievingly. 'Eh, pull the other one, our Dee.'

'Well, I did,' Deirdre said shortly. 'You won't let our Ellen go to France, will you, Mam? I don't want her to go to France.'

'I don't want her to go either, but she's norra child, chuck,' Ada said gently. 'I can't tell her what to do now, like I did when she were your age. But she'll be as safe in a hospital over there as she is here, I dare say. And now let's stop worryin' about things what we can't change an' get this stew a-goin'. The joint'll have to go to the baker's first thing tomorrer mornin', so's he can roast it for our Sunday dinner.'

*   *   *

Ellen closed the kitchen door firmly behind her and went straight up to the room she shared with

364

Deirdre. She knew that Ada must worry about Fred and Bertie, who were both at sea, but her mother tried to keep such worries to herself and so far—Ellen crossed her fingers—the boys had been all right. Dick was still at home, fortunately. He was quite an old married man now, with two small children and a job at the Bankhall Distillery on the corner of Juniper Street, and Ozzie was a clerk in the shipping offices down on the quayside. He was married as well, but his job was a complicated one and there had been no mention of his joining the armed forces.

So Mam's better off than some, Ellen told herself, going over to her chest of drawers and beginning to examine the clothing in the topmost drawer. Some mams had four or five sons away, whereas Ada Docherty only had a husband and two of her sons. If I go . . . why shouldn't I go, anyway? They need nurses and I'm pretty experienced, and besides, if I were married I wouldn't be at home now . . . and I have to be with Tolly!

It had been a strange relationship, though. She simply could not help herself. She loved Tolly desperately but she understood his reluctance to commit himself with the country at war and the pair of them worked off their feet. And he was better; she really thought he was. When they went to the cinema he held her hand; when they walked in the park he tucked her fingers into the crook of his elbow. He even kissed her sometimes—kisses light as the touch of a moth and, she supposed, as passionless—but long ago, on the night that the twins had so nearly been drowned, she had made up her mind. She would rather have Tolly's friendship and affection than anyone else's real

365

love. She would settle for a platonic relationship, if that was all Tolly could offer, and keep to herself the wild, surging hope that one day he would suddenly realise that what he felt for her was true love.

So the news that he had volunteered to go to France as a stretcher bearer was terribly hard to take. It was as though he had said to her: 'You mean nothing to me; I'm prepared to go far away from you and risk death, but I'm not prepared to stay with you and risk life.' Because that was the cold truth—he said he wouldn't let her get close to him in case one of them was hurt but Ellen knew, in her heart, that he was afraid of warmth and closeness. He didn't want the complications of love but preferred the cooler flame of a friendship which could be terminated, if necessary, without too much pain on either side. Ellen acknowledged that had she truly felt only friendship for him she would have waved him off to France regretfully, but with none of the tearing pain that she felt now, a pain made worse, she thought, by his carefully casual attitude towards her, which forbade her to show the emotion she felt.

But she had decided to settle for friendship, so although she had been unable to help her grief and despair showing just now, she would never let Tolly see them. And besides, wasn't she going to France as well? Didn't she intend to follow him to the ends of the earth if necessary, so that at least she could have the pleasure of his company?

Sometimes she wondered what she would do if Tolly fell in love with someone else, but she didn't worry about it, because she didn't believe it would happen. He was in love with her, he just hadn't realised it yet. And if the battlefields of France were his destiny, then they were hers, too. In the dreadful dream they had both been in France. Well, Mam said it wasn't a dream it was a nightmare, and nightmares didn't come true, they were just your mind worrying away at something. So she would go ahead with her plans and forget the stupid dream entirely. Or try to do so.

*   *   *

The ship churned on over a grey and troubled sea and Ellen stood on the deck, feeling every bit as grey and troubled herself. She was on her way to France, but not in quite the way she had planned, because although the hospital authorities had agreed that she could nurse in France, she had no idea how she would be employed, or where. She had been told, guardedly, that there was a big battle being fought shortly and that a great many nurses would be needed, but the authorities had not been prepared to expand further. What was more, she might end up a very long way from Tolly, only able to see him perhaps once or twice in twelve months.

'If you'd been able to drive . . .' the woman interviewing her had said, 'then it would have been a different story. We are very keen to recruit women ambulance drivers and one who is also an experienced nurse would have been doubly useful. But since you can't, I'm afraid I can only recommend that you are sent to France. You might find yourself on a hospital train, in one of the fall-back hospitals, or even at a clearing station near the front line. However, if the Powers that Be decide the need is greater in the receiving hospitals in England . . .'

Ellen knew there was no point in pleading or saying she might just as well stay in her present job and in fact she was one of the lucky ones. Quite shortly after her initial application she received her posting and the time of her cross-channel sailing, though she had no idea how she would be deployed. And here she was, half-way across the English channel with a clutch of other medical staff, waiting and wondering still.

When her posting had arrived, Ellen had made her way up to a particular house on Walton Road where she knew she would find the interest and understanding which she sought, for her mother had wept bitterly and the twins had begged her not to go.

'It ain't as if you're sure of bein' wi' Tolly,' Donal had said, red-eyed. ''Cos you isn't, Ellie. You could end up anywhere. Oh don't, don't go!'

'I must,' Ellen had said steadily. 'But I'll come back, chuck. The Boche don't shell as far behind the lines as hospitals.'

She knew it wasn't true, but when truth was painful you kept it from children, she told herself, making her way towards the Bartlett house.

Ellen and Liza Bartlett had been friends ever since Ellen had first begun, tentatively, to attend services at the Barracks. Liza came from a Salvationist background, so was able to help Ellen quite a lot as she gradually joined in more and more of the church activities, and the two girls speedily realised that they had a good deal in common. They were both Songsters, with strong, true voices, able to sing the solo part when

368

occasion demanded. They usually sat next to one another during services, accompanied each other on window-shopping expeditions as they grew up and spent time brushing each other's hair into new styles. They were both interested in welfare and had started work at the same time, though Liza was a slum officer with the Army, working all hours to see that the poor of the city, particularly the women and children, got as fair a deal as possible. Liza understood about Tolly and in fact had recently had a problem of her own; she had fallen in love with a young man who was not a Salvationist and had not dared to tell her parents, though she had confided at once in Ellen. So naturally enough, when Ellen wanted to tell someone her news her first thought was to go to Liza.

She found her friend up to her elbows in suds, doing her washing. Uniforms were kept spotlessly laundered by your mam, but underwear and your 'best' clothing was your own concern. Liza looked up from her work as Ellen knocked briefly on the back door and entered the kitchen. She was a sturdy, square girl with dark, very straight hair pulled back from a wide forehead, clear grey eyes and a high colour in her cheeks. She was wearing a grey cotton dress which was barely discernible beneath the huge apron she had wrapped around herself, and her feet were clad in wooden clogs which clattered as she walked across to the back door and dried herself on the roller towel on the back of it. 'Well, chuck? Any news?' she asked cheerfully. 'Let's have a cuppa, shall us? You look as though you've heard somethin' at last.'

'Yes; I've heard. I'll be off as soon as they can

arrange a sailing,' Ellen said brightly. 'Look, you go on wi' your work, Liza, and I'll make the tea. Anyone else wantin' a cup?'

'No. Mam's gone round to see me gran an' the kids are all in bed, praise be to God,' Liza said. 'Well, there's no denyin' I'll miss you, but I know it's what you want. If you're determined to mek the tea, I'll sit down for a moment. I were goin' to soak that lot for ten minutes or so anyway. They come the whiter for it, you know.' She settled down at the table with a sigh. 'Good to get the weight off me feet for a bit. Now, tell me what your mam said when you telled her. An' the twins? Have you written to Tolly, tellin' him you're headed for France? Where's they sendin' you, then?'

'I dunno, that's the trouble,' Ellen had said rather gloomily. 'You know how I feel, Liza . . . but I've no choice but to take the posting. And there's always time off . . . oh, I'll find out where Tolly is an' see him, it's just so hard to explain to the twins and Mam. Mam's that worried . . . and even Donal got a bit tearful. Dee went an' said if I were goin' so were she . . . what a business it is, eh?'

'It's a business I wouldn't mind bein' involved in,' Liza said. Her young man, Hubert Evans, had joined up some months ago and was now in France. Letters weren't a problem—her parents simply accepted that she was writing to a soldier—but even the most affectionate letters could not make up to Liza for his absence.

'You should've come nursin', wi' me,' Ellen said, warming the teapot from the big black kettle steaming over the fire. 'The only other way is ambulance drivin'—the lady interviewin' said they were desperate for lady drivers—but you can't learn that in a couple o' days, I dare say.'

'No-oo, but there is another way,' Liza said. 'Tell you in a minute. Now you tell me a bit more. Any chance of bein' posted to where Tolly is? Only don't they say stretcher bearers get sent all over? Makes it harder to find 'em.'

'That's right,' Ellen said gloomily. 'But there's hospitals and clearing stations all over—the lady interviewing me explained. And of course they're bringin' all the worst cases back home because we've got better facilities here . . . so she asked if I wouldn't go to one of the receivin' hospitals down south instead—Southampton, for instance. They need trained nurses.'

'Poor Ellie; and you couldn't explain, because they'd think you were goin' for all the wrong reasons, I s'pose. But they're sendin' you anyway, so *that's* all right. Now let me tell you what I'm thinkin' of doin'.'

'Carry on, queen,' Ellen said at once. She looked hard at her friend as she handed her a cup of tea. Liza looked remarkably cheerful for one who had more or less said that she was being left out of the adventure! Ellen sat down at the well-scrubbed kitchen table, opposite her friend, cradling her own cup between her hands. 'Go on, then. Tell!'

'The Salvationists have a group going over to France from here, to relieve the people who've been out there for the past six months or so,' Liza said. 'They'll be up at the Front, where the stretcher bearers go, I dare say. And they're centred on Rouen. I thought I might ask if I could go. They need the right sort of people, and I thought . . . I thought . . .'

'Oh, Liza!' Ellen exclaimed. 'It would be

371

marvellous if it was the two of us, and I'm sure the Army will jump at the chance of taking you over. You're such a hard worker and so ... so practical and sensible. Have you tried to get aboard? Who's doing the interviews?'

'I pretended I was interested for you,' Liza admitted, shamefaced. 'I couldn't say it was for meself until I'd had a think. But it's a Captain Raines and he'll be at the Barracks all day today if ... if anyone wants to talk to him. So if you think I could do it, how about if we could both go round there when we've finished our tea and have a word. What d'you think?'

'Oh, Liza! It would be marvellous to have you near, even if we weren't that close. I wouldn't feel anywhere near as ... well, as alone, and Mam and the twins would feel better about it too, I just know they would,' Ellen said ecstatically. 'Can we go *now*?'

Liza laughed. 'As soon as we've finished our tea, I said—an' this cup's hot! Don't worry, the Captain won't run away. Did you eat before you come up here, or could you do wi' some bread an' cheese?'

As soon as she and Liza had finished their impromptu tea they went and called on Captain Raines at the Barracks and Liza was gladly accepted as a volunteer for France. She was told that she would be under the command of the Captain, and that she must remember that she would see terrible sights and, in many cases, be unable to do anything to help.

'We talk to the men, take them hot drinks, food sometimes, and remind them that God is everywhere, even in those terrible trenches,' Captain Raines had told her. 'We bring them hope,

372

a smile, a few words of comfort. We go right up to the front lines . . . but we can't interfere, even when we see terrible things. Sometimes, Miss Barlett, not interfering is the hardest thing we have to do.' He had cleared his throat. 'I know you and Miss Docherty here are good friends, and I can guess that you would like to be able to see each other and various friends who've joined the Army from time to time, when your work and theirs allows. But regardless of such feelings, your work—and the welfare of the men we go to serve—must come first. I don't ask you if you understand that because I know you do, or I wouldn't consider taking you with us. I'm just reminding you.'

'I shan't forget,' Liza had said humbly. 'And . . . and though of course I'd like to see as much of Ellen as possible, I do understand that it may not be possible. As for . . . for other friends . . .'

'Then that's settled,' Captain Raines had said heartily. 'We've a sailing fixed, so you'll be off in a few days. Would you like me to speak to your mother?'

But Liza thought it would come best from her and the two friends had made their separate way homeward, happier in their minds now that both of them had taken the plunge into a new life.

And a new life it has been so far, and will be newer yet, Ellen thought now, staring ahead across the grey and troubled sea towards the as yet unseen shores of France.

It was odd, really, she mused, as the ship ploughed onward. Ever since she had met Tolly he had been in the forefront of her thoughts yet now, when she was actually heading towards him, she found it difficult to see, in her mind's eye, that

373

much-loved face. Which was even odder when you remembered how constantly his face had swum before her inner eye when he had gone off in the *Duchess*, to seek his fortune and learn more about himself. Then, her mental picture of him had been clear and constant. Yet now, when he was far from her and in danger, she had to go to the box of treasures which she kept in the top drawer of her clothes chest and fish out the little photograph which had been taken of the band when Tolly had been soloist in a charity concert given by the Army in order to raise funds for the troops.

Then . . . ah, then she wondered how she could ever have forgotten. The photograph wasn't a particularly clear one, but it showed Tolly's strong chin, the shape of his nose, the way his hair grew. And, most importantly, it reminded her of his expressions—sometimes amused, sometimes grave, but always . . . always *caring*, somehow. Tolly never looked at anyone with the indifference which is probably the commonest expression seen on most people's faces. After all, no matter how one might try, Ellen knew it wasn't always possible to love every single member of the human race. Only Tolly seemed to have perfected the art. Sometimes Ellen found herself wishing that Tolly wasn't quite so nice to everyone, because it was so difficult to tell oneself that he was especially fond of her, but she mostly had the good grace to banish the thought as soon as it occurred, shocked at her own shallowness. Loving one's fellow man was a rare gift; she might justifiably envy Tolly's possession of it but never grudge him.

And now, here she was, about to set foot on the same ground that Tolly trod. Then I shan't have to keep looking at the photograph, she reminded herself, because whenever I have a moment off I'll meet up with him. And she refused to remember how the war seemed to spread and spread, how the men got moved around like pieces on a chess board, how she had heard stories of brothers being in the same theatre of war for months and never meeting. It'll be different for us, because neither of us is in the Army, so we will have more freedom, she told herself. And if I do find it hard to meet up with him once I'm on the spot, there's always Liza. Liza had, in the end, gone a couple of weeks before Ellen, so it had been she waving her friend off and then returning, disconsolate, home, not at all as they had imagined. But Liza, with the Salvationists, would go right up to the front lines, the Captain had said so, and would see the stretcher bearers constantly. She might be able to tell Ellen just how to find Tolly.

And then stretcher bearers go constantly to and from hospitals and clearing stations, she reminded herself. He may not come on to the wards but hospital grapevines are the same all over the world, I expect. Once the staff who are bringing the wounded on to the wards know Tolly's a friend of mine, I'll be told whenever he's around or expected, even. So that's all right! It won't be long, now, before Tolly and I are together again.

$$* \qquad * \qquad *$$

'Nurse Docherty! Nurse! If you've finished with that row can you give me a hand over here?'

Ellen had indeed finished with her row, for the brand-new beds had all been made up with brand-

375

new sheets, pillowcases, draw-sheets and blankets and were ready, now, for whatever might come. So she went over to Nurse Robbins, who was making up the last row of all, and picked up two crisp white pillowslips.

'Thanks, Docherty,' the other girl said. 'Don't you find this depressing? All these beds, just waiting . . . it's almost as if they do it on purpose—wound and kill, I mean.'

Ellen nodded, sliding a pillow into its case and laying it carefully on the taut bottom sheet. 'Yes, I know exactly what you mean. They send those boys over the top knowing there will be hundreds of deaths and casualties, they bring doctors and nurses like us to forward clearing stations so we can patch 'em up and send 'em back . . . but I suppose it's the only way they know to fight a war.'

Nurse Robbins snorted. 'I can't help wondering whether they'd feel the same—the top brass, I mean—if they had to go over the top with the boys. Still, at least this time we're preparing for the worst and hoping for the best.' She glanced around her, then lowered her voice. 'They say tomorrow's Z-day. So by tomorrow evening a good few of these beds will probably be full.'

Nurse Robbins had been in France a year and knew what she was talking about. Ellen, who had only experienced the back-up hospitals in Britain, sighed. She had been here five days and so far all they had done was prepare. She found herself suddenly dreading the descent which would happen by dusk next day if her friend was right. At home it took time to get the wounded to their destinations and the hospitals were consequently forewarned, but here, in a forward clearing station, the men came in straight from the trenches. Here, they would see for themselves patients not already swathed in bandages and dressings, men mortally wounded, some on the point of death.

'Yes, I suppose they will,' she said now, straightening the top sheet. 'One thing though, Robbie—Sisters and Matrons over here seem far less ... oh, less pernickety than the ones back home. It'll be a relief to be allowed to nurse, instead of being given absurd instructions about the straightness of top sheets and the evils of allowing a bedpan on to the ward when doctors or surgeons are present.'

Nurse Robbins chuckled. 'Wait until tomorrow,' she advised. 'When you're run off your feet and kept on duty for shift after shift, you'll look back on those quiet peacetime days with longing. You see if I'm not right.'

CHAPTER TWELVE

August 1917

Liam couldn't sleep. It wasn't just the cold or the noise—there were men slumbering all round him, slumped among the piles of equipment which they would carry with them next morning when they went over the top—it was fear. Not fear of death either, or even of disability, but of letting himself down. Turning back and being shot as a coward— breaking down, causing failure through some unguessed-at reaction.

Others felt it too. Glancing around, he could see

the occasional bright glow as a soldier drew on a cigarette, a hunched shoulder slumped as its owner shifted in his place. But the tremendous barrage covered all sounds. I can't even hear my heartbeats, Liam thought. If my heart was to stop, sure and I'd be the last one to know, so I would!

Sighing, he thought of home: of Dublin, the court, his family. What was he *doing* here, fighting this senseless war for a country which had oppressed Ireland for centuries, which had put down the Easter Rising with great brutality some eighteen months earlier? He must be mad!

But he knew why he was here really. It had been Maggie's death, of course. His mind went back to that dreadful day three long years ago, when he'd returned from England to find Maggie. On being told by the boy on the market stall that the family was at Glasnevin he had hurried up to the cemetery. When he was young his mother had taken him up there every weekend to visit family graves so he knew the way like the back of his hand, though he had not been there for a year or two. He had turned and hurried back down to the Quays, where he had only a few hours before got off the Liverpool ferry. He crossed the Whitworth Bridge and walked up Church Street past The Broadstone, where the trains left for Galway, and on to the Phibsborough Road. Dear God, Liam thought, let me be in time, let her not be buried already! At last, however, the Deadman's public house and the watchtowers on the cemetery walls hove into view. The Prospect Gate was locked, so he had turned and gone to the main gate.

The gatekeeper saw him as he walked through. 'Still keepin' dry,' he said cheerfully, indicating the cloudy sky. 'Can I help yiz?'

'There's a funeral, a young woman, Maggie McVeigh,' Liam had stammered. 'I'm after attending if I possibly can.'

'Oh, ye've missed that,' the gateman said. 'They're all gone, they've bin gone half an hour or more. Didn't ye know the funeral was earlier?'

'I've just got back from England this mornin',' Liam told him. 'I came here as quick as I could. Can ye tell me where she's buried?'

'She's in St Brigid's plot, so she is,' the man said. 'Do you know the way? Ye'll find it easy enough— it's the only new grave down there.'

Liam thanked him and turned back to where the flower sellers sat outside the main gate. He bought some flowers and, holding them stiffly in his hand, went through the gates and down towards St Brigid's plot. He found the grave easily enough for it was as the gatekeeper said, newly turned earth and there were a number of flowers on it already. He laid his carefully on top of the mound and then felt his knees give beneath him and sat down on the path.

He could see her so clearly in his mind's eye; the dark, springy hair, the little straight nose, the sweet curve of her lips. She'd not had much of a life, his Maggie, but he'd meant to make up to her for the hardships she'd suffered: a home of her own, his love and respect, babies one day. And then they had quarrelled over his chasing after the twins. He'd left her and she'd been killed. All their hopes of a bright future come to nought, because he'd been in too much of a hurry—too impatient to take the time to explain, persuade.

And as he sat there, tears welled up in his eyes

379

and rolled down his cheeks. He tried to think what he should do now—tried in vain.

He could not have said how long he sat there weeping for his Maggie, but presently he realised that dusk was falling. He got stiffly to his feet and looked up at the big black-and-gold clock over the office. Good Lord, he'd been here hours, so he had, he'd best get a move on or he'd find himself locked in, for the big gates were closed at dusk.

Liam hurried back to the exit and the keeper opened up for him without waiting to be asked to do so. "Tis sorry I am, lad,' he said, awkwardly. 'And her so young.'

Afterwards, life at home was impossibly painful. He had tried to fit in, of course he had. He had gone back to his job at the Post Office where they had been very understanding and he had moved back into his room at home, but he could not bear to be where he had been so happy with Maggie for so long and after less than a week he had told Mammy he was leaving. 'I'm goin' to join the Army,' he said gruffly. 'It's better, Mammy, it's better. Maggie's presence is here, everywhere. Every road I walk along I've walked along with Maggie. Everyone I speak to knew her, loved her. I can't stick it, Mam, I'm best away from Dublin for a bit.'

To give his mother her due, she had understood. 'But the Army, Liam,' she said tremulously. 'Does it have to be the Army?'

'It's got to be somewhere right away from Dublin, where no one knows me,' Liam said. 'It seems the best thing right now. Anyway, Mam, everyone keeps saying it'll all be over before Christmas. If I go at once I can be in the thick of it

380

by November, and home soon enough.'

And now, just three years since he had first joined up, he was a seasoned soldier, and sometimes he thought ruefully that if it hadn't been for the little photograph of Maggie which had been taken on that day trip to Booterstown three years before, and which he kept in the breast pocket of his battledress, he might not even be able to remember the look of her face. Sometimes, when he heard other men talking about their girl-friends he felt a terrible guilty stab—had he ever really been in love with Maggie, or had it been because she was near and she loved him that he had first begun to think about marriage? He couldn't help remembering that his interest in her had not awakened until another feller had begun to notice her, and her urge to get married had always been much stronger than his. But it was no good wondering because he'd never know, better to acknowledge his loss and simply slog on through the war and tell himself that when it was over he'd begin a real life again.

The photograph wasn't quite the only thing he had of Maggie's though. When he'd gone round to Mrs Collins to talk to her about what had happened she had given him the picture. 'Maggie was mortal fond of this little old picture,' she had said. 'You'd better have it, Liam, or perhaps you might give it to your mam.'

But Liam had kept the picture—it would have been a betrayal, so it would, to give it to Mammy after what had happened—and in a way it reminded him of Maggie even more than the photo did. He remembered from the very first moment she had come to live with them how she had loved

381

it and how, gradually, he had grown to be fond of it as well. So now, although it was a little tatty, it was shoved in his knapsack and he kept it with him wherever he went.

These weren't the best of thoughts, though, so Liam sat up and nudged Steve. Steve was his best friend, a tough, cynical Liverpudlian with a great sense of humour. They had joined up together and stayed together ever since. Tomorrow they would . . .

'Hey, Steve, how much longer?'

Steve had his father's pocket watch and even if he couldn't hear what Liam was saying he must have guessed. He fished out the watch and held it so that Liam could see the face and Liam, reading it, suddenly realised that dawn had broken. The eastern sky was growing lighter, the stars overhead were paling and even as he leaned nearer to Steve, the noise stopped abruptly. The sudden silence was almost as shattering as the bombardment had been and Liam shivered and hugged his greatcoat round him.

'I suppose they expect the Boches to come out of their bolt-holes and stand around chatting, so that they can be flattened by the next lot,' Steve said. 'I'm going to get some shut-eye whilst it's quiet.'

He rolled over on to his side and after a moment Liam followed suit. He didn't expect to sleep because it was getting steadily colder as the light strengthened, but presently he began to hear noises again—the creak of a knapsack settling as a man moved his weight against it; a clatter as someone cautiously turned over; and suddenly, cows lowing in the far distance. It was a soothing, gentle sound. Liam lay back and listened, gazing up at the fading

382

stars. He knew he wouldn't sleep . . .

He woke with someone shaking him. It was Steve. 'Come on old fellow—rise and shine! Any moment now . . .' The crash of the bombardment starting again drowned his voice, but Liam had got the message. All round him men were stirring, standing, picking up various pieces of equipment, generally preparing themselves for what lay ahead. He reached for his Lee-Enfield and got stiffly to his feet, shuffling towards the ladder, feeling his guts begin to knot with fear. But once they were up and over it would pass. The queue shuffled forward and Liam put his foot on the bottom rung. Any moment . . .

*　　　*　　　*

It was still raining. It had rained throughout the advance, retreat and advance of the previous day and it was only now the stretcher bearers had been sent out to fetch in the wounded. Tolly, Chris, George and Snowy flogged through the deepest mud Tolly thought they had ever experienced. Normally two men could manage a stretcher easily, but now because of the depth of the mud and the appalling weather, they had been sent out in fours with other men standing by to help if necessary. Bomb craters were everywhere—enormous holes filled with water into which a man could easily fall with fatal results. And it was so difficult to see with this fine rain blowing into their faces all the time. Tolly, however, was feeling relatively cheerful. When he came off this shift he would be off duty for a couple of days. Behind the lines there would be dry clothes, he thought longingly, and a decent meal, perhaps even a hot bath.

'That's it, Tolly, there's bodies ahead, keep goin',' George shouted. Tolly could see that the ground in front of him was treacherous to say the least, with great holes and hillocks alternately, and with the wounded men that they had come to fetch now beginning to be visible through the increasingly heavy rain. They were going to have to take great care.

'Something moved to our left,' called Snowy. 'Can you wheel in that direction, Tolly?' The stretcher party all wheeled to the left and saw the man whom Snowy had pointed out. They drew alongside him and two of them lifted the groaning man on to the mud-speckled stretcher, while the other two held it, unable to stand it down because of the mud.

'Let's get him back to the ambulance,' gasped Chris. 'Come on! Back!' They moved round, their feet slipping in the thick mud. Tolly, in spite of the heavy hobnailed boots he wore, suddenly felt something firm beneath his foot. Thank God for the occasional stone he thought, treading heavily. The next moment there was a tremendous explosion, a searing pain in his right foot and Tolly felt himself cartwheeling through the air to land in a huddled heap in the thickness of the mud.

*   *   *

'Docherty, oh, Docherty!'

Ellen turned as Sister Rose bore down on her. 'Ah, Docherty, I'm glad to have found you. There are some stretcher bearers in the reception area. I understand you're friendly with one of them—that

384

young Salvationist chappie,' the Sister called out.

'Why thank you, Sister,' Ellen replied. 'I'm off duty in ten minutes; I'll pop along and see them.'

Tolly often accompanied casualties and Ellen tried to take these opportunities for a chat, for although she had realised, during the long year spent confronting the harsh realities of war, that what she had thought to be enduring and abiding love was nothing more than an infatuation for the first young man she had known, she was still fonder of Tolly than anyone else she had yet met. And knowing that the wounded from the latest battle at Ypres were being brought in she had been half expecting him to turn up.

Ellen walked sedately down to the reception area, for the Sister was very cross with nurses she caught running, and went up to the group of stretcher bearers who were having a quick cup of tea. 'Hallo, you lot,' she said amiably. 'Pretty bad out there, is it?' She looked round. 'Where's Tolly then—Sister said you've a message from him—he hasn't gone off without waiting for me, has he?'

The men looked uncomfortably from one to another and the oldest spoke. 'We know he's a friend of yours, nurse. Didn't Sister tell you that . . . that he's a casualty?'

'A casualty?' Ellen felt her heatbeat quicken. Even though she knew now they would never become lovers, Tolly would always be one of her dearest friends. He was a good companion and she prayed that he had only received a flesh wound. She heard her voice shake as she asked: 'What's happened?'

'We don't rightly know, but I reckon he may have copped a Blighty one. It seems that one of the chaps trod on a land mine or an unexploded bomb or something like that. There were three of them injured out of the four and they already had a casualty with them on the stretcher I believe, so they were all brought into the casualty clearing station together. It seems Tolly's injuries were bad enough for him to be shipped off to hospital as soon as he was well enough to be moved.'

Ellen shivered. 'Oh, dear God! Did anyone say how badly he was wounded?'

The man shook his head. 'No, just that he was one of the injured. You know what the gossip is like and how it travels around, so he may not be too bad—we only heard he was one of them today and apparently it happened over a week ago.'

'Which hospital has he gone to?' asked Ellen. 'Do you know?'

'St Omer, we heard,' said the man.

'Thanks for letting me know,' Ellen said gratefully. 'I'll have a word with Sister and perhaps she'll let me have some time off to go and see him. I'm sure she'll understand.'

Although the wounded were still coming in from the dressing stations the nurses were coping well. The third battle of Ypres had, like all the others, brought in a steadily mounting number of wounded men, but there were fewer each day now. If Tolly had been hurt at the beginning of the battle he'd probably have been at the hospital for some days, so she would do her best to get to St Omer as soon as she could.

She thanked the men and hurried back to the ward to find Sister Rose writing up her notes. Sister looked up as Ellen drew level with her desk. 'Ah, Docherty. Did you see your friend?'

'No, Sister, because he's in hospital—that was what the chaps came to tell me. It seems he's been taken to No.7 General Hospital near St Omer. Tolly's been like a brother to me for years—he's an orphan, you know—so I was hoping that I might have some time off to go and see him.'

'You're in luck,' Sister Rose said pleasantly. 'We're evacuating some of the patients to St Omer early tomorrow morning to make room for the casualties coming in. There will be two ambulances and Nurse Bly was going with them, but in the circumstances I'll ask her to change with you. It's not too busy, is it? There's not too much still to be done?'

'Oh no, Sister, and there are plenty of nurses here at the moment. Thank you very much—I'll be ready for an early start tomorrow morning.'

*   *   *

Tolly lay very still in his bed with his eyes focused upon the white hump of the cage which covered him from the knees down, although he was not seeing it. He was trying to assimilate what the doctor had told him earlier in the day. A nurse had drawn the screens round his bed and then the doctor, with a couple of nurses in attendance, had come in and stood by his bed whilst one of the nurses stripped the bedcovers and removed the cage. It was no good being brave. Tolly closed his eyes and waited while bandages were undone, the dressing removed and the wound revealed. He didn't open them again until the doctor addressed him. 'Looking good, Tolliver,' the doctor said genially, 'If you go on at this rate you'll be home before Christmas.' He laughed, although Tolly didn't consider the remark particularly amusing. 'In fact, my boy, I'm going to recommend that you're sent back to Blighty. You're obviously not going to be able to do any sort of work here. I suppose you must have realised that?'

Tolly nodded. 'Yes, sir,' he said.

'Well, do you want to know what the future holds for you, young man?' the doctor asked.

Again Tolly nodded. 'Yes, sir,' he repeated.

'Nurse, renew the dressings,' the doctor said and moved to one side as the nurses took over.

Tolly continued to fix his eyes on the doctor's face. 'Sir?' he said.

'Yes, yes, yes, let me think. It'll be probably another fortnight before you go down to Étaples and from there you'll be shipped back to Blighty as soon as they can find room for you. Of course, you won't be able to go straight home, it'll be at least a further couple of weeks in an English hospital for you, to settle you down and make sure your stump isn't going to play up. You'll be having an artificial leg fitted in due course but that won't be for a while yet—maybe six months. Roehampton have their work cut out to find beds right now, so in the meanwhile, my lad, as soon as the hospital in Blighty thinks you're fit, you'll be able to go home.' He raised a quizzical brow. 'Better than hospital, what?'

'Yes sir, much better,' Tolly said. 'Which hospital will I be in?'

'Can't tell you that, my lad. Where do you come from?'

'Liverpool, sir, Everton.'

'Well, we'll see if we can get you in somewhere

that way,' the doctor said easily. 'Somewhere near your family, eh?'

Yes, sir,' Tolly said. Not for the world would he have admitted to the doctor that there was no family. 'Thank you, sir.'

The doctor nodded and the nurses removed the screens from round his bed, leaving Tolly a prey to various emotions, the chief of which was worry about where he would go. It was all very well to dismiss him from hospital and tell him to go home but, strictly speaking, he didn't have a home. Lodgings, yes, but what landlady, however well intentioned, would take him into a lodging house with only one leg? The responsibility would deter most women, he thought.

The Salvationists would be good to him, of course they would. There were many members of the Army who had helped him in the past and would undoubtedly help him again. But he didn't want that sort of help, he didn't want to be a burden to anyone. What he wanted was . . .

He groaned to himself: he didn't know what he wanted. If only he had a family of his own, a mam and a dad to turn to, but he didn't, so there was no point in wishing. There was only the Ragged Boys Home and good though they'd been to him they didn't have the facilities to look after a wounded man.

For an hour after the doctor had left him Tolly fretted, but then tiredness and misery overcame him and he closed his eyes. He was gently on his way to sleep when he became aware that someone was standing by the bed. He opened his eyes and glanced to the left. A nurse stood there . . . and then he began to smile as he recognised her.

389

'Ellen!'

He tried to struggle into a sitting position but Ellen waved him back and leant over the bed and kissed his forehead gently.

'Tolly, you poor boy. The nurse told me that you've lost your . . . that you've had your foot blown off and they've had to tidy you up a bit.'

Tolly laughed a trifle bitterly. 'Tidy me up! They've taken my leg off, just below the knee.'

'Yes, love, I know. It's cruel hard. But at least you're alive, Tolly, and you're going home. Back to Blighty, she told me.'

'Oh yes. I'm going home,' Tolly said gloomily. 'But for six months or so I've got to find somewhere to live until my stump is ready to have the artificial leg put on. Once it's on, I suppose I shall be able to work or do something. I don't know.'

Ellen knelt down by the side of the bed. 'Tolly, what are you talking about? If you're going back to the Pool, you must go to my home. You know Mam would love to have you and the twins would help you in every way.'

Tolly smiled at her. Even the possibility of staying with the Dochertys was immensely cheering, but after a moment he said doubtfully, 'Well, yes, but I couldn't ask that of your mam, Ellen. It's not as if you and I . . .'

'No, no, I know there's nothing like *that* between us, but we're good friends and Mam is really fond of you, Tolly,' Ellen said reassuringly. 'You must . . . look, I'll write to her today. You must go to Mere Lane. They'll welcome you, you know they will, and they'll look after you.

390

When you're fit and well with your artificial leg and some sort of job to go to, you can choose whether you stay in Mere Lane or go. You know Mam's got room—the boys are either in the forces or away from home, there's only Dee and Donal living there now. Tolly, I'll write to Mam today, I promise you, and I'll come back as soon as I can and let you know what she says. No—better than that—I'll get her to write straight to you.'

Tolly raised his eyes to her face. 'Are . . . are you sure, Ellen? Remember I may still be there when you come home.'

Ellen grinned. 'Oh, I can bear you if the twins can. Look, Tolly, I haven't got long, 'cos I'm going back with the ambulance, but I promise you I'll be in touch in a couple of days and Mam will write as soon as she can. Now, don't look miserable and don't feel miserable, everything is going to be all right. 'Bye, love.' She bent and kissed his forehead once more, then turned and left the ward.

Tolly lay back against his pillows. Wave after wave of relief was crashing over him. He was suddenly certain that Ada Docherty and the twins would welcome him and at the very thought his worries began to fade. He'd always been a chap who could cope for himself—he'd had to—it was like that when you were orphaned. But being with the Dochertys would make all the difference. He could face whatever came with their help. He grinned at the man in the next bed who was peering curiously at him. 'That was the nearest thing to a sister I've got,' he said contentedly. 'I'll be all right, now.'

*   *   *

'Post, Mam, and it's a good one.' Deirdre came bouncing into the room and threw a handful of envelopes down on to the table in front of her mother, 'There's one from Ozzie, one from Bert and one from Ellen. How about that, eh?' She plonked herself down on the chair next to Donal and reached for the loaf. 'I wonder why letters always come in batches, Mam.'

She began to saw at the loaf with the breadknife and Sammy, who was sitting next to her, leaned across and picked up one of the envelopes and looked at it curiously. 'There's not a letter from our Dick or our Fred,' he said disappointedly. 'I thought you said from everyone.'

'Dick isn't abroad,' Deirdre said patiently. 'Pass us the marge and don't grab, Sammy; if you want some bread, tell me and I'll cut you a slice.'

'I want some bread,' Sammy said hopefully, 'and some jam.'

'Say please when you want somethin'. And there's only a bit of jam left,' Ada said, turning the envelopes over. 'Which one shall I read first, eh?' Without waiting for a reply she slit open the first envelope. 'Bert is fine,' she announced, 'only his friend Chester has been wounded.' She passed the letter to Donal who was sitting next to her and opened the next one. 'Oz is coming home on leave in a month,' she said. 'That'll be good; we haven't seen our Ozzie for a long time.'

The letters as they were opened were handed round the table although Toby, always a silent child, sat stuffing himself with bread and jam and only gave them a cursory glance.

Ada picked up the next letter and scanned it. 'This one's from Ellen,' she said, opening it. After only one glance, however, she gave a sharp exclamation. 'Oh, my word, Tolly's been hurt! Oh, the poor feller, hurt bad.'

'Pass the letter round,' said Donal. 'Come on, Mam, gi's a look at it.'

'No, Mam, read it aloud,' urged Deirdre. 'Oh, I do love Tolly—I wondered why he'd not writ to me lately. Is he in our Ellen's hospital?'

'I don't think so,' Ada said absent-mindedly. 'You shall have the letter in a minute; just let me finish.'

For once there was silence round the table as she read. Even Sammy stopped chewing and Toby stared at his mother, round-eyed. At last, however, Ada put the letter down on the table and turned towards Deirdre.

'What is it? What?' Deirdre said agitatedly. 'What's happened, Mam? Oh, he's not—he can't be . . .'

'No, no, but he's been badly injured. He's had his foot blown off and the doctors had to tek the leg off below the knee. Poor old feller.'

'I remember Tolly,' piped up Sammy. 'Ah, poor old Tolly!'

'Gosh! To lose a leg—is that a Blighty one, Mam?' said Donal. Everyone knew the meaning of such expressions by now. 'Poor ole Tolly! What'll he do?'

'Course it is,' Ada said impatiently. 'Ellen's writ to ask if we'll have him here. Poor feller, he's always so cheerful I forgit he's a norphan wi' no folks of his own. He'll need friends till he picks himself up agin.'

'Oh, Mam, we will have him, won't we?' Deirdre said eagerly. 'I'm ever so fond of Tolly.'

'Yes, of course he can come to us,' Ada said, still holding on to the letter. 'I wish Ellen could come home an' all. She's been out there long enough. It's time she took a break. Still the papers say the tide's turnin' at last, so mebbe it'll be over soon. That'd be nice, wouldn't it?'

'Yes,' Donal said. 'I'd like to see our Ellen again an' all. But we'll definitely be seein' Tolly soon, won't we, Mam?'

'Looks like it. Ellen says I'm to write direct to him, 'cos she's fifty miles away, so I'll do that when breakfast is over. Let me see now, he can have the boys' room, give him some space for once. They're forty to a ward, Ellen says. They'll have to let his wound heal afore he can be shipped home, but wi' luck he'll be in Blighty in a month or so. They're going to try an' git him into a Liverpool hospital if they can, just till his stump is healed up, then he'll come to us,' Ada said, smiling at the twins and handing them the letter. 'You've bin ever so good, writin' to your brothers, an' Ellen, an' Tolly as well. I know you'll give a hand once he's here.'

When breakfast was finished Sammy and Toby helped to clear the table and the twins set off up Mere Lane towards Heyworth Street. The war had done one good thing as far as they were concerned: both Deirdre and Donal now had a job. Not full-time jobs, of course, because they were still in school, but jobs which kept them busy after school and on Saturdays.

Deirdre was still working in her aunt's shop but

she didn't go in after school often because there was insufficient business what with rationing and shortages, and Donal was a delivery boy for one of the local butchers, working for them in the holidays and in the evenings after school, and he had a paper round in the mornings.

Both twins appreciated the extra money which their efforts brought in, although naturally they gave most of their earnings to their mother, but it seriously curtailed their time together. During the week Donal had an early breakfast and went straight to school after his paper round, then directly to the butcher's shop afterwards. On a Saturday, however, he always walked to work with his sister and usually met her outside the shop at the end of the day so they could come home together.

Sundays were of course a free day which they could have spent in each other's company but at the age of thirteen they both enjoyed the companionship of their own friends, so they made the most of the Saturday walks to and from work.

Since today was Saturday, Donal had already done his paper round and wasn't going in to the butchers until eleven, when the orders would be made up, but Deirdre would be expected in by eight-thirty so when they reached Heyworth Street they both turned left along it. Today Donal would walk his sister to work, then go and pick up one of his friends who lived conveniently close by in Waterhouse Street and they would pass the time together until he was due at his job.

'It's good about Tolly coming back, isn't it, Dee,' Donal said presently as they walked along. 'I reckon we can get all sorts of extras for him, don't you?'

'Aye,' Deirdre admitted. 'But it isn't that, Don. It's having him back—it'll be great, won't it? Do you remember when he used to play with the band in the park? We'd follow him for miles, wi' Sammy yellin' from the pram.'

'He won't be playin' in the park for a bit,' Donal observed, 'not with one leg missin'. An' he'll need both his hands for his crutches—he won't be able to play an instrument at all for a bit, will he, Dee?'

'Well, he could if you or I was to trot along beside him carrying his trumpet until he had to play; and then he could, like, prop himself up on his crutches, leavin' his hands free. Haven't you seen that chap on Everton Road, the one with a cap?'

'Oh aye,' Donal said, 'but Tolly isn't like that. He wouldn't feel right being stared at.'

'Rubbish,' Deirdre said briskly, 'Tolly wouldn't mind, but anyhow people won't stare, particularly once he's got his artificial leg. Oh, he'll be all right—just you wait and see. I do like Tolly.'

'Aye, I know you do,' Donal said. 'And so does our Ellen, eh?'

'If it weren't for our Ellen, I'd like Tolly for my sweetheart,' Deirdre confided. 'Still, there you are—they was always ever so fond, I bet they'll marry, don't you, when our Ellen gets back?'

'Yes, bound to, an' even if they don't, Tolly won't want a kid like you!' Donal said. Marriage seemed to him to be an infinitely boring subject. 'I wonder if he'll let me have a go on his crutches?'

Deirdre aimed a swipe at him. 'I won't be a kid for ever and as for the crutches, that's all you boys think about,' she said. *Will he lend me his crutches?*

He'll need them himself, you fool.'

'Not all the time, he won't,' Donal objected. 'He's not going to use them when he's sittin' in a chair. He might let me have a go on them then.'

'Yes, well, don't you pester him,' Deirdre said darkly. 'If you pester Tolly I'll chop *your* bleedin' leg off for you, so help me.'

'Shut your face, our Dee,' Donal said, grinning. 'You'll be as keen yourself to have a go on the crutches, you know you will.' They stopped outside the bakery shop. 'Well, you'd best be off in. I'm goin' to see whether Fred's up yet.'

Going into the shop, Deirdre greeted the other assistants busy behind the counter and went and hung her coat up in the back. In another year she'd be working full time, but it jolly well wouldn't be in her aunt's shop if she could possibly help it. She'd go to the munitions factory if the war was still on because the money was good, but whilst you were still in school you had to take what you were offered and the work in the shop, though arduous in some ways, wasn't particularly unpleasant.

'Deirdre, get a basket an' fetch them loaves in from the bake'ouse,' shouted one of the older women. 'There'll be a queue outside 'ere afore you know where we are.'

Deirdre, obeying, continued to think about Tolly. She did like him so much! She thought Ellen was the luckiest girl in the world to have won his affection. If it wasn't for Ellen, she thought to herself, I'd set me cap at him, even if I am a bit young. Still it was no good thinking like that: she remembered the night on the sands when she and Donal had sat in their tent and watched Ellen and Tolly kissing. You didn't kiss someone like that if

397

you weren't going to get wed and that had been ages ago; by now they'd be real fond. Of course, Ellen never said much about Tolly in her letters, except in the most casual way, but Ellen had never worn her heart on her sleeve—not in front of her younger brothers and sister, anyway. Deirdre picked up another loaf and jammed it into the big basket, sighing deeply. Ever since she'd been small she'd dreamed of marrying Tolly one day, but even if she couldn't have him for herself she'd have him for a brother-in-law and that would be pretty good.

'Come on, Dee, there's a queue forming. Get a move on, queen!'

Deirdre crammed another couple of loaves into her basket and set off for the front of the shop. At least Tolly would be home soon, even if he would never have any feeling for her apart from brotherly affection.

'Right. Thanks, Dee,' the older woman said, as Deirdre staggered into the shop. She took the basket from her. 'Now you go on back into the bake'ouse and make us some sangwidges—they'll be wantin' them almost as soon as the bleedin' doors open.'

Deirdre obeyed with alacrity—she liked making sandwiches. It could be difficult in the bakery shop with people queuing for bread and rations and moaning about the dullness of the cakes on sale, but if you were in the back, making sandwiches, you had time to think and to chat, even if you had to work pretty fast. Besides, Nellie was in the back. Nellie was a little older than her—just a couple of years—and the two girls got on well, so as soon as she was able to do so Deirdre told Nellie that Tolly was coming to stay with them.

398

'You've always been sweet on him, our Dee,' Nellie remarked, spreading margarine on slices of bread. 'We'll never hear the last of this, eh?'

'He's sweet on my sister,' Deirdre said gruffly. 'Anyway, he's only got one leg so. Donal reckons we'll get loads of extras because Tolly's a wounded soldier.'

'Well you might, at that,' Nellie agreed. 'But you never know, you said Tolly'd lost a leg—might that mek a difference to your sister?'

Deirdre sniffed scornfully. 'Our Ellen's a nurse, Nellie. She won't think like that. 'Sides that'd be a terrible thing, wouldn't it, to leave off lovin' somone just 'cos they'd lost their leg?'

'Yeah,' agreed Nellie. 'But people do change, Dee. It's bin years since you seen 'em together. They're not engaged, are they?'

'No,' agreed Deirdre, 'but we saw them kissin' once, me and Donal.'

'Kissin'—that don't mean nothin',' Nellie said scornfully. 'Didn't you know that—well, it don't mean nothin' if they 'aven't got engaged since.'

'Yes, but the war,' Deirdre pointed out. 'There weren't much they could do. They've bin' in different parts of France until fairly recently and soon she'll be in France and he'll be in Liverpool. You can't get much further apart than that.'

'No, I expect you're right,' agreed Nellie. 'Still, our Dee, you don't want to give up any idea of Tolly gettin' fond of you. Your Ellen's nursin', you say. She must ha' met a great many fellers over there. How d'you know she's norrin love with one of them?'

''Cos she'd have said,' Deirdre said smartly, slapping a round of chopped ham on a slice of

399

margarined bread. 'Anyway, it don't really matter. I'm really goin' to enjoy havin' him home, and I'm not goin' to let Donal parade him round the shops like a raree-show seein' what extras he can get,' she added crossly. 'Trust a boy to think of a thing like that! Chuck us some more bread, queen.'

*　　　*　　　*

It was a beautiful golden October day and Ellen had for once managed to get a whole day off from the hospital and she and Patsy had decided to walk into the country and have a picnic. The countryside which surrounded her present hospital was wooded and the fields which, a month earlier, had waved with golden grain were now stubbled or had been ploughed, and the two girls were in holiday mood. They had managed to persuade one of the cooks to allow them to make sandwiches in the hospital kitchens, a seed cake had been bought from the local village and bottles had been filled with weak lemonade, and now they were determined to enjoy their day and forget the war.

'We might have a move down to the coast before winter,' Patsy said as they walked along. 'I wouldn't mind a bit of seaside air.'

'Nor me,' Ellen said. 'Still you couldn't get anywhere much more beautiful than this.'

'No, it is lovely,' agreed Patsy. The two of them were walking along a quiet, dusty lane and had stopped to lean over a five-barred gate and examine the view.

'Odd, how peaceful it looks,' Ellen said thoughtfully. 'I just hope it doesn't get overrun when the fighting starts again.'

'We pushed them back here, so they'll attack somewhere else, I expect,' Patsy said. 'When we reach the wood ahead should we come off the road a bit and wander through the trees?'

'Yes, that would be lovely.'

The two girls continued on their way, trying desperately hard not to think about the war, the hospital or any of the other things which had happened to them of late. Although the battle of Passchendaele was largely behind them there were always the injured to be nursed and it sometimes seemed to them that their work never lessened.

They reached the wood and turned down a narrow path between the trees. Over their heads the boughs were still in leaf, although the many colours of autumn had overtaken the green of summer and Ellen guessed that the first high winds would strip the trees of their colourful burden. They walked on for a short way, then Ellen looked to the left and saw a clearing in the trees. She pulled at Patsy's arm. 'Patsy, look.'

Patsy followed her friend's gaze. 'The clearing? So what?'

'Blackberries, millions of them. Oh, I love blackberries!'

'So do I—we must take some back to the hospital. Tell you what, if we eat our food first then we can put the blackberries in the basket,' Patsy suggested. 'Cookie will be pleased and it'll be a lovely change for the fellers to have some fresh fruit.'

'Good idea,' Ellen said, as they emerged from the trees. 'Look, there's a stream. Shall we sit down beside it and have our sandwiches?'

'Well, let's walk along beside it for a little way,'

Patsy said. 'It's a bit early for lunch.'

The stream was as delightful as the girls could have wished. It ran over a rocky bed between gentle green banks upon which foliage crowded close to the water.

Ellen knew that Patsy was right and that they shouldn't have lunch too soon, so they continued to walk beside the water until they came to a part where the stream widened out into a tiny beach, surrounded by cool green grass.

'Here we are,' said Ellen, settling herself on the bank above the little beach. 'This is ideal. Come on, get the food out.'

'It's perfect,' Patsy agreed. 'We can stand the bottles in the water—it'll keep them cool.'

The picnic was good. It was lovely to sit on the cool grass and eat the food they had prepared, whilst around them birds sang softly in the undergrowth and the little stream chattered. Presently, full of delicious food, the girls rolled over on to their backs and lay looking up at the blue sky through the canopy of branches overhead.

'We mustn't go to sleep—just a little doze, eh?' Ellen said presently. 'But a rest won't hurt—not too long, though, because we've got to get back before it's dark. Later we can have a paddle to cool our tootsies.'

'Well, we won't go to sleep then,' Patsy said. 'We'll just close our eyes for a minute or two.'

Ellen closed her eyes and the next thing she knew she was awoken by the sound of a sharp exclamation. Opening her eyes, she saw two young soldiers slipping and sliding their way into the grassy hollow, staring at them as if they had never seen nurses before. She sat up hastily and shook

Patsy, feeling thoroughly embarrassed as she realised how dishevelled they were. The boys, however, were obviously equally taken aback. The one who had come down first, who had soft, dark hair falling over his face and a pair of bright, mischievous eyes, said rather lamely, 'Oh! Sorry I am to disturb you gorls, we t'ought we was alone. We're on a week's R and R and we like to come here, me and me mate, when we've got time off. Never seen another soul here, have we, Steve?'

The lad called Steve, coming along behind, echoed the apologies. 'Fancy uz findin' de sleepin' beauty,' he said in unmistakable scouse accents. 'Two sleepin' beauties, Liam.' Both boys and the girls laughed.

'Not that beautiful,' Ellen said ruefully, well aware of her crumpled uniform dress, sleep-flushed face and untidy hair. 'Still, we don't often get the chance to relax.'

'No, nobody works harder than you girls,' agreed Steve, the scouse boy. He glanced from one to the other interrogatively. 'All right if we join you?'

'Yes, please do,' Ellen said. She smiled up at him. 'Isn't this a perfect spot? This is the first time we've been here—we don't have a lorra time off. You've been here before, you said?'

'Oh aye, the day before yesterday it was,' Steve said. He sat down on the grass and his companion followed suit. 'Well, we'd better introduce ourselves. I'm Steve Pryor and this is Liam Nolan. In case you hadn't guessed, girls, he's from Dublin.'

Ellen laughed. 'The brogue gives it away,' she said teasingly, 'but it's nice to hear a voice from nearer to home. We're both from the 'Pool, Patsy an' me.'

'Are you now?' said Steve. 'So am I—as if you didn't know the moment I opened me mouth!'

'Whereabouts in Liverpool do you live?' Ellen was asking. As she spoke she became very aware that the second young man, the Irish one, had his eyes fixed on her face with a burning intensity. She glanced towards him and quickly back to Steve. Did she have a smut on her nose? Was there something wrong? But she continued to address the young Liverpudlian. 'I'm from Everton; what about you?'

'I 'ail from the Scottie,' Steve said laughing. 'Can't you tell?'

Ellen laughed too. 'No, no,' she said. 'We all sound alike to me. Well, it's nice to meet you, fellers. Oh, I'm Ellen Docherty and this is me friend Patsy Blythe from Toxteth. Did you have a picnic, something to eat?'

'No, we just had a couple of sandwiches afore we left,' Steve said. 'Why, have youse got somethin' left over?'

'We have, there's some seed cake. Would you like a bit?'

Both young men nodded eagerly and Patsy dived into the box and produced the crumbly cake which was left, dividing it into two and handing a piece to each of the soldiers. As soon as they had eaten the cake the men glanced quickly at each other and began to untie the laces on their heavy boots.

Liam turned to the girls with a gentle smile. 'We roll up our trousers at this point and have a paddle, so we do,' he informed them rather shyly. 'Are you goin' to join us?' The girls looked at each other. Then they smiled at their companions.

'We were thinkin' of havin' a paddle,' Patsy admitted. 'But then you turned up . . .'

404

'Oh come on—youse were asleep,' Steve said, 'Anyway, we'll paddle now, yeh?'

'Yes, sure,' said Patsy. The two girls turned discreetly away from the boys, shed their shoes, undid their stockings, rolled them down and took them off, then the four of them waded into the water. It was deliciously cool and comforting to hot feet, though they had to avoid the rocks.

'I feel like a five-year-old again,' Ellen said, 'Goin' down to Seaforth Sands and paddlin' in the sea for the first time; or in the Mersey acourse. It's great paddlin' in the Mersey, if you climb down the chains on the old bridge, the swing bridge, an' don't mind the mud.'

'Ah, you've done that,' Steve said. 'Me an' all.'

'Me too,' Patsy said. 'Hasn't every girl? Every little boy and girl?'

'Not so many of the girls,' Ellen said. 'New Brighton for them. More posh.' The four of them laughed companionably.

'Would you like to wade a wee way upstream?' Liam said presently to Ellen, 'Come on, let the other two explore the other way. No messin' around. No funny business. Just have a look and see where it goes.'

'Right,' said Ellen. 'I'd like to see where it goes. Have you gone upstream before?'

'Well, we have,' Liam admitted. 'You can't get very far—the banks get too overgrown and the water goes deep, I'll show you. But it's nice, so it is.'

Holding up her skirts with one hand Ellen followed Liam up the stream and, as he had said, the undergrowth began to crowd closer to the banks until they reached a deep pool with willows hanging over it, which effectively stopped any

405

further exploration by water. As they turned round to go back Ellen became aware once more of Liam's eyes on her face. 'You do stare,' she said, half laughing. 'Would you know me again?'

'I . . . I . . . almost think I knew you before,' Liam said hesitantly. 'You're awful like someone I knew, so you are.'

'That is the oldest line in the world,' Ellen said, laughing. 'Unless I'm like your mam, of course.'

'No—not me mam—a friend . . .' Liam said slowly. 'A good friend—shall I show you her likeness?'

'Yes, sure,' Ellen said.

Liam fished around in the pocket of his battledress and pulled out a small photograph which, after looking at it for a minute, he handed to her.

The photograph showed a girl with a boy—undoubtedly Liam himself—on a beach. The girl was facing towards the camera and after a long, careful look Ellen could see what Liam meant. The girl had long, thick, very curly hair just like her own and a similarly shaped face. She handed the photograph back. 'Yes, I know what you mean, there does seem to be a certain likeness,' she said lightly. 'Your girlfriend?'

'In a way,' Liam said. 'She was killed. We was brought up together as kids. I'd known her . . . ten years . . . somethin' like that. We were good friends.'

'I'm sorry,' Ellen said quietly. 'Was she a nurse, or involved in the war in any way?'

'No, she was killed in an accident,' Liam said bluntly. 'I try not to think about that. Now, what plans have you two got for the rest of the day?

406

Steve and I thought we might pick some blackberries. That's why we come back—for a feed of 'em. Would you like some, to make up for givin' us your cake?'

'Oh, if you're going to pick blackberries, so are we,' Ellen said eagerly. 'We decided to have our food early so we could use the basket for the fruit.'

'Oh, great—well, let's get back to the others then.'

Back on the bank once more, sitting down and drying her legs as best she could with her handkerchief, and rolling on her stockings, Ellen realised that paddling in the stream had definitely broken the ice. Steve and Patsy were talking as if they had known each other all their lives and she felt comfortable and at ease with Liam. Covertly she watched him as he sat on the bank, relacing his boots and chatting to his friend. She decided he was nice to look at, with his thick dark hair falling across a tanned brow. His eyes were cobalt blue and rimmed with thick black lashes, and his chin had a deep cleft in it. He was several inches taller than herself and slim, but his shoulders were broad, his hands strong. He looks ... reliable ... she decided, fastening her own shoes and getting to her feet. And his voice is lovely, soft and melodious— I'd like to know him better.

But right now, they were off to gather blackberries so she had better stop mooning or she'd get left behind and that would never do!

The bramble patch, when they reached it, proved to be enormous and rich with huge blackberries. The boys insisted on putting their fruit in with Patsy's and Ellen's in the picnic basket but were happy to eat some as they picked.

'Sure an' 'tis terrible for your skin,' said Liam to Ellen, displaying hands purpled with the berry juice, 'and for your clothes. That's your uniform dress—what happened to you? Look, it's ruined entirely, so it is.'

'Oh don't say that,' Ellen said reproachfully. 'It's not ruined, just, just . . .'

'Let me push into the bushes; my uniform's tough,' Liam said. 'You stay on the outside and pick from there.'

They soon filled the basket, thoroughly enjoying the work and each other's company, and in the course of their blackberry picking managed to glean a good deal of information about each other. Liam was in the infantry, as was Steve, and the girls told the boys about their nursing and the various hospitals they had worked in.

'Tell you what,' Ellen said, as they made their way wearily out of the clearing at last. 'We'll get cookie to make a couple of big blackberry pies. Would you fellers like one too?'

'Aye, wouldn't we so,' Liam said at once. 'But how are you goin' to get it to us?'

'You'll have to come to the hospital—no, not the hospital, the village, there's a café in the village,' Ellen said. 'Could you come there one evening? Could you manage to come . . . say at . . . oh, gosh, what shifts are we on, Patsy?'

Walking slowly back through the trees they worked out which shift they would be working in three days' time. By then they were sure the pies would have been made.

'Meet us in the village café about eight in the evening the day after tomorrow,' Ellen said at last, 'and we'll hand over the pie. Will your duties allow

408

that?'

'Sure they will. Apart from the duty guard we're free evenings. We could talk about meetin' again, maybe,' Liam said hopefully. 'I . . . I'd like to see you again, Ellen.'

'And I'd like to meet you,' Ellen said shyly. 'But I dare say now that this latest battle on this part of the front is over you'll be packed up and moved somewhere else.'

'Oh aye, very likely,' Liam agreed. 'But whilst we're here we could mebbe meet up. And if we are moved, we could write.'

'I'd like that too,' Ellen said. 'Mind you, I write to several of the fellers, but I'd like to write to you as well.'

Steve and Patsy had drawn a little ahead and highly daring Liam put his arm on Ellen's elbow, drawing her to a halt. 'Do you have a feller, Miss Docherty . . . do you have a sweetheart?' he asked.

'No,' Ellen said decidedly. 'Not a sweetheart, though I've a deal of good friends, but . . . No, there's no one special.'

Liam nodded and sighed with satisfaction. 'Isn't that just fine now. Then I'll see you in three days,' he said, 'in the café in the village. I'll look forward to it, Miss Docherty.'

'And me, Mr Nolan,' Ellen said, and knew she spoke no more than the truth. Liam Nolan was already important to her, though she had only known him a few hours. But people fall in love between one minute and the next, she told herself as they walked briskly along the road. Why not me?

It was almost dusk by the time they reached the village and Liam made this an excuse to tuck her hand into the crook of his elbow. Ellen felt a tingle rush through her and smiled shyly up at him. She had not felt like this over Tolly, not even when she had kissed him, she realised. When they reached the point at which their ways parted she took his hand in both of hers. 'Thank you for your company, Mr Nolan,' she said. 'And I'll see you quite soon now.'

'Me name's Liam,' the young man said, 'and you're Ellen, are you not?'

'Yes, that's right,' she replied. 'Take care of yourself now, Liam.' And on the word she turned away and walked briskly up the path towards the hospital.

*   *   *

Walking back to their quarters, Liam and Steve talked desultorily about their day, but once Liam was in his bunk he allowed his thoughts to return in a more intimate manner to the girl he had just left. He liked her very much. In fact she was the first girl he had thought of seriously since losing Maggie and this made him feel almost guilty, though only for a moment. Maggie had loved him, possibly considerably more than he had loved her, he thought guiltily. She would be only too happy to know that he was beginning to make a life for himself once more. Maggie had loved family life; she had wanted children of her own one day. She would not grudge him a sweetheart.

He fell asleep soon afterwards, tired by his energetic day, but the next morning, the first thing he did was to pull out the little photograph and look at it long and hard. Strange! Was she really rather like Maggie, this Ellen Docherty, or was it

410

just his wishful thinking? He knew deep in some inner part of himself that his attraction towards her had little to do with the likeness, however. He liked Ellen Docherty for herself and would have done so under any circumstances, he was sure of it. And, what was more, when he had taken her hand he had felt a thrill of something far stronger than mere friendship.

Liam replaced the photograph in his pocket and set off for breakfast. He felt younger somehow, lighter almost, with the prospect of meeting the girl again in a few days. Maggie wouldn't grudge him happiness, he told himself once more as he joined the queue for breakfast, his irons in one fist and his plate in the other. She had always been generous. Anyway, he realised now his affection for and affair with Maggie had been that of a boy for a girl, whereas the feelings he had for Ellen were that of a young man for a young woman. He had misled Maggie, perhaps, and he would always feel a vague sense of guilt over her death although it had been no doing of his, but he had to move on, he had to live the rest of his life without her.

He had only known Ellen for a few hours, but she had lit a little flame in him which warmed him still. She would, he reflected, be easy to love, already he could see clearly, in his mind's eye, the small, pointed chin, the big eyes of her, and the sweet curves of her kissable mouth. Three more days and he'd see her again!

''Old out yer plate, you 'alfwit, I nearly threw them beans all over yer bloody 'ands.' The cook who had spoken to him as he reached the head of the queue grinned knowingly. 'Wot, cat got yer tongue? Or is you in love?'

411

'Sorry I am, Corp,' Liam said, holding out his plate. 'Me mind was miles away, so it was.'

'I'll forgive you: thousands wouldn't. Bread?'

*   *   *

It was a beautiful winter's day for once, with bright sunshine lighting up the frosted trees and only the thinnest covering of snow. Liam strolled along, humming a tune beneath his breath, at peace with the world. He was going to meet Ellen.

They had met three times, by appointment, and seen each other half-a-dozen times on the ward, because as soon as he found out where she worked, he had become a most assiduous visitor to any of her patients that he happened to know, but this was not the most satisfactory way of meeting. Sister quickly became suspicious, for a start, and often he visited only to find that Ellen's shift had been changed, or she had been lent to another ward. So now it was letters, careful plans and even more careful meetings.

Liam was puzzled by the fact that the nurses were not allowed to 'fraternise' with soldiers, either in or out of hospital. It seemed quite mad to him that two people who were fond of one another were officially denied the chance to test their friendship, see if it would turn, with more meetings, into something warmer, fonder. It was all so damned hole-in-the-corner, keeping well away from the hospital, never so much as taking the girl's hand where you could be seen, sneaking back there in the dark so that the senior nursing staff would not realise that a girl had a beau.

But this time everything should be all right,
412

because they were going to meet in the refreshment room at the railway station in the local market town, catching different buses to get there. The refreshment rooms were usually full of service men and they felt sure they would not be noticed there. This would mean that they could enjoy each other's company without forever looking over their shoulders.

And already Liam was more than just fond of Ellen. She meant more to him than anyone else had ever done, apart from Maggie, and he was no longer certain that the love he had felt for Maggie would have endured. He was a very different young man from the one Maggie had loved, far more decisive and self-disciplined. Indeed, he had been made up to corporal the previous autumn and taking decisions, leading his men, came naturally.

As for Ellen, he had thought her very like Maggie when they had first met, but closer acquaintance had pointed up the differences not only of character, but also of looks. Ellen's skin was pale as milk, but she had tiny golden freckles across her nose and when you looked at her dark hair in sunlight you could see reddish tints. What was more, her eyes, which looked so dark at first glance, were in fact a very deep blue, almost violet. She was taller than Maggie as well, and she had an air of authority which his sweet little first love had lacked and Liam believed that, had she lived, her clinging ways might have become trying.

What was more, he had soon realised that Ellen was very much better at hiding her feelings than Maggie had been. He *thought* she was fond of him, but he could not be sure. Ellen was nice to everyone, polite, kind. On their second meeting he
413

had kissed her and she had not drawn away, but neither, he thought, had she returned his kiss with much enthusiasm. He supposed that expecting a show of affection at a second meeting had been presumptuous of him—but even then, he had been pretty sure that Ellen Docherty was the girl for him. And today, he told himself grimly as his bus drew into the station square and he heard an approaching train in the distance, he would find out whether he was the man for Ellen . . . or he hoped he would.

However, he worried over coming out into the open. Suppose he asked her and she said 'no'? How would he deal with that? He could scarcely arrange another meeting with someone who . . .

He jumped down from the bus and looked to right and left. At the door of the refreshment rooms a slender, dark girl, whose hair, in the sunshine, showed reddish tints, stood waiting.

Liam gave another look around, just to be on the safe side, and walked past her into the noisy, crowded room. She followed and they squeezed into a table for two against the wall. He smiled into those dark-blue eyes and saw—or thought he saw—warm affection in their depths. Highly daring, he took both her hands in his, leaned forward and kissed her lightly on the cheek.

She moved her head and for an instant their lips met. Heart pounding, Liam kissed the soft, parted mouth, wishing desperately that he could pull her to him, crushing her against his khaki battledress, feeling through the embrace her delicate yet strong young body. Almost at once he released her to glance round, but no one seemed to be looking at them. Everyone was intent on their own business, even the waitress who presently approached the table.

Liam bought two *cafés au lait,* and as soon as they arrived he turned once more to Ellen, speaking to her under the hubbub of conversation, exclamation and laughter which surrounded them. 'Anyone see you?'

She shook her head. 'No, I'm sure we're all right. What'll we do? It's a nice day for once.'

'We'll drink our coffee for a start. Then we'll take a stroll round the town, get ourselves a meal somewhere quiet. We might walk into the country if the weather holds.'

The weather held. The small town, crowded with peasants in black and soldiers in uniform, seemed anonymous enough to hide them and they found a market and strolled amongst the stalls until, at last, Liam took her hand and led her down a side-street which, after a short way, turned into a sleepy country road.

'There's an inn a bit further on,' he told her. 'One of the fellers says you can get a dacint sort of meal there, so you can.'

'Lovely,' Ellen said, snuggling up to him as they walked. 'Isn't it quiet here, Liam, when you think of the town, so crowded and noisy?'

'It is,' Liam said. He drew her into a gateway and they leaned on the mossy gate, gazing out over rolling pasture, with the frost lifting under the strength of the noonday sun. 'Ellen . . . what'll you do when peace breaks out?'

Ellen shot a sideways glance at him. 'Go home, I suppose. To Liverpool. A-and you? What'll you do?'

'I'm t'inkin of gettin' wed,' Liam murmured. 'If

415

me gorl agrees, that is.' He squeezed her hand, then turned her to face him. She was staring up at him, wide-eyed, and he put a finger gently on her small, straight nose. 'Well, what d'you say, Ellen? Will you make me the happiest feller on earth? Shall we get wed?'

'We've not known each other for long, Liam,' Ellen pointed out. 'What's more, we only know the . . . the army side of each other, if you get me meanin'. You know Nurse Ellen Docherty an' I know Corporal Nolan. We're different people at home, I don't doubt.'

Liam shook his head chidingly at her. 'Now aren't you speakin' a lot o' nonsense?' he said gently. 'I scarce know you on the wards, you've never nursed me, nor was I ever your patient. I'm in love wit' Ellen Docherty, so I am, a pretty, sweet, tender young girl who happens to be a nurse. And you, I hope to God, are in love wit' Liam Nolan, eldest son of me mammy, who would do anything for you, Ellie.'

Ellen put her arms up round his neck and stood on tiptoe, but spoke before their lips could meet. 'You're right, Liam. I am in love wi' you, and I'll marry you gladly, but if you change your mind when we get home . . .'

'Me mind's firm as a rock, so it is,' Liam assured her. 'Oh, I wish I could buy you a ring an' we could marry at once, but it wouldn't be fair on our families, an' the Army might make a fuss, so it might. But as soon as the war ends an' we go home we'll tie the knot. Agreed?'

'Agreed,' Ellen said solemnly. 'As for a ring, there's time for that, plenty of time. Well, Liam Nolan, you certainly have surprised me! You're so

416

sensible an' practical an' level-headed . . .'

'So I am. And 'tis sensible an' practical an' level-headed I'm bein', gettin' you to agree to marry me,' Liam said contentedly. 'Let's seal our bargain, eh?'

He bent his head and their lips met. He strained Ellen's slim body against his khaki battledress and thought he had never been happier. When at last they broke the kiss he told her so, putting his arm round her shoulders and leading her along the country roadway once more.

'I'm happy too, dearest,' Ellen said softly. 'It'll make the work less pointless when I think that I'm helpin' to end the war so's we can be together. But oh, Liam, for my sake, take care!'

'And you,' Liam reminded her. 'I know how dangerous your job can be. But we've something worth waiting for now. Peace means we'll be together for always, not just in little snatches and odd moments.'

And arm in arm they continued up the road, oblivious, for once, of the possibility of watching eyes.

CHAPTER THIRTEEN

1918

'I'm just off, Mam,' Deirdre called as she slipped through the front door and into Mere Lane. 'I'm in good time, so I'll go for Tolly.'

'Right you are, queen,' her mother shouted back. Because of rationing and the inevitable food shortages that the war had brought, Ada's help was no longer needed at the sadly understocked cake shop, so she was working in a munitions factory on Great Nelson Street, which meant that sometimes she and Deirdre walked to work together. Deirdre had worked at Jacobs biscuit factory on Dryden Street ever since she had left school, a far cry, she had told her mother ruefully, from the farm that she and Donal had longed for.

'But if you was to find gold at the end of the rainbow right at the start of your workin' life, you'd not appreciate it the same as if it came after hard work, an' tryin',' her mother had said. 'It's in me mind that you'll marry a farmer, mebbe, or perhaps Donal will get hisself a farm an' you'll keep house for him. That 'ud be rainbows' ends for the pair of ye!'

And Donal, Deirdre thought wistfully as she turned left along the dark pavement—for in November she walked both to and from work in the dark—was well on the way to his own particular rainbow's end. He had continued to work for the butcher who had employed him part time once he left school, but not for very long. His employer had taken to sending him to the lairage, in Birkenhead, to pick out likely beasts for the shop and quite soon, because of the shortage of able-bodied young men in the trade, he had been offered a full-time job in the lairage in Birkenhead. It meant more money and better prospects, but the best thing about it was that it included assisting the grizzled old man who journeyed out to the Welsh farms to select both cattle and lambs for slaughter and Donal was openly hoping that he would get taken on by one of the farmers once he was a bit older.

So Donal was happy, but the job at the lairage

meant that he had to leave the house at an incredibly early hour in the morning and scarcely ever got home before ten at night.

Deirdre missed him badly, of course she did, but when Tolly first came out of hospital he had stayed with them for a few weeks and liked to practise walking with his sticks, swinging companionably along the pavement at her side. That way, he walked her some of the way to work and often came and met her coming out, too.

But then, Deirdre reflected sourly now, disaster had struck. Tolly had met up once more with Liza Bartlett, who had nursed him when he first came back to Liverpool. And once his wooden leg had been fitted and he had managed to get a job, he had thanked the Dochertys kindly for their hospitality and told them that it was best he moved out now, learned independence.

Deirdre hadn't suspected a thing at first, when he told them that he'd got a room on St Domingo Road, over a small tobacconist shop. She had not realised that, because of the war, Mrs Bartlett had moved from her old home and taken on the shop, which had previously been run by her elderly uncle. And of course, she told herself now, proximity had done the rest. Tolly was on the best of terms with Liza, the pair of them sang with the Songsters together, went up to the Citadel together . . . and though there was nothing in it, because Tolly was Ellen's feller, it still made Deirdre uneasy that Tolly was so much in Liza's company.

So whenever she could, she reminded him, if obliquely, of his obligations by walking part of the way to work with him and by calling for him on her way home too.

Tolly was a clerk in Gaddish's dairy, on Priory Road, and since Deirdre had to pass it each day, that was excuse enough to call for him whenever she and her mother were not able to go together, because of Ada's shifts. Sometimes she thought there was a shade of reluctance in Tolly's face as he saw her waiting for him, but she scolded herself for a too-vivid imagination. Tolly was her dear friend and Ellen's feller, he didn't really want to go about with Liza, it was just that they were both Salvationists and lived in the same house. So call for him she would . . . she owed it to Ellen, she told herself confusedly.

She reached the end of Mere Lane and turned right into St Domingo Road. The Bartlett shop was out of her way, but not by very much and she particularly wanted to remind Tolly that Ellen would be coming home very soon. Everyone knew the war was as good as over; by the coming Christmas Ellen would he back with them . . . and the boys, of course. Not that Tolly needed reminding, she told herself. He was an honourable bloke and would never let anyone down, but two days previously she had seen him in the street with Liza, her hand tucked into his elbow, their heads close. Anyone who hadn't known, Deirdre had told herself angrily, would have leapt to a very false conclusion. It behoved her to keep an eye on them for their own sake as well as for Ellen's.

She reached the corner of Penrose Street and broke into a run to get across before an approaching bicycle, her winter boots clattering on the frosty surface. The bicycle rider hallooed cheerfully.

'Mornin' chuck! You're goin' in the wrong

direction . . . decided not to do no work today, eh?'
It was Ethel, who worked beside her at the packing
bench and had been at school with her too. Ethel
put her feet down and trundled to a stop. 'Want a
lift on me bike, Dee?'

'No thanks, Eth,' Deirdre said, grinning at her
friend. 'I'm fetchin' our Tolly to the dairy. I do it
most mornin's. Am I late or is you early?'

'Dunno . . . guess I'm early. Me mam always tries
to drive me out afore she gets the kids off to
school,' Ethel said. She sniffed and rubbed her
watering eyes. 'I've gorra cold comin' on, I reckon.
Well, see you later, then.'

'I hope it ain't flu,' Deirdre called after her as
her friend wobbled off down Heyworth Street.
'There's a lorra flu about, I've heard.'

'Wouldn't mind a day or two off,' Ethel shouted
back. 'See you then, gal!'

Deirdre yelled a reply and set off once more, not
tempted to look into the windows of shops she was
passing since the lamplight reflected off the
window glass and made it difficult to see within.
Besides, she wanted to reach the Bartletts' place
before Tolly left. He liked to be at work a quarter
of an hour before his official time so that he could,
as he phrased it, 'sort myself out', but she should
catch him, she usually did.

She ran the last twenty yards along the pavement
and turned into the small shop. It was lit by an oil
lamp which gave out heat as well as light, so it was
pleasant in there after the chill outside. It was also
quite full, for Mrs Bartlett sold home-made toffee
as well as cigarettes and newspapers, and her shop
was consequently well-patronised.

In fact, Mrs Bartlett, serving busily, did not
421

notice her for a moment, but as soon as she did she smiled her broad and friendly smile and turned to shout up the stairs behind her, 'Tolly, your bezzie's 'ere!'

Deirdre grinned. She would not have described herself as Tolly's best pal, but she was pleased that Mrs Bartlett had called her that for more reasons than one. She felt guilty over one thing: Ellen's defection from the Salvation Army. The younger members of the family scarcely ever went to a church of any description, but Ellen had even worn the Salvationist uniform. Then, unexpectedly, she had written home to say, half defiantly Deirdre thought, that she had returned to the Catholic faith and had been attending a nearby Catholic church with her friends and had enjoyed the service. Mam had been pleased. 'The Salvationists are good folk; look what care they took over Tolly,' she had said. 'But I'll be happier wi' Ellen back where she belongs, back in the fold. Gals tek odd notions in their heads when they first fall for a feller.'

Deirdre had been less certain that Ellen was really returning to the fold. Surely she had not given up on Tolly? Still, she reminded herself, Tolly didn't know of her sister's defection and once she was home, if she decided to revert to her former habits, the Army would not know, any more than Tolly would, so that would be all right. Because in her heart she knew that Tolly would not want to marry a girl who was not a member of his church, and it worried her that Ellen's defection might be a temporary thing and might spoil their reunion, if Tolly ever came to hear of it. Not that he was prejudiced, she reminded herself hastily as he clattered down the stairs and into the shop. But if

422

Ellen decided once again to go to the Catholic church by St Edward's College on St Domingo Road just past the free library, instead of to the Citadel . . . ?

'Mornin', Dee,' Tolly said, interrupting her thoughts. 'Is it rainin'?'

'No, but it's cold; you'll need your scarf,' Deirdre said. She had bought him that scarf out of her first wages and had missed seeing him in it during the summer. 'Oh!' Her scarf, the one she had given him, had been a cheery green with yellow tassels, but the one he wound round his neck now was blue, with cream stripes at either end.

Tolly pulled on a pair of brown gloves and came out from behind the counter looking a trifle self-conscious. 'Gorra new one,' he said rather uneasily. 'Liza bought it from one of the patients what's keen on knittin'. Me other one's kept for best,' he added hastily, obviously taking in Deirdre's downcast face. 'Now come on, gal, best foot forward or the pair of us'll be late. See you later, Mrs B.'

Outside, the cold nipped at Deirdre's nose and she pulled her own scarf up to cover her mouth, then pushed it down again. 'How's your leg today, Tolly?'

Tolly grinned and took her arm to cross the side-road. 'Pretty good,' he said as he almost always did. 'Reckon you can't tell it's a wooden one unless you know. I've gorra limp, but that could be a wound, eh?'

'Sure it could,' Deirdre said truthfully. 'You haven't half come on, our Tolly! You can walk faster'n me if you put your mind to it.'

'Well, as fast as you, anyway,' Tolly said as they hurried along the gleaming pavement. 'You lookin'

423

forward to your sister comin' home?'

'We all are,' Deirdre said. He had raised the subject himself so there was no harm in her asking a question or two. 'Are you, Tolly? Lookin' forward to seein' our Ellen again after all this time?'

'Yes, indeed. So's Liza,' Tolly said heartily. 'They write, you know. Regular as clockwork.'

'Do they? But I reckon Ellen writes to you oftener, don't she, Tolly?' Deirdre asked craftily. Now was her chance to remind him of his obligations! But the wind was promptly taken out of her sails.

'No, she scarcely ever writes to me, 'cos she knows Liza reads me her letters,' Tolly said serenely. 'I add a note on the bottom, like, when Liza writes, though. And I know all the news that way. No point in her writin' two letters when one will do.'

'No, I suppose not,' Deirdre said uncertainly just as they swung out across Heyworth Street and turned into Priory Road. 'It just seems odd, Tolly, that our Ellen don't write to you before she writes to Liza.'

'It's not odd at all; they've always been good pals and now they're both in nursin' they've a lot in common,' Tolly said. He reached the yard with the shippon on one side of it and the office buildings on the other. 'See you tomorrer then, queen.'

'Or tonight. I'll come tonight to see if you've finished,' Deirdre said quickly. 'Then we can walk back together, Tolly, and . . .'

'Not tonight, chuck. I'm . . . I'm goin' out tonight,' Tolly said as he turned into the yard. 'See you.'

And Deirdre was left standing on the pavement,

424

staring after him.

*   *   *

Deirdre and Ethel were on their assembly lines, working busily, when half-way through the morning the factory whistle sounded. And it didn't just blow off one blast, to let workers know that they should be in their places, or should be going home, it went on and on . . .

'Hello! What's up?' Eth asked, her busy fingers continuing to pack as she spoke, however. 'It ain't time for our whistle yet, nor for anyone's, come to that. What's goin' on, our Dee?'

'Bloomin' thing's gorritself stuck,' Deirdre grumbled, screwing up her eyes and ducking her head, for the sound was loud. 'You sure it ain't our whistle, Eth? Sounds bleedin' like it to me!'

'Course I'm not sure,' Eth admitted. 'My Gawd, what's that when it's at 'ome?'

'That' was the clangour of church bells, ringing so loud that they all but drowned the factory hooter, and a moment or so later other sounds came to their ears—small explosions, cars' hooters, trams' bells . . .

'It's the peace!' someone further up the room shouted suddenly. 'Mark my words, it's the bleedin' pleace, that's wharrit is. Come on, gairls!'

Deirdre looked round, bewildered. Everywhere on the factory floor, girls were pulling off the caps which concealed their hair, dropping their work and making for the doors. One or two of the older girls—supervisors, senior hands—called a protest, tried to persuade the people nearest them to stay with their lines, but no one was taking any notice.

425

Deirdre, joining the shouting, cheering crowd, with Eth close at her side, pushed her way out of the door too and was soon in the street. It was black with people, mostly cheering and waving something—head-scarves, aprons, even flags—and the traffic had come to a standstill, unable to progress through the crowds, but for once everyone was smiling. Tram-drivers grinned from ear to ear and rang their bells, a motor-van driver hooted his horn ... and above the shouts and cheers of the crowd the factory whistle continued to blast out and the church bells rang their joyful peal.

'Is it the peace?' Deirdre said breathlessly to a policeman, his helmet down over one eye, his cape pulled askew. 'Is it really the peace at last?'

The policeman grinned. 'Aye, they signed the Armistice at eleven o'clock and so the war's over,' he said breathlessly. 'My, what a day, eh? Where's you off to, then?'

'We's goin' home,' Eth said. 'Wonder where they got the fireworks from?'

'Nelson Street; the Chinks have crackers, fizzers an' God knows what besides stored away for their New Year celebrations,' the policeman told them. 'They'll have brought them out to celebrate the peace, though.'

'An' I dare say Mam's munitions place might have a few bangers goin' spare, now the war's over,' Deirdre said, linking her arm firmly in her friend's. 'Come on, Eth, let's see if we can get home.'

'See if we can? Course we can, you an' me. We'll wiggle and squiggle through the crowds like a coupla tadpoles through a reed-bed,' Eth said thickly. 'Tell the truth, Dee, I'll be glad to get back to me mam; me 'ead's fair swimmin' an' me 'anker-

426

chief's wetter'n the River Mersey in flood.' Eth spent her holidays with an aunt who kept a small farm out at Upton and knew all about the country. "Sides, there'll be all sorts o' parties an' frolics planned for this evenin'. I want to join in, so I does.'

So the two girls, arms linked, began to fight their way through the crowd in the direction of home.

* * *

It took them longer than they expected to get back to Heyworth Street and instead of parting once they reached it, Deirdre decided to go home with her friend. 'You ain't so good, Eth,' she said as they emerged from Priory Road. 'I'll come back wit' you, see you into bed. No, don't go sayin' you won't miss out on the fun tonight. You'll be best in the warm.'

'I know it,' Eth said gratefully as they ploughed across a Heyworth Street on which all the traffic was at a standstill once more. 'I reckon it is flu. Oh, an' I did want to share in the fun.'

'Mebbe, if you rest till, say, five o'clock, you'll be better,' Deirdre suggested hopefully. 'I'll come back then, see how you are, queen.'

But once she had seen her friend into her mother's cosy, noisy kitchen, Deirdre made her way to Mere Lane, with very little real hope of seeing Ethel out and enjoying herself that evening.

'She's got the flu, an' I just hope she hasn't give it to me an' all,' Deirdre told her mother as the family—those of them still at home—gathered round the table for a meal later that afternoon. Sammy and Toby had been allowed out of school early—or possibly, Deirdre thought, the teachers had been unable to stop the entire school leaving the premises—and were eating scrag-end stew and boiled potatoes with great enthusiasm. 'Are you goin' to let the lads come out when we've et, Mam?'

'I'll come out an' all,' Ada said. 'Reckon there'll be high old doin's this evenin', judgin' by the noise outside right now. They aren't goin' to want us at work, that I can guarantee.'

Deirdre, in the middle of her meal, stopped eating abruptly. 'Tolly! Reckon he'll be free too, our Mam?'

'Bound to be,' Ada said, helping herself to another potato. 'Eat up, all of you; I've put Donal's share aside, he can have it when he gets home, even though I dessay it'll be nearer tomorrer mornin' than today when he catches that bloomin' ferry.'

'Depends where he was when the peace started,' Deirdre observed, following her mother's example. 'Eat all you can, you little fellers,' she added, addressing Sammy and Toby, ''cos it's my belief that you won't eat again till tomorrer breakfast!'

'We'll all call for Tolly,' Ada decided, inspired. 'We'll ask him back for a late supper ... Me credit's good, we'll have a bit of a party.'

'Right. I'll go round there, an' bring him along,' Deirdre said briskly, finishing up the last of the gravy on her plate with half a round of thickly cut bread. 'Wharrif he's with a pal though, our Mam? Can it stretch to one more?' She had it in mind to ask Liza too, if that was the only way to get Tolly. 'He might be with Liza Bartlett, I dessay.'

'Oh aye, another one or two won't mek no

difference,' Ada said cheerfully. She was earning more money than she could have dreamed of four years earlier and never minded spending some of it on others. 'Right, queen, you go for Tolly an' the lads an' I will meet up wi' the pair of ye at nine o'clock tonight, back here. Awright?'

Deirdre agreed eagerly and set off once more into the crowded streets, her eyes darting everywhere for a glimpse of Tolly.

But for most of that evening she found it impossible to search for any one person, you simply went with the flow. She called on Eth's mam, and was told that Ethel was much too ill to go out and that the youngest member of the family, five-year-old Freddy, was also poorly.

'They've got flu, there's no doubt of it,' Mrs Rathbone said gloomily. 'Still, we've caught it early, I reckon. I got a bottle from the pharmy. He reckons if I keep 'em warm an' quiet it won't last above a week. Off you go, young Dee, an' enjoy yourself. Lerroff a firecracker or two for me, will ye?'

Deirdre, laughing, promised to do so and was soon back in Heyworth Street once more, making her way up, this time, in the direction of Mere Lane. She had given up on Tolly, but was working up quite an appetite and wondering hopefully what party food her mother had managed to get hold of when, through the throng, she caught sight of Donal, hair on end, his chin gleaming with grease, a large piece of sausage in one hand. He saw her and dived through the crowd.

'Dee! I say, wharra go, eh? Want a fire cracker? I was give half a dozen an' I've still gorra couple left.'

'Gi's a bite of that sausage an' all,' Deirdre
429

shrieked, grabbing her twin by the arm. 'Mam's havin' a party at home, wi' lots of food, so we'll be awright once we get back to Mere Lane, but right now I'm starved!'

'Sure,' Donal said good-naturedly. 'Who's comin' to the party, then, eh?'

'Oh, Tolly, us . . . neighbours, I reckon,' Deirdre shouted. 'Only I haven't seen neither hide nor hair of Tolly since we walked to work this . . . Well, wouldn't you know it? There he is!'

And there he was, with his arm round Liza, doing what looked like a dance with a dozen other people and waving a bottle of beer with the hand that wasn't squeezing Liza's shoulders.

Deirdre fought her way over to him and clutched his sleeve. 'Tolly!' she shouted. 'Mam's havin' a bit of a party at home; can you come? You an' Liza, I mean.'

'We'll be there,' Tolly shouted back. 'Nine, you say? Right, we'll be there. Got somethin' to show you an' your mam, anyroad.'

So Deirdre and Donal made their way back to Mere Lane, assuring their mother and a crowd of neighbours and friends that Tolly and Liza would be along any time now.

And so they were. Tolly entered the room, blinking at the light, with an arm around Liza Bartlett's plump shoulders. 'Evenin', Mrs Docherty. Evenin', all,' he said breezily. He took hold of Liza's hand and held it out for everyone to see. 'We're engaged to be married, me an' Liza here!'

There were shouts of congratulation and more bottles of beer were opened and poured. Neither Tolly nor Liza drank as a rule but they shared a small glass of stout, beaming at everyone.

Deirdre saw, from a quick look round, that she was the only person surprised and dismayed by their news, and as soon as possible she made her way to Tolly's side whilst Liza was showing her little ruby engagement ring around. 'Tolly! What was you thinkin' of?' she demanded furiously. 'Wharrabout our Ellen, eh? What'll she say when she knows you've been an' gone an' got engaged to that Liza?'

'She'll wish us happy, as you should, Dee,' Tolly said courteously. 'Why, she's Liza's best friend as well as me own pal. Your sister would no sooner grudge us our happiness than . . . than you would!'

'Well, I do,' Deirdre hissed. 'You an' Ellen's been sweethearts for years, Tolly. How can you turn to someone else when our Ellen's off in France, nursin' the wounded?'

Tolly sighed. 'Your Ellen's gorra feller of her own,' he said quietly. 'Hasn't she told you? But anyway, chuck, she an' I agreed we wouldn't suit months an' months back. Didn't she tell you?'

'N-no, she didn't,' Deirdre said, considerably surprised and taken aback by this statement. 'Why, she writ to me mam askin' that we tek you in when you first come back to Blighty. We thought . . . I thought . . .'

'Well, think again,' Tolly said quietly. 'I were always mortal fond o' Ellen, but it were . . . it were a brotherly fondness, I suppose. The way I feel about Liza . . . it's different.'

'Oh,' Deirdre said inadequately. 'Well, I wish you happy too, o' course. But . . . but Ellen hasn't said nothin' about havin' a feller. Honest, Tolly.'

'She'll have to say somethin' soon,' Tolly

431

observed. 'Since she's bringin' him back wi' her when they come back to Blighty. I dessay your mam knows, queen, even if you don't. So have you forgiven me for arrangin' to marry Liza?'

'Of course,' Deirdre said rather stiffly. 'I hope you'll be very happy.'

She sounded doubtful, but Tolly only laughed, then bent and kissed her cheek. 'We shall be, don't you worry,' he said lightly. 'An' the whole Docherty family will dance at our wedding, see if they don't!'

'Cripes! When's the weddin' then, Tolly?' Deirdre asked. 'Are you goin' to wait until our Ellen's back?'

'Of course. Who else will be bridesmaid but your Ellen?' Tolly said gravely. 'An' then it'll be Ellen's turn, see if it ain't. An' you'll be bridesmaid, Dee!'

*   *   *

Tolly was right over Ellen's reaction to his news, Deirdre had to admit it. She wrote at once, saying she was delighted, would certainly act as bridesmaid for her dear friend Liza if she was home in time and telling Ada shyly that she would be bringing a friend home when she came; a young Irishman called Liam Nolan.

'Fancy her tellin' Liza first,' Deirdre said rather crossly to Donal. 'You'd ha' thought she'd tell Mam or us first, not a stranger.'

But Donal had pointed out that Liza was no stranger but an old friend. 'And some things are easier to tell a friend than your mam or your little sister,' he pointed out.

And then they got the letter from Ellen, telling them the expected date of her return in March.

'She an' Liam should be home around the same time as your brothers,' Ada said. 'It's a long time to wait but it'll give us a chance to do somethin' special. Tell you what, we'll have a party, we'll get the whole fambly round, an' friends, an' the neighbours. Yes, we'll have a real big welcome home party!'

*   *   *

Seamus charged up the stairs, flung open the kitchen door and stormed into the room, his cheeks pink with wrath, his eyes sparkling. His mother, peeling potatoes at the table by the window, turned and stared at him. 'All right, are ye, Seamus? Where's your brother?'

'You tell me,' Seamus said bitterly, throwing his coat in the rough direction of the coat-stand and scowling blackly when it fell to the floor. 'You'll never believe it, Mammy—he's quit again!'

'Quit?' Aisling said mildly. 'Quit work early, d'you mean? Well and isn't that just like Garvan now, when Mr Reilly gave the lot of you a bonus on Armistice Day and you took most of the day off? I wonder what he's up to now? He's not shown his face here yet.'

'He hasn't left early, he's left work,' Seamus growled. 'Quit the job, Mammy, not even give notice, just told them he'll not be comin' back. And it's the best-paid job the pair of us ever got, so it is. And Mr Reilly wouldn't have took Garvan on if I hadn't promised to make him behave. Oh, I could give him a good wallop, so I could! The ingratitude, Mammy! I shan't know how to face the Reillys tomorrow.'

Aisling sighed. 'And now I suppose you've quit as well, so there'll be two jobs wantin',' she said resignedly. 'Well, if you want to give Garvan a tap you can join the queue. It seemed just the job for him, too, what wit' bein' in the open air half the time, an' mixin' wit' folk the other half. Still, now the war's over an' the fellers will all be comin' home, I dare say you'd ha' lost the jobs regardless.'

'No we wouldn't, Mammy,' Seamus said dully. 'And I've not quit, not this time. I told Garv if he walked out again he could do so alone and I meant it. Mammy, I've a future with the firm, Mr Reilly as good as told us so. Well, I'm stayin' on and so I told Mr Reilly this afternoon, before I came home. Garvan's eighteen, same as I am. He'll have to learn to stand on his own two feet 'stead of tramplin' mine. If he believes I'd t'row a dacint job like this one down the pan he must t'ink I came up the Liffey on the last lily! Besides, there's . . . there's other considerations.'

'Oh, well, if you're still in work then it's not quite so bad,' Aisling said. She finished peeling the potatoes and looked hopefully round at her son. 'Did you see Ticky as you came t'rough the courtyard? I could do wit' a hand to get the meal on the table.'

Ticky, at twelve, was a handful and resentful of being asked to do what he considered to be 'girl's work', but Seamus got to his feet, picked up his coat and slung it over one shoulder. 'I'll fetch him up for you,' he said. 'I'd better go an' see if I can find Garvan, I suppose. I wonder if he's down at the docks? He's still hankerin' for a job down there, though small hope he'd have of keepin' it, wit' the troops comin' home any day now.'

434

'Right. Thanks, Shay,' his mammy said and, as he opened the door, she turned towards him. 'There's not ... not another reason for Garvan's givin' his notice, is there, son? It's ... it's nothin' ... personal ... like?'

'Ask Garv,' Seamus growled and made his escape, clattering down the stairs and out into the courtyard, feeling that he'd evaded some acute—and embarrassing—questions by the skin of his teeth. He stood in the middle of the courtyard and roared for Ticky and, when his brother did not appear, dived into the next block of housing and whipped up to the first-floor landing. Sure enough, a small gang of boys, including Ticky, sat in a semicircle, with a variety of ill-made clay marbles before them.

'Ticky, go home,' Seamus ordered his younger brother. 'Mammy needs a hand, so she does.'

'But I'm busy ...' began Ticky defensively, only to feel his collar grabbed in a firm hand. 'All right, all right, I'm goin',' he said at once, freeing himself. 'But it ain't fair, you an' Garv never help Mammy, it's always me.'

'We're in work,' Seamus began, then stopped. What was the use of justifying himself to his small brother, who knew very well why he was called upon to help in the house from time to time? He hustled Ticky down the stairs and out into their own apartment block, saw him up the stairs, then turned back to the courtyard once more. He had better try to find Garvan; for all his brother's vaunted independence, this would be the first time he had gone job-hunting alone. If he was job-hunting, that was.

The streets were unlikely to appeal to his twin as

435

somewhere to find work, however, Seamus realised. He would have gone to the docks, or the tram depot, or to one of Dublin's many markets. Twins, Seamus reflected sourly, are supposed to be able to read each other's minds—well, he could not imagine where he would find Garvan, and if his brother could read his, Seamus's, mind he would stay well out of the way for a while. Still. He would try the quays first.

As he made his way through the crowded market stalls on Francis Street, Seamus kept a weather eye cocked for Garvan. He had little doubt that if his twin was here, discussing the possibility of casual work with one of the stall-holders, he would see him. Twins could not walk close by each other and not be aware of the other's presence, Seamus knew from experience. But he traversed the length of the street without a glimpse of the familiar figure, so continued, with a sigh, towards the quays.

Although he believed it was chiefly perversity which had caused Garvan to leave the huge, family-run store on O'Connell Street where they worked mostly as delivery boys but also as 'help' in the brand-new bicycle department, he was uneasily aware that he had kept one important factor from his mother. Trixie Reilly. The only child of Mr Thomais Reilly, she was a year younger than the twins and worked in the store as well, learning the business, her father frequently told anyone interested. He had no sons and intended that Trixie—whose real name was Beatrix—should take over the running of the store when he grew too old to manage it himself. And Trixie and Seamus had taken one look at each other and decided that they wanted to be friends. They had, Seamus thought

436

now, a similar sense of humour, they both enjoyed bike rides, the cinema, dancing . . . and to Seamus's astonished pleasure Mr Reilly had raised no objection to his beloved only daughter beginning to go about with an errand boy. 'It's good that you've a friend, as other girls have,' he had told Trixie. 'So long as you behave yourself and keep things on a friendly footing . . .'

He wouldn't have said the same to Garvan, Seamus knew. Garvan tended to treat girls in a cavalier fashion, which was odd when Seamus remembered how guilt-ridden and miserable Garvan had been for many months after Maggie's death.

He had told Seamus once that, had it not been for him, Maggie would still be alive. 'Whose idea was it to pretend to run away, so Mammy would take her back?' he had demanded. 'Mine, of course. And who heard her call, that day in the street, but pretended not to? Me. So she ran into the road to get my attention . . . straight under that bloody 'bus.'

'But you weren't to know . . . and Maggie wouldn't hold it against you,' Seamus had said gently. 'She's forgiven you long since.'

'Aye; 'tis meself I can't forgive,' Garvan said simply. 'She's everywhere in Dublin, Shay. Everywhere we go, she took us; everyone we know, she knew too. I can't forget her.'

'Nor me,' Seamus had said at once. 'Nor want, Garv.'

So it was partly for this reason that he had stuck closer than a corn plaster to his brother, had left jobs when his twin did, had sometimes done two people's work in order to hide the fact that Garvan

437

had sloped off for a day's fishing, or a walk round Phoenix Park, rather than work.

But no more. Maggie had been dead over three years and although Garvan did take a girl out from time to time there was no disguising that he treated them pretty badly, one way and another. Seamus suspected that his twin made demands on girls which they were not prepared to meet and dropped them with insulting suddenness. He had tried telling Garvan that Maggie, of all people, would disapprove of this behaviour, but it seemed to cut no ice. 'You can't compare them little tarts wit' our Maggie,' Garvan had said. And when Seamus asked him to make up a foursome with some decent friend of Trixie's he refused, not bothering to invent an excuse or a previous engagement, merely saying that he did not want to go. 'I've got better t'ings to do wit' me life than to spend it dancin' attendance on some ould gorl,' he had said sullenly, when Seamus had tried to persuade him to come along. 'I can't understand you, Shay. It's not as if she was even pretty, like Bridie McShay or Edie Abel.'

'I t'ink she's prettier than either of 'em,' Seamus had said honestly. 'They're ... they're kind o' flashy, Garv. Trixie's a dote.'

'She's ginger,' Garvan muttered. 'Spotty, an' all. Just because she's the boss's daughter ...'

It had been the cause of their first serious fight and though, after suffering a couple of days of his twin's icy silence, Garvan had had the grace to apologise, to admit that Trixie was 'all right really, if you didn't mind the gingery look', it still hung between them in a sense. Seamus knew that Garvan was jealous of his affection for Trixie, that

438

his twin sensed the parting of their ways which would come as they grew older and resented it, but he had done his best to ease the situation by only seeing Trixie once or twice a week and making a habit of always asking Garvan along, or meeting him after their date.

He had thought he was successful, had believed that Garvan was becoming reconciled to Trixie, red hair and all, but now he doubted it. Garvan had decided to play his trump card, to separate his twin from an alliance of which he did not approve, and had thrown in the job.

Always, before, the twins had stayed together at work, never approaching a possible employer singly, but always as a pair. And now Garvan must be fairly sure that, though Seamus would grumble, he would do the same. Well, he had told him and told him that he wouldn't, but Garvan had gone anyway. Now was the time to reiterate his remarks and show Garvan that he was on his own . . . unless he backed down, of course, went round to Mr Reilly's beautiful house in Phoenix Park and said it had all been a mistake, that he'd spoken rashly and out of turn and that he would be grateful for his job back, please.

Seamus knew, of course, that Mr Reilly was highly unlikely to know that Garvan had quit, though he would be told next morning when he arrived for work, for their boss never missed appearing at the store at least once a day. But if Garvan went round tonight . . .

It was odd how he found himself in Phoenix Park, almost as though he believed that Garvan would be hovering outside the Reilly house, but arrive there he did. And the first person he saw as he approached the Wellington Monument was his twin, leaning against the plinth of the statue and shying bits of gravel at a flock of pigeons who were arguing over someone's cast-down sandwiches.

Garvan pretended not to see him, but Seamus knew better and went and leaned too, close by his twin. He waited a moment without speaking, then said gruffly: 'Well, you've done it now, Garv. What'll you do? If you was to change your mind, sure an' isn't Mr Reilly the best of fellers? He'd not hold it against ye, he'd speak to Mr Mulvaney . . .'

Garvan straightened up and the two brothers began to stroll along the path together.

'I don't want me job back,' Garvan said. 'Haven't you an' me done all right before, now? Christmas is comin', there'll be jobs a-plenty standin' the markets, sellin' door to door, fetchin' spuds in from the country an' sellin' them to the fancy restaurants on O'Connell Street. 'Sides, you don't suppose the ould feller 'ud keep us on once the troops get back, d'ye? We'll be out on our arses faster'n greased lightning once there's older men to tek our place.'

'That's a fool remark, Garv,' Seamus said quietly. 'Men don't want work as errand boys nor counter hands and besides, Mr Reilly isn't like that. Our jobs are safe an' you know it.'

'Oh, safe,' Garvan said scoffingly, abruptly changing tack. 'Who cares for that? We've never gone for safety, you an' me, Shay. Why, comin' up to Christmas we'll be workin' all hours, makin' twice the money we could wit' old Reilly. Use your loaf, ould Shay.'

'I am, because Christmas lasts a few weeks, not the whole year. What'll you do in January, eh? When the snow comes, an' the markets shrink, an' folk stay at home o' nights?'

'Move on. Find somethin' else,' Garvan said easily. 'I've a fancy to leave Dublin for a few months longer. What we need is a change of scene, Shay. Why don't we go to Limerick? Or Belfast? Or why not London? There's navvyin' work over the water which would keep us outdoors for months an' months, an' plenty of money an' they say the wimmin's friendly.'

'I told you, Garv, that I'd not leave the store, an' I meaned every word of it,' Seamus interrupted. 'An' I'm sweet on Trixie an' she on me, as well you know. Is it likely that I'd tek off for foreign parts an' t'row away the first dacint opportunity I've ever had of a proper job?'

'But Shay, it won't be the same wit'out me, you know it. We've always been together, so we have, from the day we was born. You'll not stay stuck in the store wit' me on the road, makin' money hand o'er fist, enjoyin' a free life again.'

'I'm stayin' in me dacint job, and I'm stayin' wit' me girl,' Seamus said firmly. 'Mebbe it's for the best, Garv. Mebbe we'd do best apart.'

Garvan stared at him, his eyes gradually hardening, then shrugged and turned away with an elaborate unconcern which did not fool Seamus for a moment. 'Right. You stay an' see where it gets you,' he said. 'Just because the boss's daughter likes the look o' you, an' you're prepared to put up wit' the foxy, gingery crittur, that doesn't mean I have to go along wit' you. I'm out an' I'm stayin' out.'

'Right. Well, are ye comin' home now, then? I won't quarrel wit' you, Garv, though you're clearly doin' your best to make me, but you'd best stop insultin' Trixie, me fine boyo, or I'll see you regret

441

it,' Seamus said, with a calmness he did not feel. 'Come on home, now. Mammy'll have our teas on the table and nothin' meks her crosser than our lettin' good food spoil.'

'I'm not coming in till later,' Garvan said, refusing the olive branch. 'I've got to find me a job afore I face the ould wan.'

'Wise,' Seamus said, giving his twin a half-grin. 'Mammy worries about money wit' Ticky goin' through a pair o' trousers a week, an' Liam still away, to say nothin' of Kenny married an' livin' up to Goldenbridge. Still, she'll be glad that mine'll keep comin' in, regardless.'

The two boys slowed their walk. They had reached the dog pond and Seamus stooped and picked up a pebble, chucking it into the glistening water.

'Aye, you'll be mammy's darlin' now,' Garvan said sneeringly. 'But wait'll I start showerin' her wit' me earnin's, it'll be a different story then. An' when she hears about Trixie, an' knows why you're stayin' on at the store.'

'Leave it, Garv, or I'll chuck you into the bleedin' pond,' Seamus said unwisely and in two moments the pair of them were fighting like a couple of mongrel dogs, growling and battering as though they were sworn enemies instead of two brothers who had rarely, until now, had a bad word for one another.

After ten minutes, however, they parted as if by common consent and stood, breathless, panting, both with an incipient black eye and Seamus with a shirt torn from collar to tail, eyeing one another measuringly.

'No point in fighting, we're too evenly matched

and we know each other's minds too well,' Garvan said at length. 'I t'ink you're wrong an' you t'ink I am, but we'd best agree to differ or we'll be needin' crutches.'

'True. See you later then, Garv,' Seamus said, turning away.

But Garvan kept pace alongside him. 'You'll be passin' the market so we might as well go along that far together,' he said almost amicably. 'Besides, you might see sense an' change your mind!'

Seamus only laughed and the two of them set out towards Parkgate Street and the river, ignoring their bruises and talking, not about their working future, but about a film being shown at the Tivoli on Francis Street, which they had both wanted to see. When they reached Thomas Street they parted and Seamus hurried through the dark streets thinking hopefully of his dinner.

At home once more, Mrs Nolan did not comment on Seamus's bruises, though she screeched at the sight of his shirt. 'I hope your brother intends to mend that slit,' she said aggrievedly as Seamus hung his coat on the rack. 'Did ye win, son? Is he goin' to knuckle down to work at Reilly's after all?'

But she did not look surprised when Seamus shook his head.

'No, Mammy. We've agreed it might be best if we were parted for a bit durin' workin' hours at any rate. Mebbe this change is no bad t'ing. He's restless, is Garvan, an' mebbe I'm not.'

'Hm,' Mrs Nolan said. She was draining potatoes into a bowl and finished her task before turning to her son. 'I never got the chance to tell you earlier, but I've had a bit of a blow meself, so I have. Liam's writ that he's courtin' an English gorl, so he's not comin' home right off. He's goin' back to Liverpool to meet the gorl's fambly.'

Seamus whistled. 'An English gorl! After all the troubles, what's he thinkin' of?'

'She'll be first-generation English—her name's Ellen Docherty—but how he thinks he can support a wife.'

Seamus shrugged. 'That's Liam's business, so it is, an' now where's me dinner? I'm starved, so I am. Oh, and Garv's job-huntin', but he'll be along later.'

CHAPTER FOURTEEN

March 1919

It was the day before Ellen's arrival home and Ada was making fruit loaves for the party. The war was over and her factory was returning to peacetime production, so she was back at the shop, but still earning reasonably good money. There was, nevertheless, a good deal of hardship, both for the men returning from abroad and for those who were no longer needed in their once well-paid jobs. Food was still rationed and as soldiers returned the need to house them became more and more desperate. Beggars, many in the tattered remains of military uniform, were becoming commonplace, and the bright optimism which had greeted Armistice Day was beginning to dissipate as the 'flu epidemic increased and the shortages did not improve.

But the Dochertys, with the elder members still working, were better off than most, and now, at the table, Deirdre was peering over Sammy's shoulder as he did his arithmetic homework and Toby, now a sturdy ten-year-old, was making paper chains out of scrap paper, for they intended to decorate the parlour with anything bright they could lay hands on.

'Sammy, love, will you pop these loaves down to the bakery on the corner of Mission Road? There's a dozen . . . can you manage 'em? They're not too big.'

Sammy got up from his place at the table and looked at the round loaves, then up at his mother. 'Mam, I casn't carry that many on me own, it 'ud break me arms off at the elbows! Can't Tobe come too?'

'If I let the pair of ye out of me sight . . .' Ada was beginning, when Deirdre straightened up and smiled across at her.

'It's awright, Mam, Tobe's doin' pretty well, so soon's he's finished he can lay the table for tea. I'll go wi' Sammy. Come on, our Sam, it won't tek us more'n five minutes if we run in both directions.'

'I aren't runnin' to the bakery wi' that lot,' Sammy objected, struggling into his coat. 'They's heavy, Dee.'

Deirdre laughed. 'True. Awright, Mam, we'll be ten or fifteen minutes, likely. Want any messages whiles I'm out? Anythin' you've not got for tomorrer?'

'No, you're awright, queen,' Ada said. 'Tell the baker we'll call for the loaves first thing, if that's all right. Or you can get 'em after tea, if you like.'

'We'll see what time we finish tea—wharris it,

anyway?' Deirdre asked, piling the loaves closer on the big tray. 'It's gettin' nice an' springlike out, but there's still a nip in the air. I'm starvin'!'

Ada laughed. 'I'm goin' to mek do tonight,' she said. 'Save your appetite for tomorrer, young 'un. We'll 'ave blind scouse, though. At least it's hot.'

'An' if we go for the loaves, after, could we have a slice for us puddin's?' Sammy suggested hopefully, hefting his own burden. 'Cor, these loaves weigh somethin' awful.'

Ada opened the door for them and Deirdre sailed through, grinning over her shoulder at her small brother trailing behind, one boot unlaced, his socks round his ankles. 'Don't tell our mam she makes heavy bread or you'll be lucky to get a crumb,' she said, clattering across the tiny backyard. 'Best foot forward, our Sammy! Even blind scouse'll taste good to me after this.'

The baker was busy, but he came across the kitchen, sweat shining on his forehead, and took the loaves from them. 'I'll charge a farden a loaf for them littl'uns,' he said. 'Why so many, chuck?'

Deirdre explained that it was for a party, since her sister was arriving back from the war next day. 'And me brothers said they'd not have a party until everyone were back,' she continued. 'So tomorrer we're havin' a real bit of a do for 'em. The whole street's comin', just about.'

'A party? Well, gi's a penny an' we'll call it square,' the baker said. 'Ready in an hour. That do you?'

Deirdre said that would be fine and she and Sammy left the warm, sweet-smelling shop rather reluctantly and proceeded to jog through the busy streets. They reached home in record time and went round the back, sniffing appreciatively as the smell of the meatless stew came to their nostrils.

'Mam'll put an Oxo cube in, that'll give it a bit more taste,' Deirdre said, opening the back door. 'Come on, Sammy, it's on the table! Did you save some for our Donny, Mam?'

'A dacent plateful,' Ada said. 'But I put the rest out, knowin' how hungry you said you were. Come on, get dug in. I let Toby start bein' as he eats slower than the rest of us.'

'Currant loaves ready in an hour,' Deirdre said, hanging her coat on the hook behind the door and taking her place at the table. 'I'll tek a big string bag, or a coupla paper carriers an' bring 'em back in that, then I can meet up wi' Donny at the same time. We'll walk home together, he can carry one o' the bags.'

'Right, luv,' her mother said, picking up her own spoon and fork and beginning to eat. 'Only ... suppose Donny's goin' out somewhere? You never know.'

'I do,' Deirdre said complacently. 'He'd ha' told me if he were goin' out. 'Sides, he's too busy wi' the spring lambs an' all.'

Donal and his latest boss had gone into business for themselves, much to Ada's amusement. They had bought some weaned lambs, rented a small meadow not too far from the lairage and were fattening their new acquisitions there, going up to the meadow each night after work, laden with any bits of hay, straw or cast-down cabbage or carrot they had been able to find around the street market stalls. Donal was not only sure that they would sell the lambs for a good profit next Christmas, he intended to slaughter one of them for the family, so

447

that they would be able to feast on meat over the holiday.

'Right, then. But don't hang around if it starts to get late,' her mother advised. 'I'm keepin' Sammy off school tomorrer, so's he can help unload the ale when the pub deliver the barrel. An' I'll want him to keep his eye on it, else the neighbours'll start in on it afore our Ellen's so much as stepped ashore.'

'Right, Mam,' Deirdre said obediently. 'Eh, this scouse's a treat! Jest what the doctor ordered!'

Later, when the washing up and clearing away had been done and the two small boys despatched to bed, Deirdre put her coat on again and took two paper carriers and a string bag down from the dresser. 'I'll be goin' for Donny then, Mam,' she said. 'An' for the fruit loaves, acourse.' She glanced at the kitchen clock, ticking away on the wall above the dresser. 'It's gone an hour, so the bread'll be ready.'

'Good girl,' Ada said absently. She was sitting down for what was probably the first time that day, Deirdre reflected, knitting a sweater for Toby. She had got the wool by purchasing three old jumpers from Paddy's market, unravelling them, then washing the best wool and rewinding it and, though the colours were not a perfect match, Deirdre doubted that anyone would notice. Mam was a first-rate knitter, she thought, buttoning her coat and clattering across the yard. She had knitted Deirdre a matching jumper and skirt in a variety of different coloured stripes and it was a much-cherished garment. In fact, Deirdre would wear it to the party next day.

She was still thinking about the party as she walked out of the bakery, all her bags positively

448

bulging with currant loaves. Donal usually got home by about eight to eight-thirty, and it was eight-fifteen now. I'll just stroll down to the tram stop and back, Deirdre told herself. Without quite knowing why, she was sure that Donal would be catching the tram tonight and she was proved right when one squealed to a halt by her and a crowd of people got off, her brother amongst them. He was clearly labouring under some considerable excitement, for he fairly pounced on her, beginning to gabble so fast that Deirdre had to tell him to talk slower before she could understand a word.

'What's bit you?' she enquired truculently, trying to make Donal take the heavy string bag from her. 'Catch a holt of this, Donny, we'll talk as we go. Now. What's up?'

'Our Ellie's up,' Donal said, grinning like a Cheshire cat. 'She's come 'ome, Dee!'

'I know that,' Deirdre said briefly, setting off along the pavement in the direction of Mere Lane. 'That's to say I dessay she's well on her way, but . . .'

'She's bleedin' here, I tell you,' Donal shouted, red-faced. 'I gorron the tram at the Pier Head, same's I allus do, an' when we reached the London Road stop there were a fair crowd—I 'spec' a train had just come in—an' there were our Ellen, waitin' in the queue for the tram. I were on top, so I yelled an' that, but she were talkin' to some feller an' never heard me. An' when I tried to push me way off the bleedin' tram the folk wouldn't let me by . . . what'll we do, Dee? What's our Mam gorrin the house for supper?'

'Oh, lor, it's blind scouse, 'cos Mam thinks they're comin' back tomorrer,' Dee recalled. 'An' only enough for you, our Donny! What'll we do? If

449

they catch the next tram they won't be more'n a few minutes behind us. There's a lorra trams runnin' at this time o' night.'

'Fish an' chips!' Donal declared suddenly. 'We've got some time to spare; the next tram's not for ten minutes—if they gerron it, that is. You know what our Ellen is, she does hate to shove.'

'Money?' Deirdre said briefly.

Donald patted his pocket, looking smug. 'I've a few bob,' he said with assumed nonchalance. 'Enough for fish an' chips all round, I reckon. Come on! We've gorra get back before they do!'

$$*\qquad*\qquad*$$

They made it, too, though by the skin of their teeth. They burst in through the back door and hurled the newspaper packages on to the table whilst their mother began to protest that this was no time to go treatin' theirselves, an' she'd thank them to take that stuff off of her kitchen table.

'You'll be glad of it presently,' Dee said briefly. 'Tek off your apron, Mam, an' run a comb through your hair. An' get those paper chains off the table, young Toby, or you'll gerrem all over grease from the chips.'

'Wharron earth . . . ?' Ada began, but she obeyed, nevertheless, taking off her apron and laying it across the back of a chair and beginning to tidy her hair with her hands, whilst Donal swept paper chains, poster paints and brushes off the table and over to the draining board, ignoring Toby's furious protests.

'There you are,' he said breathlessly. 'Plates, Dee . . . they'll be arrivin' . . .'

450

'Donal! Deirdre! If you don't explain this very minute . . .' Ada was beginning crossly when the back door burst open for the second time in two minutes and a familiar figure entered, closely followed by a total stranger. Ada screamed and flew across the kitchen into her elder daughter's arms, whilst the twins danced around shouting a welcome and Toby and Sammy stared, open-mouthed, at the sister they had not clapped eyes on for three years.

'Oh, Mam, Mam,' Ellen was crying. Tears were running down her face, Deirdre saw with interest. 'Oh, it's been so long . . . it's so good to be home . . . Oh, Mam, this is me feller . . . come in, Liam, don't hover in the doorway!'

Deirdre watched with approval as her elder sister released her mother and seized the arm of the very tall, dark-haired young soldier and dragged him right into the room. 'Liam, this is me mam, the redhead is me sister Dee and this feller's Donal, her twin. The little feller wi' paint all over his face is Toby and the other one's Sammy. Mam, me an' Liam's goin' to be married.'

'Well, that's nice . . . pleased to meet you, Liam,' Ada said faintly, taking his hand. 'Wharra surprise, chucks! We'd a big party planned for tomorrer, wi' all the fambly comin', an' friends an' neighbours, too. Oh my Gawd, I reckon you'll be starved an' all I've gorris a few odds an' ends an' a little pan o' blind scouse. Oh, I'm so ashamed of meself, but you did say tomorrer.'

'Our Mam's gorra a head like a perishin' sieve; if we weren't just a-sayin' as how you'd enjoy a fish supper,' Donal said agreeably. 'Dee, where's them plates, girl?'

451

There wasn't time to get anyone else round—nor enough fish and chips, as Donal pointed out—so they sat down round the table almost at once, with Ada bustling about, one minute kissing Ellen, the next dividing one piece of fish between Sammy and Toby, the next asking Liam about his family, then running to the cupboard for bread and margarine, and making everyone a nice cup of tea, with conny onny in it since they had run out of fresh milk.

Deirdre saw that Donal had been right to get the fish and chips. Eating a meal is a great breaker of the ice, and once they were sat down with a plateful in front of them the small boys stopped gawping at their sister's young man, Ada stopped worrying that she was not entertaining her daughter's friend properly and they all began to act naturally. The sauce bottle and the vinegar were passed round and Liam was loud in his appreciation of this unexpected supper, whilst Donal had to explain all over again how he'd been on the top deck of the tram when it stopped at the London Road stop and had seen Ellen and Liam in the crowd which had been unsuccessful in boarding the tram.

'And we knew as how Mam weren't expectin' them till tomorrer,' Deirdre said with relish. 'And all she'd gorrin the cupboard was the pan o' blind scouse for Donny. An' I'd been for the bun loaves, so we went an' got fish an' fried potatoes, enough for us all, an' then we fair tore home, so's to be indoors first.'

Then Ellen had to explain how they came to be a day earlier than they had expected and Liam,

452

having begun to talk a little more easily, was finally put to the question. It's like the bleedin' Spanish Inquisition, Dee thought. She had done the Inquisition in her last term at school and remembered it still. But of course it was just interest and Liam seemed happy enough to answer their questions.

Yes, he had brothers, though no sisters. Yes, there were twins in his family too—Seamus and Garvan were going on nineteen and like as two peas in a pod, though Seamus was, on the whole, considered a good boy and Garvan was a young devil.

'Even now they're so old?' Donal asked, for nineteen seems old when you've only just attained fifteen.

Liam chuckled. 'I've not seen 'em since I went to France,' he said. 'Probably they's both angels now, like the pair of ye, Donal. But perhaps you'll meet 'em some day, for if Ellen and meself live in Ireland you'll be wantin' to visit from time to time, no doubt?'

'Visit? Oh, but aren't you goin' to settle down here?' Ada asked. 'Course, work isn't goin' to be so easy now the troops are all comin' home . . .'

'Easy? Mam, we saw a soldier beggin' outside Lime Street station,' Ellen said, her voice sounding more sad than shocked. 'The poor devil had no legs . . . I never thought I'd see such a thing. And everyone's sayin' that jobs are hard to get, even for men who've won distinction fighting the Hun.'

'Oh, the country's still in a muddle,' Ada said easily. 'They'll sort things out; they'll start buildin' houses an' makin' provision for the troops. But as I told the lads there, it's more important than ever

453

for them to get a good education, so's they can get a job when their turn comes.'

'I can read a treat,' Toby said boastfully. 'Even the newspaper. Shall I read a bit to you, Ellen?'

He picked up a sheet of the *Evening Echo*, which had been wrapped around the chips, turned it right way up and began to read.

PUBLIC NOTICE
If the parents or guardians of Deirdre and Donal, twins, believed to be residing in the Everton district of Liverpool will contact the undersigned they may learn something to their advantage.

Locke, Bagnold and Locke,
Solicitors,
Lime Street Passage,
Liverpool.

He looked proudly around the table and Liam was just beginning to say heartily that sure an' wasn't that the neatest piece of readin' he'd heard for years, so it was, when Ellen jumped to her feet and reached for the paper. 'He must have read it wrong,' she said rather breathlessly. 'Deirdre and Donal . . . twins . . . there must be a mistake.'

'I never read it wrong,' Toby protested and started to read it again.

Ellen found the advertisement and she and Liam read it too, Ellen's nose almost resting on the page, for the newsprint was blurred with fat from the chips.

'*If the parents or guardians of Deirdre and Donal, twins, believed to be residing in the Everton district of Liverpool . . .*' She broke off. 'What have you two been up to this time?'

The twins had gone white.

'We haven't done nothing we shouldn't—not lately,' Deirdre said stoutly. 'Besides, it says *"something to their advantage"*, and in books that means a 'heritance or something, don't it? But that's an old paper . . . probably it were years ago.'

Ada in her turn took the page and turned it over. 'No, it's only a month old,' she said, having perused the top right-hand corner. 'Well, this is excitin' an' no mistake! What've you two been up to, eh? Saved a millionaire from jumpin' in the river, or give your last 'a'penny to a poor old woman what's a duchess in disguise?'

'Dunno,' Deirdre said stolidly, chewing, whilst Donal merely looked bewildered and rather annoyed. 'We'll go round to Lime Street Passage tomorrer though, eh, Donal? Find out what's happenin'?'

'We'll go Saturday; I'm off at noon,' Donal said. 'I don't want to lose me job, Mam. Nothin' ain't worth losin' your job for.'

'Lose your job nothin', Donny,' Deirdre said crisply. 'Tomorrer's the party—remember? You an' me's gorran afternoon off.'

Donal stared at her, much struck. 'So we have,' he admitted. 'Right then, we'll go tomorrer afternoon an' see these fellers Locke an' Bagnold. Can you come an' all, Mam? Only I don't know as I fancy just me an' Dee turnin' up in some posh offices.'

'Well, I'll have no end of work for the party . . .' their mother began doubtfully, to be promptly interrupted by Ellen.

'Mam, I'm home now,' she said at once. 'An' so's Liam. The two of us will do all the preparin' you

455

would have done, if you'll tell us what you want. We'd like to, wouldn't we, Liam?'

'Sure an' it 'ud be a fine t'ing to help wit' a party,' Liam agreed. 'I'd be honoured to help, so I would.'

'We-ell, if you're sure,' Ada said. 'Thanks very much, then, both. Me an' the kids'll soon find out what's what. I wonder whether I should take their birth sustificate wi' me?'

'Yes, I think you should,' Ellen agreed. 'And your own, Mam, or your marriage lines. Something to . . . to prove identity, I think they call it. Isn't it excitin', though? We'll be dyin' for you to come home an' tell us all about it!'

*   *   *

As soon as they had eaten their midday meal next day, the small party set out, Ada grimly clinging on to the twins' birth certificate and her own marriage lines. There had been much discussion as to whether they should go 'smart' or 'natural', but Ada had finally managed to persuade the twins that they would feel more at home in the solicitor's office if they wore their best, so it was with Donal smarting under the unaccustomed stiff collar and too-tight trousers of his best suit and Deirdre in Ellen's best coat, which was a bit too large for her, and her own red tam-o'-shanter, which she felt was too childish, that they at last sallied forth.

'If I'd ha' known that I were goin' to be half strangled I don't think I'd ha' agreed to come along,' Donal groaned, trying to get his hand down between his throat and the collar and failing dismally. 'It 'ud better be good, that's all I can say.'

456

'It says in the advertisement *something to your advantage*,' Deirdre reminded him. 'Look, it's a lark, any old how.'

And since Donal was forced to agree with her, and to acknowledge that he'd rather be going off to find out what it was all about than spending his time helping Ellen with the homecoming tea, tempers improved as they drew nearer their goal.

'Come on and do try to look happy, Donal,' their mother urged as they found the right door and read the brass plate affixed to it. 'If we go in there lookin' guilty as all get-out they'll think we're shammin' it, and you ain't Deirdre an' Donal at all.'

Horrified by the mere thought that his curiosity was not about to be satisfied, Donal stood up straighter and squared his shoulders resolutely, then fixed his female relatives with the most unnatural smile Deirdre had ever seen on her brother's countenance. 'Right you is,' he said through his crocodile grin. 'Let's be havin' you, Dee—smile, gal! Smile, Mam.'

And thus encouraged, the three of them opened the door and filed into the offices beyond.

*   *   *

'I like your mam an' the twins is great,' Liam said as he and Ellen began to slice bread and butter it. 'And your brother Bertie's a nice feller, an' all. Seems to me I'm a lucky bloke to be marryin' into a family like the Dochertys, me darlin'.'

Ellen looked up from her swift slicing and smiled, the rose rushing to her cheeks. Liam loved her even more when she blushed, he thought, and leaned over to kiss the tip of her nose, then got on with his buttering. When everyone stopped work, they'd be round here, Mrs Docherty had warned them, so it behoved them to be ready in good time.

'I'm glad you like 'em, Liam,' Ellen said shyly. 'An' it's plain as the nose on me face that they like you too. An' you'll meet the rest this evenin'—all but Uncle Willie. He's livin' way up north, in Darlington, where his wife comes from. But you'll meet everyone else—me aunts an' cousins too.'

'An' you'll meet mine when we go to Dublin, so you will,' Liam said equably. 'They'll love you like I do, acushla. Any more loaves to slice?'

'Yes, dozens,' Ellen said with a slight groan. 'Never mind, when we've done the loaves we'll have a break, shall we? I could do wi' a nice cup o' tea, to tell you the truth. An' I wouldn't mind a slice of currant loaf, either.'

'Nor me,' Liam said. He went to the parlour and fetched a tray of loaves through, then came back, eyeing his beloved uncertainly for a moment. 'Ellen, when we were in France an' you told me about your home, it didn't seem to matter that you had a whole house all to yourselves an' us Nolans just had a couple o' rooms. But now I've seen it . . .'

'I know, you can see it's nothin' special,' Ellen said with a smile. 'But it's a palace compared to the little house in the court where Mam brought us all up.'

'Aye, you said.' Liam looked around him at the big, untidy, comfortable kitchen, then glanced back at the parlour, which was so smart and beautifully furnished, at the short, square hall, and at the stairs which led to the bedrooms on the first floor, and included another staircase, leading up to a garret divided into two on the second floor. He remembered their rooms, so much more commodious than the dreadful quarters which a good many Dubliners accepted as their lot, and frowned to himself, standing the loaves down on the kitchen table and picking up the bread-knife. 'We're not badly off by some standards, but . . . this is a palace compared wit' Claymore Alley, honest to God, so it is.'

Ellen sighed and put down her knife, then looked across the table at Liam, her eyes steady. 'I'm not marryin' your family, Liam, nor your home,' she said gently. 'And you'd not planned to live with them in Claymore Alley, had you? After we're married, I mean.'

'No, I t'ought we'd get a room of our own,' Liam said. 'But it wouldn't be much of a room, not at first. And when I see this house . . .'

'You worry too much,' Ellen said. She came round the table and put her arms round Liam, then kissed his chin. 'It's you I'm marryin', Liam, not your . . . your circumstances. And besides, if things don't go right for us in Dublin we'll come back here—right?'

'To be sure. If they've not kept me job for me,' Liam agreed. 'Of course, 'tis not certain that I'd get a job here, either, but I'd have a rare good try, so I would.'

'There. Then that's settled,' Ellen said, going round to her own side of the table once more and picking up her knife. 'We'll go and see the priest tomorrow and get the wedding arranged. That's what we both want, isn't it?'

'It is,' Liam said, smiling lovingly at the girl opposite him. He loved her so much, but if she'd wanted to back out of their agreement he would

459

not have blamed her. Their future, he thought despairingly, was just a big question mark. But wasn't it always so, when two people wed? And they'd make a go of it, he knew they would. He leaned over and squeezed her hand. 'Love you,' he said.

*   *   *

Deirdre didn't know quite what she had expected to happen once they had explained their business to the elderly man in the front office, but it was not to be asked to wait for half an hour, 'Until Mr Locke is free to see you.' However, that was what happened and as the three Dochertys sat there, unable to chat amongst themselves because the gentleman who had spoken to them was dictating letters to a young girl with frizzy blonde hair, Deirdre began to know an overpowering urge to run out of the room and forget all about the mysterious advertisement. And looking at her mother and brother, she was pretty sure they felt the same. In fact they might have done so had it not been for the fact that the gentleman had taken the birth certificate and Ada's marriage lines from them when they entered and had shown no disposition to give them back again. So when at last the door opened and a youngish man poked his head into the room and said, 'Would you send 'em up please, Mr Clark?' she almost hoped that her mother would say they would not bother after all and ask for their documents back.

But Ada was made of sterner stuff. She stood up, jerked her head at the twins and followed the young man out of the room, up some stairs and

460

along a short corridor. He stopped outside a door, tapped on the panel, opened it and said into the room: 'Mrs Docherty and the twins, Mr Locke,' then stood to one side, ushering them into the room and closing the door firmly behind them.

Deirdre looked apprehensively at the man behind the desk. He was stern-looking, with thick grey hair and spectacles. But having looked, he smiled quite pleasantly and came round the desk, shaking hands with all three of them and introducing himself as Mr Locke.

Then, in a voice which was dry but not unfriendly, he bade them sit down on the three upright wooden chairs arranged in front of his desk and sat down again himself. 'I've examined your documents, Mrs Docherty, and it seems to me that you are probably the person we are seeking,' he said. 'But in fact we are, in this instance, only the agents for the solicitors who will actually deal with the matter in question. They are a firm situated in Clare, in Southern Ireland, by the name of . . .'

'Clare?' Deirdre interrupted. She half stood up. 'Oh, sir, is it me pal? Bill McBride his name is, he come from County Clare and . . .' She stopped short.

Mr Locke was positively beaming at her. 'There!' he said in a satisfied voice. 'Not only are you genuinely Deirdre and Donal of the Heyworth Street area of Everton, but you must be the ones I was instructed to find. No one else would know of Mr William McBride! Now that is *very* good news, and will make my job considerably easier. You see, the main task my firm was given was to find you and to pay your expenses to reach County Clare— in point of fact the town of Ennis—where you will

461

be told just what this is all about.'

Ada frowned. 'Surely no one would expect us to set off for Ireland without knowin' why or wherefore?' she said in a clipped, anxious voice. 'We've all got jobs, Mr Locke, besides me being responsible for the younger children still. We's not goin' off on a wild-goose chase, not for all the expenses you mention.'

'No, no, no, Mrs Docherty, don't think we're not aware of the problems,' Mr Locke said soothingly. 'I'm at liberty to tell you straight away that, should you be able to prove that you are the mother of the Deirdre and Donal mentioned in Mr McBride's will . . .'

'Is Bill dead, then?' Deirdre asked sadly. 'Oh, I am sorry . . . we was real fond of Bill, Donny an' me.'

'Yes, I'm afraid he died close on a year ago,' Mr Locke said gently. 'And clearly, he was as fond of you and your brother as you were fond of him, since by the terms of his will he has left you two farms with the farmhouses and all the land attached thereto.'

'Wha-aat?' exclaimed Ada, whilst Donal whistled expressively through his front teeth and nudged his sister excitedly. 'Left the twins a farm— two farms? But . . . but din't Mr McBride have relatives? I thought our Dee told me he had a brother . . .'

'Yes, he did. But his brother predeceased him by several years and latterly Mr McBride has been running both farms, with the help of various farm-workers and a manager. However, I can tell you very little more I'm afraid, save that one of the farms is in excellent heart and thriving, whilst the

462

other is well enough, I understand. Now, Mrs Docherty, I'm sure you can see that this is not an opportunity to be lightly cast aside? In fact, it is a wonderful chance for your family, for Mr McBride has given you what amounts to *carte blanche* over what you do with the properties. As I understand it, Mr McBride has left them in trust for the twins until they are twenty-one, when they become theirs absolutely, with you, Mrs Docherty, as trustee. This means that you cannot simply sell them until the twins are twenty-one, and then they too will have to say they want the farms sold.'

'There's no way we'd sell a farm, would we, Donny?' Dee put in, feeling her cheeks warm with excitement and seeing, by her twin's glowing face, that he too was astounded by their good fortune. 'Why, Donny's rearin' lambs right now on a bit o' land he's rented from a farmer on the Wirral. There's nothin' either of us wants more than land of our own. Ain't that right, Donny?'

'Yes, *sir*,' Donal breathed raptly, addressing Mr Locke. 'Ever since we was nippers we've wanted land . . . a farm . . . something like that. Why, when we lived in Evangelist Court we helped Bill to make a garden, din't we, Dee? An . . . an' Bill said we were naturals, he said we had green fingers, we could make most things grow.'

'Excellent, excellent,' Mr Locke said, beaming. 'Well, Mrs Docherty? I think that ferry and train fares for you and the twins, plus full board in an hotel for a fortnight, ought to be sufficient, don't you? And money for those left behind, of course. Because all being well—and I'm sure it will be—the firm of Donovan and McCready, the Irish solicitors who instructed me, will see that you have monies to cover all your other expenses, including what you might call pocket-money, once you reach Ennis.'

'That sounds very fair, sir,' Ada said cautiously. 'But I've a dacent job I don't want to lose and there's them in me fambly what wouldn't go off to Ireland and live on a farm, not if it were ever so. They've jobs, you see, what can't be left . . . an' the older boys are away, married . . . to say nothin' of me man, not home yet. He's in the Navy, he's no farmer.'

'I do understand, Mrs Docherty,' Mr Locke said earnestly. 'What I want you to do now is to go away and discuss with your family, in particular these twins and the younger children, what you wish to do. Then, in a couple of days if you can come back to me and tell me of your decision I will arrange for the purchase of ferry tickets and so on. Will that suit?'

'That 'ud be grand, sir,' Ada said thankfully. 'Me daughter Ellen's just come home from France, wi' the young gentleman she means to marry . . . I'd like to get that sorted out afore mekin' a decision about leavin' the Pool, even for a couple o' weeks.'

'That's sensible. I'm sure that Messrs Donovan and McCready, having waited so long already, won't object to a trifle more delay,' Mr Locke said cheerfully. 'Well, I'll bid you a very good afternoon and shall look forward to hearing your decision as to when you'll leave—not *if*, Mrs Docherty, but *when*—in the next few days.'

He saw them down the stairs and along the corridor, then out of the door and down to the corner, nodding very pleasantly to them before he returned to his offices.

For a moment the three of them just stood there,

464

staring at each other, then Deirdre broke the silence. 'Well I'm damned!' she said explosively. 'I can't believe it happened—it's like a bleedin' dream come true, our Mam! Cor, I can't wait to see their faces when we tell 'em where we've been an' what's a-comin' to us.'

*　　　*　　　*

It was a lucky thing that the party had been planned for that evening, since it gave Ada the chance to talk to her whole family and to make a decision.

'It's a grand chance for the kids, Mam, an' for you,' Dick assured her as soon as they had been regaled with the story of the advertisement and its consequences. 'Things ain't goin' to be easy for anyone, not now the war's over an' all the troops are comin' home. Jobs'll be that hard to find—and to keep—that you'd be mad not to go over, see what's what. But us older ones . . . we've gorrour own lives to lead. Wives, in-laws . . . we wouldn't want to leave England.'

'Well, I'm norrall that keen on farm-livin' meself,' Ada admitted, keeping her voice down. 'I'm Everton born an' bred, I don't see meself tekin' kindly to bogs an' sheep an' . . . an' pigs. Lerralone no neighbours comin' in for a screw o' tea when they run short, or a handful o' currants. Then there's your Auntie Anne—she's been real good to me, I know the business now like the palm of me 'and, an' if she goes before me, I'll 'herit the cake shop, she's showed me her will. But the twins is more'n keen, they're afire to go, an' I sounded out Ellen an' her young feller as soon as we got

465

back from the s'licitors, an' she an' her Liam said they'd go as me proxy, so to speak, if that were what I wanted.'

Ozzie, who had been listening, frowned. 'But won't they need all the 'elp they can get, Mam?' he asked. 'I thought as 'ow these Irish farms was fambly affairs, that a man relied on 'is sons to work for 'im. That's 'ow I allus understood it, anyroad.'

'I dunno about that, but Bill's been runnin' the place wi' workers an' a manager for years, apparently,' Ada said. 'Anyway, the important thing is to go over an' see what's what. I 'splained about not bein' able to sell till the twins are twenty-one, didn't I?'

'You did. An' I can see the sense of it,' Dick allowed. 'It 'ud be 'ard on the little feller if he were keen to farm an' you sold up afore he were old enough to start workin'. But you'll go fust-off, won't you, Mam? Though you'll have to either tek the littl'uns or get Ellen to look after 'em, I suppose. Unless you'd trust 'em to one of us?'

But after a day or so to think it over Ada decided what she would rather do, and put it to her family at teatime, as Ellen and Liam, the twins and the two small boys sat round the table, eating meat pie and mashed potatoes. 'I want you an' Ellen to go in me place, Liam,' she explained. 'You've said you want to take our Ellen home to see your fambly— well, you can kill two birds wi' one stone that way— you can have a day or two wi' your mam an' then you can go on to the solicitors in Ennis.'

'But what about you, Mam?' Deirdre demanded rather thickly. She had just loaded her mouth with meat pie. 'You want to see the place, an' talk to the solicitors, don't you? They'll read the will an'
466

'splain wharrit all means, Mr Locke said so.'

'Oh aye, but Ellen will tell me everythin' when she comes back,' Ada said soothingly. 'You don't mind tekin' Ellen instead of me, do you, queen?'

'No, course not . . . but Mam . . . don't you want to come?' Deirdre asked, considerably astonished. She would not have missed the chance for a fortune she realised. 'An' think of seein' the farm, the little lambs, pigs . . . the fields . . . oh, Mam!'

'I know, queen,' Ada said rather guiltily. 'But the fact is, I don't know as I'd ever take to farmin' . . . not meself, like. But if the rest of you can manage wi'out me . . . well, for a whiles, say . . . then I'm best 'ere, keepin' me job warm an' seein' as the younger ones go on wi' their eddication.'

'Oh, but Mam . . .' Deirdre began, only to be drawn to one side by Ellen.

'Look, Dee, if you think you couldn't manage wi' only Liam an' me to help, then say so,' Ellen said. 'But don't push Mam too hard, norrat first. She'll come round when things are more settled, but right now, she's scared o' the whole idea. We'll go over there, just the four of us, and sort things out. Then we'll be able to tell Mam she's nothin' to fear and perhaps persuade her to come over for a holiday, first off.'

So it was arranged.

'But you two ain't goin' afore you've tied the knot,' Ada told her eldest daughter firmly. 'There'd be talk—it 'ud give a wrong impression and you know what folk is like. I want you married afore you goes off anywhere, wi' anyone.'

And though she laughed, Ellen agreed, so she and Liam decided to have a quiet wedding just as soon as it could be arranged, and this time Ellen,

Liam and Ada went off to Lime Street Passage and explained how things stood to Mr Locke, who promptly put matters in hand.

'I'm glad you're going with the youngsters, young man,' Mr Locke said to Liam. 'Being Irish yourself, you'll know all the ins and outs of it, I dare say, and will be able to advise them how they are to go on.'

Liam smiled gently and Ellen, stifling a giggle, did not tell Mr Locke that all Irishmen are not natural-born farmers, nor that Liam had spent most of his life in the city of Dublin and probably knew a good deal less about farming than young Donal.

'It's all arranged,' she told her mother when they returned to Mere Lane that night. 'It's a shame Liam's family can't be with us, but it's just not possible: there's no time. We'll marry on the Tuesday and set off for Ireland on the Thursday. We'll spend a few days wi' Mrs Nolan an' the children, and go by train and bus to Ennis. Oh, Mam, I can't help bein' excited—I just hope the twins behave theirselves, mind.'

'Oh, I'm sure they will,' said Ada, with a cheerful confidence she was far from feeling. Donal and Deirdre were full of themselves, as high as kites on excitement and anticipation. 'Just you give 'em a good clack if they play up—tell Liam to tan their bums for 'em, that'll mek 'em think twice.'

And so it was arranged and the Docherty family began to plan the wedding breakfast.

*　　　*　　　*

In the end it was May before the newly-weds and the twins set off for Clare, and then it was not

468

merely for the visit that Ada had foreseen, but for an indefinite stay. The reason was simple; the farm manager had been offered another job by a cousin who had a very large sheep station in Australia and, though willing to remain at the farm for the weeks left before his passage to that country, he did not wish to stay indefinitely. So the Dochertys and Liam had discussed the matter and decided that they had no choice. If they were ever to make a go of the two properties they must start work there as soon as possible, in order that they might learn the ropes before Mr Catlin, the manager, left.

'After all, it's norras though we don't mean to stay,' Donal said. 'Once I'm there . . . well, I shall need to stay put, what wi' summer comin' on, an' stock to look after an' that.'

But they had had some help. Donal went, with Liam, to one of the sheep farms he visited in the course of his work and they had a long chat with the farmer who had rented him his sheep pasture, a rosy-faced, middle-aged man called Bert Nobbs, who was happy to help a young feller who was going into farming—and who might buy stock off him one of these fine days.

'You're right not to leave the place once you arrive,' he assured them. 'And at first, at any rate, it looks as though wages will be your biggest outlay, so if you can work as a family, it'll pay you. You already know a good deal about sheep, I grant you, but you've yet to discover what thrives best in Clare. I can't tell you that for most of me stock is bought this side o' the water.' He looked at Liam. 'Now as to workers, I know all the young Dochertys are settled, he said so, but what about your fam'ly, young feller-me-lad? Any strong young chap what

469

could do wi' some country air an' country food in return for workin' on the farm?'

'Aye, that's possible,' agreed Liam. 'Just at first, mind. They're all city born, like the Dochertys.'

'An' what about yourself?' the farmer enquired. 'Young Docherty tells me you're just back from France. Got a job to go back to?'

'I don't know,' Liam said gloomily. 'I dussen't tell 'em I'm back, not until I can claim me job an' start work at once. But I've me doubts, to be honest. Mebbe I'm best stickin' wi' the Dochertys, if they want me. And besides, I'm marryin' shortly, so I am, an' me wife won't want to leave her brother an' sister strugglin' on the farm alone, not for a year or three.'

'Good, good. Well, don't be ashamed to ask for advice when you reach Clare, an' then tek it. You're tekin' your lambs wi' you, I understand?'

'Aye, 'cos I've two rams an' four ewes,' Donal explained—unnecessarily, since Mr Nobbs had kept an eye on his small flock for him when he was unable to be with them and much approved of his choice. 'It'll be the beginnin' of me flock . . . if the present one's norrup to wharr I want, tharris.'

'Right. Well, then, they say the best manure for the land is the farmer's boot—you know what that means? You've got to be there, keep your eye on everyone and everything and that way you'll succeed. Drop me a line now an' then, let me know how you go on.'

Donal agreed to it, so they were packing all their possessions, not intending to be back in Liverpool for some considerable while.

'Though Mam will come out to us in a few months, I dessay,' Deirdre said a little forlornly.

She loved Ellen dearly and was already fond of Liam, but much though she longed for a country life, she knew she would miss her old friends and relatives. 'And anyway, Mr Nobbs says women do as much work on most farms as men—I'll enjoy that.'

Because of the arrangements which had to be made the time fairly flew, and suddenly the wedding was about to take place. Deirdre was a bridesmaid in a pale-green dress and Liza, now Mrs Tolliver, was matron of honour in pink. To save money, Ellen wore the dress which Liza had married in, but no one minded. Indeed, it looked quite different, for it had to be altered to fit so Ada had added a wide lace hem to lengthen it and had embroidered white roses round the low neck. 'No one will know or care that it ain't new,' she assured her daughter comfortably. 'And isn't your weddin' ring the prettiest thing now? Where did Liam gerrit?'

'From George's, on Scotland Road,' Ellen told her mother. They were all sitting in the kitchen on the eve of the wedding, talking comfortably. Liza was there, and Tolly, who had agreed to be best man, and Dick, who was to give the bride away. 'I wish I could ha' give Liam a ring too, Mam, but we dussen't. Not wi' going to Ireland an' all. We felt we oughtn't to spend any more money, not yet awhile.'

'Goodness,' Ada said, jumping to her feet. 'That's put me in mind o' something . . . wait you a moment.'

She left the room and returned presently with a small wooden box in her hand. She sat down on the arm of Ellen's chair, opened it and delved about inside, presently emerging triumphantly with a large and heavy gold ring which she handed to her astonished daughter. 'There—wharrabout that then, eh? You can have that for Liam, until you can get one of your own, I mean. It belonged to your great-grandfather, then your father wore it until he died. I didn't give it to Mick, because he'd a signet ring of his own.'

'Oh, Mam, he might've been killed in the war,' Deirdre said reproachfully. 'Can I have a look at the ring?' She held out a hand and Ellen, who had been fingering it with awe, handed it to her younger sister. 'What's the initials, Mam? It ain't a D for Docherty, that's for sure.'

'No, it's not, because your great-grandmother was married twice,' Ada explained. 'Didn't I ever tell you? She came to England as a widow expectin' her first child, an' had a little lad, your grandfather, Dee. The ring had belonged to her first husband . . . I never did hear his name . . . an' she gave it to your grandfather, who took the name of Flanaghan, who was my gran's second husband. But he kept the ring an' handed it on to me as the eldest child at me weddin'. An' I give it to your father, who wore it till he died.'

'I 'member 'im wearin' it,' Dick put in suddenly. 'Lor', it's nigh on twenty year since he died, but I 'member it, glintin' on 'is 'and when 'e played wi' us.' He looked down at his own broad, calloused hand, with a thin gold ring on the third finger. 'Course, my Esther bought me a ring . . . it's nice as it's goin' back to Ireland, Mam.'

Deirdre had been turning the ring over and over, and now she said curiously: 'I wonder what the pattern means, Mam? Or is it a whole lot of capital

Ms, all joined together?'

'Likely it is, bein' Irish,' Ada said. 'Pretty, ain't it, done in a circle like that? Looks like a dandelion, a bit. Still, so long as it fits the bill . . .'

*   *   *

Ellen surveyed herself in the glass in her mother's room. She was pale—but brides were always pale, weren't they? She knew she loved Liam, that they were right for each other, and yet . . . and yet . . . she was going away from the city she loved and the people who loved her, with Liam, who wasn't even related to her, and the twins, who could be such holy terrors. Was she doing the right thing? Had Mam been right to insist on their marrying before they left for Ireland? And now that she thought about it, it was all very well to say that she and Liam were right for each other. How did she know? She had never seen him in a temper, or doing an ordinary job of work, even. For all she knew he might grow violent when crossed! He might try to hit her! He might bully the twins, ill-treat the farm animals, drink too much . . .

These depressing reflections were interrupted by Deirdre, bouncing into the room with her red curls brushed into a flaming bush and her eyes snapping with temper. 'Mam says I must plait me hair, an' that bleedin' Liam agrees wi' her,' she stormed. 'I won't plait me hair, I want it like Liza's got hers! An' Liza's here, she arrived ten minutes ago . . . she's gorra crown thing on top of her head . . . why can't I have one o' them?'

Immediately, all Ellen's fears faded and looked as foolish as a candle flame in daylight. How could

473

she ever have imagined, even for one moment, that Liam was anything but the dearest feller she'd ever known, the gentlest, the kindest? 'You're a little idiot, Dee Docherty,' she said. 'Liza's gorra *coronet*, norra crown, an' don't you know how them coronet things is made? You pull all your hair to one side and plait it, and wind it round your head an' fix it in place wi' them artificial rosebuds we bought at Blacklers. Oh, come here, I'll do it for you.'

'Oh! Well, why didn't they say?' Deirdre grumbled. 'Does I look awright, Ellie? Liam looks a treat—an' you're jus' like a fairy princess . . . you look ever so much prettier than Liza did in that dress, honest to God you do.'

'Thank you, queen,' Ellen said, picking up her sister's heavy fall of dark-red curls and beginning to braid them. 'Now stay nice an' still for me, an' you'll have one o' them coronets in no time. Got the roses handy?'

'No. I threw 'em down when Mam said I were to plait me hair,' Deirdre admitted, going slightly pink. 'Wonder who I'll marry, Ellie? Ain't it strange to think it'll probably be an Irishman too—just like Liam, if I'm lucky.'

'They broke the mould when they made Liam,' Ellen said, smiling. 'He's the best, Dee. Aha . . . someone's comin' up the stairs . . . I'll ask 'em to fetch up your roses.'

When the door opened it was Liza, standing framed in the doorway with her pink dress neatly buttoned and her hands full of white satin roses. She smiled at Ellen, then addressed herself to Deirdre. 'I thought you'd be needin' these, queen,' she said gently. 'It's always the same on a weddin' day—it was the same when Tolly an' me got

474

hitched—tempers fray an' folk say things they're sorry for, after. My, but your hair looks a treat done that way! And as soon as you're ready we oughter be mekin' our way—Tolly an' Liam left just now, an' Donny says his neck'll bust clean out o' that stiff collar if we don't gerra move on. You ready?'

Deirdre, rendered sunny once more by a glimpse of herself in the mirror, said she was and Ellen followed her out of the room, suddenly full of eagerness to arrive at the church—and see Liam. It would be all right, she knew it would—and the sooner the knot was tied and they were man and wife the sooner she could prove it to herself.

She tripped lightly down the stairs and when, in the living-room, Dick offered her his arm she was able to smile up at him with perfect confidence.

'Ready, queen?' her brother said. 'You're a picture, Ellie Docherty—and it's the last time I'll call you that!'

'I'm ready, Dickie,' Ellen assured him. 'In fact, I can't wait!'

*   *   *

The wedding went off without a hitch and Deirdre, in her pale-green silk, was the life and soul of the reception. Partly, she thought, it was because this was in the nature of a farewell party and also because she and Donal were absolutely on fire to get to Ireland.

'Me home's nothin' special,' Liam had warned them. 'Mammy's put Ticky in with the twins so as to give us a room to ourselves. Donal will share wit' Ticky and the twins, so he will, an' he won't mind

475

that—they'll git along just fine.'

'An' we shan't be there long, shall we, Liam?' Deirdre had said. 'Only a few days. So Seamus an' Garvan won't be too put out be us.'

'Seamus is an easygoin' feller,' Liam assured her. 'An' Garvan's not so bad. Knowin' me brother Garv, in fact, chance is he'll be away from home anyway. Mammy told me a while back that he was standin' the markets and roamin' about all over. Oh, we'll all manage very well.'

Deirdre was rather looking forward to meeting the twins. She was a twin herself and was interested to know how Garvan was taking Seamus's being in love, for apparently he had a regular girl-friend and intended to marry her when they were old enough.

I don't think I'd much like the thought of Donal marryin' whiles I were still on me own, Deirdre told herself honestly. An' we ain't 'dentical twins. Still, if Garvan's not there he's not; there's nothin' I can do about it.

So when the time came to say goodbye to her brothers and to her mother, Deirdre shed tears and clung convulsively to Ada and promised that she would come back when 'everything's sorted', but she wasn't truly unhappy. Anticipation of what was to come was too strong—and besides, she was taking Donal and Ellen, her favourite people, with her.

They reached Dublin at four o'clock on a beautiful May afternoon and it was only then that Deirdre realised she was a foreigner in a foreign land, for all that this was a part of Great Britain. She occasionally had trouble in understanding Liam when he used a strange expression, but she speedily realised that the people in the street were

476

speaking in a brogue so thick that it might have been a foreign tongue. As they crossed the River Liffey by the Wellington Bridge, and saw the wide quays crowded with people, she clutched Donal's hand, pulling him back from the others for a moment.

'Suppose us can't understand a word they say, Donny?' she said plaintively. 'That feller shoutin' his mackerel might as well be doin' it in Dutch for all I could catch!'

'Likely it'll be worse in Clare,' Donal said cheerfully, shaking her hand off his arm. 'Don't grab, Dee. No one's goin' to eat you.'

'But I love to talk, Donny,' Deirdre said, near to tears. 'Likely they won't understand me, either. Oh, I wish I'd never come!'

'No you don't,' Donal said bracingly. 'You just have to listen more careful, queen, and it'll be the same for all of us, I reckon. Liam's been mixin' wi' other British soldiers, an' I reckon he's had to calm his brogue down a bit to be understood. Don't worry ... an' his mam works in a smart shop— you'll understand her all right.'

'Well, I just hope you're right,' Dee said, but she felt more cheerful. She lowered her voice to a whisper. 'You'll stick by me, won't you, though, Donny, when we reach the Nolans' house? I won't be scared if you do.'

Donal sighed exaggeratedly. 'I'll stick by you,' he promised. 'An' in half an hour you'll be wantin' me to leave you alone so you can gossip wi' someone.'

Content on that score, Deirdre hurried to catch up with the others once more, then tugged Liam's sleeve. 'What's that, Liam?'

'It's the castle,' Liam said briefly, following her

pointing finger. 'I wish you could see O'Connell Street . . . but it's not on our way and the bags are heavy. Dublin's a small city compared wit' Liverpool, but it's a grand place, so it is. I'll show you round tomorrow, we'll tek a tram ride, go to Phoenix Park and buy ice-creams, go round the markets . . . oh aye, we're not here for long so we must mek the best of what time we have.'

'That'll be nice,' Deirdre said obediently, though she thought that so far Dublin did not seem particularly exciting. After all, she'd known Princes Park all her life and could not imagine anything much bigger or better. 'Is it far to Claymore Alley now, Liam?'

'No,' Liam said briefly. 'This is Parliament Street and when we get to the castle we turn into Lord Edward Street and then sort of twist our way through the Liberties until we're home.'

'Parly! Like at home,' Donal said. 'What d'you call it, Liam?'

Ellen, listening, laughed. 'Dubliners don't shorten everything like we do, chuck,' she said. 'They call it Parliament Street!'

The twins laughed too, but their bags were heavy and Deirdre at any rate, shifting her load from one hand to the other, was only half interested in her surroundings. She had been surprised that the buildings which lined the Liffey were neither huge nor impressive, like the Liver Building back home, but she was prepared to accept that Dublin was different. And meanwhile, she would be very glad to find herself at the Nolans' home so that she could put down her burden, slump in a chair and have a nice cup of tea.

'This is Corn Market,' Liam said presently. 'And

478

ahead of us, on the right, is our church, the one we'd have married in, Ellen, if we'd decided to tie the knot over here. It's on Thomas Street, but we're quicker to turn down Francis Street, right here, and cut through. There, now we're nearly home!'

*   *   *

Ellen did not know quite what she had expected, but she was pleasantly surprised once they reached the Nolans' home. Before then, however, she had been a little amazed at the number of dirty, ill-clad children playing around the tenements and back streets. Neither Evangelist Court nor Mere Lane was exactly upper class, but most of the children were better dressed and cleaner than these little ones.

She did not say this to Liam, but he must have guessed what she was thinking, for he took her hand and squeezed it reassuringly. 'It's spring and we're mortal short o' dacint housin',' he said under his breath. 'Folk sleep more to a room here than they do your way . . . I did warn ye! But you'll see that the kids are well nourished for the most part, an' the women send 'em to school dressed as well as they can afford. It's just when they're playin' that boots an' good clothes get took off 'em.'

But then they reached Claymore Alley and the tall house with its small, square entrance. Liam hurried them up the stairs and opened a door . . . and they were there!

The door led straight into a kitchen, a large room with a bright fire burning in spite of the warmth of the day. A woman was arranging cups

479

on the large wooden table in the centre of the room and she looked up and smiled as they came in. 'Liam! Sure an' didn't I t'ink you'd be along soon, if the ship docked when she usually does, and isn't it a fine day now and not the sort of day to hold up a sailin'?' she demanded, her face brightening into a smile. 'Come an' give me a kiss, son ... and this'll be ...' She stared at Ellen for a moment, then a hand flew to her heart. 'Dear God, and aren't you—' she broke off, then resumed with an obvious effort. 'Aren't you just the sort of pretty girl I've always wanted me son to marry? Ellen, welcome to your home!'

She was a pretty, dark-haired woman with a neat figure and she was wearing a russet-brown dress with a pearly brooch at the V of the neck. She kissed Liam, then Ellen, and Ellen, who had secretly dreaded this moment, was aware of a warmth and friendliness emanating from her mother-in-law. She was also aware that she had in some way been a shock to Mrs Nolan. Smiling, admiring the large, airy kitchen, telling Mrs Nolan about their journey, she wondered whether the older woman had assumed that she would be blonde, or plumper, or even younger or older. But it was pointless to worry; she would find out in the fullness of time if she asked the right questions.

As soon as they had put their bags down and been properly introduced, Mrs Nolan insisted that they go through to the parlour, a room so beautifully furnished and so immaculately kept that Ellen actually gasped. Mrs Nolan, clearly very proud of her room, fairly beamed at her. 'I've always kept the youngsters out of me parlour, until they was growed, that is,' she said. 'But when we

480

have the ceilidh to welcome you tomorrer, alanna, we'll open it up and have half the world in. Ah, here's Liam's little brother. Ticky, come and be introduced, me son.'

Ticky beamed at them all, kissed Liam moistly on the cheek and came towards Ellen when his mother bade him, only to pause, looking up at her with wide eyes. 'Mammy, isn't she the image of our Maggie?' he said. 'Just like I 'member her—an' just like the photy you've got standin' below the Holy picture in your room!'

So *that* was it, Ellen realised, remembering the photograph which Liam had once showed her. He had told her about Maggie, who had worked for his mammy, who had been going to marry him . . . but it had been ages ago, when they had first met; she'd not thought about that Maggie—or their resemblance—for years.

''Tis only the hair,' Mrs Nolan said hurriedly. 'An' mebbe the shape of the face . . .' She turned to Ellen. 'Forgive us, alanna, but at first glance, you know, it was quite a shock.'

'It's all right, Mrs Nolan,' Ellen said quickly. 'I remember now, Liam showed me a photograph taken on a beach somewhere of himself and his . . . his friend. We both thought there was a likeness.'

''Tis just the hair,' Mrs Nolan said again, adding: 'And now I'll get some tay and soda bread; you must be t'irsty, all of ye, after that long journey.'

*   *   *

The rest of the day had gone well, Deirdre thought, as she lay in bed that night, trying to keep a decent distance from Mrs Nolan, for she was sharing the

481

bed with her. Seamus had come home and been friendly and amusing, and the other brother, Kenny, who was married and living out at Goldenbridge, wherever that might be, had come round with his wife and small baby, assuring his mother that they would all come to the ceilidh the following day. They had had a good hot meal and, because the evenings were light still, had been taken on a short tour of the neighbourhood, Seamus walking between her and Donal and telling them stories about the people who lived and worked in the various streets and houses. He had offered to take them further afield at the weekend, for this was his Saturday afternoon off, but he had been evasive about his twin brother.

'He works all over,' he said in answer to Donal's query. 'But don't worry, you'll see him before you go off to Ennis, so you will. Sure an' Garvan's as curious as the next. He'll be wantin' to tek a look at these brand-new English relatives of his.'

Deirdre did not intend to admit that she was curious too, but she did ask Seamus if he and Garvan were really identical.

Seamus had looked embarrassed and shrugged. 'Like enough to fool people when we'd a mind,' he said at last. 'But when we're together . . . now I wouldn't say we were identical, exactly.'

Thinking it over, however, Deirdre decided that she liked Seamus very much and thought the rest of the family a pleasant lot. And what was more, this family were very much in sympathy with her intense interest in Clare and what they would find there.

'My fambly come from the Burren, way back,' Mrs Nolan had told her as they prepared for bed.

'Liam's great-grandmother left Clare long ago—at the time of the famine, I dare say—and never returned, but I've always had a hankerin' for the country, so I have. Mebbe we'll come and pay you a visit once you're settled.'

'That would be lovely, if everything goes all right wi' the solicitors in Ennis,' Deirdre had said. 'Mind, the fellers in Liverpool said it were just a formality, because we were the right people, an' that. But they said that if the place were too much for us, or very run-down, we'd need to know the solicitors in Ennis, so's we could sort it out.'

'Sure an' you'll be fine, the lot of ye,' Mrs Nolan murmured sleepily. 'Tomorrer I want Ellen to come to O'Connell Street wit' me, so's I can buy her somethin' useful or pretty for a weddin' present. Would you be after comin' wit' us, alanna?'

Deirdre had said she would go, but she hoped that it wouldn't take all day to buy whatever it was. She hated shopping, especially when there was a whole new city to explore outside, and Seamus had promised to tell Donal how to find the bird market, which should be a bit of fun, Deirdre thought.

She decided that she would plan a reason for not accompanying Ellen and Mrs Nolan and lay for a while, plotting to herself. But she had had a long day and, much sooner than she wished, she slid into the land of dreams.

*   *   *

Once the Nolans and the Dochertys got used to each other the days passed in no time. They met scores of friends and relatives at the ceilidh and

483

were showered with invitations to visit and, on their last day in Dublin, Seamus went out early, presumably to Mass, and returned with Garvan in tow.

They were very alike, Deirdre felt, but she thought that Seamus was the handsomer of the two. Garvan had a dark, brooding look and a sarcastic twist to his lips, and almost the first thing he said to her, when they were alone for a moment, was 'I s'pose you don't wear a hat much, even though you're a bleedin' Englishwoman—scared of settin' light to it wit' that flamin' hair!'

Deirdre had given him a cold glare and ignored him after that, but now, it appeared, she was going to be unable to do so, for Donal wanted to go to the cattle market and Seamus had offered to take him, Liam and Ellen were off on some ploy of their own, Mrs Nolan was busy indoors . . . and Garvan, with an ill grace, had offered to 'show the young wan somethin' a bit livelier than ould O'Connell Street or the Cat'olic cathedral'.

It would have been rude to say she'd rather do almost anything than go anywhere with a feller who made personal remarks about her red hair, but Deirdre was determined not to be rude. Besides, she thought that the offer was in the nature of an olive branch and should be taken courteously. However, having agreed to go, she saw no reason why she should not warn Garvan that she would not allow him to insult her once they were alone. 'No more of your cheek, feller,' she said briskly as they walked, side by side, down Francis Street, weaving their way between the stalls which lined it. 'For stand it I will not. I'll give you a thick ear an' a bloody nose if you try it, what's more, an' you can

484

explain *that* away to your mammy!'

Garvan had given her a startled glance and grinned, though he had vouchsafed no reply.

After waiting a moment, Deirdre asked curiously: 'What've you gorragin red hair, anyway? You give me a dirty look soon's you saw me—no need, as I could see.'

His look, this time, had a trace of admiration in it, though he frowned and tried to look cross. 'Quick, aren't ye?' he said in a sneery sort of voice. ''Tis clear you've not met Seamus's girl-friend yet.'

'No, but Donal has,' Deirdre said, remembering. 'So she's got red hair, has she? I thought Donny grinned like an eejit when he mentioned they'd seen her. But what's that got to do with it? Your brother wouldn't choose some little tart; I reckon she's nice. He is!'

That made Garvan grin and he was much better when he grinned, Deirdre decided. But it clearly didn't change his opinion of girls with red hair, and herself and Seamus's young lady in particular.

'Oh, nice,' he said scornfully. 'I just don't see what he wants to get tangled wit' a girl for, that's all. All girls do is make a feller marry 'em, an' then they hang on his sleeve an' have babies an' ruin his freedom, that's what they do.'

'You might as well say fellers ruin girls' freedom,' Deirdre said obstinately. 'An' it teks two to mek a baby, Garvan Nolan, or hasn't no one told you the facts of life yet?'

Garvan wanted to laugh, she could tell, and this of course made him angrier. It is always infuriating to want to laugh when you're trying to be serious and to vent your annoyance on someone. 'Girls aren't ever free, not in the way a feller can be,' he growled. 'Besides, who needs girls?'

'Your brother does, seemingly,' Deirdre said. 'Surely you like some girls, don't you, Garvan?'

He stopped in his tracks at that, right beside a fat woman in black with a huge basket of lilac and laburnum. He stared unseeingly at the flowers, then bent down and picked out a bunch of lilac, purple, pale-blue and white, and dug in his pocket for the necessary coins. 'You come wit' me, gorl, an' you'll find out what use I've got for women,' he said in a low tone. 'Come on . . . there's a tram!'

'You said we could go down to the quays,' Deirdre said breathlessly. 'An' then you said you'd show me Phoenix Park.' She followed him up the stairs and on to the top deck, of the tram, slumping on to one of the hard wooden seats. 'You din't say nothin' about no tram rides.'

'I'm goin' to show you somethin',' Garvan said obstinately. 'It won't tek but a moment if we go an' come back be tram. Then you can go to the quays, or to Phoenix Park or both . . . if you still want to, that is.'

Deirdre decided that she had better humour him, so she began to talk lightly of this and that, commenting on the buildings they passed, though she did herself no good in Garvan's eyes by saying involuntarily and with no thought of being rude, 'Mind you, I thought Dublin would be bigger an' more imposin' than Liverpool, but it ain't. It's smaller and more . . . more countrified, I s'pose you could say. Still, small things is nicer'n large in some ways.'

Garvan snorted. 'Wait'll you see Phoenix Park, that's all,' he said darkly. 'Come on, we get down here, so we do.'

They left the tram, crossed the road and went through an imposing gateway, and at this point Deirdre stopped short and caught hold of Garvan's sleeve. 'Wait on, this here's a cemetery! What d'you want to bring me here for?'

Garvan turned and glared down at her. He was tall and brown-skinned from working constantly in the open, and suddenly it occurred to Deirdre that perhaps she should not be here with him—after all, she scarcely knew the feller and the huge graveyard was almost deserted.

'To show you somethin',' he said. 'Don't worry, I'm not goin' to turn into a vampire an' bite your t'roat out.'

Deirdre giggled. She had told the twins that morning about the cinema show she and Donny had seen just before they left Liverpool and how she'd been afraid to go upstairs to bed that night. 'No, I know *that*,' she said scornfully. 'But I just don't see . . . oh, awright, I'm comin'.'

He clearly knew his way unerringly, that was one good thing, Deirdre thought, as they threaded their way across the huge cemetery. They stopped by a small mound without a headstone and Garvan picked up the stone vase which lay there and put the lilac into it, then jerked his head at her to follow him. 'I'll put some water in it,' he said. 'There's a tap. Come with me.'

Deirdre followed and watched in silence as he filled the vase and carried it back to the grave. Then she said rather uncertainly: 'Is it your da, Garvan? Or your gran? It's very nice of you to buy flowers to put . . .'

He interrupted her without apology, staring at the lilac in the vase, not looking at her. 'It's Maggie

McVeigh, the gorl you've seen in the photograph. She . . . she brought us up, me an' Shay. So now you know what happens to gorls who are fond of me. I . . . I kill 'em, like I did Maggie.'

Deirdre thought for a moment, then snorted rudely. This must stop, she decided. What did he think she was, an eejit? Of course he hadn't killed the girl, he was just trying to frighten her! 'You didn't kill anyone, Garvan, so stop givin' yourself airs an' graces an' come down to earth! She was Liam's gorl, what's more, not yourn, an' he don't go around givin' hisself airs an' sayin' he killed her.'

She expected Garvan to take offence, but he simply said quietly, 'I did cause her death though, Deirdre. She was workin' at the market, an' she saw me across the street and shouted, an' . . . an' I pretended not to hear, so I did. An' she ran into the road . . . a bus killed her, but it were my fault, all my fault.'

'Yes, I dare say you was partly to blame,' Deirdre said slowly, having given the matter some thought. 'But just because you were stupid, that don't mean you caused her death. Me mam's always tellin' us to look careful-like before we crosses a road. Your Maggie could ha' been killed any time if she was quick to act an' slower to think o' danger.'

There was a long pause. Garvan stared at Deirdre across the grave and Deirdre stared straight back, refusing to drop her eyes even though Garvan's were hot and angry. 'Ye-es,' he said slowly at last. 'But it were me . . .'

Deirdre cut in at once, with brutal truthfulness. 'No, it weren't you, Garvan Nolan! You din't push her under the bleedin' bus, nor you didn't shout to her to cross the bleedin' road. So stop makin' yourself important by pretendin' that she died 'cos of you. That's almost worse'n killin' someone, if you ask me.'

'Why, you nasty little redheaded English tart,' Garvan gasped. 'I've a good mind to give you a drubbin', girl or no girl! How dare you say such t'ings to me!'

He was a good nine inches taller than Deirdre and a lot stronger, as well as being four years the older, but Deirdre did not intend to back down now. 'Why not do a proper job an' kill *me*, if you're so sure of yourself?' she taunted. 'You could do it easy, then you'd have a real death to boast about.'

'Boast? *Boast*?' Garvan leaned towards her, his eyes narrowed into slits, his voice dropping to a hiss. 'Why you nasty, foxy little bitch, killin' you would be a boastin' matter, that's for sure! Likely the lads of Liverpool would crown me king jest for gettin' rid of your sharp tongue!'

Deirdre was about to reply in kind when the humour of the situation struck her and she began to giggle, then to laugh out loud, clutching her waist and doubling up at the absurdity of it. Garvan held out for a moment, but laughter such as hers was irresistible and despite himself, he gave a muffled snort and had to turn his head away.

Deirdre, wiping the tears from her eyes with the backs of her hands, walked round and joined him, looking into his face. 'This is no place for a fight,' she said briskly. 'Shall us go somewhere else, Garvan?'

'You're a terrible gorl, Deirdre Docherty,' Garvan replied with as much severity as he could muster. 'Sure and you'll get the pair of us t'rown out, so you will, wit' no choice of leavin' of our own

489

accord.' He took her arm and turned her towards the cemetery gates. 'An' mebbe you're right at that, mebbe I've bin usin' what happened to Maggie as a kind of excuse when t'ings went wrong for me. But guilt's a terrible thing, so it is, an' didn't I feel I'd wrecked two lives, me brother's an' poor Maggie's? Still, Liam's makin' a new start an' so will I. Now, would ye like to see the Smithfield? We might catch up wit' your brother, so we might.'

'Yes, I'd like that,' Deirdre said easily, falling into step beside him, 'But don't forgit we're goin' to Phoenix Park later.'

'As if ye'd let me forget,' Garvan mocked. 'Sure an' it would be nag, nag, nag until you found yerself where you wanted to be. Come on then, we'd best get a move on if we're to find your brother.'

*　　　*　　　*

They did not find Donal but they had an excellent day. Garvan, who never seemed to be short of a tanner or two despite his many and varied occupations—or perhaps because of them—treated Deirdre to fish and chips at a small eating house by the cattle market and later, to an ice-cream from a cart in Phoenix Park. And whatever they were doing and wherever they went, they talked incessantly and very soon Deirdre realised she was enjoying Garvan's company as if she had known him and liked him all her life. And seeing his animated face and hearing his frequent chuckle, she was pretty sure that her companion was enjoying himself too—perhaps for the first time for a long while. It seemed to her, in fact, that the scene in the cemetery had acted on Garvan as a

490

purge, getting rid of the festering guilt over Maggie's death which had haunted him for so long.

Indeed, by the time they were wending their way home through the narrow streets of the Liberties once more, they were in such accord that she asked him impulsively if he had ever worked on the land, for she had noticed at the Smithfield that he seemed both knowledgeable about and interested in all they saw.

'I like to work outdoors,' Garvan admitted. 'That's why I stand the markets or muck out the shippons or drive cattle.'

'Then why don't you come with us?' Deirdre suggested eagerly. 'It'd be a rare ole game if you came too. I'd like it, honest to God I would, an' Donal would be glad of someone who knew a bit, same as he does.'

'Aw, you're coddin' me,' Garvan said slowly. 'Donal and Liam won't want anyone else.'

Deirdre laughed. 'Course they will. We's not nearly enough to run two farms. 'Sides it'll be a case of the more the merrier, if you asks me.'

There was a short silence whilst the two of them continued to stroll along the pavement, then Garvan fetched a deep sigh and turned to face her. 'No, it wouldn't work. I'm a city feller at heart, I dare say. Turn right here, it's a short cut, so it is. We'll be home in no time now.'

'But I'm not askin' you to stay for *ever*,' Deirdre pointed out reasonably. 'Just for a bit, Garv, until we're settled in, like. And then, if you find you like the work . . .'

'Can you see me, workin' side be side wit' your brother an' mine?' Garvan said derisively. 'They'd not stand for me ways for two minutes wit'out

491

drivin' me mad, naggin' at me to do t'ings their way. No, no, I'm best here in Dublin, so I am.'

And though Deirdre tried for the rest of the walk home he stuck to his guns and continued to insist that it would never work, that the others would not want him, that he would be as out of place as a fish in a field.

'Oh, have it your own way, then,' Deirdre muttered at last as they climbed the stairs to the Nolan home. 'But you're mekin' a mistake, I'm tellin' you.'

'No, I'm not. I know meself too well,' Garvan said promptly. 'I couldn't take orders from me brother, nor from a pipsqueak five years me junior. Now stop naggin', you little witch, or we'll fall out, so we shall. And I don't want to fall out wit' you, because red hair or no, you're not a bad kid at all at all.'

'All right then,' Deirdre said. 'But mark my words, Garv, if you don't come with us you'll be missing one heck of an adventure! Put that in your pipe an' smoke it, Mr Clever!'

CHAPTER FIFTEEN

They had got up at the crack of dawn, in great excitement, and Aisling Nolan and Ellen had busied themselves with preparing a packed meal to eat on the train.

'I'll miss ye,' Aisling had said as they worked, and had been surprised to find that she really meant it. 'But as soon as you're settled me an' Ticky'll be after comin' for a visit, like you said. Eh,

492

but it'll be grand to see Clare—all me life, whiles me gran were alive, we heard about Clare as though it were the Promised Land. Yes, I envy you, so I do.'

'We'll be glad to have you,' Ellen said. She put down her buttery knife and leaned across the table to take her mother-in-law's hand for a moment. 'You've been mortal good to us Dochertys, takin' over your beautiful home the way we have, an' we've not felt strangers for a moment, despite us bein' English. There!'

Aisling laughed. 'Sure an' wasn't I waitin' to dislike the lot of ye?' she said honestly. 'And wasn't I disarmed the moment I set eyes on ye? You're the very girl for my Liam, so you are, an' between ourselves, alanna, I've a feelin' that you're goin' to be good for our Garvan too. In fact, between us two again, nothin' could be better for Garvan than to get away from Dublin. Nor for Seamus, neither,' she added. 'Life isn't as aisy for twins as you might t'ink . . . but you'll be knowin' that, wit' Deirdre an' Donal on your hands. The t'ing is, my lads have been inseparable all their lives an' suddenly, isn't there another interest in Seamus's life that's even more important than his brother? For he's in a way to bein' serious about young Beatrix, you know. And havin' Garvan nearby, always wit' a jealous eye on his carryin's on, weren't helpin' none. I'm sure the best t'ing for both of me boys is to get away from each other, lead their own lives for a bit. An' you takin' Garvan, what's always been difficult, away wit' you will give Seamus a chance that he'd all but give up on, so he had.'

'I hope so,' Ellen said. 'But we're takin' Garvan for our own sakes too, remember. Another pair of

493

hands—and especially hands which know what they're doing!—will be a tremendous help. Mind you, Dee's a young devil; she'll lead him a dance one way and another, so I can't guarantee he'll stay the course.'

Aisling nodded decisively. 'So I t'ought,' she said. 'More power to her elbow, I say. And knowin' Garvan, it's the very treatment he needs, so he does.

'But there's somethin' I been meanin' to say to you, Ellen, when I got you to meself. It's . . . it's not easy for me to tell you this, but I felt I must. I . . . I wasn't kind to young Maggie McVeigh, not when I found out she was after marryin' me boy. In fact, I was downright wicked. But I tried to get her back, say how sorry I was, put t'ings on the right footing, and sure I never got the chance, for didn't she up and die on us?'

'I know, Liam told me,' Ellen said, manfully repressing a smile at her mother-in-law's turn of phrase. 'Well, all I can say is if it made you easier on me I'm grateful. But—Liam hasn't said much — didn't you think Maggie was suitable for Liam, then?'

'It wasn't that so much as the fact that she come from a quare fambly, so she did. The McVeighs died in a very sad way . . . but Maggie's sister is no better'n she should be, an' her mammy was what I'd call feckless. I didn't want me son to end up wit' a girl who might revert to her mammy's ways the moment she got out from under me roof.'

'I see,' Ellen said and glanced across at the older woman just as Aisling glanced up at her. They smiled and Aisling, impelled by heaven knew what desire to get it off her chest, added: 'And truth to

494

tell, alanna, I wasn't any too sure how I'd manage wit'out me son's money an' support comin' in. But now, havin' managed wit'out him for years, I can afford to be generous.'

Ellen couldn't help laughing, but she liked Liam's mother the better, she told herself, for her honesty. And the two of them continued to work together harmoniously until the sandwiches were all made and packed into a basket, together with a number of small iced buns and two tall bottles of cold tea.

Whilst they had prepared the food the rest of the party had been busy as well. Deirdre, Donal and Garvan had finished their packing and Seamus had gone off to borrow a handcart to carry their belongings along to Kingsbridge station for the first part of their journey.

It was Seamus thundering up the stairs, in fact, which alerted Ellen and Aisling to the fact that they must leave.

'I'll get me coat,' Aisling said breathlessly, carrying the basket out on to the landing. 'Liam will fetch down your bags, alanna, and no doubt Donal will help Deirdre with hers. Garvan's been ready this past hour, pacing up and down the courtyard waiting for his brother.'

Ellen picked the basket up—it was heavy—just as Deirdre emerged from her room, her face bright with anticipation, her coat slung round her shoulders, for the morning was warm although it was not yet sunup. 'Oh, Ellie, ain't it excitin'?' she asked. 'Donny's taken the bags, I've just got me birds to bring, then I'm all ready.'

Rather to Ellen's dismay, Donny had spent some of his money on a large cardboard box with airholes in the top, inside which a dozen or so fluffy yellow chicks now resided, and had insisted, when reprimanded, that it was really a present for his sister and a useful one at that.

'You wouldn't let me bring me lambs, told me I must sell 'em an' buy more when we were settled,' he said mutinously, when Ellen tried to tell him that the birds would only be a nuisance and an added responsibility. 'Every farm needs poultry, don't it? An' poultry's usually the women's business. So Dee's startin' off on the right foot, wi' a nice little flock o' hens.'

'They're probably all cockerels,' Liam said. 'Then what'll you do wit' them, me fine bucko?'

But Donal refused to be cast down by this pessimistic utterance. 'We'll eat 'em, roast, for us dinners,' he said cheerfully. 'Besides, there's twelve of 'em—I don't think they can all be cockerels, Liam.'

'Don't try arguin' wi' the twins, Liam,' Ellen advised him. 'For they'd argue the hind leg off a donkey even if they were totally in the wrong. Besides, they're the ones who'll be lookin' after their wretched livestock all the way from Dublin to the Burren. I dare say by the time we arrive they'll be wishin' they'd listened to your advice—but they won't admit it, if I know them.'

So now Deirdre hugged the cardboard box to her bosom and listened lovingly to the cheeps from within, and Donal carried a squelchy bag full of bran mash, boiled vegetable peelings and various household scraps to feed them with, whilst Seamus pushed the handcart laden with their luggage and the others strode on ahead through the streets which were beginning to brighten as the sun slowly rose.

It was odd to see Francis Street deserted and to turn left into Thomas Street, quiet as the grave with not a soul stirring. Even the Guinness Brewery was quiet still, and when they reached the fountain at the edge of James Street and turned into Steevens Lane they saw a gentle white mist curling up from the distant Liffey, and by the time they turned into St John's Road and saw the imposing station building in front of them the sun had come up and was gilding the dome which towered above the entrance.

The station was not deserted, as the rest of the city had been, but neither was it full of people. Porters strolled about, a man with a brush was attacking the foyer and there was a short line of people waiting to buy their tickets from the man behind the small glazed window.

'I'll get the tickets,' Liam said. 'The rest of you get on to the platform . . . an' if the train comes in before I'm back wit' you, try to get a carriage to ourselves.'

But they were in plenty of time and stood in a small group on the platform, whilst Aisling sniffed and said in a tearful voice that she didn't know what she'd do without them, she was sure, and Seamus first unloaded all the luggage, then loaded it up again, reasoning that it would be easier to run along to the luggage van with the handcart than with each of them burdened with bags.

The train came in with a great deal of noise and fuss; Ellen kissed her mother-in-law, smiled at Seamus, pushed the luggage into the van and persuaded Deirdre to part with the chicks, for the time being at any rate. They found an empty carriage and settled themselves. Aisling was crying, Liam comforting her. Seamus shook Garvan's hand and they both roared with laughter over some shared joke, though Garvan was pale and Seamus kept blinking. The engine driver was getting up steam, people were piling aboard, others were waving . . . the train was moving! Ellen and Deirdre hung out of the window waving to the two on the platform, then Deirdre got a smut in her eye and came inboard, giving Garvan a chance for a brief wave before he collapsed on to a seat and produced a comic paper from his pocket.

'Well, we're off,' Liam said in a flat sort of voice which did not conceal his excitement. 'Ennis, here we come, we do indeed.'

'Not just Ennis . . . the Burren, here we come,' Donal said. 'Wish you'd let me bring me lambs . . . they was good lambs, now someone else is lookin' after 'em and waitin' for the money to roll in.'

'Oh shut your face,' Deirdre said rudely, jabbing him with an elbow. 'Want a humbug? I've gorra whole bagful here!'

They settled down for the journey, spreading themselves over the carriage, glad it was not a corridor train, each boundlessly, endlessly excited at the thought of the adventure before them. Even Garvan, still wondering how he had come to let himself be cajoled and persuaded into becoming a part of this expedition, began to feel a delightful anticipation coursing through him. They were off— and whatever happened in Ennis, it was unlikely to be dull!

*   *   *

Left on the platform, Seamus and his mother waved until the train was out of sight, then grinned rather sheepishly at each other.

'Goin' to miss your brothers, Shay?' his mother said half teasingly. 'Sure and I'd never have t'ought to see you *encouragin'* your twin to leave Dublin, go off wit' an English family, but you did encourage him, didn't you so?'

'I did, Mammy,' Seamus admitted, turning the empty handcart in the direction of St John's Road once more. 'It's the best t'ing that could have happened for both of us, Mammy, because now we'll be able to go on likin' each other. But I tell you straight, Mammy, that if Garv had stayed, and gone on despisin' my girl and mekin' our lives difficult, it would ha' been war between us.'

'I guessed it.' Aisling nodded. 'Strange, isn't it, son, that the pair of ye seem to have found yourselves girl-friends wit' red hair? Though your Beatrix is a deal gentler and prettier than Deirdre, so she is.'

Seamus frowned, then shook his head. 'Mammy, Deirdre's a child, so she is. Garvan isn't interested in her at all at all—nor in any woman.'

'That's what you say now, my son,' Aisling said serenely as they emerged on the still-empty pavement. 'But give it a year or two—she's fifteen, is Deirdre, and that isn't a child.'

'Mebbe not. But you're not after tryin' to convince me that Garvan's got his eye on her, are you?' Seamus said incredulously, wheeling his handcart across the road. 'Holy Mother, Mammy, he's had a dozen opportunities to go out wit' some o' the prettiest girls in the store and turned 'em all down flat. Why should he feel differently over a

499

wee redhead—an' an English girl at that?'

'Why indeed?' Aisling said a trifle tartly, hurrying to keep pace with her long-legged son. 'You t'ink you know Garvan better than anyone else could—but 'tis clear you don't know human nature, nor that what repels one, attracts another. I'm tellin' you, Shay, Garvan's not gone all the way to Clare because he's a fancy for farmwork.'

'Well, we'll see who's right in a few weeks, when Garv comes saunterin' back, sayin' he's had enough of farmin', so he has, and expectin' you to dance attendance on him again,' Seamus said rather acidly.

'True,' Aisling said absently. 'Now you tek the handcart back to the Iveagh market an' then come home for a bite to eat afore you start work. I'll go round to the Brownes' place an' see if Ticky's comin' home for breakfast.'

Ticky had spent the previous night with his pal, Joey, so that he would not be disturbed by the leaving preparations next day, and Aisling guessed that he would be eager to get back to his own home and find out how the trip to the station had gone. Indeed, he had begged to be allowed to accompany them, but his mother had decided that it was too early for the child to be up, so Mrs Browne's invitation for Ticky to share Joey's bed had been gratefully received.

'Right,' Seamus said. 'And anyway, it's grateful I am to the girl for persuadin' Garv to go wit' them. It'll give Trixie an' me a chance to be alone for a change. I'll see you later, Mammy.'

*   *   *

500

As the train wound its slow way across the Irish countryside, Deirdre sat with her nose all but glued to the window, knowing that this was an experience she would never forget if she lived to be a hundred. What she was seeing, as the small stations ambled by, was a landscape and a way of life which was entirely foreign to her—and was as entrancing as only new and foreign things can be.

The countryside was in blossom, with every tree and hedge breaking into tender new leaf, the hawthorn a mass of foaming white, the apple trees pink, the ground beneath the branches of each small copse misty with bluebells. She saw tiny cob cottages, children in ragged clothing playing in the dust, other children toiling in the fields. She saw ducks on ponds, pigs in sties, cattle and sheep in fields, as well as rabbits, quietly grazing on upland meadows, a red fox stopping half-way across a field to gaze with startled eyes at the great, steam-belching monster roaring by and horses, mules and donkeys by the score. The train stopped at Kildare, Portlaoise, Roscrea, Nenagh, as well as a dozen other, smaller stations, and passengers came on board or disembarked, calling to each other, laughing, joking.

And Deirdre loved it all. It was so peaceful, the people themselves seeming slower moving, softer spoken, than either their Dublin counterparts or the folk that Deirdre had left behind in Liverpool. A keen observer, it soon occurred to her that faces were different in a more basic sense too. Cheekbones were broader, eyes, often set wide apart, calmer, and the pace of those walking through the streets and across country platforms seemed more leisurely, as though there was no particular rush. If you got there tomorrow instead of today, would anyone die because of it? She saw the country people working hard, sometimes very hard, but she did not see them hurrying. She saw brooks half hidden by hazels and willows, fields where young crops were already well grown, half-ruined castles and stately manor houses, as well as the tiny farms crouching in the lee of the gentle hills, and cabins where hens and pigs, unkennelled, wandered in and out of the family's living accommodation.

And then she saw mountains. 'What's them?' she said to Garvan, who was sitting beside her, staring out every bit as hard as she. 'Them hills?'

'They'll be the Arra mountains,' Garvan said. 'We're nearly in Limerick ... best be gettin' our t'ings together.'

'Cripes, the time's gone quick,' Deirdre said. 'How far is it to Ennis from Limerick, Garv?'

'A fair way,' Garvan admitted. 'But there's a bus. We'll be catchin' that.'

'You know very well, Dee,' her brother put in rather reproachfully from the seat opposite. 'You moithered Ellen half to death until she'd gone over the journey wi' us five or six times. It's train to Limerick, bus to Ennis, then another bus to Corofin, an' mebbe a pony-cart from there to the McBride place.'

'I know, really,' Deirdre said, grinning. 'But I keep wantin' to hear it all over again. Can you realise we're here, Donny? Actually in Ireland, near Limerick, an' gettin' closer to the Burren by the minute?'

'Yes, just about,' her twin was saying prosaically as the train began to slow. 'Look lively, everyone . . . what's the solicitor's name again?'

Deirdre giggled. 'You moithered Ellen a thousand times, askin' her that,' she said, in a good imitation of Donal's own censorious tone five minutes earlier. 'You're as excited as meself, Donal Docherty, so don't go pretendin' to be so high an' mighty! Come on, everyone, the train's stoppin', it's stoppin'! We've reached Limerick.'

*   *   *

After that, time seemed fairly to whizz past. They found the lodging house which Mr Donovan, the solicitor dealing with their case, had told them was clean, reasonable and friendly. Ellen rang the bell and they were ushered into a neat parlour and welcomed by a fat, friendly woman called Mrs O'Rourke, who showed them the simple bedrooms she had reserved for them and explained that they might sit in the parlour, but would take their meals in the dining-room, which was adjoining the kitchen, so that the food did not have a chance to get cold, as she put it.

They left their baggage in their rooms, cleaned themselves up after the journey—Deirdre and Donal had managed to collect more than their fair share of smuts—and set off for the solicitor's office. Messrs Donovan and McCready occupied the first floor of an office above a hardware shop and they soon found themselves being shown to hard wooden chairs before a very large desk behind which sat a very small man, with twinkling eyes and pince-nez spectacles.

He beamed at them. 'You're very welcome, ladies and gentlemen,' he said as soon as they were settled. 'Now I believe you were told by my colleague in Liverpool that you had inherited two farms. Strictly speaking, you only inherit the McBride place because the other farm still belongs to the Feeneys, should any of their descendants ever turn up. But the McBrides have been farming the Feeneys' place on their behalf ever since they left and for all practical purposes you will continue to do the same. Now, Mrs Nolan, since you're *in loco parentis* I'll address myself to you, but I'm sure the young people . . .' he smiled at the twins, sitting forward on their chairs . . . will let me know if they disagree with what I've said, or simply don't understand it.'

Ellen blushed—she still found being referred to as 'Mrs Nolan' a bit odd, but nice. 'I'm sure they will,' Ellen said, sounding a trifle rueful. 'Neither my brother nor my sister, Mr Donovan, is in the habit of letting themselves be overawed by their surroundings. Now I'll just show you our . . . umm . . . identifying documentation, I think the other solicitor called it.'

She handed the bundle of papers her mother had given her to Liam, who stood up and was in the act of handing it, in his turn, to the solicitor, when Mr Donovan exclaimed sharply. He stood up and stared at Liam's hand, outstretched and with the papers in his grasp. 'Young man . . . that ring! Where did you get it?'

'Me mother-in-law gave it to me wife, so she could give it to me,' Liam said, considerably startled by this strange question. 'It's an old ring . . . her mammy's property, I believe. Why, sir?'

'May I see it?' Mr Donovan held out his own hand and took the ring as Liam slid it, not without difficulty, over his knuckle and dropped it into the other man's palm. 'Well—this is really the most extraordinary thing! How I wish Mr McBride could be here now!'

'Why?' Deirdre asked baldly, standing up herself and peering first at the solicitor's face and then at the ring in his hand. 'It's only an ole signet ring, Mam said. Our grandad had it from his mam and Gran gave it to Mam when Grandad died, an' then Mam give it to our dad, only he died . . . What's 'strordinary about it?'

'It's the engraving,' Mr Donovan said almost reverently. He held the ring out so they could all see the curious, spiky circle engraved upon it where, usually, initials would have been plain. 'If you look carefully . . .'

'It's a dandelion, ain't it?' Deirdre cut in impatiently. 'Or some such thing.'

'No, alanna, it's no such thing, though I admit it looks a little like. It's initials. It's capital Ms, engraved in a circle, and the heir of the McBride house always wears such a ring. In fact, Fergus McBride passed his ring, in his will, to your friend Bill McBride who was buried wearing it, since it was by then generally agreed that the McBride family had died out. But Fergus's ring was a comparatively new one. Do you know why? Can you guess?'

'I 'opes it weren't stole by one of us ancestors,' Donal said with considerable foreboding. 'That ain't it, is it, mister?'

Mr Donovan laughed. 'No indeed, me laddo. The story, as I was told it, was that the elder brother of your friend Bill McBride was betrothed to a young woman by the name of Grainne Feeney. But due to the sad circumstance of his being badly injured during a tempest of unusual ferocity, the young couple were unable to marry. Instead, when they said their farewells, he gave her the ring he wore on his finger. And so far as is known, that ring has never been seen in Ireland since,' he finished.

'And . . . and that is it?' Deirdre said faintly, pointing to the ring on his palm. 'The ring that William McBride gave to Grainne? Bill told us the story, Mr Donovan, it were ever so sad, but of course we din't know our mam had a gold ring at all, apart from her own weddin' one. Then does it mean we's really the descendants of Grainne Feeney? Is that what it means?'

'I truly think so,' Mr Donovan said gravely. He turned to Ellen. 'Mrs Nolan, what did your mother tell you about her grandmother? Did she ever mention a name, or how she came to possess this ring?'

'She told us when she gave it to me for Liam that her grandmother had come to Liverpool from Ireland because she had been widowed in some . . . some natural disaster,' Ellen said, having thought for a moment. 'She said that her gran's first child took the name of Flanaghan, though he was not, in fact, the child of the marriage that her grandmother later made. Could . . . could it be that my great-grandmother ran away because she was expecting William McBride's child? Was that why he gave her the ring?'

'I doubt whether we shall ever know that for sure, my dear,' the solicitor said quietly. 'But it was certainly what Bill and his brother believed, and they believed it because, in his turn, their father thought it was what had happened. The old man felt deeply guilty that he had allowed the girl to go, knowing that she had been promised to his son, without at least offering financial help. That was why he took over the Feeney holding, when it became clear that the family were never going to return. He always banked the money he made from it—for Burren land, when properly farmed, produces some of the finest sheep; both their wool and their meat are top quality — so there will be money enough to set the holding to rights once you've got the time to work on it.' He came round the desk and gave Liam back the ring, then returned to his seat, slowly shaking his head. 'If only Bill were here and could see you all and know that his hunch had been right, that he had found the Feeneys after all! It would have made him very happy.'

'Perhaps he does know, mister,' Deirdre said. An' if we mek a go of it it'll be thanks to Bill, I'm tellin' you. He started us off makin' gardings, growin' things, an' he telled Donal about farmin'—that was what started me brother off wantin' to rear sheep. He took us over the water an' showed us what a good lowland farm should be like, an' he were always on about beasts an' the country ways. He telled us a lot, eh, Donal?'

'He did that,' Donal agreed. 'He were a great gun, were Bill.'

Mr Donovan smiled and nodded. 'Aye, and he improved the place no end during his time on it,' he agreed. 'He was a better farmer than his elder brother, no doubt about that. But now to your next move, for you must see that I'm completely satisfied as to your right and title to both properties. You've booked yourselves into a lodging for tonight?'

'We went to the place you recommended as soon as the bus dropped us off, so we did,' Liam said at once. 'The lady's mekin' us a hot meal for five o'clock.'

'That's grand. I've arranged for someone from the McBride place to meet you off the bus at Corofin in the morning with a horse and cart to take you to the farms. Will that suit? I think, now, that the sooner you reach your property the better.'

* * *

The horse and cart wound its way alongside a small stream, the driver gesturing ahead of them with his whip and turning round to address his passengers seated along both sides of the wagon on the polished wooden seats. 'Sure an' isn't dat de prettiest sight now? 'Tis a fine house, indade— more like a manor dan a farm. What do ye t'ink of it, eh? Mr Donovan was after tellin' me dat it was your great-great-somet'ing-or-other owned it, an' youse is the heirs.' He sighed deeply. ''Tis lucky you are, I'm t'inkin'.'

But the Nolans and Dochertys were too busy gazing at the house crouched at the foot of the gentle hill. They were at the McBride place at last. A solid house, built foursquare to withstand the worst of the weather, with the hill at its back and a good, thick wood of oak, ash and beech at its front. It was tiled and some sort of creeper softened the rosy old bricks, and from here they could see that at the back were a range of solid outbuildings built to form a square around a courtyard, stables, dairy, shippon ... everything a farm needed. There was even a flower garden in the front, they could see the neatly planted beds from here.

'How far's the Feeney place?' Deirdre said, looking around her. 'I know it's by the stream because when Bill told us the story, Grainne got her water from the stream; they didn't have a well nor nothin'.'

''Tis a fair step afoot,' their driver said. 'But in the wagon I can have ye 'dere in the twinkling of a bedpost, so I can.'

'Right,' Ellen said, speaking for all of them. 'We'll go right now, if it's all right with you.'

*   *   *

It was a lovely afternoon. Birds sang, a gentle breeze blew and the long golden rays of the sun would have made most things appear beautiful. But the Burren as they reached it was in bloom, which was enough to stun anyone into silence, and as they drove along, they simply stopped talking and stared.

'It's the strangest thing I ever did see,' Donal said at last. 'Look how the stones are covered with flowers—tiny ones, medium ones and some quite big ones. Even the moss is all different colours—no wonder Bill wanted to come back, Dee. I've never seen nothin' like it, I can't tek me eyes off it.'

'Look at that wall,' Ellen said. 'It's every colour under the sun, yet you can see it's just a thin slab of rock, six foot high and no more'n an inch wide . . . oh, and the grass in that medder's such a bright green! Mr Donovan said the land rears the best sheep in all Ireland . . . can you doubt it, when you look at the colour an' richness o' the grass?'

'Aye, an' if that's a medder . . .' Donal said,

509

turning away from the stream, 'then the Feeney place can't be far off . . . look, is that . . .'

Deirdre glanced in the direction he indicated. A low, one-storey cottage hugged the ground, the grasses and wild flowers high enough to touch the windowsills. The walls were white, the thatch, although mossy and bird-tattered, was the golden-beige of dried reed and the shutters still had signs of paint long blistered and gone. And it was, because of the stream before it and the land behind, instantly recognisable.

There was a simultaneous gasp from Deirdre and Garvan. 'It's the picture!' they both said, almost in the same breath. 'It's me mam's picture!'

After a moment's stunned pause, Deirdre turned to Garvan. 'I didn't know you'd seen the picture—I didn't think Ellen had brought it out yet.'

'I haven't,' Ellen said, looking bewildered.

'I don't know nothin' about Ellen's picture, I'm talkin' about me mammy's picture, what came down to her from me gran,' Garvan said slowly. 'It's a real clever t'ing—it used to hang in Maggie's room. It showed a cottage just like this one, wit' the stream before it an' the slabs o' stone an' the colours behind, an' it weren't painted, nor drawn, it were . . .'

'Stitched, out o' cunning little bits an' pieces o' cloth?' Deirdre said for him. 'Like ours, Garv? Ours shows the place in springtime, just like now.'

'Ours is autumn,' Garvan said dreamily. 'All browns an' golds an' greys . . . but the sky's blue, an' the sunshine's over everyt'ing, so it is. Well, ain't that the strangest t'ing you ever did hear, now? How come we've both of us got a picture of this cottage?'

510

'Could it be that our grans were related—sisters, or somet'ing?' Liam said after a moment. 'No, that's not likely. But s'pose they were at the same school . . . or near neighbours? Would that mek sense of it?'

'Only if the school was held in that cottage,' Ellen said, pointing across the stream. 'I know it's the wildest of coincidences, but . . . it sounds to me as though them pictures were made by the same person. Or one was copied from the other. Which could mean our families were connected, way back.'

'And why not, alanna?' the driver put in. He had been listening to the conversation with keen interest. 'I'm a Ryan, as I've mebbe mentioned, and we've lived on the Burren for ever, so we're after knowin' a t'ing or two. The way I've heard it the Feeneys were a big fambly, so they were. An' wit' a name like Docherty youse is bound to be of Irish distraction. So your gran could ha' married a Docherty, an' her sister a Nolan. See? As for the pictures, de Feeneys lost most of dere t'ings at de time of de storm, but de girls would keep somet'ing small, dat dey valued, like them pictures. Oh aye, it makes sense, so it does.'

'When we unpack we'll tek a look at our picture,' Liam said. 'Then Ellen can tell us if it's made as hers is. Isn't it grand, now, to t'ink mebbe all of us is findin' our roots again? Ellie?'

'Yes, grand,' Ellen said slowly. 'You brought the picture then, Liam?'

'Aye. Mrs Collins gave it me, after Maggie's death. I guess I t'ought you'd like it.' He stood up and held out his hands to Ellen. 'Are we goin' to tek a closer look? I doubt the place is locked up, bein' so far from everyt'ing.'

Ellen stood up too and let him hand her down, whilst the younger ones swarmed over the sides of the wagon and dropped down, discovering the stepping stones with cries of pleasure.

'There would have been a little bridge here once,' Deirdre said as she jumped from stone to stone. 'We could build another . . .' She reached the bank, scrambled up it and headed determinedly for the cottage. 'Right, now I'm goin' to look inside . . . look all round everywhere, at everythin'. Ain't it a pretty place? An' there's still glass in the windows . . . an' the door's solid, but there's a dacent-lookin' latch. I think you were right, Liam, we'll get inside without trouble.'

They did. The latch groaned and protested but it lifted and they stole inside, the older ones hanging back good-naturedly to let the youngsters go first. Donal went ahead and Deirdre and Garvan followed, she unashamedly gripping his hand. Suddenly it seemed like trespassing, she felt there might be someone inside who would ask what the devil they thought they were doing, coming unasked into private property . . .

But there was no one. Nothing. The interior of the cottage was dark, divided into four rooms, one very large, the rest smaller. But all were completely and utterly empty. In fact . . .

'Beasts have been stabled here,' Garvan said disgustedly, standing on one foot and examining the sole of his shoe in the muted light coming through the small window panes. 'In the last year or so, I mean. Well, what a t'ing to do to a good little house!'

'Hens, too,' Deirdre quavered as her quick
512

movement stirred a pile of hay and feathers into momentary unlikely life. 'Oh, how Grainne would hate to think of her little home bein' used for hens an' sheep. Bill telled us how hard she worked to keep the place neat an' tidy, how she cooked and preserved an' stacked up veggies for the winter . . .'

'If she were like most farmers she probably let the hens pop in an' out as they wanted,' Garvan observed frankly. 'Sure an' country folk aren't as fussy as you townies—a hen can clean up your floor real nice if you've spilt peelin's or bits o' food on it, so it can. There'll mebbe be a spot or two of chicken manure, but Grainne would have swept that out quick enough wit' her twiggy broom. Sheep though . . . that's another t'ing . . . an' cattle, an' if I read the signs right they've been here awright.'

'Well, they won't come here no longer,' Deirdre said fiercely. 'We won't let 'em, will we, Ellen? We'll purrit right, won't we? A nice bit o' linoleum on the floors, an' new shutters . . . some furniture, mebbe . . . an' we can clean out the chimbley, so's we can have a fire . . .'

'We'll do it all in time,' Ellen said comfortably. 'But first we've the big house to sort out.' She wandered across the room to the big stone fireplace. 'I reckon the picture would have hung above the fireplace,' she said. 'No, I'm wrong—if there really were two they'd have hung one on either side of the fireplace, where the settles would have been once. Didn't Bill say nothin' about pictures, Dee?'

'I b'lieve he did,' Donal said, answering for his sister who stood in frowning abstraction, clearly racking her memory. 'But I don't know as we took much notice, not havin' seen our mam's picture then. She din't fetch it down from the attic until you had a room of your own, did she, Ellie? An' that weren't till we moved to Mere Lane. But no worry, we'll have all the time in the world to sort out the mystery once we're settled into the McBride place.'

'True,' Liam said. 'Come an' look at the outbuildings, Ellen, see if we can patch 'em up wit'out too much trouble. If all we've been told is true, the best sheep come from the Burren, so they do, so we'll need a shelter up here for when we're lambing.'

The two older ones and Donal went out, back into the sunny yard, and Deirdre turned to Garvan. 'Do you know, Garv,' she said slowly, 'I never got no feelin' in me insides when we first saw the McBride place, ''cept that it were a proper good farm. But the moment me eyes clapped on this 'ere little house, I felt . . . I felt as if I *knowed* it, an' . . . an' loved it, too. Odd, ain't it?'

'No, not that odd; I felt the same. It's knowin' the pictures, perhaps, an' feelin', like I did when I were a nipper, that I'd find that white cottage one o' these days,' Garvan said. 'Tell you what, Seamus is me brother an' me best friend, but I'll not miss him here, not like I would anywhere else.'

'No, 'cos it's *your* place too,' Deirdre said at once. 'Garv, I want to do this place up an' one day, I want to live here. It's a sad place now, but can't you feel how warm an' friendly an' . . . an' *happy* it were once? Wi' the kids playin' out by the stream an' in the yard, knowin' the countryside like the backs o' their hands, lovin' what they'd made o' the place, plannin' what to do next . . .'

'We're all goin' to have our work cut out these next few years to keep the McBride place in good heart,' Garvan said. 'But I'm wit' you, Dee me darlin', though there'll be a deal of opposition, so there will. Liam an' Ellen won't want to move into a tumbledown cabin wit' only a stream for their water an' not a field ploughed or sown.'

'I meant you an' me an' Donal,' Deirdre said impatiently. 'Ellen's already talkin' about gettin' our mam over to run the house, wi' Sammy an' Toby, too. Mr Donovan says there's a good livin' at the McBride place for a big fambly, but 'tis the Feeney place what calls to me. An' they'll be glad enough to see us independent, you mark my words. Well? Are you wit' me? Donal will back us up, honest to God he will.'

She looked up at Garvan as they emerged from the gloom of the house into the golden sunshine of the yard and saw the slow smile spread across his face.

'We'll give it a go,' he said gleefully. 'Just as soon as the others can spare us, which may not be for a while. Hey, Donny!'

It did not take a moment to explain the plan to Donal who was immediately in favour. 'You're on, Garv, Dee,' he agreed at once. 'Oh, I can't wait to get started. I reckon they'll agree pretty fast once Mam comes to give a hand.'

They returned to the stream, crossed it and joined the others in the wagon. Liam and Ellen were holding hands and gazing into each other's eyes—sloppy stuff, Dee thought scornfully, but then what could you expect? They were newly-weds, and everyone knew newly-weds were soft in the head.

As they scrambled into the wagon a cloud drifted across the sky overhead and a fine soft rain began to fall. It would not be much, Deirdre told herself, settling down comfortably between Garvan and Donal, because there was sunshine too and the sky overhead was still a soft and radiant blue ... and besides what did a little rain matter?

'Come up, me ould lad!' Mr Ryan shouted and flicked his whip above the patient cob's broad back, and Dee felt a hand reach for hers and an arm turn her a little so that, together, she and Garvan were looking back at the Feeney place.

From this distance it looked all white and gold, as though it were new-built and waiting to welcome them home, and even as they watched faint tints formed in the drifting rain and tinged the thatch and the white walls with colour—every colour known to man.

'Will you look at that, alanna?' Garvan said softly into her ear. 'A rainbow's lucky ... look, it's paintin' our house till it's as beautiful as the Burren.'

Dee nodded. 'When I were little me mam used to tell me I'd find me rainbow's end one day,' she said softly. 'An' we have, Garvan.'